The Puller

Michael Hodges

SEVERED PRESS
HOBART TASMANIA

The Puller

For Sarah, and the compassionate amongst us.

The Beginning

The school bell rang, startling Matt Kearns with its cold metallic rattling. He slammed his biology book shut and hurried out of the classroom. As the last chaotic notes faded down the hallway, he felt something was wrong. There was no specific image to latch onto, he just knew.

The big glass doors at the end of the hallway beckoned him, leading him from the concrete tomb that was Walnut Grove High. He kicked open the doors, sunlight flooding onto his skin. *Relief.*

"Hi Matt," Amber Lynne said. She was leaning against the brick wall and chomping watermelon Bubblicious. He could smell the gum from where he stood.

"Hey," he said.

"Did ya see the big ruckus over at the athletic field?" she asked before blowing a bubble.

Pop!

"Lots of shouting," Amber said. "Prob boys fighting. You know how guys are." Amber rolled her eyes.

Matt bent down, pulled his jean cuff from the lip of his right boot, and leaned his biology book against the wall. As he jogged over to the athletic field, a small crowd gathered on the trimmed grass, mostly lacrosse players in full gear. Many of them were shouting. After reaching the group, Matt nudged his way into the center.

"Get that SUCKER!" Abe Johnson shouted.

"Haha it doesn't know what to do!" shouted another male voice.

Then Betsy Armstrong chimed in, her angsty voice as shrill as ever. "Watch out for its teeth! It's got a lotta teeth!"

As Matt inched forward, something yipped and whimpered from the middle of the group, a sad, pleading vocalization that immediately drew him further into the mix. When he reached the inner circle, Mike Armstrong loomed there in full lacrosse gear, jamming his lacrosse stick at an object on the ground. Matt sided up to Mike and followed the end of the lacrosse stick to the netting.

A coyote.

A big coyote with a beautiful, thick coat.

All two hundred and twenty pounds of Mike Armstrong leaned into the lacrosse stick, smashing the wooden netting frame to the earth, preventing the coyote's head from escaping. When the coyote tried to back its head out from under the net, Mike jerked the stick harder until the traumatized coyote gave in. Matt had the sickening sensation the douchebag was enjoying it.

The coyote yipped and growled as its ribcage pulsed. Its bronze eyes glared from behind the netting, a beautiful prisoner that had made a dreadful mistake. Every few seconds the coyote bared its teeth as its upper lip quivered.

Matt studied the crowd, their faces red and contorted, spittle flying from their lips as they cheered. Something seized him, an unexplainable pressure. The maniacal cheering faded, the faces and clothes morphing from color to black and white. The grass bled crimson. The sky grayed and molted. Mike Armstrong turned monochrome, the whites of his eyes vivid. Everything had changed color except for the coyote. Its earth tone coat slick in the sunlight, its vibrant pink tongue. Then it all became slow motion, the yelps, the reaching, the shouting.

Another student emerged from the crowd dressed in lacrosse gear: Ben Jacobsen, athletic star of Walnut Grove and serial meathead. Ben sprinted towards the coyote, lacrosse stick high above his head. *Don't think so*, Matt said. He knocked Ben to the side, but Ben kept momentum and smashed the coyote's head.

"Get that bastard!" a male student shouted. "Get that vermin off our field!"

Matt recovered from his attempted sideswipe and ripped the lacrosse stick from Ben's hand.

For a moment Ben stood there, eyeballing Matt, incredulous. "What the hell you doing?" he asked while cocking his arm back to deliver a punch. Matt ducked the punch and swept Ben's lacrosse stick across his knees, eliciting a sick crunch. Ben collapsed, holding his legs and screaming. The screams intertwined with the yipping and growling coyote. Glinting blood now matted its furry head.

Undeterred, Mike continued to force the coyote's head against the ground. The coyote kicked its back legs, throwing bits of grass and dirt.

Matt whirled and slammed Ben's stick across Mike's skull, triggering a hollow *thonk*. After a brief stagger, Mike lifted his lacrosse stick and swung it behind him, catching Matt across the shoulder and knocking him to the side.

The faces in the crowd transformed from cruel, self-satisfied domination to twisted confusion.

"Get him Mike! He took a swing at YOU," Betsy Armstrong shouted.

Sensing an opening thanks to Betsy, Mike took another powerful swing, nailing Matt square in the jaw. His world blurred and swam, his hearing rang, and then dialed back into focus.

"Shouldn't have done that," Mike yelled, eyes wild as he prepared for another swing, holding his stick high over his beet red face. But the look on Mike's faced changed from one of victorious rage to bewilderment. And then his face contorted into a scream a Hollywood starlet would be proud of.

From the ground, ripping flesh and frenetic growling, rising in intensity. The coyote, now free of the lacrosse netting, tore into Mike's ankle, nipping his tendon in half like a pair of scissors to string. As the coyote took its revenge on the downed lacrosse player, Matt noticed its eyes, brimming with rage but also containing a certain wisdom that he would never have expected. The coyote's muzzle and coat was slathered with blood, although whether the blood was Mike Armstrong's or the coyote's, he could not tell.

Mike swung around to smash the coyote, but collapsed when he placed his weight on the severed tendon. His ankle lay limp and bloody as he screamed on the ground. As Mike reached for his injured ankle the coyote slashed at his hand. When Mike pulled his hand away, only three fingers came back.

Cursing and mumbling, Ben Jacobsen crawled over to the coyote and swung his stick one-handed onto its head. The coyote yipped and retreated, then shook its bloody head, spraying crimson droplets onto the faces of the onlookers. The coyote gazed at Matt, lifted its snout into the air, and sneezed twice. Then the coyote limped to tree line at the edge of the athletic field.

The students behind Matt grew quiet. The only sounds left were the self-pity cries of Mike Armstrong and Ben Jacobsen's watery sobbing.

Matt dropped the lacrosse stick and it hit the ground like a bone cut loose from a whale.

Mike scowled up at him, his lips blubbery and slick. "Asshole!"

Then Betsy Armstrong got in his face, wagging a finger at him. She smelled of starch and makeup. "I'm calling the police," she said. "You're not allowed to hurt athletes." She ran over to Mike, examined his severed fingers and cried. "You'll pay for this! LOOK at his hand! He won't be able to play! LOOK at his hand!"

Matt tuned Betsy out and checked the southern end of the field. The coyote sat at the wood's edge, eyeing Matt as its tongue lolled. Then the coyote slunk into the vegetation, bushy tail suspended above the weeds until it was no more.

He figured the coyote would be alright, give or take a few bumps on the head. Matt limped away from the stunned crowd and the world slowly segued from black and white to color. The sound of car engines washed into the audio spectrum like cool waves.

***

It turned out Ben Jacobsen had a broken leg and a sprained knee. His high school sports career was in question. Mike Armstrong's fingers were never found. Matt assumed they were eaten by the coyote, snatched up like chicken McNuggets from the grassy salad of the athletic field. Mike's tendon needed surgery, something that would take a long time to recover from.

When Matt heard the news he didn't exactly feel remorseful. They were doing *the wrong thing* and he stepped in to do *the right thing*. His father had always told him *the right thing* was always harder to do.

His father was right.

Matt was more concerned with a trapper the town had hired. The coyote would be *euthanized,* a chickenshit way of saying "killed" (probably by a .22 to the head). He wondered how they'd know which coyote it was. They'd end up killing a bunch to find the one.

The police had come to his house and asked questions, but no charges were filed. Some of the students had testified that Matt was attacked first, and this absolved him of any wrongdoing. This was not the case with Walnut Grove High. An emergency meeting was called between the school and Matt's parents.

Principal Anderson was a short man who fancied three-piece suits. He was bald and covered it with a toupee. His cheeks looked like that of a chipmunk storing seeds. "You've been a pretty good student, Matt. Not *grade A* but good nonetheless. We've looked at all options for you here at Walnut Grove, but we think it is best for you to move on," Principal Anderson said, licking his thumb and finger to help separate the papers in his file.

Matt sat back in the chair, rubbing his hiking boots together, heel to toe.

"What about a suspension?" Mrs. Kearns pleaded, a tear-damp paper towel balled into her small fist. "Our son was attacked". She was a conservatively beautiful woman, and her pleading was not lost on Principal Anderson.

But Anderson was not in the mood for convincing. "We've been informed that if Matt is not removed there'll be a joint lawsuit filed against the school on behalf of Ben Anderson and Mike Armstrong." Principle Anderson said.

Mrs. Kearns furrowed her brow. "Well, who cares? They can't do that, can they, John?" she asked, looking at his father, her eyes glistening.

Matt's father nodded. Big John, they called him. But not big enough to do a damn thing in this situation. "They can. But we can file a countersuit. This isn't over," his father said.

Principal Anderson sighed. "I'm afraid it is, Mr. Kearns. We've exhausted all possible options."

Matt looked on, mouth agape, dismayed that *doing the right thing* merited expulsion. He bore down on Principal Anderson with his eyes and pointed a finger at the table. "You're telling me that I'm being expelled for defending myself and a helpless animal? I was in danger, Mr. Anderson. *And* protecting the dignity of the school by stopping psychotic behavior. Please, I'll do anything to rectify this."

"I'm sorry," Principle Anderson said, shifting his beady eyes from Matt to his father. "You folks *are* aware that *both* Ben's parents are trial lawyers? The school doesn't want a drawn-out legal battle and I don't think you folks do either." Principal Anderson leaned back in his leather chair, satisfied with the dagger he'd unleashed.

A pall crept into the room, and then his mother and father rose from the table. His mother placed her gentle hand on his shoulder and whispered. "Come on Matthew, it's time to go."

That was the end of Matt Kearn's career at Walnut Grove High. He'd opted to finish his senior year at a computer-based satellite school. He flew through the courses, earning his diploma in June.

Two weeks later, a few residents reported seeing the trapper leave the area, empty cages rattling in the back of his truck.

Journey

Matt Kearns gazed out the windshield, the truck headlights slicing through the Michigan darkness. Moths and mayflies fluttered in the beams along the sloping embankment. He cracked the window and breathed deep. Clean gusts of air curled the edges of three photographs taped to his dashboard. Green glow from the instrument cluster illuminated the photos like museum pieces. The first photo was of his father and him, each hoisting a fresh brook trout. The second photo was of his ex-girlfriend, Stacey. The third photo was of his childhood dog, Elmo.

They were all dead.

His father from lung cancer, and his ex-girlfriend from a drunk named Ed Higgins. The inebriated Ed Higgins ran her over while she was jogging in Ruger Park. She never heard the drunken slob coming thanks to her ear buds. Elmo, good old Elmo, had been taken by cancer as well, but he didn't go as quietly as his father. There wasn't much quiet about Elmo. He'd been a protective, if not psychotic Shih Tzu.

Matt sighed and took in the Northwoods air, which always had a way of clearing his thoughts. He gripped the wheel and sighed again.

Trucks beat you up. At least that's how they used to be before they became luxury couches on wheels. Matt liked his trucks the old fashioned way, the kind that kicked your tail on the highway and gobbled up logging roads. Like the truck he was driving now, a trusty old Toyota 4x4 he'd inherited from his father. He shook his head and couldn't help but smile for a change. Here he was, heading up to the beloved shack for nine days of peace and quiet. And maybe along the way he'd figure out his life, and finally decide if he should go back to college.

The drive from Chicago was close to eight hours and uneventful until reaching the Ottawa National Forest. The "Ottawa" as it was known to locals was a million sprawling acres of undeveloped federal land on the Wisconsin/Michigan border. Long stretches of red pine, jack pine, and aspen dominated the drive. One of the reasons for this trip was the fishing on the Black River, a cutting stream with a slate rock bottom and numerous waterfalls. It was September, and the Coho salmon would be spawning upriver, eager to strike any flashing lure dangled in the clear pools. The other reason for the trip was to heal. Stacey had left this world sixty-four days ago. Elmo one hundred and twenty days, and his father six months now. He thought the sorrow had fractured his mind for good, and even his mother noticed he wasn't doing well. She insisted he go north. She knew this was where Matt was *Matt*.

I'm getting too old for these drives, he thought even though he was twenty-one. He snorted at this, knowing full well it was nonsense. The three hours of sleep the night before might have something to do with it. *Might*.

The four cylinder engine rumbled on, not a force at highway speeds but a real fuel sipper. As he entered the Ottawa National Forest, the big pines increased. The Forest Service liked to keep the roadside trees tall while logging the hell out of the forest beyond view of travelers. If someone were to hike fifty yards in, they'd see stumps and clear cuts. They'd also notice an abundance of stunted poplar and other overcrowding hardwood trees. These took the place of the giant old growth white pine and hemlock that had covered most of the Northwoods. He'd explored a huge portion of the area as a child, and over the years, he'd come to know this country as his home. He'd built up his legs hiking the ravines and rocky ridges of the Huron Mountains.

Despite logging, the Ottawa and Hurons managed to maintain populations of wolves. Native wolverines and mountain lions had long been extirpated from the ecosystem, the result of over-trapping and speciesism-based persecution. His community college biology teacher, Mr. Emerson, was always impressed with Matt's knowledge of flora and fauna, and they often had lengthy conversations about the U.P. These were the school moments he remembered with fondness, the exchanges with teachers where you were equals, just two adults having a conversation.

High road densities in the once roadless forest facilitated the elimination of many predator species via poaching. Former roadless areas were whittled down to nothing over decades. The only remaining unroaded lands were a few 20,000 acre wilderness areas protected by the federal government.

Matt had plans to explore the intriguing Huron Mountains further, always interested by the possibility they may well be the oldest mountain range on earth and at one point as high as the Rockies. Now they were just 2000 foot rocky knobs. But there was always something about them he found captivating. Isolated stands of old growth hemlock reached from ravines and granite-shrouded patches of soil. Wind-battered red pines clung to cliffs. These places were the opposite of the Midwest: scenic. Remote. The old hunting shack he was heading to this very moment sat in the shadow of the Huron's, in a wide forested valley cut by the Black River and its numerous falls and glinting pools. The "shack", as it was known, was surrounded by a defunct apple orchard that now produced miniature, tart apples. Bordering the orchard stood a forest of aspen, alder, balsam fir, and spruce. Springs and bogs supplied the Black River with water all season, refreshing the riverbed even as summer and fall wicked away the water. To the west of the shack loomed Twenty Mile bog. The rest of the area consisted of thick forest, home to fisher, black bears, wolves, and owls. These creatures made the Northwoods what it was. The idea that they still existed made him smile. Coming from the Chicago suburbs, this was a paradise teeming with life and adventure.

Matt ran his hand through his brown hair and searched for some music to accompany the darkness that had crept over the land. In the fading light, the instrument cluster bloomed like a spaceship panel.

Green Day? Neil Young? Eh...not yet. Pink Floyd? Yes. If his parent's generation did one thing right, it was rock music. No, they didn't just do it right, they kicked all sorts of ass.

Matt inserted the disc into the Pioneer CD player and "Let There Be More Light" pounced through the speakers.

He rolled down the window by a third and breathed cool Northwood's air. Such a contrast from Chicagoland.

The Toyota pickup rolled down empty U.S. 2. The locals were either at home watching TV or at a convenient watering hole, usually called "Insert Name Here showing possession" Northwoods Tavern. One of the benefits of this wild locale was the lack of people, so traveling on an empty road was a kick.

As Matt reached for the heater switch a stout white-tailed deer leapt in front of the truck. He hit the brakes and gripped the steering wheel. Tires shrieked and the sick smell of burning rubber stung his nose. The unlucky deer let out a sheep-like cry as the driver's side hood skimmed its left rump. The deer's eyes widened to the size of tea cubs as it sprinted up the embankment to the spruce trees. The truck screeched to a stop, rubber smoke wafting in front of the headlights. The chattering four cylinder and radio penetrated the sudden stillness.

Matt rolled his window down. The deer was nowhere to be found. He turned the music down, grabbed the heavy-duty flashlight from under the seat, and inspected the truck's grille. No visible damage, no blood and no deer hair. For good measure he walked over to the embankment, shining the flashlight into the ditch, working a good fifty yards in front of and behind the truck. If he found the deer he'd ease it out of this world one way or another. He hated people who ran over animals without looking back to see if they were still suffering. Running over an animal didn't mean it was dead, not at all. A year ago in Glacier National Park (on a trip with Stacey) he'd seen a red squirrel run over by a car doing forty in a twenty-five mph zone. Only the back legs of the red squirrel were run over. The squirrel had chirped and cried, valiantly pulling itself a few feet before collapsing in a heap on the road, still alive. Another red squirrel had scurried onto the pavement and tried to pull the crippled squirrel off the road. He remembered watching in horror as the scene unfolded, the desperate chittering of the healthy red squirrel, and the terrible screams of the injured one. When the healthy red squirrel had given up, he'd returned to his vehicle and proceeded to drive over the injured squirrel, ending its life before any more suffering could occur.

He'd never forgotten that squirrel. Sometimes he pictured it in his mind, its eyes bulging. Sometimes he could still hear the chirping as it tried to warn others of the danger, its striking cinnamon fur ruffling in the wind and the tiny, pink sliver of tongue like a tender plant root. But worst of all was how the squirrel looked up at him with its mouth open, a hint of teeth showing and the fear in its eyes right before death took it. That incident made him question a lot of things. One of those things was God. What kind of God would allow such a thing to happen? It didn't make any sense. But then not much made sense to him—especially things like rules and the behavior of his peers and supposed authority figures. There was always friction with the world no matter how hard he tried. In many ways, he sensed a stronger bond with the creatures of the woods than he did with people—except for the ones he was already close to.

Some would find that disturbing or introverted but for him that was reality. That was what he saw out of his own two eyes and felt with his own heart. Did he exhibit an underlying anxiety when near people? Maybe. But it's not like he was a loner. He had friends, but quality over quantity. He sensed that pull, that bit of fear in many social situations—probably why he kept a core group of friends and didn't venture often into new social territory.

What he did prefer was hiking in wilderness areas. There were trips with his ex-girlfriend Stacey to Glacier National Park in Montana and Yellowstone National Park in Wyoming. They'd go during spring break sometimes, when most kids went to sunny beaches. Less people, too, snow or not. He could hear himself think in the woods and mountains, could spread his arms and kick back.

Balance.

The country out in Montana was still wild. A 20,000 acre wilderness area was nothing out there. You could find 2 million acres wilderness complexes and spend years exploring. Back in the Northwoods, back in the Ottawa you were amongst endless logging roads. Less than one percent of the old growth forest remained. Most of the big animals that had sauntered across the Northwoods were ghosts. But for some reason, this place still had such a *strong* feeling of home. He liked it. No, he *loved* it. All the little streams gleaming in the forest. The clumsy porcupines fumbling around in tree tops and bald eagles swooping from hidden lake to hidden lake.

A benefit of the Northwoods was the eight hour drive from the Chicago suburbs. You had to travel twenty-two hours to reach Yellowstone. For a working man, this was all the difference in the world. He busted his ass six days a week in the summer for Stinson Construction. This entailed pouring concrete foundations for McMansions in the suburbs. The labor was difficult at times but he found it soothing. Being outside was always preferable to sitting indoors in crummy office air.

You have to spread your wings, his father would often tell him.

He couldn't spread his wings in some little office. No room. He couldn't spread his wings in high school, either (or the alternative computer-based school). Both buildings had always seemed like prison to him. Even worse was the dearth of windows. The only natural light entered from the ends of long hallways, piping into the halls and then pulling back as if to say *I'm not going in there*. So the light waited for him outside the doors, as the Northwoods waited for him. Stepping outside, he was reborn.

Even with the disdain for high school he did well, playing soccer and getting okay grades and dating pretty girls. Until *The Incident*...something he didn't talk much about, or even want to remember. The most vivid recollection he had from *The Incident* was the look he got from his father when returning home that fateful day. His father had stormed out of the house. His mother, always one to plug the gaps and paint over the cracks hugged Matt when his father had left.

It's for the best, Matthew, she'd said. *He will be back. Time will heal this.*

She was right, as she often was. Time did heal it. But time couldn't heal his father's cancer. "Big John," they'd called him. Big John liked to smoke and smoke he did. And Big John didn't just smoke the lights, he went right for Marlboro Reds at two packs a day.

Big John had big hands. And a big everything else. His father was assertive, but offering encouragement where needed. It was his father who'd taught him about the outdoors. He was the one who initiated the quick trips up north. The "bonsai" trips as they were referred to were fast three day trips up to the shack. His father would have the gear packed the night before, coolers and duffel bags stuffed with smoked sausage, canned goods, hash browns, camping equipment, and fishing gear. The old flannel sleeping bags were so bulky they'd take up half the pickup bed. Having everything packed the night before allowed them to head out when his father got off work from the phone company at three p.m. Big John was pretty damn slick with telecommunications. He was trained by the Army, even stationed in Turkey for a while, working on several top secret radio jamming projects that he couldn't discuss.

Just know that what I know, people don't want you to know, he'd say when prodded.

Sometimes he could tell his father was full of shit because his upper lip stiffened and his eyes widened. But that never happened when Matt brought up the Army. He never got it out of him, even on his deathbed.

The bonsai trips were scheduled around the working man. By leaving at three p.m. on a Friday, they could drive eight hours to the shack and get a decent night's sleep. They'd stay for Saturday and Sunday, leaving Sunday night at seven. This would allow them to get back by three a.m., enough for three or four hours of sleep before his father had to go to work.

There was always competition among Matt's friends to come up north, and his father would sometimes allow a couple to tag along. When this happened, he'd set up cots in the back of the pickup. Having the camper shell facilitated the cot system. Matt and his friends would watch the world change at their feet through the rear window. Sometimes it was like they were launched in a rocket, the world sucked away behind them, cars, lights, and traffic diminishing as they headed north. They'd bounce in the cots and sleeping bags during rough patches like astronauts punching through the atmosphere. Then the pine trees appeared like ghosts and the cars were few. A new world. A cleaner world.

Matt shined the flashlight to the eastern tree line, illuminating the sweeping branches of spruce and occasional spider web. The deer was gone. *Probably alright*, he thought. He'd had close encounters before and even smacked into a deer near Big Timber,

Montana. The area was known as "deer alley", home to outlandish numbers of mule deer under the shadow of the Crazy Mountains. The deer in that accident had also disappeared, but he'd assumed it wasn't going to make it when he'd seen the smashed front end of the truck. But that was another land, far away from the Ottawa National Forest and the Huron Mountains—a land that wasn't cut up.

He walked back to the truck and got in. Despite having close to 200,000 miles, the vehicle started just fine. He admired it as much as you could admire any material item. The old Toyota 4x4 had seen him through high school, numerous girlfriends, construction work, and innumerable camping trips. That wasn't even counting the trips his father had made up north with it. The truck was beginning to rust and the muffler never sounded right no matter the amount of repair work. Acceleration wasn't so hot, either. He guessed his truck was dying. Maybe this was the last trip.

The little four cylinder engine purred, accompanied by cacophonous swamp frogs out of sight behind tree line. He smiled, at last back in the Northwoods with his trusty steed. He rubbed the grey plastic dashboard a few times as if to say "good girl," the way you would to a horse. He felt a little crazy doing it, but whatever.

The pickup rolled into the night along the empty highway, still an hour from the shack. It'd get there. It always got there.

The fresh Northwoods air always made him ravenous. Matt grabbed the chocolate-covered wafer cookies he'd taken from his mother's place. Sometimes he stopped over to grab food before trips. He liked the way her food tasted, liked the smell of the kitchen. Even if he went out and bought the exact cookies, they wouldn't taste the same. It was some sort of voodoo mother magic.

His mother had moved to a condo in the suburbs after his father died. For the time being, he'd been allowed to stay in the family house as it was prepped for sale. There were ways of delaying the realtors though....

He always thought of his mother as that tall pretty woman with dark hair. His little league baseball coaches always gawked at her. They'd ask him if that was *really* his mom. this was amusing the first fifty times. It happened so often he stopped answering them—instead choosing to furrow his brow at them. His mother's favorite activity was sewing and she even had her own room dedicated to it. She'd win Halloween costume contests and lavish Matt and his sister Andrea with the prizes. One year it was a PlayStation video game system, and he still remembered staying up to one a.m. playing Resident Evil with Andrea, the cold October wind scattering leaves against the glass patio doors.

The cooking wasn't the only thing that he used to go over to his mom's place for. His childhood dog, Elmo had lived there part-time after his father died. Matt and Andrea shared him the rest of the time. The poor old pup had been dragged in three directions at once. How he'd loved Elmo, taking him for long walks and giving him way too many treats.

But there was no Elmo at his mother's place this time, no face-wide grin and wagging tail. He still had Elmo's ashes in the house, on the corner of his dresser in a red aluminum case with a floral design.

Mile after mile, headlights revealed the landscape. A pair of glowing eyes hovered up the western embankment at tree line. A raccoon. They used to be uncommon here, but he'd read that climate change was pushing them north. He glanced to the oncoming lane. No cars. His mother always warned him about keeping too tight to the oncoming lane. *Stay away from the death lane,* she'd said, eyes pleading. It's not as if he had a choice. Most Northwood's roads were two lanes. You *had* to be near the death lane.

The temperature dropped and thick fog crept over the road. Cold air filled his lungs as he shifted the truck into fourth gear, then third, then second. He peered into the foggy night, searching for the right turn onto Julip Road. the thick boreal forest did not make it easy. Another five hundred feet of ferns and aspen, and Julip Road emerged from the fog, wide at the highway like a river mouth. Gravel spilled out onto the asphalt, washed down by rain from the highlands.

His trusty 4x4 attacked the gravel, chewed it up, and spit rocks behind it. The steep road tilted him to the fog-consumed sky, and his arms shook from the washboard. Julip Road would take him into the highlands, away from the low country that bordered Lake Superior. As the road climbed, aspen and spruce crowded the truck. Fog enveloped the headlights like a blanket over a flashlight. The trees stood like respected elders in the darkness, their branches reaching across the ragged embankment in a pagan greeting. Frogs leapt from puddles in the road, desperate to escape the beams and tires. Voles skittered across the gravel like cartoon animals, their feet flying behind them. Matt always braked. Didn't require much effort. He rolled down his window and stuck his nose into the wind, catching the scent of sweet flag and pungent earth.

After eight miles of narrowing, rough road he brought the truck to a stop and turned right. The truck climbed a dirt two track hidden by golden grass. The grass whispered against the truck's side panels and clamored against the undercarriage. Soon the headlights revealed a small clearing and a haggard shack. A great horned owl swooped from a behemoth aspen next to the shack and disappeared into the fog.

Once he was sure the truck was parked on a flat enough surface (the emergency brake needed repair), he shut the engine off and put the truck in gear. Matt stepped into the cool night, the owl hooting behind the fog wall at the edge of the orchard. No stars tonight. Even the moon was obscured. Wind nudged a patch of fog, revealing the path to the top of the orchard. The honey scent of yarrow permeated the breeze.

He went behind the seat of the truck and took his blue backpack. Then he shouldered the hefty pack and lumbered towards the enormous wooden shack door.

Sleep will come easy tonight, he thought.

Iron Daily News February 21, 2014
What's Killing the Moose?

Sandy Jones, Outdoor Reporter
Ironville, Michigan – New data fresh from the Department of Natural Resources shows the Michigan moose population continues to decline.

Aerial survey results revealed a precipitous drop this year, with a total count of one thousand moose compared to last year's two thousand. Officials have not determined an exact cause although climate change and tick infestation are being investigated.

Researchers say they have never witnessed such a large drop. Officials are preparing to close the moose hunting season until a cause can be determined. Several town hall meetings will be held across the region in an effort to explain why the moose are disappearing and a possible hunting season closure.

Officials claim there is no reason for panic and that predicting animal populations is not an exact science. Michael Eggerts, field biologist for the Michigan DNR has been working the area for the last twenty years and was one of the principal architects of the original Michigan moose reintroduction. "Yes, the moose numbers are falling." Eggerts said. "Yes we have serious concerns about this issue. But that doesn't mean we need to panic."

Michigan sits at the southern limits of moose habitat and may become inhospitable to the animals as temperatures warm. Moose are heat-sensitive, and temperature graphs the last twenty years show a warm spike....

On air transcription from Ironville's KBIL "The Moose" 660 AM
Location: Ironville, Michigan
KBIL "The Moose" 660 AM
8:30 p.m. to 9:30 p.m.
Program title: Jim Gibbon's Talkland
Details: Golden oldies and open lines

Jim Gibbons, Ironville DJ: Welcome back folks. Tonight we're running open lines. If you have something to talk about, feel free to let your fingers do the punching and dial us in. Please turn down your radio so we don't have the echo echo echo. Okay, first caller, you're on Talkland with Jim Gibbons. Please state your location and name.

Caller: Hello, Jim.

Jim: Could you please turn down your radio, caller? I'm getting some feedback. Please state your name and location.

Caller: Oh…gosh I'm sorry…is that better? This is…this is Betsy from Ironville.

Jim: Yes, yes that's much better Betsy. Thanks for calling Talkland tonight. What's on your mind?

Betsy: Well, I was wondering if you were going to speak tomorrow night at the town hall meeting. It's about the building permits. My husband and I want to build a third storage shed on our property, back at the forest line and the county says we need a hundred dollar permit to do that. I don't think that's right and I want you to come down and speak for us.

Jim: Thanks Betsy, but I have no plans to speak at the meeting. But I do have to ask why so many storage sheds?

Betsy: My husband and I never throw a thing out. He keeps all our old shutters and doors. When he does the roof on our place, we keep the old shingles stored away. We also need more room to store the grandkids' snowmobiles and jet skis.

Jim: So what do you do with the old shingles?

Betsy: We store them.

Jim: Do you use them?

Betsy: No. We keep them around in case we need to use 'em. You do the same I bet.

Jim: Ah no I don't. Betsy, I think you might want to throw your junk out and not build a third storage shed. Have you thought about that?

Betsy: Just who the hell are you to tell us what—

Jim: Alrighty, next caller, you're on Talkland.

Caller: Hey Jim. This is Erickson from up on Huron Road.

Jim: Whoa, way up there, eh Erickson? I didn't know they had reception out there yet. What's on your mind tonight?

Erickson: I was wondering if you knew about the moose problem.

Jim: Yes, yes I'm aware. From what I can remember they are dropping like flies. The paper is printing up a storm. The hunters are getting riled up and some of the animal activists want to stop the hunt.

Erickson: Ayup. There used to be a bunch of moose around here. We saw them every morning at Harry's Pond. Now they don't come around much. You spend time on these roads. Seen any?

Jim: No, not for quite some time. I like not seeing them. Who wants a moose through the windshield? I know I don't. (pause) Our good producer just informed me that biologist Eggerts is going to be interviewed on 660 AM Tuesday afternoon. Are you tuning in?

Erickson: You bet. But only because I want to see if Eggerts is gonna keep lying. (heavy breathing).

Jim: (snickering) What's he lying about Erickson? Let us in on your secret.

Erickson: The moose aren't dying from the warming. They're dying from another animal.

Jim: (snickering) How do you know this? Do you have proof?

Erickson: My dad and I were up in the Hurons near Mill Bridge bucketing berries. We found this real nice patch of blueberries, enough to fill all our buckets. Dad went up the hill, just to where the edge of the berry patch met the big hemlocks. Then he looked up and screamed. I've never seen him do that.

Jim: (laughter) So what was it, Erickson? Bigfoot or a black helicopter?

Erickson: (long pause and heavy breathing) A moose carcass. It was strung out over a branch fifty feet up the tree. Now you tell me Jim, you ever see an eagle do that?

Jim: No, of course not. But I'm not sure where this is going, Erickson. If you are just trying to make things up to scare—

Erickson: It's not made up. It's the God's honest truth, swear on my ma.

Jim: What about a cougar? They're known to drag prey into trees.

Erickson: There hasn't been cougar around here since one hundred years.

Jim: I hate to tell you this Erickson but a cougar makes more sense than anything else. There's no other explanation.

Erickson: A cougar can't pull a moose into a tree. The only animal can do that is a grizzly bear, and they only have those out west. No black bear could pull a full grown moose fifty feet up a tree. This was a big bull, Jim. And since there are no cougars, where does that leave us?

Jim: Well it leaves us with no explanation of any kind. But I ask again caller, where is your proof? We need more than your word. Don't you have a digital camera? Everyone has those now. Did you get video?

Erickson: My pa and I went back and borrowed John Lusten's video cam he uses for the YouTube. When we got back to the tree, the moose carcass was gone.

Jim: Gone? Now you tell me how a moose carcass just disappears from a tree?

Erickson: You tell me how a moose carcass gets fifty feet in the air. You tell me.

Jim: Caller, I can tell you how a moose carcass gets fifty feet up a tree. It's called *your imagination*. That's exactly how it got there. THANK YOU Erickson for entertaining Talkland with your preposterous story tonight. Those who want facts should tune in for biologist Eggerts' interview on Tuesday. We'll be back with more Talkland after these words from our local sponsors....

-------CUT transcription -----------

The Trapper

"Careful what you trap up here, fella. You may not like what ya catch." -Skeet Ackerson

After a substantial breakfast of hot cakes and hash browns, Matt made his way north on Julip Road. The graders had worked hard this year, pushing the edges back even further and smoothing the road for logging trucks. They'd pushed so hard that sometimes scarred tree roots jammed through the sandy embankment like steroidal earth worms. There was a lot of that sort of thing around here, a blatant disregard for the land and its wild inhabitants.

The clean morning air invigorated him. A couple years ago, he'd gone online and checked the EPA air quality ratings for the U.S. The reports indicated the Northwoods had a CLASS ONE rating, the best you could get. States with larger cities were rated the worst, especially if they were near refineries.

The Toyota rambled downhill towards Lake Superior, passing rutted cherry stem two-tracks that dissected the U.P. forest like rogue arteries. There weren't many places without some kind of logging road or ATV route. Most of the wilderness had long been hacked out of the landscape, or at least as it was defined by the U.S. Forest Service. Real wilderness didn't have roads. Oh, a few places remained and Matt knew them well. They were a rugged drive from the shack, but he did visit them. The granite knobs and ridges of the Huron Mountains visible from the orchard was one such place. Today he was heading in the opposite direction, away from the Hurons and down to the mouth of the Black River where he'd try his luck fly fishing. The Black was a clear trout stream that flowed at a ridiculous pitch from the Hurons into Lake Superior. The river bordered the eastern boundary of the shack property, but this was far above the barrier falls that prevented the salmon from swimming upstream. The salmon had no choice but to gather downstream of the craggy thirty foot drop. Below the falls swirled an impressive pool surrounded on three sides by moss-covered cliffs. The cliffs towered over the falls and were dotted with the occasional stout hemlock that had managed to survive the axe. The slate streambed made it slick and dangerous to walk, and jagged rows of slate spiked from the water like the plates on a stegosaurus. Large slot channels ran on for fifty feet in some places.

Matt dreamed of this place often.

Sometimes the landscape details were foggy. Other times everything cleared, enough to see drops of moisture beading on the bright-green moss. Sometimes the people he cared about appeared, often standing knee deep in the pool below Black Falls. He'd call out to them, but they wouldn't speak. His mother and father. Stacey. His sister. Friends from high school.

At last he reached Highway 5 and turned right, passing over the Black River, clear water spilling out of the woodland and glinting in the sun. A hundred yards down Highway 5 brought him to a dirt parking lot on the right side of the road.

Matt got out of the truck, pressed the lever behind the seat, and took the nylon tube which held his four piece fly rod. He put on his tan fishing vest, reached into the front right pocket, and pulled out his silver fly reel. The rod was a gift from Stacey for a trip to Montana. Matt squeezed the case and fought back the images of her.

He slid the burgundy fly rod from the case, relishing the craftsmanship. He set the reel to the rod seat and then attached the other sections of the rod—each one smaller and lighter than the last. The simplicity pleased him. It was nice to not be obsessing on depressing things.

The tip section was fragile in his hand. Hell, everything seemed fragile lately. He ran the fishing line up through the fly rod guides, careful not to let the line fall back through. Once the line was through the top guide, he pinched it with his other hand and pulled the line taught, forcing the reel to unwind. When enough line was out, he tied on a pattern that worked well on this river—a bushy red and white humpy fly.

Matt sighed, locked the truck, and headed up trail to Black River Falls.

The lower forest of Huron country consisted of birch trees, aspen, and other hardwoods. Most of the trees were small although near the river they fattened and provided an extensive canopy. Patches of blueberry and lady fern dotted the forest floor. In the past, this area was predominately white pine, red pine, and hemlock with a dash of beech and aspen. Here along the river (now protected from logging) a few of those big pines remained. They appeared as freaks of nature, their trunks dwarfing others and their crowns looming above the rest. The first of these big pines was a four hundred year old hemlock known as *Lazarus*, and it marked the entrance to the Black River Canyon trail. Matt rested his fly rod against the beast and gave it a hearty pat. Then he steered his gaze up through the layered branches and needles. An unseen red squirrel chittered from high up in the crown. Matt smiled.

This had been a sacred trail of sorts since he was a child. His father had taken him up into the Black Canyon numerous times. During those trips the canyon walls seemed much higher and the water deeper. Now they felt comfortable, although he couldn't help but sometimes feel as if he was a giant that had outgrown his childhood home.

He climbed higher, watching his steps with the felt-soled wading boots. Soon the trail ascended, bringing him closer to the canopy of the trees down the slope. A pileated woodpecker swooped up a tree and gripped the bark with its claws, smooth as could be. A vertical runway. Heck, *we* couldn't even do that yet.

Rushing water whispered to him from far below. Shimmering glimpses of the Black appeared to his right, between old growth hemlocks that speared the ravine walls.

Welcome home, he said to himself.

As beat up as these woods were, a bond still existed, a thing that had established itself without his consent. He was brought here as a boy and *that was that*. The landscape had burrowed into him for life. No cure, no remediation. All he could do was accept.

The ravine to his right steepened and revealed less light than the ridge he hiked. Fifty feet ahead squatted a burned-out stump that marked the descent point to Black Falls. Matt held the long part of the fly rod out behind him, tip up. If he fell forward with the rod pointing in front of him the tip would splinter into the ground. Then he half-sat and scooted down the ravine wall, gear in his fishing vest jingling like a bumped Christmas tree. As he slid down the ravine, his boots furrowed aside layers of pine needles and sandy soil. The shady trunks made excellent places to slow momentum provided he was not going too fast and played the landing just right. Occasionally a red squirrel chittered and tried to drop cones on him. He laughed. *Little devious buggers.* Ever since the red squirrel incident in Glacier National Park, he'd been in awe of how intelligent they were.

The falls pool gleamed from below, the foamy back eddy swirling in-between two hemlocks. Another hundred foot drop and he'd be on the rocky spit of land that bordered the pool.

When he was younger, he and his father would sometimes swim the pool. The water was clear for most of the year except for spring runoff. Two slick logs stood upright at the base of the falls, rising along the slate face and stopping just short of the lip. They'd been this way for as long as he could remember. The water surging off the lip ran diagonal between two gouged channels of slate. Glistening rock walls sloped into the pool on three sides and were layered with pine needles and moss, which predominated closer to the water. A steep and suspect trail wound its way up the left side of the falls and upriver. In order to get to this questionable trail a hiker had to balance on a section of exposed slate fins bordering a sheer rock wall. The protrusions looked like a submerged stegosaurus. He'd tried it without much luck several years back— he had to of been twelve, maybe thirteen. Getting in and out of the Black River Canyon was not easy. In order to be here, you had to *want* to be here.

Grateful to be on flat land again he took a seat on a dried cedar log at the high water mark. He opened his backpack, took a swig of soda, and surveyed the water for rising fish.

Nothing.

He stood, inched towards the edge of the pool, and kneeled. This was something he'd learned over the years when approaching clear water. You don't want to let the fish know you're there. If they do, pack your fly rod and go home. He unhooked the fly from the holder, pulled out extra line, and dipped the rod behind him, then forward. He did this several times until thirty feet of line sailed in the air. Then, one final push and the line arced forward in a well-formed loop. The red humpy propelled straight and true, nipping the water with nary a circle. Matt watched the bushy fly, eyes locked in hawk-like focus.

Nothing.

He continued to work the pool, but no takers. He even tried the "lucky spot", as his father had coined it. It was the hardest water to reach, a pocket hidden between the sheer rock face of the falls and the two protruding logs. The bigger fish used this as shelter and a feeding area. No eagle or bear would try and swipe the trout from such a precarious position. But on this particular day, the "lucky spot" wasn't so lucky. It didn't matter, though. He was entranced by the rhythms of nature, the cadence of falling water, the gurgling over multihued substrate.

Something screeched high up in the trees, breaking his meditative state. Maybe a barred owl, but he couldn't be sure.

A beautiful day, he said to the woods. He gazed into the hypnotic pool, his thoughts pure and free. There was nothing but this canyon and the beauty. Or so he thought.

"Hey guy, you got your fishin' license?" a gruff male voice asked behind him.

Matt jumped and whirled, trying not to show fear when he realized it was just another outdoorsman. The man looked to be in his fifties with slick, black hair, a thin face, and a long nose. The man wore an orange hunter's vest and held the chains of several steel traps in his right hand. The trap receptacles swayed above the rocks like small iron plates. The circular outline of a tin of chewing tobacco pressed against the right chest pocket of the orange vest.

"You got your fishin' license, guy?" the man asked again.

Matt cleared his throat. "Always. Why, are you a warden?" He doubted this guy was a warden, but you never knew up here.

"I'm asking because they a waste of money, guy," the man said, laughing. "I don't give no crap if you ain't got a license. But be careful, if the warden shows up he'll pinch ya. He pinched me and

Davey last year. You don't wanna get pinched. Watch yer back, guy."

"I have a license," Matt said.

"You ain't trappin'?" the man asked.

"Nope."

"Everybody traps up here, guy. Woods are full of 'em. You can't walk ten feet without steppin' on one."

"I'll watch where I walk, thanks." Matt felt an urge to search the forest, disabling whatever traps he could find. This wasn't the frontier anymore. People didn't need to kill these critters in such a brutal fashion to survive the winter.

"Trappin' in the Yooper's a tradition, guy," the man said, his left eyelid twitching.

The stench of stale beer, the kind of smell that slowly takes over a keg party as the night wears on, wafted towards Matt. He waved, as if that would dismiss the man and the smell. "Okay, thanks, but I have no interest in trapping."

The man's face scrunched up and reddened. "Bullshit you ain't trapping, guy. You got a set in your truck? I saw it back at the lot." The man held up his left arm. A series of trap lines clanked from it, little plates of death rattling at the bottom.

Yeah, things were starting to get slightly uncomfortable. Why was this stranger poking around his truck? Weird bordering on unsettling. "I don't trap," Matt said. "Don't plan to, don't want to."

The trapper listed to the left and slurred his words. Then he laughed, revealing a fermenting wad of chew in the back of his mouth. Black specks plugged the gaps in his teeth.

"Well, whether you do or ya don't, be careful of what you trap up here fella. You may not like what ya catch," he said.

Matt kicked his boot toe into the gravel. "I'll take that into consideration." Matt looked up the ravine, then kicked his boot into the gravel again, clear signs he was done with the conversation. Did he need to actually turn his back on the guy so he got the message?

The man's eyes narrowed. "By the way guy, what's your name? I saw your plates and I know you're a F.I.B."

"F.I.B." was a term some Northwoods locals used to describe visitors from Illinois. It was short for *Freaking Illinois Brat*, or *Fucking Illinois Brat* if so inclined.

Matt straightened his posture and glared at the man. Maybe now he'd get the message. "I'm Matt, not FIB. And FIB has become sort of a cliché, don't you think?"

The man spit a black globule onto the dried log, just missing a scurrying black ant. "Ain't no quiche if it's true. By the way, name's Skeet. Skeet Ackerson. I'm over on Jessup Road, last graded till the Hurons."

Matt chuckled. *Quiche?* The gaffe put him at ease and made him hungry at the same time.

"Alright, nice to meet you, Skeet. Good luck on your hunt," he said with as much enthusiasm as a boy telling his parents that yes, he'll eat the green beans after all.

Skeet squinted up into the canopy, then scanned the woods as if something was traveling from tree to tree. "Be careful out here, guy. I been trapping these woods since '72. They feel sick. F.I.B. or not, we all gotta survive in this economy, right guy?"

Matt thought it unusual to make peace while also serving an insult, but accepted anyway. "Yep," he offered.

Skeet fixed his gaze on him, and for the first time in the conversation Matt sensed fear in his voice.

"Oh, and guy, stay out of the Hurons. Davey was up drinking near the wilderness boundary two weeks ago and said he saw somethin' he never seen before...well, more like *heard* something. Said it was like an elephant moving through the edge of the clear-cut. Scared him straight out of there so bad he almost smashed two trees with his Chevy before getting back to his place. I come over and he's got the front door barricaded. I could see his eyeball looking out a slit in the planks, blinking and the pupil darting like a tadpole. That's how he knew it was me. I talked him into letting me in and he had all his guns on the card table, popped and ready. He was pacing back and forth, too. Never seen Davey like that. Never. I asked him if it was a big bear, he said it wasn't nothin' close to a bear of any kind. We seen plenty of bear up here guy, plenty. This wasn't no bear. No bear can get past me and Davey."

Matt didn't care for the tone of Skeet's voice, and he was surprised to conclude this didn't sound like a standard booze story. Those all had a familiar theme. These were guys who drove the woods drunk and armed. They feared little. It was everyone else who feared *them*. For these bullies to be spooked? What would it take?

"Well guy, I got some lines to check. Watch your back and not just for the warden. These woods are running a fever, guy."

Skeet turned his back to him and grunted his way up the eastern ravine wall. Matt was shocked at how fast he made it up, like a bear. Skeet's silhouette appeared up on the ridge, and for a second Matt thought he saw him looking down towards the pool.

Then he was gone.

The Shack

On the way back from Black Falls a porcupine ambled across Julip Road, and Matt swerved to avoid it. The porcupine sauntered across the road as if it couldn't be bothered. Porcupines didn't have much to fear, but he knew of one animal they don't want to run across—a fisher. He'd read that fishers have a way of flipping porcupines and attacking their soft underbelly.

The spiky animal slogged up the bank into the cinnamon ferns, where it gawked back at him, eyes wide and questioning. The right side of its mouth quivered underneath the right eye, creating an uncanny human impression of fear. Then it straightened its head and shambled into the ferns and bog birch. A moment later crows rustled in the tree tops, their wings like dry newspaper.

The drive from Highway 5 to the shack was eight bumpy-ass miles and mostly a straight run down Julip Road, passing a few bogs within the ever-present boreal forest. Most of the forest on the stretch was second-growth hardwood trees. Red pine, white pine, and hemlock made rare appearances. Fifteen years ago the sides of the road were thick with hemlock but the loggers had gotten those, too. Matt remembered seeing their gnarled branches while looking out the back of his father's pickup. Now the road was much wider and pine-less. Tourists in sedans and station wagons gave up about a quarter-mile down Julip Road from the Highway 5 junction. It was just too much. Those that did make the drive to the Huron Mountain wilderness boundary were few. Sometimes it could be a week before you heard another motor.

A few temporary logging roads emanated from Julip Road. These side roads produced more two tracks to access even more timber. Most of the forest was penetrated by this cherry stem system. He often wondered how many animals had denning areas disturbed by mechanized activity and where they'd go to avoid it. The answer to that was of course pretty simple: the bogs and remote roadless areas in the Huron Mountains. The bogs held old timber, usually white pine and hemlock. These were often on the periphery or in raised pockets of dry land in the bog's center. Obviously ideal places for animals to raise their young.

Matt reached the shack property and turned right up the steep two track. Tall grass swished against the chassis of the truck.

In ten seconds he was parked in front of the shack. When he shut off the engine, he was overcome by how quiet everything was. And so still.

He *loved* it.

The truck door creaked open and he stood to survey the land that had swirled in his blood for so long. Goosebumps peppered his arms as he remembered how he and his father tossed a football around in this very spot.

The shack was an ancient log structure, twenty by twenty feet, with hand-crafted, small diameter logs. An asphalt shingle roof hung over the sides and front by five feet. The south, west, and east walls each contained a single window. All the windows featured simple, wooden lattices opened by undoing a brass latch and swinging the panes inward. Ratty curtains made of red burlap clung to the southern and eastern windows.

A pile of wood and an aging wheelbarrow sat along the western outside wall. A basic Coleman grill—the kind you see on a thousand porches—leaned against the firewood. A massive aspen tree towered over the eastern side of the shack, its branches splaying in all directions. It was one of the most impressive aspen Matt had seen, and he'd seen quite a few. Its white bark was smooth and matte. The leaves looked like jumbo silver dollars. On windy days the leaves fluttered and sang like a balsa wood chime.

Behind the shack to the north was the widest part of the orchard. The apple trees no longer produced sweet apples. Instead they delivered tart little monsters that made your mouth pucker. Eventually this part of the orchard joined the encompassing forest, rising to greet it to the north. The shack's west side was also orchard, rolling out into open high ground. A short path led from the shack uphill towards the property high point. A single, wooden leaning post marked the top of the high point, nothing more than two posts and a horizontal piece of wood connecting them. The leaning post stood as a symbol from a time long ago when the property was an active apple orchard and farm. It had been a hitching post, but now was a place to put beer, cigarettes, whiskey bottles, and lighters. Next to the post, embedded into charred soil was a fire pit. The view from here was one of the best in the U.P., and that was no exaggeration.

Matt loved it, always had. The Midwest wasn't known for rugged, scenic views, but *this* was an exception. Everyone who first glimpsed this spot seemed to be in a trance. From this vantage point one could gaze across miles of seamless hardwood forest to the south. The forest stretched on until it piled against the ancient Huron Mountains, like someone had bunched up a vibrant rug. The Hurons, rising like a sleeping giant in broken granite ridges, dominated the horizon.

To the west of the high point, the orchard dipped into lowlands, and eventually Twenty Mile Bog, one of the least inaccessible locations in all the Northwoods. The trees deep in the bog had never met the axe. Twenty Mile had always been a source of strange noises. Moose and bear could be heard huffing and snapping branches. Fishers darted around the bog, using the dead fall as forest highways. Bobcats found the orchard and bog edges to be prime hunting grounds, often stalking numerous grouse that used the tall grass to hide. The rare goshawk nested high in older bog trees, hunting along the orchard edges, surprising rabbits and grouse with ambush tactics.

The ten acre orchard was walled by dense vegetation on all sides. The transition zone was distinct. Open terrain filled with knee-high grass collided with walls of spruce, fir, birch, alder, and aspen. Over time, Matt guessed the forest would swallow the orchard, reclaiming it. After all, the orchard was carved out of the forest to begin with. Nature sought what was always hers. That's how it worked. *Maybe she'd reclaim us all in the end,* he thought.

As Matt hiked the property, the sun warmed his bones and spirit. A breeze sighed across the valley from the Hurons, rustling alder and chokecherry. He saw the breeze coming a minute before he felt it. That's how it was here.

The front of the shack faced a huge, dead oak. This truly was one of the monsters of the Northwoods, all silver and weathered.

Most of the branches were gone. Thirty feet of trunk remained with remnant branch spears sticking out like a madman raising his arms into the air. Woodpeckers often hammered away on the leviathan in search of insects. Behind the dead oak dipped a steep, grassy bowl—the location of the original farm house which was lost to a fire. His father had told him the previous owner fell asleep in bed with a cigarette. Built into the slope on the far side of the bowl was a crumbling wooden structure that once held pigs and chickens. Next to the pen, also embedded into the slope was a carpentry room that also served as an ice room, the chips and shavings swept into a floor hole to help maintain the ice's temperature.

Matt had always wondered how the old farm managed to survive. This was not farm country. The methods imparted upon the land were tenuous at best. This was ten acres hammered out of the wilderness, and getting to town took an hour. But the owners didn't need to go to town. They raised chickens and pigs and grew apples. They procured drinking water from the Black River across Julip Road. They built an honest living out here in the middle of nowhere.

But what a fragile existence, he thought.

This thought was reinforced by the ghost-like structures that lingered, the leaning post, and crumbling logs half-buried in patches of sandy soil in the orchard. He once walked down into the grassy bowl and noticed flexing wood under his boots—remnants of the farmhouse.

He often wondered about living up here, if he could pull it off. The main problem was a lack of jobs. The former tenants of this land didn't worry about that though, did they? He found their ability to survive out here romantic, if not admirable. He wanted that for himself someday.

The shack stood as the last intact structure of the old farm operations. Despite a little mold, it was holding up fine. Lake Superior casted a humidifying spell on these highlands, and sometimes he'd wake to find the property ensconced in fog. No doubt this contributed to the damp smell.

A few yards southeast of the shack was a sloping section of grassland that made up the two track driveway. Matt followed the driveway down to Julip Road. Directly across the road was a half-acre section of the property besieged by a jungle of maple, birch, and enormous Goldie's fern. Walking through that soup was always a challenge. You couldn't see anything below your waist as the ferns obscured the ground. Anyone trudging through the salad had no idea if they were going to surprise an animal. He often thought he'd stir up a sleeping bear back in that jumble, maybe even a mother with cubs. So why not just avoid it? Water. The Black was much smaller up here at the shack, but substantial enough to roar during spring runoff. Rotting logs, moss, and beaked sedge made up the stream banks. Trickling springs seeped between ferns here and there, some forming sink holes filled with thick, black mud. They reminded him of tar pits. A few years back, his friend Trent had fallen into one. It wasn't pretty. When Matt pulled him out, the pit had taken both of his hiking boots. They'd named that sinkhole "Merril", after the boot manufacturer.

In order to fill the water buckets, you had to inch down the unstable bank. If you slipped and fell, enjoy five feet of ice-cold water. This section of the Black was narrow but deceptively deep. Boulders nudged past the surface like curious turtles. The water percolated through dark, undercut banks and then out onto sunny riffles. Brook trout nipped the surface for bugs, the bigger fish making a distinct popping noise as their jaws smacked the surface. The upper Black was known for frequent sightings of mother black bears with cubs in tow. Perhaps this was a good place to keep cool with all the springs and moist vegetation.

Beyond the official property, the Black snaked through boreal forest. Matt could hurl a rock east and it would cross the stream four times. In some cases, only a few feet of earth separated the stream. These slower sections contained mounds of sand (known as boot-eaters) and thicker mats of algae. But most of the river up here in the highlands was gravel and slate. A half-mile upstream a series of waterfalls cascaded over grooved slate, framed by jack pine and hemlock. The river followed a series of steps and a thirty foot drop-sheet before sluicing into a wide pool contained within angular cuts of grey and black slate. This was Matt and his father's swimming hole and bathtub. Fat brook trout finned in the clear depths, although Matt had noticed a decrease in their numbers over the years. He often observed them six feet down, pressing right up against the rock shelf where it met the gravel bottom. The skill required to catch one of these taunting trout was beyond reasonable acquisition. They scattered when a fly line was cast upon the pool, no matter how careful. A fisherman had to approach from upstream, standing on the thirty foot slate sheet and spooling out line, letting the current take the fly to pool's edges.

Upstream from the falls the river narrowed, bullied into chutes by fantastic slate formations. Higher up than even that the river disappeared into a tangle of alder, and beyond that the mist-shrouded bog and cliffs of the Hurons. Matt always figured this portion held the biggest fish, but no one dared push back into that jungle. Black flies were a nuisance in this part of the U.P. thanks to the moisture from Lake Superior and all the standing water. Mosquitoes were almost as bad. These obstacles, when combined with spiders in the alders, made exploring the upper river a challenge.

All was not well for the Black, however. Matt had noticed sediment piling up on the streambed where it hadn't been years previous. The bigger fish were few and far between these days. The water had also grown warmer to the touch. Jumping into the pool had always been a heart-exploding experience no matter the time of year. The past few seasons it was not the freezing head rush it used to be. Submerged boulders that had once been slime free now donned a thick, mucus-like substance. He'd heard reports of climate change affecting the U.P. moose and thought the same thing may be affecting his beloved river. Visitors had also noticed the evening frog choruses growing weaker and inconsistent.

Matt walked back up the driveway while sipping his Sprite. After lifting the enormous metal latch on the shack door, he leaned against it, listening to it creak. One time he'd asked his father why the door was so damn big. His father had explained to him the shack was never meant to be a place of residence. Instead, it was designed as storage for tools and other equipment.

Inside the shack, mustiness greeted him like a friendly wet lab. The big door took up half the southern wall, the other half consisting of a window and a tall, narrow table with wheels. A black cast iron stove took up the corner, its exhaust pipe snaking up the logs. The wheeled table under the front window held a portable camp stove—the kind you attached green propane tanks to. A drawer held corroded and misshapen silverware, cast-offs from kitchens back in the suburbs. Below the drawer sat two plastic bins used for washing dishes.

Matt strode over to the east side of the shack and sat down on the couch, if he could still call it that. "The couch" was a plaid grungy thing from who-knows-when. An east-facing window above the couch revealed the mega-aspen. Beyond the aspen listed a grey-planked outhouse. His father used to say the outhouse was one good wind from being firewood.

A shelf above the window sagged with all kinds of trinkets: knives, knife sharpeners, strike tip matches, a compass, an old bear trap, dozens of fading copies of National Geographic, lantern mantles, lamp oil, boxes of tea, two first aid kits and a bunch of lighters hawked from the local taverns.

A bulging slate fireplace at least eight feet wide hogged most of the north wall. The multi-hued rocks embedded in the fireplace had been taken from the Black . Bulbous hunks of rock all along the face made for impromptu shelving. Those who liked to smoke used the shelves for packs of smokes and lighters. One protruding rock could even hold a bottle of whiskey. A full grown man could sit inside the firebox, Indian-style.

A field identification poster of SALMON AND TROUT OF THE GREAT LAKES was taped to the rock above the firebox. An out-dated calendar featuring various busty women holding chainsaws was taped next to the fish poster. Matt had always found this calendar tacky, but after a few days in the woods by himself, the poster changed from tacky to *awesome*. Sure, all the fresh air triggered his hunger, but it affected other things, too. Fumes and pesticides from heavy development and agriculture played a larger role in dulling senses than people realized. Coming up north was like removing a heavy coat.

Against the western wall loomed a triple bunk bed, made possible by the sloping, attic-less ceiling. The shack was deceptively diminutive from outside, but the open design was inviting and semi-spacious once you entered.

The triple bunk was legendary on all levels. The highest bunk was closest to the birds that liked to peck the roof. The top log was also a super highway for mice, and their chamfering and pitter-pattering could be heard all night. Also, the roof slope made the top bunk claustrophobic. If a person rolled to the left they'd face the corner where log met roof. If they rolled to the right? Well, prepare for a long drop.

Matt and his friends had played games designed around who got stuck with the top bunk. One of the games was called "Sucker's Bunk". This involved three or four shot glasses (depending on how many people you were with). When the glasses were filled with 7-UP (his father didn't let him drink whiskey at the time), one person would count down from three. Participants had to pound the shot and slam it back down onto the table. The last person to slam their glass down was "awarded" the top bunk. This was of course followed by cries of horror from the owner of the slow hand. Losers of Sucker's Bunk often opted to sleep on the grungy red couch instead. Matt wouldn't tell them the couch was also a highway for mice. Perhaps the mice even preferred the couch to the top log.

A few seasons back his good friend Trent had lost Sucker's Bunk and chose the couch. At two in the morning, Trent had woken, screaming. Matt had shone his flashlight in time to see a fat mouse perched atop Trent's chest, staring right at him with beady eyes and twitching whiskers. The mouse did not move until Trent attempted to swat it.

It's looking right into my eyes! Right into them! You guys see this shit? Trent had shouted.

The mice were no big deal to those who knew the shack well. But they made for amusing newbie fare. They'd all laughed their asses off as the mouse had climbed the wall and disappeared out the roof.

Other times guests rolled right off the top bunk, crashing onto the floor or swinging into the lower bunks with acrobatic moves of desperation.

Growing up, the triple bunk held Fart Wars, intentional freak-outs, and Burp-Fests. Matt remembered one childhood friend who was particularly good at fart-rattling the thin plywood that held each mattress. Eric Holmes was a big kid, real big. The theory was that Eric possessed a combination of bone density, flexible ass cheeks, and brute intestinal strength in order to produce such legendary farts.

The people frightened of small critters were the most fun. Matt would scratch the logs with his fingernail as they drifted off, eliciting nervous gasps of *what was that?* and *you guys hear that?* He'd just laugh to himself. His father had done the same things to him. Nothing wrong with passing down a family tradition. His father had been hazed by Ron (his father's best pal, and the one who bought the property after the farmhouse burned). Ron had paid $2500 for the land and what was left of the farm. Ron shared the keys as best friends do. Matt's father had his own copy and could go whenever he wished. There were no exceptions—the place was as good as his. And it was one of the few faraway places Matt's parents let him drive to once he got his license.

Matt gulped his soda and gazed at the trinkets and fading logs. So many memories, enough to lift his spirits. To the left of the triple bunk bed on the west wall stood a beautiful hutch. The top half was a glass cupboard, and inside were dishes, but nothing fancy. There wasn't much fancy about the shack except for the fireplace. Below the glass cupboard on the hutch was a wooden ledge that held a sturdy green lantern. Below this a series of battered drawers that held knives, segments of rope, and duct tape. The hutches' wood contained a reddish quality and was smooth to the touch. The glass panes in the cupboard nothing more than thin layers of frost. He got the impression they'd break at any moment. On the log wall between the triple bunk bed and hutch three hefty nails were pounded into place, holding a frying pan, a waffle pan, and a flat, square pan. On the floor beneath the pans was a white construction bucket with a straightened coat hanger across the top. Needled on the straightened hangar was a soda can smeared with peanut butter. Antifreeze coated the bucket's bottom. This was the shack mouse trap—a foul device that you were supposed to clean out upon arrival. Sometimes he'd find up to a half-dozen mice. The idea was the mice would walk out onto the wire, lick the peanut butter, then spin off the soda can to a green, oozy death.

It was not a fast death.

He'd always felt that humans should afford the most painless solution possible when dealing with something as finite as ending a life. The antifreeze could also kill other animals. Ron dumped the bucket's morbid contents into a hole on the property, mouse-soaked antifreeze and all. If another creature came and ate the poisoned mice, it too would be poisoned. On top of that, you don't want the antifreeze running off downhill into the Black. It was a crappy system all around.

The pans hanging between the bunk and the hutch were sometimes the home of garter snakes. One morning, while his father and Ron cooked corned beef hash and eggs, a certain large snake had been stretched along the pans, its silvery belly slung and bowed between the nails. His father had walked over to the snake, grabbed its tail, and ushered it out the shack into the tall grass.

Under the lowest bunk was a clay pigeon launcher and a box of crumbling clay pigeons. Shooting clay pigeons from the leaning post was a popular past time. Watching the yellow discs spin at warp speeds into the U.P. sky, only to be obliterated into a thousand pieces was something everyone got into. The sessions often involved beer sipping, smoking, and shirtless white guys getting bad sun burns. There hadn't been any shooting contests the last year. His father was gone and Ron seemed to lose his enthusiasm for the place after he died. Matt didn't own a shotgun and there wasn't one in the shack. Besides, he just wasn't a gun guy. Even if he was, the shack wasn't a place you wanted to leave valuable items. Thieves could rob the place and be in Arkansas (or further) by the time anyone found out. The closest neighbor was Bob Sanders, four miles away over in Silver River country. Matt rarely saw Sanders except for the occasional fishing trip to the Silver. Sanders also had a place back in town, an hour southwest of the shack. Matt wondered why he had a house in town and then another an hour away. But hey, who was he to judge?

Soon Matt would head over to the Silver River for a chance at the elusive Coho salmon. A challenge is always a good thing. Keeps the mind sharp. The Silver was twice the size of the Black and contained many more pools. He'd be walking past Sanders' place to access the Silver since his property bordered one of the choice pools. It was either that or bog walking. Yeah, tough choice.

Matt stood, placed his empty Sprite can on the cherry wood table, and headed to the door. His hiking boots thudded against the musty floor, which gave way as he stepped down.

The bolt on the door was a gigantic iron contraption designed to keep out curious black bears. Matt lifted the iron beam and pushed the door open, letting sunlight wash onto his face. The sound of chittering birds and rustling grass greeted him.

The Traveler

The coyote left behind the narrow strip of suburban broadleaf forest. She trotted across Hemson Road, dodging a rusting Ford Taurus, then through thickets along muddy Worthington River. She followed the bank for miles, careful to move under cover of darkness. Humans had trouble spotting her in the brush, and she knew this.

She trotted along a corn field, the pungent scent of rodents thick in the air. She perked up, ears twitching as the wind rattled a section of corn husks. She tilted her head sideways, ears detecting a rodent where the moist soil met the forested river corridor. Her ears straightened and she pounced. In a smooth motion her head arched back as she gobbled down a corn rat. She trotted back into the corridor, licking her chops.

At sunset she picked up speed, racing past downed river birch, glistening crayfish mounds, and dew-speckled spider webs. She didn't much care for spiders, yipping when she felt them crawling on her fur.

Something was pushing her north. It wasn't a mate (she already had one, thank you very much) and it wasn't to claim new territory. A powerful sensation drove her, although she guessed the humans didn't care too much about that. They always watched her, men everywhere with spotting scopes or guns. Many of them wanted to shoot her. She never understood why. She'd lost siblings to the metal wasps and traps, tried to help as they chewed off their own paws or dragged themselves into the woodlands with shattered hips. Once, she hauled one of these injured ones to the river and drowned him. She had cried out for two moons. She didn't know what else to do.

Panting, she curled up under a fallen yellow birch and scratched her ears with her back paw. Then she pattered down to the river, her bushy tail high as she bent down to lap water. She didn't the water was polluted. This was all she ever had. It tasted fine and made her feel more alert. She knew dogs had the best endurance, that she could outlast any woodchuck or human. She disappeared through the inky vegetation like a furry torpedo, never to rise.

***

The sun rose above Baraboo Wisconsin, revealing the farm fields with photographer's light. Frost and pesticides gleamed across the slick fields like a thin layer of ice.

Eric Gnomes woke to the sound of his chickens squawking. He slid on his Carhartt's and took the .22 from the closet.

God damn coyotes again, Gnomes thought, jamming the banana clip into the receptacle. He liked the feel of a gun in his hands. It made him feel powerful in a world where he often felt powerless.

The chickens squawked again and he hustled out the back door, letting it slam into place, a strip of white paint settling onto the porch. He huffed down to the chicken coop, the last few strands of his hair blowing high on his crown. As he ran he scanned the coop fence for damage. He couldn't see the chickens, but knew they were huddled inside the coop, flapping their wings and panicking. He unlatched the entry gate and swung open the wire door. THE HUNT WAS ON. Gnomes hurried over to the coop, pointed the rifle into the dark entrance and peered inside. His eyes slowly adjusted to the dim area near the back wall. In the middle of his prize chickens sat a healthy coyote, as if it was doing no wrong, no wrong at all. To Gnome, a coyote was nothing but nature's jester, a thing sent to mock him, to rile him.

"Hey, rat face!" he yelled.

The coyote turned her head, a dead chicken swinging in her jaw by its broken neck. The coyote's eyes grew to the size of silver dollars. She leapt up a chicken stairway and onto the egg laying cages, dead chicken swinging. Gnomes pulled the trigger and bullets sprayed the coop. Each shot a cracking, icy whip. White feathers billowed into the air as the chickens clucked and knocked into each other, a pillow fight gone wrong. A clutch of his prized chickens blew past him as he continued to fire. Bullets ripped into flesh and bones cracked. Gnomes clenched his teeth amidst the muzzle flash and recoil, unfazed by the chaos. His rifle was no normal .22.No, boy. He'd had it modified by Terry Garr, a local militia member. *You ain't got no standard pea shootin' .22 now, boy,* Garr had said.

Satisfied with the barrage and the dense aroma of gunpowder, Gnomes released the trigger, saving two bullets in the clip. When the feathers settled he counted four dead chickens, and a whole lotta blood splattering the far wall.

There was no sign of the coyote.

Gnomes crouched to get a better view of the upper nesting platforms, sticking his head into the coop and gazing towards the dark corners. A single, white feather floated down to him like the ghost of chickens past. The dander quivered as it glided, calming him like a mother calms her crying baby with song. As he gazed at the hypnotic feather, two saucers of light bloomed from a dark corner. A second later they narrowed into amber slots. Adrenaline streaked up his spine and he yanked his head back, smacking it against the overhang. His jaw rattled and he started to fade. The coyote growled and leapt from the dark corner onto the shit-stained floor. Gnomes held up his rifle, ignoring the stabbing pain at the back of his head and lined up a shot. The rifle barrel swooned. The first shot was high, the bullet thwacking into the wall. He pulled the trigger again, the shot low, hitting the filthy floor. The coyote bolted for the coop opening. Gnomes swung the rifle at the pest, hitting it square in the hips with the barrel. The coyote yipped and ran past. Gnomes whirled, knowing the coyote wasn't smart enough to find the open gate. With that in mind, Gnomes seized the gun barrel so he could smash the coyote with the stock like a mallet. And it would feel damn, good too. The ole' jester getting a load of Eric Gnomes.

The coyote paced the corners of the chicken pen, looking for an exit.

"Stupid rat," Gnomes said, shambling over to the coyote, a trickle of blood on the back of his neck. "Can't find the exit, can you?"

The coyote pawed the fence halfway up, then down to all fours again. She moved with precision, but also desperation. Several of the panicking chickens fluttered and squawked on the other side of the pen, wanting nothing to do with her.

***

She had her tail to the man, but could hear him approaching. She was proud of her hearing. A moment later, the man reared up with the rifle. She acted like she didn't know he was there, but she did. When she heard his steps quicken and felt the ground shake, she spun at his feet, biting into the ankle as hard as she could. As Gnomes reached for his ankle, she ripped into his exposed forearm, spraying blood onto her shiny coat. Gnomes screamed and collapsed, the rifle thudding onto the dirt.

She ran up and down the fence perimeter, at last finding the opening she'd dug earlier. She squeezed into it, grunting and grimacing her way through the hole. Then she sprinted into the river corridor, safer in the birch and alder, safer from the prying eyes of man. It seemed she could never get away. They were everywhere, all the time. She just wanted to be with her pack. There'd be no chicken to eat. Energy wasted. The man yelled back there, furious. They were always so angry.

The stars guided her along the river corridor as she followed the sensations driving her north. She had no idea what these sensations were, but she felt them within her completely.

Soon the men were less, although the country was still thick with them. The nights were cooler and she didn't pant as much. The river corridor widened, the forests deepened. The days shuttered past, a blur of rodents, crayfish, and the pull of running water. The water tasted better, too. She came upon animals she had not seen before—a slow, giant rat with spikes growing out of it. She wanted to eat it, but the barbs stung her nose. She had to lower her head and step on the barbs with her paws to take them out. Her nose still hurt. Along the river, the biggest birds she'd ever seen glided and swooped. They had white heads and yellow beaks. They frightened her, but soon she saw enough of them to know they only wanted dead things. They didn't make things die.

She made things die, though. She gobbled up crayfish, muskrats, rabbits, and sometimes even insects—but no spiders, never spiders. The thought of the creatures made her twitchy.

The trees along the river changed. There were lots of new trees with sharp leaves and strong scents. She liked the smell of these. She also liked the extra-large rabbits with the big feet. She'd never seen them before.

The nights grew colder and the people less. She wandered farther from the river and still remained hidden from men. One night she even slept far from the water.

She curled up against a sappy tree trunk, tucking her snout under her tail. She woke with frost upon her coat and shook it off. Trotting back to the river, she saw something she hadn't seen before. It was black with broad shoulders and an even bigger rump. This animal frightened her. Its claws were enormous. Her eyes darted, looking for cover. She shook and paced and ran, then stopped to look back but the great creature didn't even notice her. Just in case, she stayed far away. She could smell the thing. It stunk up the woods.

As the days wore on, she saw more of these beasts, both large and small. The small ones were clumsy. Come to think of it, so were the big ones. She learned they weren't clever but she needed to keep some distance. They didn't like her at all. That was fine by her. As long as they kept apart all was right.

Food was good here. Lots of it. She wanted to bring her mate up here, show him the freedom. They were mated for life, as all good coyotes are.

The men here were few. So were the hard trails and metal colliders. This was good coyote country.

She woke under a fir tree, the branches preventing rain from dripping on her. A scent drifted in the wind and she stood and waited for the animal to show itself. Her ears pointed straight forward and her eyes widened. She heard the gentle sound of branches swishing against fur and then bending back in place.

Panting came from the south and a flash of teeth appeared between fluttering leaves.

She growled and backed up, prepared for battle.

When the stranger emerged from the blueberry bushes she yipped and circled. The other coyote did the same. They met noses and licked each other's snouts.

It was her mate.

They ran and licked and yipped, cleaning each other's coats and playing. They sprinted out into a field and bounded after each other, tails hoisted, paws and legs splayed out.

They chased voles into burrows and caught some of them, snapping them up and gobbling them down. She paused, stuck her muzzle into the air and twitched her nose. A scent blew down from the north, something she knew she had to follow. Her mate gazed at her, his fur ruffling in the breeze.

She led the way and he followed.

Bob Sanders

The Toyota pickup raced down the driveway and spun out onto Julip Road. At the last second Matt yanked the wheel to the right, towards the highlands.

Soon the road narrowed and hunks of slate protruded from the dirt like fossils. He rode the cloth bench seat like a rodeo horse as the truck creaked and lurched. After a mile he hung a right at a muddy two track besieged by tag alder and chokecherry. As the road dipped, water flooded the low spots. Bog country.

The pickup was decked with skid plates and high clearance, so he wasn't too worried. Soon spruce and fir clotted the roadside, although calling this a road at all was generous. Branches fingered the truck and swung back into place. Blotches of mud squelched on the windshield and sprayed up in the rearview.

Now *this* was his idea of a proper road.

He smiled and steadied the wheel.

When the muddy two track met the graded Silver Road, he stopped the truck. Silver Road would take him to the pool behind Sanders' place. Matt turned left, jamming the gas pedal just to see gravel kick out in his side view mirror.

"Go get em, girl. Show 'em you still have something left," he said.

His trusty truck obliged.

A half-mile south along Silver Road, the blue paint of Sanders' cottage clashed with the forest.

After hurrying into his fishing gear, Matt locked up and headed towards Sanders' place. He didn't want to park too close to the property. You never knew what might happen around Bob. As he hiked along the road, a gray jay chittered on a branch to his left. He paused and watched the delicate but vociferous bird. This might be the closest he'd ever gotten to one. When he reached his hand out, the gray jay chittered again and flew off, turning its head and studying him with beady black eyes as it penetrated the thick woods.

Spirits lifted by the close encounter, Matt walked the roadside opposite the house, making sure Sanders could see him from a long way off. Sanders wasn't the kind of guy you wanted to surprise. Big time.

The porch door slid open and a young woman stood there, smiling. She was surprisingly attractive with short blonde hair, rosy cheeks, and a china doll nose. She had to be twenty years younger than Sanders, the corners of her lips always ticked up into a near-smile.

"Doin' some fishin, are ya?" she said.

Matt nodded. "You mind if I cut through to fish the Silver?"

"Nope," she said, smiling with her eyes. "But it's not my land, eh? It's Bob's land."

Sanders appeared from behind the woman and spastically gestured to Matt. He was wearing a red Hawaiian shirt and blue jeans. Still in his fifties, Sanders was lean and well-tanned. His pepper hair was cut military style, and he sported a ridiculous handlebar moustache. And of course the classic Yooper accent. How could Matt ever forget that.

"Long time no see eh?" Sanders said. "You want something to wet the ole pucker? There's Millers in the cooler. By the by, this here is Melinda."

"Nice to meet you," Matt said, leaning his fly rod against the wall and shaking Melinda's petite hand.

"Come on in," Sanders said, waving enthusiastically. "We got some snacks too, peanut butter and Ritz. You gotta be hungry, eh? Hell, stay as long as ya want. We got a real feast. There's bear jerky, spray cheez-whiz, although Melinda here calls it gee-whiz cause it gives me the runs so bad."

Sanders reached out his hand and Matt shook it. The grip was too strong in a way that hinted at overcompensation.

Dead animals decorated the cottage. If you could call dead animals decorations. Stuffed deer heads stared back from the walls with glassy doll eyes. Black bear hides spread across the southern wall, a family by the looks of it. Charming. A fisher mounted on a piece of driftwood across a mantle. In the corner sat a record player with a stack of vinyl. Ravels of chamfered wire led to two dodgy speakers. Sanders compound bow leaned against the east wall next to two side by side futons. Overall, the cottage was a thrown-together place but felt strangely comfortable. Maybe it was the good air. There was something about the Northwoods that demystified material items. An imperfect, small home like this was acceptable in the tangle of forest and hills. In fact, it seemed preferable. Who needs a big house when you've got paradise right out the door? People didn't spend much time inside. But oh, in the suburbs of Chicago they were sealed in their homes like tombs.

"Grab a seat, eh?" Sanders said, pointing to one of the futons, a can of cheez-whiz and a half-eaten package of Ritz in the other.

When Matt sat, Melinda leaned over and rubbed her hand along his back, her blond hair fanning over half her Nordic face. "I'll get ya a cool one, eh?"

"I don't mind getting my own," he said, making eye contact.

"I'm not hung up on political correctness," she said. "Lite or MGD?"

He felt like a jackass, but he had to admit her cerulean eyes were more than capable of making him feel certain ways. "MGD," he replied, hoping she hadn't detected his uncomfortable pause.

Sanders sat down on the futon next to Matt, roll of crackers in hand, a big grin stretching out his handlebar moustache. "Ritz?"

"Thanks, but I just ate." Matt focused on the dead fisher, wondering why Sanders had it mounted since it was illegal to kill them. "Where'd you get the fisher?" he asked, regretting the words as soon as they passed his lips.

Sanders eyed him and took a crumbly bite of Ritz. Bits of cracker crumbs caught in his moustache. "You don't need a license to hunt fisher, eh? You just need one to show up in your yard!" Sanders let out a roar of laughter.

"Always fighting the animals, eh? What'd they ever do to you?" Melinda said, brushing the front of her yellow sundress.

Sanders ditched his smile as his face reddened. "I'll tell you what they did, Mrs. Sass-back. They fookin' came into my yard! All these fookin' animals better stay out, eh? The porcupines, the rabbits, the deer, the possum, the raccoons, the wolf, the coyote the bear, all of 'em! I'm tired of them eating it all up. The God damned rabbits ate half the garden this summer. The deer come in here and eat up my greens and shit all over the place. Even the fence 'round the garden doesn't keep them away, eh?"

Melinda handed Matt a cold beer, her lovely bangs caressing her face as she leaned over. "Here you go, hon."

He cracked the tab and swallowed the foamy mess. Delicious. A cold beer always tasted better in the Northwoods. As Melinda passed him, he smelled orange fragrance.

Sanders slapped Matt on the knee, then stood and motioned for him to follow. In the adjoining room, Sanders went to the window and pointed outside with his long and skinny arm. "See that? That's my garden. Do you see what's behind it?"

Matt peered out the window into the yard. A tall woodpile was set up in the shape of a "V". Contained within the "V" space was a pile of bruised apples.

"That's what I call my *do right*, eh?" Sanders said, chuckling. "The deer or bear step in my yard, go to eat those apples and I do 'em right there." Sanders pointed to another compound bow in the corner. Next to the bow leaned a .308 Winchester and on the floor a Colt Python .357.

"I just open this window here quite as can be, and shoot on 'em. With an arrow in 'em they try to run straight ahead. This is where the wood pile comes in, eh? They run right into it and I have time to shoot another arrow into their bee-hind."

Matt clenched his fists. He knew Sanders had issues, but never figured him as a poacher. But now was not the time to say or do anything. Sanders was clearly losing it and a confrontation with such a person wasn't the brightest idea—especially with all this weaponry laying around.

"Those poor deer," Melinda said from the kitchen.

"Too many of em anyway, eh? Fook 'em."

Sanders strode into the kitchen with great, long steps and grabbed a beer from the cooler. He cracked the tab and took several gulps, then burped. "These animals up here, Matty, You gotta show 'em who's boss, eh? Sooner or later they'll run the place if you let 'em. You give an inch and they take a mile. They'll come back with their buddies like teenagers at a kegger. Especially the damn rabbits."

Matt cleared his throat and regretted his words as soon as they passed his beer-moistened lips: "If you don't like rabbits why would you kill the fishers and coyotes? They eat rabbits," he said.

Sanders turned to him, anger welling in his eyes. The target of his anger was not Matt, however. It was the animals. Always the animals.

"Because the fisher and coyote eat the fawns. And I don't want nobody eating my deer. I eat venison year 'round. Why go to the store when I got a supermarket up here, eh?"

Matt's beer was losing its flavor, or maybe it was Sanders' attitude that was spoiling it. Melinda emerged from the bathroom in nothing but a peach-colored towel, her hair slicked back.

"How about a sauna?" she said.

Matt realized Melinda was quite effective at diffusing tension with her charm.

Sanders's mood changed at once. "You bet your Swedish ass I do," he said. "Come on Matty, let's check out the new hot box. Put her together this spring."

He wanted to fish, and to kind of get away from Sanders, but Sanders was a good craftsman and Matt had always wanted a sauna. He felt better when he walked out of one—somehow more pure. "Just for a second," he said.

They exited the cottage and followed a quaint slate path to the backyard. Birds flittered deep in the forest. The Silver River gleamed to the right, no more than twenty yards from the cabin, its high banks corralling water past balsam fir and sugar maple. Everything was bathed in gentle canopy shade.

As expected, Sanders had done a fine job with the sauna. He'd carved a moon with two stars above the soft, lush cherry wood door. Overall, the fit and finish was notable.

"Come on in," Sanders said, a big grin stretching out his handlebar. After opening the door for them, Sanders stripped down to his checkered boxers. "You aren't coming in here like that, are ya?" he asked Matt.

"Yeah, I'm only in for a second, then I need to get fishing."

Sanders hung his clothes on two wooden dowels. "Well I never heard of a guy going into a sauna fully rigged up," Sanders said.

Melinda took a seat in the corner, not taking up much room and tucking the pink towel underneath her. Sanders stood in the middle, and Matt sat near the door. This was a practice of his since his high school days.

Sanders gulped his beer, belched, then gripped a wooden ladle and dipped it into a construction bucket filled with river water. "We need to get her going, eh?" Sanders said, his bony knees popping as he took his long steps towards the heating unit.

The sauna was indeed a piece of work, quality wherever you looked. Smooth dowels held towels and clothing. The pine bench was comfortable, almost soft. A sign had been nailed to the wall near the heating unit. It pictured a cartoonish-looking man with a mega-boner about to mount a woman who was bent over and putting a log into a fireplace. Below the picture was the sentence, HOW A YOOPER PUTS A LOG INTO THE FIRE.

Sanders watched him reading the sign. "That's how we do it up north, eh?"

Matt let out a fake laugh and shifted to sincere thoughts. "You've got a hell of a sauna, Bob. How long did it take you?"

Sanders reached into his boxers and scratched his balls. "Bout two months comin' up every weekend. And thanks, she's grand, eh?" Then Sanders sat down between Melinda and Matt, his knees cracking.

Melinda shivered and seemed to make herself smaller, like a bird. "It's cold in here," she said, adjusting her towel and gazing down at her pink toenails.

How Sanders landed Melinda, Matt had no idea. Maybe that Yooper magic he'd heard so much about.

"She's as fast as she can go," Sanders replied to Melinda. "Have some patience, eh?"

Silence came between them, the kind of quiet only wild lands can produce. Sanders gently placed his hand on Matt's thigh and looked into his eyes. "Hey, about that putting a log in the fire, that isn't no joke," he said, upper lip quivering.

Matt stood and brushed Sanders' hand away. "Gotta run. The trout wait for no one."

"Aw you going already?" Melinda said, kicking her diminutive feet up. "Come on, we're just about to have some fun."

"Thanks guys!" Matt opened the door and hurried out. He trotted along the slate path, Sanders' rising voice behind him.

"Come back anytime you want, eh? There'll always be a cold beer with your name on it."

"What did you do to scare him off?" Melinda asked, her voice muffled by cedar and the hissing heater.

Matt took his fly rod from the wall and approached the Silver. He could still hear Sanders and Melinda chattering back there in their little wooden box with the carved moon and stars. A Yooper spaceship.

He found a riffle and forged to the other side, the multihued stones shimmering near his boots, a grouse thumping its wings from some unseen glade. The more he hiked, the more the Northwoods overtook Melinda and Sanders until there was only the wind in the trees.

Ernie

On the way back from the Silver, a peculiar flashing in the woods caught Matt's attention. He cut the engine, leaned over, and rolled down the passenger window. A series of growls and gasps emitted from the shadows. Tufts of fur flew into the air, mixing with pine needles and leaves. Between each growl, the rattling of metal.

He got out and crept towards the noise.

The low growling rose in pitch and frequency. Heart pounding, he spread apart the bushes enough to see. There, in a small clearing leapt a fisher, its rear paw caught in the jaws of a steel trap. The fisher valiantly tried to pull away, only to be slammed back down again by its nemesis chain.

The thick metal chain led from the trap jaws to a hefty nail in a hemlock. There was no conceivable way the fisher would ever pull free. Although the Mustelidae family was known for its pound-for-pound toughness, the fisher simply didn't have the mass to pull free. After a few seconds, the fisher bit its own paw in desperation, and Matt realized his presence was not helping. He stepped behind the trees, allowing only his face to be seen. The fisher's black eyes locked onto him as it bared its teeth and growled. Matt was impressed by the sleek fisher, a bullet of a face pinned back by symmetrical ears and offset by white teeth made for puncturing rodents. The fisher continued its desperate maneuvers, darting and twisting with the speed of a minnow, its thick tail curling and uncurling. A series of offset claw swipes ravaged the hemlock.

No reason at all for this, Matt thought. Trappers were supposed to check their traps every twenty-four hours. He guessed the fisher had been here for at least a day.

He shuddered at the thought of the trapper sitting in his house, slugging down a Pabst Blue Ribbon and watching Judge Judy while this animal suffered. So he marched to his truck and took a flathead screwdriver from under the seat. As Matt returned to the trapped fisher, he removed his flannel and held it out in front of him while speaking quietly to the fisher.

It's okay, he said. *You're going to be just fine. We'll get you out of here and you can go about your day.*

He had to wonder what the fisher was thinking as he crept closer. How would *he* feel in this situation? Not so great. Terrified, actually. Without delay, Matt leapt forward and shielded the fisher with the flannel.

Growling, spitting, hissing below the fabric.

He did the only thing he could and sat on the animal—allowing just enough room for the fisher to breathe. Then Matt located the trapped paw by feeling the length of steel chain under the flannel. The fisher growled from deep within its lungs. There was no time to lose. Although wild animals were tough, handling them often produced erratic effects. Soon Matt found the paw, moist and bloody from the trap. After peeling the flannel back just enough, he jammed the screwdriver between the trap's iron jaws. The paw flopped out, swollen and bloody. The angry fisher stretched its back legs and kicked with both paws at once.

He took a deep breath. *One, two, three…go!*

Matt bolted up and away from his flannel. When he was a few feet away, a little brown head poked out of the shirt. The fisher stared at him and sniffed the air. After a good whiff, the fisher shot out of the flannel. Wasting no time, it streaked through the understory, visible for a moment as a long sleek band of dark brown. The last he heard of it was a jubilant chittering from deep within the trees.

Elated, Matt retrieved his flannel and gave it a few good shakes. Then he took the screwdriver, walked over to the tree, and pried the nail out. Next he gathered the trap chain into a coil and threw it over his shoulder.

Yeah, you can get a new nail, too, asshole, he thought as he pocketed the nail.

***

The fishing on the Silver had been terrible. Matt wondered if the cold front had put the fish down. The bad news was that cold fronts up here had a reputation for lasting weeks. He could extend his trip if he wanted to. His boss—James McAdams—had always given him shit for not taking enough vacation. And as he knew, the trout waited for no one. They were always a challenge. But they'd become more of a challenge the last fifteen years. With the silted streams, warmer temps, and lower water flows, they'd become very difficult to catch indeed.

Once, while snorkeling the Black pool as a kid he saw them in their own world, spotted and beautiful, darting through the water like flashing cutlery. Some of them pecked at his feet, their little trout lips nipping his skin like sandy marbles.

Dusk cast its pall across the Northwoods. White-tailed deer appeared on the side of Julip Road, chewing on fescue sedge and parasol sedge. High in the sky, a large-winged bird soared. A bald eagle. The Northwoods was a refuge for the majestic eagles when DDT had almost wiped them out. Authorities who should've known better had claimed DDT was safe. It was decades later until everyone realized the truth: DDT was killing the eagles by weakening egg shells. It seemed to him mankind's ability to produce chemicals far exceeded its ability to test for side effects.

He pointed the truck up the shack driveway and rolled to a stop twenty feet from the front door. The sun at last dipped behind the trees, flooding pink across the cirrus clouds.

Matt went to the shack's west side and flipped the wheelbarrow over, taking care to stay away from any critters that may have been living underneath. He had plenty of experience with critters leaping at you when you least expect it. Last year, when he and Trent picked up the canoe from the bottom of the orchard, an ermine ran the length of the vessel and jumped off the bow towards Trent's head. He'd screamed and dropped the canoe. It had landed on his foot. He'd screamed again. Over the years they'd found snakes in sneakers, weasels in the woodpile, bats in the shack, and mice nestled boxes of pancake mix. Anything was a candidate for home, and the animals had no problem relocating.

The firewood smelled moldy and had a damp texture. *Hard fire tonight*, Matt thought as he lifted the quarter-cut logs into the wheelbarrow. As he did, something scurried off the pile, tiny feet pattering on birch bark. Maybe a mouse or weasel. Spiders fled the woodpile each time he removed a log. He'd grab an end, turning it in his hand and inspecting for spiders before grasping all the way.

Hidden in the middle of the woodpile was an axe—its blade protected from the elements by a sleeve made from birch bark and leather strips. Matt yanked the sleeve off, listening to the delicate sweep of the bark, then placed the axe into the wheelbarrow. He checked his pockets for a lighter and smiled as his fingers touched smooth plastic.

Satisfied with his firewood situation, Matt opened shack door and retrieved a copy of the Ironville Daily. He lifted a log on the wheelbarrow, placed the paper underneath, and returned the log. Then he pushed the rig up the path towards the old leaning post. His forearms flexed below his rolled-up checkered flannel, the wrist veins bulging like the broken granite country to the south.

Once at the post he parked the wheelbarrow next to the fire pit. Chunks of slate ringed the pit, hauled up from the Black by his father and Ron ten years ago. The thought of his father hand-picking those rocks out of the river and carrying them up here tightened his chest. He closed his eyes in an effort to shake the memory. There were so many here, a flood of them. He wondered if it was possible to wallow down memory lane and never come back.

He pictured his father trudging uphill from the Black, shirtless and red-faced, glistening rocks in his hands. The call of a crow from the aspen. The gentle roll of wind from the Huron's. Grasshoppers buzzing in the tall, golden grass. The Yooper.

Miss you, Matt said to the landscape.

And what a landscape it was. The forest spread out before him, the uneven canopy painted in sunset hues. A blue heron skimmed the trees, heading east, the distant granite outcroppings of the Huron Range glowing in various shades of pastel.

Matt shivered, then turned to split an aspen log. The inside of the wood was dry and smooth. The last log, a grungy balsam fir, took many more chops.

Breathing hard from exertion, Matt hunched over the pit and arranged the fresh kindling into a teepee. He separated pages from the newspaper and rolled them into cones, then inserted each piece into the teepee's base. His tongue crept between his tightened lips as he did this, and he caught himself and sucked it back in. He was a grown up now, not some little kid.

Almost dark now. Matt thumbed the lighter, the wheel spikes compressing his skin. He lit each paper cone as he circled the pit. *You need synergy*, his father always said. *If you don't have synergy, you don't have shit.*

Soon the birch bark popped like Rice Crispies. Embers flourished into the sky and disappeared between Altair and Venus. Matt pulled up one of the fat stumps that circled the pit and sat.

Night swept in on him, obscuring the Hurons and the lower forest. Guttural sounds came from downhill to the west, out in the bog. Maybe a moose, but he wasn't sure. He knew of the struggling moose population, and that this area was part of the core population zone. The shack stood only a few miles from the reintroduction site in the Huron Wilderness. The ancient cliffs that made up the border of the wilderness lay out there in the night, protecting virgin timber. If value was indeed determined by rarity, then the Huron Wilderness was priceless by Midwest standards. Unfortunately, the wilderness was only twenty-five thousand acres, surrounded by a sea of logging roads and second-growth forest.

Regardless, Matt took great comfort in knowing it was there.

To him, all of this country emanated from that wild core. Everything was better off from the existence of wilderness, including him.

The grunting from down in the bog intensified, and a branch snapped. It sounded like an elephant cracking a femur. Whatever it was had inched closer.

Keeping his gaze on the low forest, Matt reached into his flannel pocket and pulled out his elastic headlamp. This style of lamp freed his hands for camp chores and working on his truck. It beat lipping a flashlight and slobbering all over it. Matt pressed the switch and gazed downhill to the west. A saber of light followed his every move. That was the beauty of it.

Soon, two tennis ball sized-eyes shone behind the wall of chokecherry and tag alder. Matt followed the shimmering eyes to an enormous rump.

A black bear. A huge black bear.

Goosebumps peppered his forearms and legs, and at once he felt more awake, like he'd gulped a cup of coffee. He suspected this bear was "Ernie", a six hundred pound behemoth that was the stuff of shack legends. Shack visitors had often found enormous scat on the game paths crisscrossing the orchard. The funny thing was they'd always found the scat at the highest points, as if the bear appreciated a good view while doing its thing.

His father and Ron used to try and scare Matt and his friends with Ernie tales. Supposedly Ernie had once tried to open the shack door when Ron was there by himself. And who could forget the story of Ernie breaking into Ron's camper shell and running off with a ham? Matt had doubted these stories, assuming they were the product of too much booze around the campfire. If *this* was Ernie out there in the dark, he wasn't very frightening. Ernie looked gentle as could be, darting out his long tongue and grasping branches plump with chokecherries. Ernie didn't seem to mind him, and Matt in turn was glad to finally see the legend. After several minutes, Ernie slumped off into the berry bushes.

Certain he was in no danger, Matt placed a crispy piece of kindling on the fire and a fat log. The embers took on a nice, red glow. All sorts of shapes and patterns materialized in the fire—ones the human brain was accustomed to seeing, such as faces. One particular face in the embers he didn't care for, a bulbous face with a wide forehead that seemed to glare at him. The embers burned so hot the face bloomed in neon. The jaw hung prominent, with several ropes of braided hair dangling from the chin, the eyes beset with cat-like inquisitiveness. The thing had three mouths, all circular and with sharp teeth like the lampreys that had devastated the Great Lakes fishery. The middle mouth was set in the usual human place. The other two mouths, about half the size of the original, occupied the cheeks and opened and closed like fish lips out of water.

The embers pulsed as the eyes stared at him.

A chill coursed down his limbs, but not the pleasant goose bump kind.

Matt turned his attention to another spot in the fire. This time he saw a hand sticking out of the embers, open palmed, fingers splayed. The hand looked strong and rough—the sign of a man who'd worked hard.

He realized it was his father's hand.

A wave of memories overcame him and he clenched his fists.

No more staring into the embers, he thought, turning from the hypnotic fire. Something flashed in his peripheral vision. The fiery, open hand jumped from one side of the fire to the other and smacked the eerie face.

The fire popped and embers shot into the sky.

The hand was gone, but the face remained. The eyes were bigger, angrier, the circular mouths opening and closing.

Go. Leave the woods now, he thought.

The woods are not your friend this year, Matthew Kearns, a little voice told him.

Matt blinked, his mouth hanging slack. He knew the voice. Knew it all too well. He'd even seen doctors for it. The doctors had sad the voice was triggered by bad anxiety. At first he and his parents doubted them all, but they were right in the end. It was there when he was a boy, it was there when his father died, when Elmo died, and when Stacy died. And here it was now. He'd been spooked by the face in the fire and it triggered the anxiety. Not uncommon when camping alone. *You've done this plenty of times, big boy,* he thought.

Matt straightened his posture and peered beyond the fire into the dark orchard and apple trees.

Skeet's comments at the Black River floated into his mind. *Davey was up near the wilderness. Something big scared him off, something real big. These woods are sick.*

Nonsense, Matt thought, gazing into the fire.

The face had grown larger.

The center mouth opened, revealing two forked tongues intertwined like mating snakes. The tips of the tongues hung limp between sharp rows of teeth. Beyond the tongues bleak darkness. As he stared, the face swelled like an inflating balloon. Next to the face, several smaller shapes formed. They appeared to be tribal humans, some held bows, arrows ready to launch. Some rode massive horse-like animals. Their hair cascaded past their buttocks. Matt blinked and the tribal army surrounded the face. The eyes on the swelling face looked to the side in horror.

Never should've taken those mushrooms last year at Trent's party , he thought. *I'm having some sort of flashback, that's all.* His forehead warmed and moistened from sitting close to the fire. Or was it his nerves?

Just when he was about it lose it, the meanest, lowest growl he'd ever heard rattled from behind him.

Matt stood at once, flicked the switch on his headlamp, and pivoted downhill towards Ernie. The great bear was halfway up the hill, staring in the direction of the campfire.

Matt swallowed and backed away, almost tripping over the stump seat. His legs were rubbery, feeble.

Whoa boy, take it easy there, okay? he said.

He'd learned in Yellowstone that running from a bear was the worst thing you could do, as it triggered a chase instinct. You were better off playing dead with grizzly bears. This wasn't a grizzly bear, though. Ernie was a full-fledged black bear. The experts said that when a black bear attacks, you need to fight back. Black bears stalk and attack humans because they are hungry, unlike grizzly bears who are territorial.

As Ernie approached, Matt reached into his side pocket for his knife. It wouldn't do much, but gripping it made him feel better.

Ernie let loose another rattling growl, each note connected by a series of lower notes. The bear's ears were pinned back. Never a good sign.

Adrenaline soaked Matt's nerves, leading to irrational thoughts that may lead to a mistake. He took a deep breath and watched the bear, prepared to flee or fight. But Ernie wasn't looking at him. Oh no, Ernie wasn't paying attention to him *at all*.

Ernie was staring into the fire.

Right at the ballooning face.

Angry Ernie stalked up the hill, all six hundred plus pounds of his massive body. The ground quaked under Matt's feet each time the bear stepped forward. Soon the details on Ernie's face were revealed by the flames, a muscular warrior in the night riddled with battle scars.

Matt backed away from Ernie and down the orchard slope, knowing bears couldn't run as well downhill. When he reached the bottom the scene above him turned unexplainable. There before him loomed Ernie—the bear of legends—apprehensive and growling at fire's edge.

The night sky thrived behind Ernie, framing him in the shimmering of all that is.

A bone deep sense of earth and place tugged on his soul.

Why does Ernie see the face in the fire if you're only imagining it, Matthew? A little voice asked in his head. *Is the bear imagining it too?*

Matt stepped back.

Ernie's growl raged into a spittle-dispensing roar. The bear clamped his jaws shut and glowered at the fire.

Sparks popped from the flames, in the direction of Ernie.

Ernie let loose a high-pitched yip as if wounded, then stood on hind legs, roaring and pouncing down onto the fire with colossal front paws. Huge chunks of fiery wood spun across the orchard like flaming helicopter blades. Matt ducked. A twenty foot column of fuming embers plumed into the air, flickering amongst the pinprick lights of the Milky Way before fading to dull ash.

Ernie stood there, sniffing the air through the smoke entrails, paws in the charcoal as embers rained down on him.

The bear backed off the fire, several embers glowing in his rich fur. Ernie didn't seem fazed, instead grunting and studying the orchard. Confident in the result, the bear ambled down the hill, back towards the bog.

As Ernie sauntered downhill, Matt climbed back up. Embers sizzled in the bear's fur and the rank scent of burning hair filled Matt's nose. He followed Ernie with his headlamp as the bear entered the wall of chokecherry and alder and disappeared.

Matt slowly turned to the fire pit, his mouth agape. The face was gone.

Maybe the legendary stories of Ernie are true, he thought. *This is one crazy ass bear.* He spit the taste of ash out of his mouth and laughed. *I've got one to add to the mix, too, Dad. But I think this one might be a bit better than anything you and Ron came up with. Yes indeed.*

Matt held his breath, and heard Ernie ambling through the bog, snapping branches out past the lone balsam fir. The great bear was heading west.

There was nothing Matt could ever do to explain what he saw. A black bear had just herded him off a campfire and then proceeded to destroy it. *When does that ever happen? Has it ever happened? Why?* he thought.

With the face gone, it was easier for him to imagine it was all a coincidence. It was easier to conclude that Ernie just didn't like campfires.

A bear that puts out campfires? Come on, Matthew, the little anxiety voice said.

Shut up, Matt said.

As the legendary bear drifted west, night birds sprang from the trees Ernie passed under. Some of them flew over the orchard, peering down at Matt as he collected the flaming wood, now scattered in an eighty foot circumference around the fire pit like crash-landed fireflies.

Colors

When he got too cold, and the moment had been allowed to settle in, Matt followed the path to the shack, shoulders slumped and heels dragging.

So that was Ernie, huh Dad? he thought. Good ole' Ernie. He never believed any of those stories, but now he was sorry for ever doubting his father.

The wind shifted from the Hurons and his skin prickled. *The face was nothing,* he thought. *A flashback.* Still, why did Ernie look like he was staring right at it? Matt puffed his chest out and took a deep breath. The only monsters he knew were tiny, cancerous cells, and other people.

His headlamp cast a violet light upon the wooden door, making it look artificial. He grabbed the iron handle and the door creaked open, revealing a dark womb. Something scurried off into the corner, probably a mouse. He reached onto the shelf and took the box of strike tip matches. The match sticks rattled inside the delicate cardboard box as he took the lantern, swinging it a bit while placing his ear to the base. On the last swing he placed the lantern on the cherry wood table. Matt twirled two butterfly nuts on top of the lantern and removed the glass. He pinched a match, closed the inner box and tilted it to the side. The match head dragged along the coarse strip and came to life, effusing a warm glow that contrasted with the artificial light of his headlamp. He positioned the flame under each fragile, white-netted sack. Then Matt replaced the protective glass and tweaked the fuel nozzle. The lantern hissed and dazzled the shack, chasing off every patch of darkness.

"Now we're cooking with gas," he said.

The lantern had a way of removing the chill from the fire incident. He gazed at the immense slate fireplace, marveling at the way light revealed cuts and scrapes in the rocks in high-definition.

Listen to the stillness, he thought.

Nothing made a sound but his own breathing and the quiet lantern hiss. Dorothy, we aren't in the suburbs anymore.

He let his mind go blank and closed his eyes, leaning back in the bone-hard chair. Aspen leaves caressed the roof. A thin whistle of wind from the south found weaknesses in the logs. The door on the outhouse creaked. The orchard grass sighed as the wind brushed it like the mane of a horse.

Back home something was always making noise: cars, lights, people stomping around. This was where he wanted to be.

Matt got up from the chair and walked over to the southern window. He brushed away the ratty burlap curtain and pinned it to a nail above the pane. He peered into the night, catching part of his reflection. Above his head loomed the dead oak with its reaching branches—a frightening sight to a first-time visitor. In the dark it resembled a huge creature lurching towards the shack, hands held high in a fit of insanity or rage or both. He saw it only as the fossilized, dead oak that the woodpeckers loved. Once, long ago, it had provided shade for the farmhouse.

His attention turned to the table and the paper sack that held his late dinner. He reached inside and picked out deluxe Kraft mac and cheese. Below that was a can of white chicken breast. He opened the wobbly drawer and took the ancient looking can opener. It cracked the metal lid like an octopus beak to a crab's shell.

Slock!

He pulled one of the pans off the wall and poured a jug of water into it—fresh from the Black. The water contained little chunks of sediment that sloshed around. Next he attached a green propane canister to the dual burner camp stove and screwed it onto the protruding valve. This old camp stove was a Kearn family heirloom. It'd been in the family for decades and now showed rust patches. A little dancing bear sticker decorated the lid—the product of a tour with the Grateful Dead in the nineties. His father had loaned it to a friend who'd quit his job for a summer. The friend then used the stove to cook vegan hot dogs and sold them in the parking lot extravaganzas the Dead followers were known for.

Matt lifted the smashed metal fastener and pried the lid open. The lid creaked like a rusty coffin. But instead of Dracula or a mummy, a place to cook tasty treats was revealed.

Hmmm…boil the water first or put the noodles in and then boil? Matt, you're a good cook, said no one ever. Either way, it was too late. The mac and cheese was mushy. If he worked at a restaurant, he'd be fired on the spot.

He devoured the glop regardless, the fork clanking in the pan like that rip-off ring toss game at the carnival.

Satiated, he studied the triple bunk bed and his red, extra-long sleeping bag splayed out on the bottom bunk—the best bunk. *No Sucker's Bunk tonight,* he thought with a hint of sadness. Then he glanced at the couch and pictured the mouse sitting on Trent's chest and laughed.

After stretching the headlamp over his head, he killed the lantern. The mantles grew dull like heroin eyes.

Matt stripped down to his checkered boxers and t-shirt and crawled inside his toasty sleeping bag. While his bag was officially rated at zero degrees, it was more like a thirty-two degree bag in reality. Anything less than that and you'd wish you had either a blanket or another bag. The Yooper wasn't the Rockies where night time September temps could get ridiculous.

A bit too hyper yet for sleep, Matt examined the planks that supported the middle bunk bed. Numerous shapes and patterns swirled on the wood. It didn't looked stable, but no one ever fell through.

In the triple bunk bed, you *never* wanted to be under the guy who ate beans or the corned beef hash. Omelets were also something you had to look out for. The damn egg farts were the worst. Powerful farts rattled the wood like a train to a loose trestle.

Matt rolled to his left, switched off his lamp, and tucked it into the corner where the shack wall met bed frame. Pitch black, now. Only his breath and the wind.

An animal scratched softly outside, maybe a raccoon on the logs.

Some time later he woke to a strange glowing, a swirl of purple and green tinged with white. The peculiar light reflected off the glossy tablecloth and in the windows. Matt unzipped his sleeping bag, careful not to make noise. He placed his feet onto the musty floor, quiet as a ninja. The lights on the center table bloomed.

Is this a dream? he thought.

He reached out, his hand like a ghost's, the light shimmering on his fingernails and then back to the table. The brightest light seemed to come from the southern window. He rubbed his eyes, just to make sure he wasn't asleep. The entire southern window was bathed in purple, green, and gooey white. Resting his hands on the camp stove, he stared out. The glass panes caught the colors and twisted them. He put his fingertips to the glass, his mouth slack. He wondered again about the mushrooms at Trent's party. *Tracers, they called them.* But he wasn't on anything. Matt gazed out to the dead oak, its branches bathed in the vivid light. At last he understood, feeling embarrassed that he hadn't known right away.

The Northern Lights. The Aurora Borealis.

He and his father had observed them on several occasions from the orchard, always mesmerized. After lacing his boots, Matt clomped across the floor and lifted the steel bolt. Looking up at the sky, he stumbled towards the dead oak, marveling at the display. Pulsating reds, yellows, greens, purples, pinks, and hot-whites consumed the sky as if at war,

Dad, I wish you could see this, he thought. He wished Stacey could see it too, and Elmo.

Although the display was beyond normal comprehension, bordering on absurdist surreal, there was a definite structure to the whole thing. The top of the sky was an orb with a gelatinous-looking center. This center oozed and pulsated, but stayed within a certain circumference. Every few seconds the orb lit with a bright, white charge. Radiating down from the orb to the horizon were sky-covering curtains of light. The curtains glittered and rotated like mini blind slats opening and closing, except every time the slats moved, red, green, purple, and white dripped off the edges and slathered the sky below. Frenetic bombasts of white light shot from the orb to the bottom of the curtains like the 80's arcade game *Tempest*.

Matt raised his right hand to his face and observed details in his palm and fingernails even though it was the middle of the night.

Across the horizon, the bottom third of the light curtains shifted to fluorescent emerald as the gaseous edges dripped milky, fading streaks of white.

Without thinking, Matt ran up the path to the leaning post for an unobstructed view. There was no need for his headlamp, not tonight. The aspen and apple trees sighed in the wind, their leaves encased in a soft emerald glow. Towering light curtains spread out across the universe, dropping all the way down to the tree tops. It looked like the curtains were right there in the lower forest, brushing the fir, chokecherry, and aspen in lush strokes of emerald and white. Night birds that normally couldn't be seen flew low over the trees, their wings sharp knives against the slats of light. The green silhouette of an owl glided to the south.

Matt traced the light curtains from the tree tops to the orb in the sky's center. White flashes radiated down in nano-seconds, but the curtains absorbed new colors. The midsections banded with sparkling magenta, the upper curtains a deep amethyst as the central orb pulsed and swirled with the rich colors of a storm planet.

Across the southern valley the Huron Mountains absorbed the vibrancy, the exposed rock along the ancient ridges like the ribcage of a psychedelic whale. Sentinel stands of the old, uncut hemlocks spiked into the green sky, their silhouettes jagged before the shifting curtains.

Matt stood there with his jaw unhinged, lit up like a rock star. He leaned against the post, both arms resting on the battered piece of wood. He could even read all the symbols and letters visitors had carved into the wood over the years. One in particular caught his attention: *The right thing is almost always more difficult.* He had no idea who wrote it.

Matt returned his gaze to the Hurons. He'd never seen such an impressive display, not even the late fall of 2005. Not only were the woods aglow at two in the morning, but numerous species of birds had begun to grow restless with the unforeseen exposure. They flittered across the sky in a panic, some in flocks, some alone. The swooshing of wings filled the air. Bats, surprised by the light set cruise control back to their roosts. The sound of ruffling feathers surprised him from behind. He whirled, and thirty feet above him, a mature bald eagle flapped its way south towards the Huron Mountains. The great bird flew so close Matt glimpsed green reflections in its eyes. He assumed the eagle had been roosting in a nearby tree—perhaps on the edge of the orchard. As the eagle flapped across the southern valley, it dwarfed the other bird silhouettes. Soon the sky was thick with hundreds of birds flying in different directions. Pileated woodpeckers, black cap chickadees, gray jays, ravens, crows, white-breasted nuthatches, turkey vultures, red-tailed hawks, pine warblers, chipping sparrows, you name it they were out there.

None of the birds were calling out or making noise.

It was then Matt felt a sensation he hadn't in a long time. Many years ago, along the Huron River, he'd slipped on a shelf of slate, then slammed his head on the edge before falling in. His father had been right there, and had saved his life. In-between the icy water and the slip, there'd been a vacuous moment of expectant silence. This expectant silence was exactly what he felt as the birds hurried into the night.

Maybe they're just trying to get to where they're going without fuss? he thought.

No, no, the little anxiety voice told him, deep in his mind. *They aren't making noise because they don't want to draw attention, Matthew. They don't want to be caught.*

"Nonsense," he said out loud, as if doing so would quell the voice.

A goshawk buzzed his head. *Wooooosh.* The goshawk's crimson eye ogled him as it streaked for the other end of the orchard, dagger wings and fanned tail cutting through the green air.

Where's it going, Matthew? the little voice asked. *Why is that goshawk out in the open at two in the morning? Think about it.*

Matt stood from the post, as if changing position would make the voice go away. Wings buffeted the air around him. Birds of all sizes and species swarmed the sky, their scattering silhouettes against the gigantic curtains of northern lights.

To the southwest, where the orchard met the wall of chokecherry, several balsam firs marked a game path that led to the bog. It was there a trophy white-tailed deer scraped and picked its antlers against a trunk. The buck's hide was green from the lights, turning it into a woods specter.

Matt shifted his attention back to the sky, turning in a circle, soaking in the curtains from orb to treetops. He wanted to remember as much of this as he could. His father would've done the same thing. To put it simply, very few people got to see this kind of spectacle. And it wasn't some gimmick in a movie. No sir, this was the real deal.

A strange sensation hit him, like he'd just stepped off an elevator. Then he realized the ground was shaking under his feet. He went over to touch the leaning post and it too was vibrating. The U.P. was not known for earthquakes, but it was possible. As he removed his hand from the leaning post, a tremendous boom echoed from the Hurons. Matt's first instinct was to hold his hands to his ears, but then he realized it was too late. As his ears rang, he tried to form an association with the sound, and the closest he could muster was an enraged elephant mixed with freight train.

His nerves bubbled up in his throat, and he swallowed away the bile. He worried that the voice might return. He took deep breaths, his feet uneasy on the earth, his mind betraying him at sub-levels, ready to order his feet to go at any second. *Okay, calm down,* he thought. *You know there are no trains in the area. Could've been a quake shifting some rocks up in the Hurons. This is tough country under the soil, real rugged. Precambrian stuff.*

The sound came again.

Huuuooohar.

Matt cradled his ears, half for protection, half for denial. When he removed his hands and touched the post, it no longer shook. He scanned the southern valley towards the Hurons, looking for anything that might've created such a noise.

The birds had disappeared from the sky.

The noise came from a bad thing, the little anxiety voice said. *A very bad thing. Run.*

A jolt of adrenaline seized him, sending electric warnings to his brain. He moved one foot, preparing to follow the advice, then stopped.

"Just a small earthquake," he said. "Stop scaring yourself. Everyone gets spooked in the woods. Everyone." And then, just to squash the little voice forever, he screamed across the valley. "Come get me! Come and freaking get me! I'm all alone up here in the orchard, near the Black River!"

His words echoed into the enormous light curtains. The pulsating orb in the sky's center ebbed and flowed, then shot flashes of hot-white light to the horizon.

Matt laughed. Tonight had been strange. Maybe if he hadn't taken those mushrooms at Trent's party. Whatever was left of them was probably working its way through his system. That was it. Of course. The mushrooms from two months ago explained everything.

Soon, the enchanting light display calmed his nerves. There was no way it couldn't. This was his home. He was where he wanted to be. The unparalleled beauty triggered thoughts he didn't care to think—thoughts of his father and Stacey. He pivoted in a circle, absorbing the sky and spectacle, trying to tune his mind out. Completing the turn, he felt something tiny crawling on his leg. A tick was perched on his muscular calf. The tick had not dug into his skin yet, so he flicked it away with his wrist.

Should've put some pants on, he thought, shivering and crossing his arms. He walked back down the path, humbled by the display and shaken by the earthquake. Two extreme natural events such as these happening at the same time was improbable. But hey, this was the U.P. It wasn't exactly a normal place.

Don't forget the birds, Matthew, the little anxiety voice said. *They didn't want to be caught, and neither do you.*

Matt let the creaky shack door drown out the voice in his head. He crawled into his sleeping bag and turned on his side so he could see the shafts of northern lights breaking into the room. As the minutes passed, the lights dimmed. All that remained was white light—as if a child had sucked the green juice out of a Flavorice pop—dancing outside the windows. Soon his eyelids grew heavy, the train sound on a loop in his mind. The last, scant reflections of northern lights receded from the cherry wood table, then ghosted out the southern window like the tentacles of a retreating octopus.

***

At two a.m., Matt woke to claws scratching on glass.

He froze, not wanting whatever it was to see him. His heart pounded so hard the sleeping bag fabric matched its rhythm. He moved his head in tiny increments, his bed head swishing against the nylon. Some sort of creature was on the other side of the eastern window, scratching the glass with its paws. He could barely make out the face of the thing in the darkness.

scritch scritch scritch

The animal scratched harder.

He got the feeling it did so because it knew he saw it.

Chills trickled down his arms and legs. He strained into the darkness, trying his best to make out facial details. Slowly, a basic shape formed.

A raccoon, he thought with a sense of relief. Then the animal turned its face, revealing a short, flat snout.

Not a raccoon. Small bear? Has to be a bear cub. He stood from the bunk, thinking he might scare the animal away.

Then it barked.

"What the hell?"

Matt leaned towards the window, his eyes bulging A furry face with round eyes stared back. The hair was mix of white and grey.

No, he thought. *It can't be. This isn't funny, or amusing, or any of those things. Just no.*

The creature barked again.

scritch scritch scritch

The animal's claws screeched down the glass onto the logs. Matt's eyes stung with fresh tears as he grabbed his headlamp and stretched it over his head. Then he ran for the big door, swinging it open as such a door could be swung. He ran to the east side of the shack near the big aspen, headlamp shining where the animal would've been.

Nothing there.

In his peripheral vision he saw a flash of white fur, low to the ground, sprinting down the two track driveway towards Julip Road. He sprinted after it, the two track dirt soft under his bare feet. His defined quads pumped under the boxers, his breath economical. The lamp beam bounced along with the movement of his head. And then he slipped on the soil where the driveway steepened and fell on his ass. His teeth rattled and for a moment the world faded. After several seconds of discombobulation, he recovered his bearings, scrambled to his feet and reached Julip Road. Panting and scraping came from the dark road, towards the direction of Lake Superior. Matt turned in that direction, throwing a beam of light. There, far down the road he saw a little white and grey dog sprinting and barking.

Freaking impossible, he thought. *Can't be him.*

Of course it's Elmo, the little voice said. *What else looks like that, Matthew? Don't you think it's strange Elmo is all the way up here—especially since he's dead?*

Matt cradled his head and shut his eyes tight, as if that would make the little doggie disappear. When he opened his eyes, the little dog was gone.

A wave of guilt and remorse smacked him, and he ran south, searching for tracks or sign that the pooch had gone into the forest. He couldn't find any. He focused his headlamp light cone into the woods again and again, wondering if the little dog could've gotten lost. Matt combed fifty yards deep on both sides of the road amongst the sedges and ferns. No tracks or fur. He'd picked up a few ticks and spider webs, though. After brushing off the insects, he sighed and shone the lamp south down Julip, expecting to see the glowing eyes of Elmo.

Nothing.

Matt shuffled up the driveway, cold and tired.

It could've been a coyote, he thought. *Or an albino fisher.* Albino animals did exist in the Northwoods—sometimes they showed up in photographs on the walls of local shops. Albinism was a rare skin condition that made animals (including people) white. Also, his father and Ron had seen albino deer a few times in the area. Albinism had its negative aspects, such as hunting season. Albino animals didn't survive long up here, standing out against the greenery.

Follow your old friend, the little anxiety voice said.

"I'm tired," Matt said. "Too tired. And besides, Elmo is gone."

He waited for a response from the irritating voice, but there was only silence.

It had been a hell of a night. He was beat up, his senses overworked. Matt closed the gargantuan door and reached into the blue cooler for the fat bottle of Crown Royal. He wasn't much of a drinker, but this was sort of tradition up north. He unscrewed the cap and put the glass to his lips. The brusque fluid soothed his nerves and warmed him. With his senses dulled, he slid inside his sleeping bag, keeping his headlamp on. He checked the window over the grungy couch. Nothing.

Soon he drifted off, three last words trailing across the musty shack: *Miss you, Elmo.*

Day One

Matt checked his watch. 10 a.m.

Shit.

He twisted out of his bag, wincing as he stretched. His arms were laced with puffy scratches from his foray into the forest last evening. The physical pain was easy to ignore as his thoughts turned to Elmo and what he'd seen in the night.

Elmo had not been a wimp. A German Sheppard that decided to visit the yard one day and of course was chased off. The family had watched from the big living room window, bursting out in laughter at little white and brown Elmo, on the heels of the big Sheppard.

Elmo charged many dogs that made the mistake of roaming through their yard, a fierce defender of the their hilly yard on Smokey Road. Elmo assumed his rightful throne behind the screen door, looking down upon the neighborhood. Anything that came by the house was barked at. No one in the Kearns family had any explanation for his behavior. Matt assumed Elmo was born as an alpha, and there wasn't much anyone could do. Elmo even scared him sometimes with how he'd bark at strangers. Yet at the same time, Elmo was loving and gentle with the family.

Once, Elmo had escaped out the screen door when a Rottweiler trotted up the walk. The Rottweiler had stood its ground, and Elmo slammed into the much larger dog in a tumbling ball of fury, slashing and biting. As the Rotty clamped its jaws onto Elmo's back, Elmo had yipped and shrieked. Upon seeing Matt sprint into the yard to "defend" Elmo, the Rotty had looked up. This was all Elmo needed. Without hesitation, Elmo leaped up and bit the Rotty's nose, causing it to cry out. Then the Rotty took off down the hill, with Elmo in pursuit. The Kearns had heard the commotion and ran outside, wondering what the hell was going on. His father appeared first, broomstick in hand. There had been no need for the broomstick on that day though. Elmo was the victor, sitting in the neighbor's yard, staring down the Rotty as it wandered into the forest.

Elmo lived for danger, and had no regard for cars. He'd often chase them up and down the hill. One evening, Matt had just finished eating dinner when he went out into the yard to look for his baseball mitt. Unaware that Elmo was hiding behind the main door, Matt opened the screen door. Elmo raced out into the street just as a car sped up Smokey Road. Matt remembered shouting as a barking Elmo slid underneath the driver's side door of the speeding car. The driver, a horrified spectacle-wearing man, swerved towards the curb.

Andrea had come running.

"Matthew? Matthew! What happened? Where's Elmo?" she'd said.

She'd stormed down the hill in her Bib overalls, tears glistening her cheeks. Matt had stood in shock at the side of the car. Their dog was dead. Elmo was dead.

The driver opened his door and started apologizing. Then the driver was cut off mid-sentence as a noise was heard under the vehicle, a sort of *gruff, gruff* and then the scrape of claws on asphalt. A furry white and brown mess shot out from under the driver's side door and then leapt inside the vehicle.

"He's alive, Elmo is alive!" Andrea had cried.

The perplexed driver had been in danger of being licked to death by an Ewok.

Elmo liked slides, too. Matt could never figure out why. If Elmo couldn't get up the stairs to reach the top of the slide, Matt or Andrea would pick him up and place him at the top. Once placed upon the lofty perch, Elmo would inch forward and let gravity take him. You couldn't pass a playground without him tugging his leash towards the sand.

New Jersey didn't last long. Matt and Andrea had made fantastic friends in the rolling green hills and it was difficult to leave. His father was transferred to Illinois, back to the suburbs of Chicago. Matt was saddened to leave his pals and the comfortable woods of northern New Jersey, but it also felt meant-to-be, whatever that truly was. He sensed it in his bones. His mother was the saddest of all about the move, telling them it was the best thing in the long run, but Matt wasn't buying it—Junior High age or not. They had lasted two years in New Jersey. It was a blessed time.

The transfer back to Illinois was jarring. The new school was built without much thought, and there wasn't a window in sight. Madison Junior high was a series of giant brick and concrete walls, and a circular center with the administrative offices right in the middle like a bull's eye. Between classes, students walked the circle, exiting at four points into different sets of steps leading towards other voluminous concrete rooms.

There was no sunlight. On their first day, Matt and Andrea sat side by side on the office bench as the students of this new world swirled around them in the circular passageway. Making new friends was rough, as the kids were nothing like New Jersey kids. The cliques were tighter, the atmosphere less friendly, the smiles fewer. Kids were doing things they had never heard of, like huffing paint.

The days were long inside the concrete tomb that passed for a junior high. The best part of the day for Matt and Andrea was walking towards their house, fresh off the school bus and seeing that big white and brown ball of fur sprinting towards them.

"Elmoooooo," Andrea would shout. "Elmooooooo!"

Eventually the friends would come. And like always, some faded away like that sandal you just lost in the river but can't quite reach. Sometimes, the fade wasn't until thirty years later, sometimes it was next year. Jim Bowden was one of those friends. Jim liked to cause a bit of trouble. Jim looked like trouble too, usually in a smart ass t-shirt and faded blue jeans. His face wasn't always clean, like he had something better to do than wash. It wasn't stupid trouble, more like mad scientist trouble, which was fine because it was creative. Because of this, they could look back on the hijinks with a sense of pride. Good work was good work, regardless of intentions. Tossing smoke bombs into the auditorium during gym class might not have been the smartest prank, but it was an epic one. Of that were was no doubt.

"Throw it, pussy," Jim had said, stuttering from nervousness as they sat cross legged on the gym floor.

"You throw it, asshole," Matt had said, voice cracking.

"You throw this hellacious smoke bomb as soon as Mr. Gaunt turns his back and you'll be a legend."

Matt liked that framing. Mr. Gaunt, their good-natured gym teacher didn't need the hassle, but at that point it didn't matter. Mr. Gaunt was just an innocent bystander in the way of an epic prank. Matt had gripped the ping pong-sized smoke bomb they got from Derek Cho, the stocky kid with glasses from home room. Without hesitation Matt lit the bomb and rolled it under the bleachers, the wick spitting sparks and hissing. Soon enough, smoke began wafting between the wooden bleacher slats.

Within a minute, the entire gymnasium had filled with smoke. The students who were cross legged on the floor leaped like panicked frogs. A few students ran for the exits. Teachers scuttled, waving their hands, clipboards flying. Random shouts of confusion and shrieks of surprise penetrated the dense smoke.

When the smoke was at its thickest, and the confusion at its most frantic, Matt and Jim had burst out laughing. Their laughter intensified when Derek Cho hobbled into the gym doorway and shouted at the top of his lungs, "Holy hell what have you guys done? WHAT HAVE YOU GUYS DONE?" This of course triggered suspicion from assistant principal Mary Higgins. She grabbed Derek by the arm and had begun an impromptu interrogation. Through the thick smoke, Matt couldn't make out much. But what he did make out seemed like slow motion: he could see Derek Cho pull his hand out of his jean pocket and point it right at him.

That was it. Punishment was swift and harsh. Mary Higgins informed Matt and his family he wouldn't be permitted to attend graduation. He'd also be forced to help the janitors after school was out for the summer, which consisted of scrapping gum off the bottom of cafeteria tables with a butter knife. Jim was there too, of course. But Jim's idea of helping the janitors was far, far different from what the school had in mind. Jim Bowden's idea was to give the janitors a few days off. His plan was simple: take a paperclip, unbend it, wrap lots of electrical tape in the center, then bend it into a U-shape. This crude device was to be inserted into the bathroom electrical socket—well out of the sight of anyone in the concrete tomb known as Madison High.

They'd walked into the bathroom with Jim cupping the sabotage device in his palm. He went to one knee, lining up the paperclip ends to the socket inputs. It seemed like forever.

POP!

A blinding flash had radiated from the socket, knocking Jim back five feet. The acrid stench of burning hair flooded the bathroom, and the lights went dark. Matt had walked over to Jim, laughing his ass off.

"You alright, man?" he'd asked.

"What you think? If I'm talking to you, I'm alright" Jim said. But it was obvious the shock had frazzled him. Matt could see it in his eyes.

He'd taken an toilet roll and used it to knock the paper clip out of the socket. The clip glowed in the dark, red hot like an ember. Matt had picked up one end of the clip and wrapped it in his shirt. When they got to an area with emergency lighting in the circular passageway, Matt dropped the clip into one of the wastebaskets. They could hear staffers trying to make sense of the situation, attempting to gather their bearings. Mary Higgins, who was still inside her office, hustled out the front doors to greet the fire truck they could hear halfway across town. She'd told Matt and Jim that they needed to go outside in case of a fire. After an hour of no electricity, she sent them home. The next day, Mary Higgins informed them that their suspension was over. The school was down for a week because of electrical repairs.

That was the end of the strangest suspension ever—one that occurred when school was over, after they'd graduated. Looking back Matt had the distinct sensation of being trapped in a place that had moved on from him, as if the rest of society had migrated to another plane of existence. It was not comforting.

That was also the last time Matt Kearns or Jim Bowden ever saw Madison Junior High, and Matt doubted if all the money in the world could get him back through those doors. They might close behind him, and he'd be there forever, scraping gum in an empty cafeteria, stranger's feet shuffling in the darkness here and there.

Through it all, Elmo waited for him, as all good pets do. Through junior high, through high school, through his intermittent college classes, through trips. Always there, regardless of social position or the blues. Looking back, he owed that dog so much. In the end, he did as much as he could for Elmo, because Elmo was always there for him. He wasn't going to let some stranger hold Elmo as he was injected with a lethal drug. He and Andrea made sure of that. The cancer had hit Elmo fast. He'd started vomiting blood and bleeding from his nose. Before that, he'd gotten stiff, arthritis taking its toll.

Four nights before he'd died, Elmo had wanted to go outside for a walk at one a.m., and for the first time in two years had worked himself into a full sprint, legs fully extended. Elmo and Matt had run down the empty suburban street, streetlamps humming, Elmo's claws scraping the pavement. A real, full-on sprint, Elmo's tongue lolling, his eyes big and full of love. Even Elmo seemed surprise he could do it. They'd run for at least five minutes, alone in the suburban night, Matt laughing and shouting with joy, encouraging Elmo on. Elmo was so amped he'd sprinted around the court four times before going inside. Matt had given him a bath, and the crazy dog ran around in the house, too. Four days before he died, he acted like he was a puppy again.

Four days.

He wished he didn't remember Elmo's death, but he did. Most prominent in these remembrances was the phone conversation he had with his sister a month after Elmo died. The dreams had been relentless.

He remembered the hollow rings.

"Hello," Andrea had said. Exhaustion thick in her voice.

"How are you?" he'd asked, weary, beaten.

"As good as can be, I guess," Andrea said. "Still hurts."

Silence overcame the line.

"I had a dream last night," Matt said. "Super clear".

"Okay…" Andrea had said.

"It was about Elmo."

Silence.

"I dreamt he'd fallen down this metal tube. I mean, real long tubing that went down into some metal chamber the size of a hospital room. When he emerged into the chamber, he was no longer a dog. He was a mountain lion. Crazy, right?"

"It's not crazy at all," she'd said. "It's beautiful."

***

Matt slid into his blue jeans and snapped the silver belt buckle. Then he pulled on his flannel and shivered. The temp felt about fifteen degrees cooler, and the musty scent of the shack was even more pronounced than usual.

He went outside to take a piss. There was no need to use the outhouse. He had to keep track of where he pissed, though. There was nothing worse than walking through wet grass and realizing it was your own urine. This had happened many times before and always triggered laughter from those who were spared the embarrassment.

Matt looked back at the old outhouse. It had seen better days. Then again, the outhouse always seemed like it had seen better days.

The brilliance of the previous night's display was replaced by a leaden, windless day. The sky was a blown-out white (what photographers referred to as *the sky of death)*. Matt listened for birds and other wildlife, but all was silent.

Strange. Woodpeckers were always working the trees. He walked the path to the leaning post to take in the landscape, a common morning ritual before breakfast. In the mornings his father and Ron would often have a smoke and a coffee at the post. Matt clenched his right fist at the thought of this.

Blackened patches of orchard grass surrounded the fire pit thanks to Ernie's temper tantrum. Everything else seemed in place. The intense curtains of northern lights had not lit the place on fire. The Hurons still loomed on the horizon, like a sleeping giant. The earthquake had not ripped them apart. All was as it should be except for one thing: no animal noises, not even an insect. If he didn't hear a bird, he could at least hear a mammal digging or hoofing around. If he couldn't hear that, he'd be able to spot insects flying.

He found nothing.

Matt shook his head and went inside the shack for breakfast.

The lumpy pancakes didn't look so hot. The bottle of Vermont syrup reminded him of his childhood, when he stayed with friends on the Jersey coast whose parents were syrup aficionados. During breakfast, he and his friend Scott were scolded by Scott's parents for using too much syrup.

No no! they'd yelled. *You pour it on your fork, and when your fork is coated in syrup, you're done, that is enough!*

Matt tilted the bottle over the lumpy cakes. "Screw you guys," he said.

The cakes didn't go down so well.

Engorged, Matt checked the floor near the blue cooler. The plastic milk jugs he'd filled the day before were low. He grabbed three of the jugs and headed down to the Black.

Crossing Julip Road, he was relieved to see his first animal of the day, a white-tailed deer. The doe paced in the road and snorted. At first he was alarmed, but then realized sometimes does act nervous and downright bizarre to distract predators who sought their fawns. It's a tactic he'd seen before, both out west and in the Northwoods. Just in case she was protecting fawns, he moved on, away from the road and towards the Black.

Goldie's ferns came up to his waist, sliming his jeans. The scent of sweet gale soothed him. He dodged several of the mud pits and perched halfway down the stream bank. The plastic milk jugs glugged as they took water.

Matt hoisted the clear jugs into the daylight, admiring the "creek wash" (as his father had called it) that swirled in the jugs. Now *this* was bottled water.

Upon returning to Julip Road, his heart sank. The pacing deer now lay still on her side. Quietly, he set the jugs on the gravel and jogged over to the animal. As he got to within ten feet, his chest tightened, as if a thick rope was squeezing him by around his shoulders. He gasped for air and went to clutch his throat but couldn't move his arms. *What the hell*, he thought. *Jesus Christ what the fucking hell.* He kicked his legs wildly and tried to move his arms, but they were blocked by powerful muscle. He screamed, but what emerged from his lips was nothing more than a windless grunt.

When he looked down at his arms, they weren't there. All he could see were his hands. He splayed and wriggled his fingers, then tried to free himself once more, but it was pointless.

A disorienting pressure squeezed his throat and he gasped. Little white and black specks polluted his vision and his thoughts seemed far away. He lurched forward, and before his body hit the ground something squeezed his torso—something BIG. The stench of rotten deer meat hit him, and he heard rough, agitated breathing. Something whipped the air above him again and again, but he could not see the agitator.

As he struggled, every part of his body was poked and prodded, as if twenty thousand dull needles had all found a spot on his skin. *Something* squeezed him again, causing his bones to creak. He'd never felt such pain, never. He tried desperately to associate it with wrestling, or bad fights, or falling from a tree, but it wasn't close to any of those things. He was being constricted by something *alive*, could feel the thing's pulse in his nerves. Through his cloudy vision he glimpsed his weird, armless hands. They were swollen and red, the oxygen supply lessening.

He tried to scream again but couldn't. He screamed for his mother, his father, for Stacy and Andrea. They would not hear him, could not hear him. He'd chose this remote place, this so called home. His next series of thoughts were that he was dying. That was all he could assume, because he'd never been near death. These symptoms, this affliction was also foreign to him. A match. A pair. It all made sense now, maybe a heart attack.

His thoughts were cut short as a head-rocking force yanked him off the road.

The deer carcass grew smaller and smaller.

Branches and leaves whipped against his body, making little tears in his shirt and slapping his face. The deer carcass disappeared behind cracking branches and ferns as he was pulled uphill. In a moment of clarity he realized he was in the woods northeast of the shack, traveling through the air backwards and towards the orchard. Something ripped in his left arm as burning pain flared. He looked down amidst the commotion and saw a maple branch protruding from his flannel like an arrow that had met its mark.

The turbidity in his stomach correlated with the velocity at which he was hurled, and he realized he was flying into the orchard through tree line. As he passed through the last row of trees, expectant silence overcame him, the kind you hear when an ice skater is up in their air on a triple twist, or a ski jumper vaults off the ramp, waiting for impact. A second later, Matt Kearns came down hard onto the orchard, next to one of the faded game trails.

All the air from his lungs expunged as the soil ate his scream. Rolling on his side, he gasped again and again. The squeezing and needle sensations had at last disappeared, and he sucked for air as spittle peppered from his lips. When at last he took in a reasonable gulp of air, his eyes darted to the edge of the forest, then around the orchard.

He tried to make sense of what had just happened, tried to apply some sort of logic or reasoning. Mr. Gallant, his high school chemistry teacher had called it "cause and effect". But all there was here was effect. He searched for potential causes, but familiarity never entered his thoughts.

Something grabbed you, the little anxiety voice said. *I don't like it when things grab you, Matthew. Should have followed your friend.*

Matt laid there, taking rich breaths and scrutinizing the orchard. "Should have followed my friend? There was no friend to follow," he said. Unless the voice was talking about Elmo. But anyone who was sane knew that wasn't Elmo last night. Matt looked down at his mangled arm and spit. Then he glanced to the tree line to make sure nothing was coming for him.

Nothing there.

He reached down, gripped the knobby part of the leafy branch, and yanked. He made a sound through gritted teeth he never thought he was capable of making, more like a wolf than a human. Then he unbuttoned his flannel cuff and gently rolled it to his elbow. The wound was deep, but not something he'd die from. Blood pooled into the fleshy gash and spilled onto his wrist. A mess of miniature tart apples surrounded him in the orchard grass, a couple of them drizzled with his blood.

This is what original sin must have looked like, he thought. At least he still had his demented sense of humor. Ron had once told him if you can't laugh, you're not much use to anyone, including yourself.

He had the worst unfunny elbow ever and his arm was numb. Instinctively, he studied t the birch trees that had spat him out.

Nothing.

A moment later bright pain slashed up his left leg. Matt pinched the edge of his bloody sock and peeled it down, revealing a gash across his ankle.

Head pounding and in disbelief, he checked his body like a cat cleaning itself.

Need to stand up, he thought. *Need to make sure I can get out of here.*

He placed his good arm against the ground and pushed himself up. His ankle and chest ached, but nothing like before. Once standing, he looked again to the northeastern edge of the orchard from where he'd flown through the trees. Suddenly his wounds didn't seem so important. What seemed important was getting the hell out of here. Every cell in his body piqued with dread, the same way he felt at the funerals for his father and Stacy. He wanted to leave, and leave now. The voice had been right. He should have gotten in his truck last night and followed the little pooch down Julip Road until he was back at the highway. The highway was safe. He didn't know why he knew that, but he did. His eyes widened like a spooked ungulate as his heart reverberated in his gums. The hairs on his forearms rose. He felt something, or someone watching him.

Should have followed your friend, the little voice said. *Friend follow friend follow friend follow.*

Once more he checked the northeastern tree line. A gust of wind swayed the tree tops all about, like pom-poms.

He ran.

Ten painful steps in, the anxiety voice shot through his brain like a cap gun. *Don't run! Running triggers chase instinct, Matthew.*

Okay, okay, slowing his gait now. He brushed mushed apple from his jeans and looked back towards the northeast tree line. Then he turned and limped towards the shack, favoring his right leg. Soon the outhouse and the big aspen came into view. At once the hair on his neck rose.

Something was watching him.

Every sizeable tree and shady patch held potential danger. Rustling leaves triggered unreasonable adrenaline surges. At last the tailgate of his truck appeared between the outhouse and the aspen trunk. It was time to get the heck out of here.

Can't rationalize this one, can you Matthew? the little voice said.

Fuck off, he thought.

Matt reached for the shack door, eyes watering. Then he pulled his hands back and cradled his head. He shut his eyes tight and opened them, glancing back at his truck and the dead oak. *This was home.* This was always where he felt safest. But now? Now he felt...like *prey.* He had the unshakable feeling he was in a fishbowl, looking through the dirty plastic at a big, distorted eye.

He checked northeast again, back uphill towards the row of birch trees that had spit him onto the orchard. Nothing. No movement in the orchard, either.

Doesn't matter, he thought. *Something was there, something BIG. I had a branch in my arm to prove it and a relocation plan I never signed up for.*

Matt limped into the shack and seized his keys.

Time to go. Time to leave his favorite place in the world.

His truck started up like it always did, despite the miles. The muffler let loose a prolonged rumble that gently shook the vehicle. He put the truck in gear and maneuvered in a multi-point-pattern so he'd be facing Julip Road. There was not going to be any backing up today, hell no.

With the hood pointed towards Julip, he stepped on the gas and raced the 4x4 downhill onto Julip road. A quick left towards Lake Superior, the trees arcing over the road ahead of him, forming a leafy tunnel.

The dead deer was gone.

Matt stomped the gas pedal, keeping it mashed to the floor mat. The truck roared down Julip Road, vegetation patterns reflecting on the black paint and chrome bumper. Overjoyed, he pumped his right fist into the air, knocking it into the glass sunroof.

Ow.

Rocks and dust flew out behind him in the rearview, masking whatever the hell that had been back there. A Twilight Zone episode, bizzaro land, whatever. He could ignore it now, pretend it never happened. He'd warn Ron, though. That would be the first thing he'd do.

Only eight miles to pavement, he thought.

The chrome grille gleamed in the daylight, his truck devouring the road like a strange but loyal robotic dog. His trusty truck, awkward on pavement but oh-so at home on dirt roads.

He wondered how he'd explain this to anyone, then realized it was impossible. No one would believe him. How could he convince others if he didn't even believe it himself? The first thing that would happen to him if he told his mother would be a recommendation for a mental ward. Andrea would believe him initially, but she'd have questions, too. Oh yeah, there'd be a ton of those. And Ron? He could just picture the look of disbelief, as if Matt was setting him up for a joke, much the same way Ron and his father used to do to him.

As he sped at unsafe speeds down Julip Road, Matt watched for animals, fearful he might smash into a moose. At such high speeds, that would be a death collision. And his mother had worried about the death lane? Ha. What about the moose lane?

"Stay back, moose!" he shouted for good measure.

Verdant birch and maple blurred by him. He licked his dry lips and reached for the jug of water in the passenger footwell, removing his eyes from the road. The engine thudded and he quickly sat back up.

The truck hesitated and lurched, making his stomach queasy.

Inexplicably, the truck grinded to a stop, dust and gravel billowing in front of the hood, pinging the paint like a kid throwing beach sand at a pail. Matt stomped the gas pedal all the way to the floor, producing a metallic whine from the engine. The meaty wheels spun in place as stench of burning rubber wafted into the cab.

The truck began to move backwards.

He stomped the pedal, pushing the old four cylinder into a fit. The truck reversed faster and faster as the gear box rattled and whined. Smoke curled all around him, obscuring his view. The stench grew nauseating as the truck groaned and shuddered like a dying whale.

Should have followed your friend, the little voice chimed in his head. *Follow friend, friend follow, follow friend, friend follow.*

Matt let go of the wheel and tried to open the door, but it wouldn't budge. He rolled the window down and as soon as he did his chest tightened like before. Whatever positive thoughts he'd had disappeared into the U.P. air like expelled tobacco smoke. In their place, the darkest of thoughts, ones that he'd never felt before. At Stacey and Big John's funeral, the bleakness was for them, for their behalf. For the first time in his life, Matt felt bleakness for himself. The view out the window blurred as something blocked it, half-reality, half not, a deceptive and clever camouflage. Needle sensations wrapped his body as he choked and gasped. Soon the world was full of black and white sparkles, every sound in his ears muted yet encased in heavy layers of reverb. As he dipped into unconsciousness, his foot slipped off the gas pedal, quieting the engine.

The forest of Julip Road streaked past him in reverse.

I'm being pulled backwards, he thought just before darkness swallowed him.

Yes you are, Matthew, the little voice said. *I'm sorry.*

His trusty 4x4 lurched, whined, and jostled in reverse over Julip Road at thirty miles per hour. Inside, Matt Kearns slumped against the driver's door. Gears grinded and wheels spun. Plumes of dust whooshed into the cab as the truck he and his father had worked on and taken care of zoomed down the road, the back tires three feet off the ground. The chassis creaked and groaned like it always had over these Northwoods logging roads, maybe for the last time.

***

Matt Kearns woke to the sensation of blowing air and the workman-like scent of oil. He opened his left eye, gazing onto the world through a film of blood.

I'm in hell, he thought.

The other eyelid refused to open. He moved his fingers to his eyebrow and touched a bump.

The heater blew lukewarm air from the driver's side vent into his mouth. His stomach curled, and he did his best to hold back.

Rivulets of oil trickled across the windshield. He blinked his bloody eye, then wiped at it with his left hand.

He turned and looked out the driver's side window only to see ants crawling between smashed blades of grass.

Upside-down, he thought. *Or on the side.*

Matt reached out to the dull light seeping through the passenger window, which now seemed like a sunroof. He groaned and pushed himself up, using the truck bench for support. Then he popped the lock on the passenger door, his body aching and his head throbbing from temple to temple.

"Keep going you wuss," he said, as if that John Wayne style of pep talk would somehow heal his injuries. And, John Wayne never saw the sands of Iwo Jima anyway. Soar or not, he pushed on the passenger door above him while climbing the seatback. Soon, he was able to get his head through the opening, enough to prop the door while pushing the rest of his body through. The plastic armrest on the door dug into his back, hard. Once clear of the door opening he let himself fall, only to have his boot catch on the door panel. He dangled for a moment, then collapsed onto the orchard grass.

Head throbbing and confused, he blinked at the leaden sky, cool air fresh upon his cheeks.

One time, back in school he'd slipped and fallen on spilled apple juice and cracked his head on the tile. He'd been discombobulated for a while, and this was sort of like that. The good news was his right eye was beginning to open, but just a bit. The blood in his left eye had cleared, too.

Matt turned to his left, making his head hurt even worse. The entire truck was on its side, the underbelly exposed. The passenger tire was still spinning. He zoned out on the rust patches corroding the metal frame and realized the engine wasn't running. On top of that, branches jabbed through the plastic windows on the pickup cap he and his father had installed. Clusters of leaves stuck out of the tailgate as if they'd grown there. The cap tailgate window was speared by a gangly maple branch that protruded like a ladder on a handyman's truck.

Dismayed at the condition of his truck, Matt wiggled his toes, making sure they weren't broken. While doing so, he noticed the tall blades of golden rod and sandy soil. The smell of *place*. An undeniable olfactory imprint. At once he knew the location, didn't even need to turn around.

He stood, slowly, examining the truck's path. A head rush hit him and he had to bend over, his fingers to his temples. Sure he wasn't going to pass out, he stood upright once more. A swath of flattened orchard grass cut between the outhouse and big aspen tree. The path led northeast across the orchard to the tree line where he'd been flung back. The birch tree crowns rustled in all directions. There was no wind.

Is that it? he thought. *Does it live in the trees?*

The rustling stopped.

Get in the shack, NOW! the little voice screamed.

Without hesitating, he hobbled to the shack door, like a bloody hunchback. Once inside he shut the door behind him and locked down the huge iron bolt. He teetered from window to window, eyes darting.

Nothing.

He glanced around the room for weapons, focusing on the bunk bed. After painfully kneeling, he dragged out the musty cardboard box from underneath the first bunk. Inside lay a faded red box of clay pigeons, an rusting steel bear trap, a hammer, and moldy-looking rope—maybe forty feet. A faded roll of duct tape was tucked in a corner. After forcing himself to his knees, he limped over to the hutch and took the biggest kitchen knife in the mix, relishing the heft in his hands.

Reassuring, Matthew? the little voice asked. *That thing just pulled your truck a mile down the road and flipped it. What do you think a kitchen knife is going to do against that?*

He gripped the knife harder. "Because there might be other things out there I haven't seen yet," he said. There. That shut the voice up. Or maybe not.

You haven't even seen this one, the anxiety voice chimed back.

How he wished Ron had left a gun at the shack. Even a .22 would be welcome.

Knife in hand, he stumbled over to the eastern window and peered out towards the aspen and outhouse. He saw something very strange—a patch of grass bent to the west, to the east, to the south…then the grass blew in a circular motion, three hundred and sixty degrees.

Board up the windows, Matthew! the little voice said.

Ignoring the pain and blood drizzling down his forearm, he grabbed one of the cherrywood chairs and placed it alongside the eastern window, using the grungy couch as a support. Next he trudged over to the west wall and removed the pans and nails. Then he took the hammer from the cardboard box and nailed the chair into the logs. The two sheets of plywood behind the cast iron stove were quite a find, so he positioned them over the southern window and nailed. He left enough of a crack to see out. He'd always found the dead oak menacing in a way, but not today, not anymore. Now there was a real boogeyman, or *boogeything* out there, toying with him like a cat toys with a chipmunk, letting him get ever so far before dragging him back. It was a bummer to think about what happened to the chipmunk in reality. Cute, seed-stuffed cheeks or not, the chipmunk, once caught, never got away. It either died from shock or was chewed to death. In many cases the chipmunk became paralyzed, causing the cat to lose interest. Therein lies the worst result. Only the fattest, dumbest cat would allow any other outcome.

A great rush of nausea hit him, and he vomited on the camp stove. Chunks of pancakes and syrup coated the dancing bear sticker and slopped off the sides.

See! We told you! Only a forkful! Scott's parents taunted in his mind. *Only a forkful! Only a forkful!*

He took a dish towel from the side rack and swept the vomit off the camp stove and onto the floor. If he was going to be trapped in here, he couldn't have vomit everywhere. He set the paper bag sideways on the floor and mopped the upchuck sauce into it.

After the last sweep, stillness crept over the shack like a medieval court hushing before the queen enters.

He thought he heard steps outside, and placed his ear to the log wall. Something was pacing the shack—the unmistakable sound of hooves on earth. A dark shape appeared in the southern window, detailing to dark fur and a long, droopy face.

"A moose," Matt said, overjoyed.

The wide-shouldered bull sported a majestic set of antlers. He was all muscle too, a real bruiser. Goosebumps rippled down Matt's limbs as the moose stopped in front of the window. Its round, fearful eye was so close as its nostrils flared. And then it pressed against the window, the chocolate-colored fur flattening against the thin glass.

"Run," he shouted at the moose. "Get out of here!"

The bull moose turned to the west, towards something out of Matt's visual range. The moose's eyes widened and it chuffed deeply as it thrust itself against the shack. For a moment the moose's petrified ungulate eyes met Matt's through the thin window. Before Matt could even pluck the slightest bit of sense from this scenario, the moose was yanked away, its enormous hooves furrowing the soil. The moose bayed and kicked as it was dragged towards the dead oak. Then it disappeared over the lip of the bowl, down into where the old farmhouse used to be. The last he saw of it was those terrified eyes staring back at him.

Up came more pancakes. This time he had the bag ready.

Sweat flecked Matt's forehead and dampened his hair near the roots. He stared out the opening in the southern window, his heart doubling up on each second. His hands trembled, his stomach a churning sea of misery.

Think, buddy, think. He scanned his thoughts for a solution like an anti-virus program scans a hard disk.

He could try to run again. There had to be other ways out. Not every possible outlet could be blocked by whatever this thing was. For some reason images of his schoolboy days flashed through his mind: stapled pieces of paper lying on a smooth desk, shiny linoleum floors and the scent of pine sol. He could smell sharpened pencils and hear department store loafers shuffling.

"Taking a test?" he whispered to himself, gazing at the dead oak. Yes, a *test*.

Sure it might kill him, but whatever was out there was going to do that, too.

Or disable you and leave you paralyzed, the anxiety voice said. *It likes to play games, Matthew.*

"Or that," he said.

He only had so much information, but he did know a few things. When he got too far out of range the creature—

The Puller, the little voice said.

"I'll call it whatever I want," he said, cradling his head with both hands and brushing his sweaty hair back.

He knew that when he went too far, he'd get that pressure on his chest and start choking. If he could somehow test the allowed roaming space by carefully pushing the boundaries, he could figure out how much room he had to work with. There was a slight chance he may not be stuck in the shack after all.

The biggie, the WHOPPER question was why was he pulled back onto the shack property twice and then freed? Why didn't the thing just kill him then and there?

Matt spit into the paper bag, grimacing at the bitter taste of bile.

One thing was certain: He'd been given space, and he had to see exactly how much he had. Either that or sit in the shack, scared as shit and growing weaker and weaker. And with no one around for miles, he couldn't expect a savior. He didn't want to cower in fear and grow weak. Oh no, he didn't want that at all. If he was going to die, it was going to be out in the sunlight. His blood would be spilled in the orchard grass, not inside the shack. He was sure of it. The problem was not being sure about anything else. There were many questions, but few answers. How big was the creature? Pretty freaking big. But how big is big? There's Sears Tower big, and then Grand Teton big.

Anything that can pull a truck like that is strong, not to mention fast. He could file that into the *Known Category* in the vanilla folder labeled *Piece Of Shit That Was Holding Him Hostage*. Fast and strong? Check. Invisible? Check. Was the creature solid or gaseous? Unknown.

And maybe the visibility is also unknown , he thought.

Certainly it was invisible to him, but perhaps it was a trick of light, a distortion capable of fooling the human eye. There was quite a difference between *invisible* and using smoke and mirrors. Smoke and mirrors can be exposed. If that was the case he just needed to find a device that reveals the trick.

Darkness began to soften the shack's rough edges, and the boarded windows didn't help. Matt slumped onto the bottom bunk, sore as an NFL running back on an October Monday.

Matt angled and twisted out of his flannel, shaking his head at the scrapes and cuts across his arms. The bump on his eye had receded, and his vision in both eyes was okay.

The gash on his arm was not.

Matt went to the shelf above the couch and took a bottle of hydrogen peroxide. He unscrewed the white cap, letting it fall to the floor. Then he tilted the plastic nozzle, allowing the liquid to drip into the wound. His face scrunched up and he muted a scream by biting the inside of his right cheek. Sure he wouldn't feel the need to scream again, he applied the hydrogen peroxide to the smaller cuts and scrapes, gnashing his teeth.

The last thing he needed was an infection. He could not escape if he was sick. That terrified him just as much as whatever was out *there*.

Panicking won't help you either Matthew, the little voice said. *Panicking won't help you at all.*

"I know," he said. "Thank you."

With his arms smarting but fresh and clean, Matt reached back onto the bunk, grabbed his headlamp, and stretched the band over his head. He flicked the switch on and snatched a copy of *National Geographic* from the shelf. Gracing the cover was a picture of a Yellowstone wolf, with the title, WOLF WARS. After a few page flips he looked up from the magazine to the chair that was barricaded the eastern window. Hints of the outhouse and the aspen appeared between the chair legs. He was at war also, except he couldn't see his enemy. It lay out there somewhere near the shack, doing whatever it liked to do. Today, it liked to hurt him. How long it would be amused by that, who could say?

It also liked to hurt that moose.

He pictured the majestic animal, its eyes wide with fear as it was dragged away, a Northwoods icon reduced to a plaything.

His eyes pooled with moisture he wiped them with the back of his hand.

Don't Matthew, the little voice said. *You have to be strong. You also need rest. You can't beat this without rest.*

He tossed the magazine against the slate fireplace and limped over to the southern window. The dead oak loomed out there in the darkness.

"Tomorrow there'll be a test," he said, sniffing.

A few minutes later Matt fired up the lantern. His bruised bones and skin warmed with each revolution of the intensity dial. In the heavenly light he thought of his family and how to contact them. He'd left his cheap pre-paid cell phone in the truck glove box, but cell phones never worked from the shack anyway. Way too far in the boonies.

As he painfully laid across the bottom bunk, he placed the knife and hammer on the outside edge of the mattress. The lantern would be left on all night. Matt crawled into his sleeping bag, sore and scratched, but not beaten. *Not yet, anyway*, he thought. And that was enough of a crack in the gloom to give him hope. Just enough.

Looking up at the thin wooden plank that supported the second bunk, he realized with a great deal of relief that the shack afforded him protection. Then his eyes closed, summoning sleep anemones which saw him through the night.

Reformed Near the Water
15 Years Ago

Big John Kearns and his good friend Ron pulled into the small gravel lot of the Huron Bay Tavern. It was an impressive place, built upon a slice of land between the big lake and the highway. John wondered if they'd needed a forklift to get the giant timbers in place. The owner, Mary Henders, had once said the logs were taken from the upper Black at the turn of the century. They were extraordinary, and John had only seen their equal in the remote Huron Mountains.

Ron took a Marlboro Red from behind his ear and lit it with a yellow Bic lighter. He drew deep and a curl of smoke wafted across the truck cab. The lone streetlamp reflected off his spectacles and illuminated his angular face in monochrome.

The night was quiet save for the faint tavern music and the gentle sloshing of Lake Superior along the rocks. The tavern windows glowed invitingly. The moon shone bright above the pitched roof, casting ambient light upon the hardwoods and balsam fir.

"Good night to be in the woods," Ron said.

John blinked. "You're slipping, Ron. It's always a good night to be in the Northwoods."

"Not slipping yet," Ron said. "And I'll prove it when I whip your ass in darts."

John chuckled. Ron definitely had his number in darts.

They exited Ron's Chevy pickup and opened the tavern door, letting Merle Haggard flood the once quiet woods.

The Huron Bay Tavern was just as impressive from the inside. Massive, vaulted timbers rose to the ceiling, towering above the spacious room. The rectangular bar was placed square in the middle with several stools and a plethora of tables and chairs surrounding it. An Alaskan king crab mount sat in one corner, the plaque indicating it was from Ice Bay. In the northeast corner loomed a tremendous brown bear mount from Kodiak Island. It stood ten feet tall with its paws out, frozen in time, teeth exposed. John stared at the thing, trying to see something in its glassy eyes. He wondered of the bear's disposition in life. What if it had been a gentle bear? They had personalities too. You had your grumps and angels, just like humans. Tonight the tavern had a few of them too, and their glassy stares weren't all that different from the stuffed brown bear.

Ron hit the jukebox with his fist. "Damn thing took my quarter."

The female bartender, slim with blonde hair and light on the makeup, shouted at him. "Hey, do I come into your place and beat on your stuff?"

Ron turned., frowning.

The bartender smiled. "Gotcha," she said.

Ron blushed. John had not seen that very often.

"What can I getcha tonight?" the bartender asked, wiping her hands on a white towel. "It's a bit late for finger food, but I can whip something up if need be."

"Two Heinekens," Ron said. He placed ten dollars on the polished wooden bar and told her to keep the change. She swooped the money away without hesitating, her hair fanning over half her face.

John whispered. "You know her?"

Ron nodded. "Angie. Best bartender in the Yooper."

Angie snorted with her back to them, tossed a sidelong glance, then plunked two green-tinted beer bottles onto the bar.

The men twisted in their seats, turning their backs to the island bar. As they sipped the delicious beer, they studied all the crap on the walls. Credence Clearwater Revival blared from the jukebox, and John thought it almost eerie, the loud music, the few people in the huge bar, and the dead animals everywhere. An empty space within an empty space. He couldn't help but be reminded of one of those old Twilight Zone episodes.

Hanging on the north wall was a fifty pound northern pike, all teeth and jaws. The bronze plaque indicated the monster had been caught in Huron Bay. Next to it, mounted on another piece of driftwood was a lake trout of similar poundage, also taken from Huron Bay.

"Place is a freaking museum," Ron said. "Can you imagine hooking into that pike?"

John shook his head and drank his beer.

"Maybe we ought to get off these rivers, get a boat and get our asses out to the big lake," Ron said.

John laughed. "Too much work. Trailer maintenance. Boat maintenance. Bla bla. It becomes a money pit and it ends up taking all your time. I like the rivers. Simple, easy."

"You had me at maintenance," Ron said.

John laughed and set his empty beer down. "Angie, two more please?"

Angie took a drag from her well-hidden cigarette and changed him out. "What are you two FIBS doing up here this time of night?" She said FIB in a way that made fun of the local usage, not actual Illinois residents.

Ron played along, feigning outrage. "Who you calling a FIB? I own land up here."

Angie laughed.

A V8 engine rumbled outside the tavern, and a harsh spotlight shone through the two picture windows facing the highway. It was some jackass with a monster truck, and the spotlights were meant for poaching, something John had seen way too often up here.

A moment later the door whipped open and a man hobbled inside, waving his finger in the air. He was dressed in knee-high hunter's boots, jeans, and a red-checkered flannel with suspenders.

"Angie, Angie, when will those clouds all disappear, eh?" the drunken man said.

"Oh God," Angie said. "It's Sanders. I'm hiding behind you two."

Ron and John laughed and sipped their beers.

"I see you two laughing, eh?" Sanders slurred. He slumped into a bar stool next to them and motioned for Angie. "Bartender, Angie, Northwoods nymph...a whiskey on the rocks, eh?"

Angie frowned. "You're crazy if you think I'm serving you in that condition."

"What are you talking bout, eh? I'm as sober as the day I came outta my momma."

Ron burst out laughing and beer spurted through his nose. John almost did the same.

Sanders eyed them with curious disdain and pointed a wobbly finger. "See, these are the drunkards, eh? They can't even hold their liquor! Look at 'em, like two school girls."

"Come on," John said. "You're out of your mind. Just admit it."

Sanders swayed in his seat and narrowed his eyes. "Alright, I admit I've had a few, *but* I'm not drunk. Only schoolgirls get drunk, eh?"

"Then where are your pigtails?" Ron asked.

"Ah, a real wise ass eh? You know what wise asses are good for? They good for a placeholder for my boot!"

John laughed so hard his face reddened. "Alright, alright. We believe you. You're not drunk, okay?"

Sanders crossed his arms and puffed out his chest, then almost teetered off the stool. "There, that wasn't so hard, was it?"

Angie handed Sanders a glass of clear liquid with a lemon squeezed onto the rim. "House special," she said.

Sanders took a drink and arched one eyebrow at Angie. "Vodka," he said.

"You bet," she said. "From Russia."

Angie winked at John and he smiled.

A ballad came on the jukebox, but John couldn't place the artist. He found the melody mesmerizing. It was one of those old-time acts, maybe from the early 50's.

"Alright, time to get serious," Sanders said, adjusting on his bar stool and shouting over the ballad. "What the he-all you two doing up here so late, ans what made you come up here t'all? *Shit-cago* is a long way from the Yooper. Or should I say FIB-CAGO?"

Ron set his beer on the counter and met Sanders' bloodshot eyes. "I came here for the same reason you did," he said. "To get away to the woods. To enjoy Mother Nature and escape the congestion. That's why I bought land up here. You know this, Bob."

Sanders looked at him, shocked. "But, in the end you have to go back, eh?" he said. "That's no good. You don't never really escape."

"Yes I do," Ron said, looking at John and waggling his finger. "I mean, *we* do."

Sanders looked around the room for a jury to help him convict his peers. But the room had emptied except for Angie.

Sanders shrugged. "Then here's to the U.P.," he said, raising his glass to Ron and John's beers. "Here's to the good times, fook the bad times, eh?"

Their glasses chinked and the music stopped. The sound of the woods at night crept into the tavern. Angie wiped down the bar sink while letting the faucet run.

"It gets *quiet* in the woods," Sanders whispered. "So quiet you can even hear the animals creepin' around. So quiet you can hear your soul shifting around as you walk."

John stared at Sanders, stunned. He had no idea he was capable of such sentiment, and his comments had hit home. Ron had noticed it too. In the deep woods, it was almost as if he could hear his inner workings, that removing noise and chaos revealed other parts of him, better parts of him.

Ron nodded. "I was up at the leaning post the other morning, and watching the valley. I actually saw the wind coming down from the Hurons in my binocs. I could see the big pines on the ridges swaying, pushing the wind my way. When the wind hit me it smelled of hemlock and red pine, sweet and pure, the best air a man has ever held in his lungs, and ever will."

"You aint shittin' eh?" Sanders said, finishing the last of his water. "Angie, I could use another, eh?"

"Sorry Bob, we're closing up," she said, wiping the wooden bar with a damp towel. "Maybe next time."

Sanders grimaced. "Angie, Angie, you can't say I never tried."

Angie rolled her eyes, and John groaned.

"Jesus Sanders you're out of your mind," Ron said.

"An empty glass is a terrible thing to waste," Sanders said.

Angie dimmed the lights at the back of the bar and Huron Bay slowly appeared in the picture window. Moonlight glimmered like a pale highway across the ripples.

The view stirred John's pleasantly buzzed mind. "Angie," he said. "Before we go, you mind if I ask you a question about this place?"

"Shoot," she said, busying herself with a set of dirty glasses.

"Who built it?"

"Long story," she said. "My great grandfather got the logs himself during the lumber craze. Took the timbers from the Hurons. He willed it to my grandfather, who willed it to my mother. She's retired and now I pretty much run the place. It's in my blood, everything about it. You guys ever get that feeling 'bout a place?"

John nodded. "The Black River and the orchard," he said. He looked around the room. "Does it do okay?"

Angie whirled and wiped her hands on her thighs. "You don't need much to live up here, and the place is paid for, so I'm doing alright."

"Nice," John said.

Sanders squirmed on his stool and pointed at the bear. "Hey, hey did you fookers know that bear ain't from around here?"

"They got it from up on Julip," Ron said, hiding his grin with his beer.

John watched Sanders, expecting him to rage.

Sanders' grimace twisted into a half-scream and then back to a grimace. "Ah, I see what you did there. Trying to push ole Sanders' buttons, eh?"

Ron chuckled.

"Well here's something you don't know," Sanders said. "My father knew Angie's father. They fought in WWII together. They knew these woods as good as anyone, even as good as me."

John didn't doubt that for a second. Sanders spent an inordinate amount of time tooling around Upper Julip and the Hurons.

Angie set a pair of glasses upside down on a rack, leaned down to Ron, and whispered in his ear. Ron's eyes widened.

"You mind if you take my truck back to the shack?" he asked John.

John looked at his friend twice, then opened his palm for the keys.

Angie gave a quick reverse hug to Ron and went back to the dishes. Then she dimmed the lights over the center bar.

"See you guys soon," she said. "And Bob, you're sleeping in your truck." She held up his keys and jingled them.

Sanders narrowed his eyes. "How in the he-all you get my keys, eh? I told you fellows she was a damn woods nymph! Trickster! Trying to get me to stay here 'cause she wants me to put a log in the fire."

Angie flashed a smile, her figure ghostlike in the darkened bar. John stood and helped Sanders through the door and into his massive truck.

"I'll see you in another life, eh?" Sanders said from behind the driver's side window. "God bless the Northwoods."

John didn't practice religion, but Sanders' words, drunken or not, couldn't have rung more true. He glanced around at his surroundings, at the moon-frosted trees and rippling water. God bless the Northwoods indeed.

Day 2

Matt woke, his eyelids fluttering, matching the pounding of his heart. His stomach churned when the exposed-bone reality of the previous day flashed in his mind. Back in *Normal Land*, it was the nightmare you woke from, setting it aside like a dirty dish as you rose from bed.

Upon seeing the barricaded eastern window, he was overcome by an immediate urge to run.

Instead he trudged to the southern window, knife in hand. The dead oak seemed to mock him from the edge of the bowl, the sky grey behind it. His truck was as it was before—flipped over and useless. He reached for the door handle, took a deep breath, and unhinged the bolt.

Nothing came to get him.

No noises, no crushing or needle sensations. Just the cold, fresh air and an urgent need to piss. This time though, he didn't bother to check where he was pissing.

The urine was dark.

Dehydration, no doubt. He limped to his truck, his fingers curling into fists. The old beast was flipped on its side like a giant tortoise. With considerable soreness, he tapped a reserve of strength, picked up a log from the firewood pile, and climbed onto the truck. Then he bent over the passenger window, ogling down into the cab like it was the hatch to a submarine. Matt wrapped his flannel around his eyes, the muscles in his forearms flexing and stinging.

"Sorry girl," he said, patting the steel door.

For a moment the log was high above his head, the rough bark scraping his hands. He slammed the log through the window, sending thousands of glass particles everywhere.

Too loud, he thought, scanning the orchard as the glass particles crumbled onto the driver's side door panel. Sure nothing was coming for him, he reached in and opened the glove box. Several maps, a book, and the original Toyota 4x4 manual fell out. His cell phone tried to, but he snapped it up as it slid out.

"Gotcha," he said, proud of himself.

Next he stood on the door, using his heightened vantage point and perhaps the metal chassis to try and amplify a signal. He never liked cell phones and always bought the cheapest ones, the shitty prepaid jobbers at Target or Walgreens. Maybe the cheapness had come back to bite him. He held the phone up, and the tiny LCD screen indicated no reception. Not a surprise. He tried anyway, dialing his mother's number, but there was nothing. Matt flipped the lid closed and then opened it, hoping for a stronger signal bar. He punched in Andrea's number and scanned the orchard for movement. Again, nothing.

Surprisingly, a crackling noise hissed through the phone, and then silence. He dialed 911. Nothing but crackling.

He needed this call but he also needed *something* else, but couldn't quite put his finger on it. He sighed, trying to lift out of the malaise. His mouth felt like cardboard and he had a hard time producing saliva, even when he tried.

Water.

That was what he needed. He looked down into the cab, but the water jug he kept on the passenger floor had spilled when the truck flipped. Then he remembered the water jugs he'd left out on Julip Road before he was first pulled into the orchard. Matt licked his lips and stared down the two track driveway, unsure of how to proceed.

The moose's terrified eyes shuttered in his mind and he turned to the bowl. The grass had been flattened in several places, as if several moose had used the bowl for daybeds, but there were no moose.

Just walk, the little voice said. *Walk until you feel something. Remember the test? Well, that's one corner of the property for you to test. You can test and get your water at the same time! That's a double win for you, Matthew.*

Without hesitating, he maneuvered off the truck and limped down the driveway. He walked five steps and waited.

Nothing.

He walked ten steps, expecting a pressure sensation. Nothing. He looked in every direction, expecting to see grass part or the treetops shake. None of these things happened.

When Matt reached the end of the driveway, he checked north and south along Julip Road before anything else. Maybe he'd spot a car, but that was unlikely since he'd hear one first.

Across the road from him sat the three water jugs, lush droplets beading on the clear plastic.

He licked his lips.

Although he was thirsty as hell, he didn't trust being this far out, not at all. Way too close to where the dead deer was.

Yeah but you got a lot farther than that in the truck, Matthew, the little voice said.

True, he thought. But maybe that was because the truck was a protective covering, like a shell.

The water beckoned and he could smell it in the air. Matt took two steps forward, stopped, and took another. Water beads trickled down the plastic, matching the sweat on his face. He licked his lips again. *Just a few more steps,* he thought. He moved quietly across Julip road, testing each step with nightmare expectations. But none of the strange sensations hit him.

Finally he reached the jugs, twisted off a blue cap, and gulped. The fluid roiled in his stomach and he fought to keep it down. As his stomach settled, he noticed his strength improving. The forest took on greater clarity. The edges and colors of the leaves defined, no longer dull. He'd been dehydrated. Not good. If he was going to get out of this, he needed to do a better job of keeping healthy.

As he gulped more Black, he watched the birches and maples on either side of the road.

He was alone.

Julip road was empty, as it often was. The only real traffic that ever passed through was the occasional logging truck and a few outdoorsmen. But this wasn't tourist season, and the chances of visitors lessened. Since today was Sunday, he doubted any logging trucks would be coming this way. He paused, his thoughts swirling, his belly distended from the water.

The occasional local hunter or fishermen might though, he thought. Sunday may not work for the logging trucks, but it might work for recreationists. His arms and legs tingled and his mind receded from the dark abyss.

The test, Matthew. Don't forget the test, the little voice whispered.

Oh, he hadn't.

No longer dehydrated, he examined the woods for solutions. As long as the creature wasn't hurting him, the confidence might remain.

He had two choices to begin this test. The first was to approach the Black River. He *had* to know if he could access water. The other choice was to head south on Julip road, towards the Hurons.

Water, the little voice said.

But he needed to walk faster. None of this tiptoe bullshit. It'd take hours to do the test at the rate he'd moved across the road.

After a deep breath Matt set out through the Goldie's fern and sedges that led to the Black. Each step made him grimace and perspire. Thick vegetation slapped against his bloodstained jeans. For the first time since being trapped, a bird chirped in the forest, a black-capped chickadee fluttered in the branches of a yellow birch.

Finally, he thought. The orchard and surrounding woods had always been full of birds.

After another deep breath and expectant silence, Matt dodged several of the pit springs and reached the Black. Then he angled down the slope, acting as if he were going to fill a water jug.

No unusual sensations overcame him.

Across the Black, wind blew the tops of the maples and balsam firs, the branches chaffing against each other like dried bones. He gripped an exposed root as support and eased into the cool water. As he stepped through the stream, several bullet shapes darted from the bank and disappeared downstream. Brook trout. He thought of his father casting for brookies in this very bend and frowned. Those were simpler times.

Certain he wasn't going to fall, he trudged in-between two boulders, water curling past his waist. The alder and lady ferns on the other side of the Black hinted at freedom.

Behind him, the ground shook as if rhinoceros had neared.

Matt twisted his torso in midstream, trying to locate the source.

Thud Thud

Half-circles emanated from water's edge as bits of dirt crumbled down the bank. For a brief, discombobulating moment, the streambed undulated beneath his feet. He knew it wasn't an earthquake. The vibrations were spaced apart, as if something was walking. Rough, elephantine breathing came from behind him on the Julip Road side of the bank. Something whipped and slashed the air high above.

Before he could make his next move, Matt'schest tightened as needles poked and prodded his skin. The air around his body distorted and bent. Slowly he began to choke, spittle peppering from his lips.

There was only one thing he could do. He calmly turned west and pushed back across the stream. Each step west eased the uncomfortable sensations, and the symptoms tapered off. Scared but encouraged, he climbed the steep bank with the assistance of a balsam root, pulling himself up like a wet rat. Then he collapsed to the bank precipice.

The ground vibrations decreased in intensity, but increased in pace. The Goldie's fern and rich sedges flattened in certain patches, and dust clouded Julip Road. Then, nothing but the birds in the canopy.

First question of the test has been answered, the little voice said. *Quite well indeed! Maybe instead of the student being intimidated, the student can do something to intimidate the test? Maybe there's a weakness, Matthew.*

There had to be something. Everything had a weakness. The difficult part was finding the weakness before dying. Yeah, that was the real trick.

Matt knew the thing was watching him, could feel its gaze upon him at all times. And he knew its breathing and ground-pounding gave it away. *Another note in the file*, he thought. It wasn't much, but he was starting to collect information. And in this situation, any knowledge gained was precious.

He fought a powerful urge to yell at the creature, to let it know he knew it was watching him.

Oh don't do that, the anxiety voice said. *The point is to collect information, not give it away. Perhaps it's best not to irritate?*

Keep every little thing you have to yourself. Surprises are tactical advantages, and you are at war for your life, Matthew.

He trudged back to the road, sickened at being handled by It.

You better get used to it, the voice said. *Unless of course you don't want more information, instead preferring to die like a confused, bleating sheep*

Matt hoisted the water jugs up the driveway, eyes darting across the orchard and tree line. His tipped truck looked like a mechanical bison, struck with tree branch arrows. He and his father had worked hard on the truck over the years, adding the bed cap, touching up the rough spots, and performing other repairs. His fingers clenched the plastic jug handles, deforming them.

Revenge without a plan isn't revenge, it's stupidity, the little voice said.

He wondered if the truck could run. He set the water inside the shack and grabbed the musty rope from the cardboard box under the bunk bed. With rope in hand he walked over to his disabled steed. Once on top, he opened the passenger door and tied the rope around the window frame. Then he tossed the rope end over the side of the truck and climbed down. Matt wrapped the end of the rope around the front axle and pulled it tight, raising the passenger door in the process. He tied a knot and stepped back

It was enough to hold.

The last thing he needed was to be trapped in the truck *and* by the creature.

In this game, always leave an exit, Matthew, the voice said. *Always.*

The exertion sent aches and pins through his body, so this time he was more careful climbing the truck. When he looked down into the cab, the keys glinted near the steering column. He lowered his sore body, using the shift stick as a halfway step. Then he placed his left leg so he was standing on the ground through the driver's side window. Glass particles crunched under his feet, reminding him of Rice Crispies. With both feet set where the driver's side window would be, he bent down. There was no need for him to be seated in the truck to start it. Although a manual transmission, his truck had come equipped with a clutch-start-cancel switch, a feature that started the truck without depressing the clutch pedal. This was ideal for situations when the driver was stuck on a hill. Pushing the clutch down meant vehicle rollback—the last thing you wanted on steep and slick terrain.

Matt reached for the switch with a shaky finger and pressed it. With his other hand he turned the key, the bronze Glacier National Park keychain tinkling against the steering column.

The test lights came up on the center console, indicating no engine damage. Matt let out a long exhale. The clutch-start-cancel switch lit up, too. After a deep breath, he turned the key. The old Toyota sputtered and shook..

"Come on," he said, his vision shimmery wit unshed tears. "You can do it!"

The venerable 22RE engine clamored to life, letting loose a discordant chorus of whines, rumbles, and pops.

Matt's limbs tingled and he couldn't help but grin. His old friend was back.

Just when he'd found the courage to smile, a shadow oozed across the dashboard. The passenger door slammed shut, shattering the side mirror. Glass tumbled towards him like silver, stinging insects. He turned away and cried out as the truck shook. Needle sensations lit his nerves afire, and it became difficult to breathe.

Turn it off dumbass! the little voice said.

Matt reached blindly for the key, touched the smooth metal, and switched it back. The engine stopped, and with it the physical symptoms.

Matt huddled there in his own truck cab, a frightened, trapped animal, each breath matching his pounding heart and the fading stomps of the creature.

He clenched his fists and grimaced. Then he waited. And waited. Occasionally a bird darted past the passenger side window.

"I'm so sorry to see you like this," he whispered to the truck. But most of all he was sorry to be trapped in a place that had always been home. He'd never really been betrayed before. It tasted sour, like a lemon, or a piece of bread that hadn't been checked for mold.

You can't blame the property or the Northwoods, Matthew, the little voice said. *You can only blame the Puller. Don't be overcome with sorrow. This is not an advantage. This is not how to win.*

When his wits returned, he stood, bumping his head against the passenger door. He pushed it open and peered out like a tank operator in enemy territory. Then he used the shifter as a step and exited the truck.

The drop from the truck was never fun, and this time was no different. After the aches subsided, he scanned the grass for tracks. There had to be something, somewhere. Within a flattened patch of orchard grass lay a print the size of a garbage can lid. Five trenches cut into the soil from the print's widest pad.

Without thinking he limped into the shack and retrieved his headlamp. Then he pinched off some orchard grass and sprinkled it into the mini-trenches. The beam from his lamp reflected off the pinched grass at the bottom. *Three feet, maybe,* he thought.

Evidence, he said to the orchard in a faux British accent, tossing his arm is if a lawyer making his final point.

Ten feet from the first track lay another print, near the shack door. Another ten feet west and another track. He followed the tracks out to the leaning post where they leapt the fire pit. A swath of flattened orchard grass led south down to the wall of chokecherry and alder.

Matt picked up the axe from the wheelbarrow, admiring the heft as he rotated the blade. Then he followed the tracks down to the vegetation wall and reached out to the chokecherry branches.

Tests can really, really suck, he thought.

Of course, without warning, needle sensations prickled his body. And next he gulped like a guppy flung from its tank.

Brilliant. Walked right into him, he thought, as precious oxygen dwindled from his brain. But wasn't he supposed to test? Didn't he have to know?

Somehow he struggled four steps backwards and the sensations faded. In-between his raspy breaths, he heard breathing that was not his own. A few leaves from a nearby stunted birch shook, but there was no wind.

He turned slowly, gripping the axe in his right hand, knuckles whitening. The air whooshed above him in methodic chops, but no clue was given as to the cause. *Funny,* he thought. *No, that's not funny. This is funny.* Midway into a casual step, he lunged towards the breathing noise, swinging the axe, his face clenched like a wolverine.

The axe found its spot, sinking into a fleshy substance and making a sick tearing noise across the orchard. Then it chinked something hard, maybe bone. Hell yeah.

Above him, the Puller blasted hot stank breath all over him, then roared, much like the train sound on the night of the northern lights.

Matt squinted up to the sky, held his arms out, and let out a maniacal laugh. "I got a piece of—"

A safe dropped on his head. At least that's what he thought it felt like. Then there was nothing except blackness.

***

In his dreams a naked female stepped into the orchard from the vegetation, her slender, pale legs contrasting with the organic hues of grass and trees. Unable to move he stood and watched, a faint whimper escaping his lips. She was beautiful, with long, blonde hair and full lips. She gazed at him, her black pupils at first frightening. But soon his fright morphed into lust. Music chimed in his head—music from a far off time, not of this place. It sounded like a reverbed flute. Goosebumps peppered his limbs and a pleasing shock spidered up his back and burst gently in his mind. He took a deep breath and noticed his pulse in his neck.

The woman held out a finger to him, her bosom heaving. All at once he realized it was Stacey, or a very close approximation. In dreams, mannerisms and physical attributes never quite duplicated real life people.

"Come," she said. "I am your friend, am I not Matthew?" She smiled at him, her lips slightly parted and ticking up at the sides.

What about my plans? he thought. What plans? All he wanted to do was screw the hell out of Stacey. This was his sole purpose in life. He didn't want to think about the funeral or all that other negative bullshit. He wanted to run to her and fuck her while pulling her hair amongst the bracken fern and leafy ground, elbows and knees and skin stained with dirt and debris as they rolled. Not only did he want to fuck her, he wanted Stacey to have his kids.

He wanted to lay with her in the orchard at night and watch the stars, naked, only gathering their warmth from each other.

At last he was able to stumble towards her, his hands and legs trembling.

"Aw, you're adorable," Stacey said, smirking. "I want you to follow me. If you follow me you can have me, Matthew." She turned her back to him, but not before throwing a sidelong glance and smile, her blonde hair stopping shy of the small of her back. Matt felt like a bear approaching its mate, waiting for the moment to get close enough so he could leap, pin her down, and bite at her neck. God, how awful was that? Was this how he treated women? No. Far from it. He'd always been a gentlemen, and cared as much about a woman's dreams, goals, and emotional needs as much as the physical. But the woods, *these* woods had a hell of a way of cutting out the bullshit and getting right down to the evolutionary grit. Procreation. Reproduction. Fucking. After all, it might be a hard winter. You might not survive. And you better sow your fucking seed before mother nature punches your card, son.

The flute music filtered through his mind, soothing and ancient. He stepped into the woods, but Stacey seemed to float over the understory ahead of him. Her hair brushed against her milky skin, the curves of her breasts protruding an inch from the profile of her back.

"I like these woods," she said in a sultry, musical tone. "They feel like home. I know they feel like home to you, too. I liked coming up here with you so much."

The pressure in his jeans was unbearable. A thin line of drool dangled from the corner of his mouth. Embarrassing, but whatever. It was a dream. He was allowed to be a fool in his dreams.

Stacey laughed, sensing his desire, but still ghosting deeper into the woods. "I can feel you. You want me so bad. Well, I want *you* so bad. You can have me in a little bit. But before you do, I want you to see something. Follow and I'll be your reward."

The lemony fragrance of sweet flag filled his nose as he trudged deeper into the forest. He felt at home here, in this magical patch of forest thick with verdant maples and the love of his life. It's what he always wanted. What warm-blooded male wouldn't want elbow room and the most amazing women he'd ever seen? When you had that, who'd give a damn about anything else.

He fixated ahead, eyes glassy and wide. Yearning and peace soothed his nerves. The paralyzing anxiety of being trapped by the Puller flitted away. He was Matt Kearns again, worry-free and full of vigor.

The intoxicating Stacey continued ahead, never looking back. Her blonde hair swayed as she walked. Her buttocks revealed a single wrinkle where they met her legs.

Spruce trees joined the maples along with a few balsam fir. The air grew rich with humidity and warm light sworded into the canopy. Frogs croaked to the west, their song coming through in waves, breaking through the comforting haze that settled around him.

Stacey stopped and turned. He melted as her eyes met his. It had been so long, and she was so beautiful.

"Come here," she said, beckoning with a long finger tipped with black nail polish. Matt limped to her, stiffening with excitement, his breath short and heavy. She held out her elegant left hand and he took it. A big, black golden buzz tingled his nerves.

"Look to the west," Stacey said, pointing with her right hand. Her grip tightened, but it was like steel wires rather than the soft cushion of a female hand. He didn't care. He tried to look west but stood there instead, gawking at her face. Her high cheek bones, full lips, and petite nose triggered a surge of lust. This was the Stacey he wanted to remember, not the bone-white Stacey in the coffin. He'd take anything over that, even this adolescent wet-dream.

She turned, her eyes meeting his. Matt dove into the black pupils, swimming in them like a shark behind a fishing boat that just poured the day's bait overboard. Dark waters slashed and churned, but he sensed no danger. He slashed at the squid-like creatures swimming up towards him, swallowing them whole. When the waves splashed into his face, he thought he'd drown, but he never did. Breathing in the warm, black sea made him grow. Soon his feet were upon the ocean floor, the sea below him like a bull moose in the bog.

"Soon you can touch me all you desire. But for now, I need you to look west." Stacey cupped his chin with her fingers and turned his head. "See? Matthew? See?"

Mist billowed from the bog, carpeting the forest floor in milky white. His feet disappeared in the haze. Goldie's fern and Blue cohosh rose out of the mist. One fern resembled a lady holding a basket, her back hunched and a scarf on her head. A big Blue cohosh mimicked a man holding a lantern, trying to find his way home.

Sweeping melancholy socked Matt in the gut and he frowned.

Stacey raised her arm into the air and the fog dissipated, slowly.

***

Matt woke to pink clouds overhead and crushing pain in his temples.

Freaking sunset, he thought, squinting at the sky. The dream now spider web wind strands, fading, fading, fading....

A lone bird raced awkwardly across the sky, maybe a loon from Albert's Lake. The bird's neck craned forward, its wings hyper-flapping. He watched, wishing he could leave like the loon. Within ten seconds the loon was out of sight, heading east over the Black.

He rose to his feet, right hand rubbing his temple.

Oh, but it was worth it, wasn't it Matthew? the little voice said. *Because guess what? You got a piece of the Puller.*

He didn't know what he'd hit with the axe, but he did know the axe hurt *something*. After a brief search he found the axe, plum-colored slime smearing the blade and drizzling down the handle. His right hand was also streaked with the substance.

He grinned.

"Gotcha," he said to the Yooper.

Drops of blood flecked the orchard grass and formed a faint trail. He strained his eyes in the fading light, trying not to lose the trail. And damn if he couldn't smell the stuff. The stench reminded him of the garbage disposal in the house when he forgot to flip the switch after a few days.

The blood trail led uphill, past the leaning post.

What he saw next frosted his heart.

The blood trail led *towards* the shack.

With the awareness of a gazelle at a watering hole, he slunk forward. This might be an ambush. A real bad freaking ambush.

Haven't they all been ambushes? the little voice asked.

Not helpful, Matt said.

I do what I can, the little voice said. *If you don't want me here, I'll leave.*

Don't go.

A moment later Matt reached the shack. So did the blood track. He tried to calm himself, then held his breath and listened.

A drop of blood splattered onto one of the slate walkway rocks his father had placed years ago. The air around him warmed like a sauna, and elephantine breathing huffed from his right.

It's next to you, Matthew, the little voice said.

Tell me something I don't know, he thought, preparing to look up at the aspen to see if he could catch an irregularity in the thing's camouflage.

Don't look up, fool! Remember surprise tactics? Besides, if the Puller knows you can see it, it might get mad enough to finish you off once and for all. Play its game. Don't reveal your hand too early.

Matt kept his head low and turned away, feigning interest towards the dead oak. Any acting class would've burst out laughing, but maybe it was enough for the Puller.

Shaking, but doing his best to straighten his hand, Matt unbuckled his belt, unzipped his pants, and pissed. As the rope of urine mixed with a drop of the creature's blood, he laughed.

Why are you laughing? the voice asked.

"Because I have more information and that makes me happy."

The Puller, Matthew. It's the Puller.

"Pull this, bitch," he said, shaking the last drop out.

That sort of behavior will get you nowhere, the voice said.

"I am nowhere," he said. "I'm in Nowhere Land making all my nowhere plans for nobody. So excuse me if manners aren't a priority, okay?"

Matt limped over to his truck and inspected the underside for leaks. As he did, the ground thudded behind him, and the familiar whipping sound returned.

Was it moving towards him? He didn't think so. Perhaps it had other games to play, elsewhere. Maybe it needed to eat.

He wondered why it had not yet eaten him.

Oh but the Puller ate the moose, didn't it Matthew? the voice said. *I think he likes you as a play thing. I fear that the taste of your flesh won't get you killed, but rather boredom. Don't let the Puller become bored.*

Matt kicked at the grass with his boot toe. That was it, wasn't it? Keep the creature occupied. It could be doing something else, off in another land, another planet, who knows the hell where. For all he knew it had no reason to keep him other than for a toy, or a game. What he needed was keep things interesting in a way that didn't get him injured or killed. A court jester, flipping balls around and *nyuck-nyucking,* doing cartwheels with a big shit-eating grin.

He thought of a line from his favorite movie, *Cool Hand Luke*: *Just shakin' the bush, boss, just shakin' the bush.* He pictured Paul Newman, skipping down the road, faux-happy and hoisting the dead turtle, looking up at Snake Eyes, eager for acceptance. He needed to put on the acting job of his life, to be ole' Luke. He also needed something else. For the first time since being trapped he was kind of hungry. No, "kind of" was an undersell. He was starving.

He hurried into the shack, the fading light ushering him into the dark room like a flashlight chasing a mouse into its hole. Then he hunched over the camp stove and cooked up some good shack grub, like he used to do with his father. This time it was a can of corned beef hash. After removing the lid with the can opener, he flung it across the room like a frisbee. The metal lid stuck into a log with a pleasant *thonk.*

Almost like a ninja star, he thought. Might be something he could use.

Oh yes, Matthew. Oh yes indeed, the little voice said.

"Enter the Ninja," he said, laughing. It was good to laugh again, trapped or not. Ron was right. Screw that thing out there. He wouldn't let it have *all* of him.

Soon darkness saturated the land and nighthawks arced the sky. The last few frogs sung from an unseen pool to the west. The lantern shone at half-power, enough to see details in the corners of the shack.

Tomorrow there'd be more tests at the northern and western boundaries. He already had a good idea of the eastern and southern boundaries. These represented a rough line following the Black River, then cutting across Julip road and forming the border between the southern valley wall of vegetation and the orchard. The rest he'd find out in due time, but the sooner the better.

Sitting on the lower bunk, he fished through his jeans pocket and pulled out his cell phone. He powered it on and it beeped with a low battery warning. There was no way to charge it in the shack. He'd have to venture out to the truck, start it, and charge the phone with the cigarette lighter. The phone felt no more useful in his hand than a rock or clump of dirt. If he started the truck it would irritate the Being like it did before. *No good, senorita. No mas.*

He shuffled his feet on the wooden floor, looking down at them. Every girlfriend he'd ever had going back to the 6th grade made fun of his feet. The second toe, longer than the big toe as well as misshapen, really threw the whole thing off. Obviously this was not a hurdle to companionship as they were his girlfriends at the time. All in all just some good-natured teasing. But it stuck the way some things do.

They are ugly feet, he thought. *Really damn ugly.*

He thought of the tracks left by the Being, the smashed orchard grass, and the deep holes.

I wonder who has uglier feet, he thought.

Before going to bed (*rest rest rest* or LOSE) he needed to try one more thing. He threw on his clothes and headlamp, then grabbed the cell phone and headed out to the truck. The headlamp illuminated sections of the truck like an exploratory submarine on a wreck. He climbed it, grasped the metal radio antenna, and powered on the cell phone.

One bar.

His heart went into his throat. Matt dialed 911 and slammed the phone to his ear.

"Ironville police."

He paused, not sure the voice was real.

"Ironville police. Please state your emergency."

"Oh my God. I-I'm trapped up on Julip road please—"

The voice dropped out and the connection died. He tried again, gripping the truck antenna for better reception. The phone indicated no bars and beeped twice. He changed position and grasped the antenna at a higher point.

Nothing.

He moved his hand up and down the antenna. No bars.

Anxiety chamfered his spine, shredding any pride or humor he'd managed earlier. He'd fought back today, and all there was to show for it was a sore noggin and a few meaningless cuts on the Being.

Maybe they heard you, the little voice said. *Maybe they're coming.*

"Maybe," he said.

He let go of the antenna, his palm sweaty and stiff. The warm sleeping bag and mattress beckoned his wracked body. If he didn't rest and heal, he had no chance. None.

Maybe I'll die in my sleep and the mice will get me, he thought. *It'd be a feast.*

He swung down the hefty interior bolt on the door, locking the Yooper behind him.

How many mice died in the bucket before you came here, Matthew? the voice asked.

He'd never checked the bucket this trip, which was strange. He leaned in-between the hutch and the triple bunk bed and peered into the bucket. Two dead mice lay stuck in the green slop at the bottom. Their fur was matted, their bodies bloating. He figured they'd stink, but that wasn't the case. Behind the bucket against the wall was a half-full jug of anti-freeze.

See that? the little voice asked. *All animals can be poisoned, Matthew. Could the Puller be poisoned too? Not too many things like anti-freeze. Not too many things at all.*

He crawled into the sleeping bag, brimming with ideas but tempered by exhaustion (*rest rest rest* or LOSE).

"Got a piece of the Being today," he muttered. "And maybe all tomorrow."

Bad Moon Rising

This thing we call a wolverine, is not a pleasant thing. The fanged beast has stolen our kills on numerous occasions, ripping down deer from our gutting ropes. One month on it still trails us, back there in the snow and mists. Although many of the men are angry, we can't help but admire its tenaciousness. The beast's energy is unmatched. Clearly, the woods belong to it, and not us. We are our destination. But this wolverine, it is the places in-between.

-Jon P. Riggins, Oregon Trail, 1830

"Hey Anneli, a cold PBR, eh?" Bob Sanders said, raising one scarred finger above the bar.

Anneli reached under the bar (and Sanders took a peek down her blouse, eh?) and popped back up with a frosted mug and a cold can of Pabst Blue Ribbon.

Sanders eyed her as she poured the cool beverage into the mug. He'd always had a thing for her he supposed. She was cut from the same Norwegian cloth that many Yoopers were—in her thirties, cropped blonde hair, meat on her bones, pretty without makeup. She was a smart one too, and Sanders figured she knew what he was thinking at all times. Some women had a way of doing that, and it creeped him out, the way they caught him staring and doubled the stare right back through his soul. They read him like witches. All of 'em. He wished he had that kind of ability. Sure, he had a sense for the animals at his place up on the Silver grade, even smelling 'em and predicting their movement in thick brush. But back in L'ander, and here in the Bayside Tavern, his senses dulled.

"Yer eyes look mighty nice today, eh?" Sanders said, working his scarred thumb on the frosty mug rim.

Anneli rolled her eyes and waved a white dishrag at him. "Knock it off," she said. "There's a ring on your finger for a reason."

Sanders held his hand in front of his face and flipped his palm a few times. "This? Ah, nothing but a friendship ring. Funny thing, eh?"

"Yeah real funny. Have you told your wife that joke?"

Sanders frowned at his beer and took a chug, the frosted handle chilling his fingers. Like dippin' his hand in the mighty Silver River.

The place was a dump. The dark-stained wood paneling and knotty pine bar showed their age, and almost no light entered save for a couple tiny windows near the door. The place smelled like mold and stale tobacco, too. The mirror behind the bar looked like it was stolen from someone's apartment bathroom, and four cracks marred the glass at various points. The sole bright spot was a polished jukebox that had everything from Credence to Hank Williams. The owners, who'd been in trouble a few times with local ordinances, claimed Bayside Tavern had a capacity of seventy people, a God damned lie. Still, he came because of Anneli and the occasional other pretty-Yooper-somethings that made the mistake of wandering in. A lion's got to go to the watering hole to find the gazelle's, eh?

What he didn't come her for were the meatheads, and L'ander had its fair share. Some might toss him in the category of *meathead*, but he had certain refined tastes and sensibilities not always apparent from his appearance.

Sanders slipped off his Miller Genuine Draft wool hat and wiped his brow. He kicked his boots on the bottom of his stool, freeing them of clinging snow. Then he unzipped his jacket , relishing the release of warm air.

Sanders drank and looked around the joint. Jan Erickson sat at the back of the bar and gave him a lazy wave. Sanders nodded and tipped his mug. He checked for more familiar faces. Patty Zorich sat with her husband Tom in one of the booths, both of them poking at their shit fries and shit burgers. As Sanders finished his look-see, he frowned. The last face he saw was that of Hoss Ratigan.

Not what he was expecting to see.

Ratigan locked eyes with Sanders as a creeping smile appeared, his eyes electric, all-knowing.

"Shit," Sanders mumbled into his beer, inching his shoulders together and turning away.

A couple weeks back at Finn's Market, he'd made a pass at Ratigan's twenty year old daughter. A real looker, the kind that could make a white-tailed buck stop and stare, cause all animals respect beauty. She'd recoiled and replied with a snotty *eeeeew*. Unfortunately that wasn't the only thing Ratigan might be pissed about. Ratigan owned several thousand acres along the lower portion of Silver Road, and he'd caught Sanders trespassing numerous times. The last time Sanders had seen Ratigan's gigantic ugly mug was in the tiny rearview mirror on his four wheeler. How could he forget Ratigan's bloated, red face shouting at him?

Sanders grumbled.

He didn't like having to leave his traps behind, and he was sure Ratigan had found them and taken them.

Sanders swung his stool so he was facing the bar. He didn't need to face Ratigan. That's what bar mirrors were for. Plus, he doubted Ratigan would pick up on that before it was too late. Sanders sipped his beer, no more panicked than a doe feeding with her fawn in their safe glade.

As anticipated, Ratigan's size 16 snowmobile boots thudded across the decaying tile floor, and soon his hulking frame appeared in the bar mirror. Describing Ratigan as a big guy was an understatement. He was six foot seven inches and at least three hundred pounds—most of it muscle. He was the prototype U.P. logger, a big axe man who owned even bigger acres.

Sanders frowned as Ratigan's beer and pretzel breath wafted towards him.

"What the hell do you think you're doing?" Ratigan asked, his brows furrowed deep as splotches of red bloomed across his face.

Dear lord he took up the whole damn mirror.

Sanders didn't answer. Instead he reached for a bowl of stale pretzels, the corner of his eye watching the giant in the cracked bar mirror.

"I SAID what the hell you doin?" Ratigan's voice was louder this time, far deeper and more powerful than a typical male voice.

Sanders shrugged. "Just havin' a beer, eh?"

Still facing the mirror, his grip tightened on the thawing beer mug. It wasn't so cold as the Silver no more.

The giant leered at him in the cracked mirror, like a funhouse spook. "Funny thing is, my girl tells me a pervert hit on her at Finn's Market. You wouldn't happen to know who that was, do you Bob?"

The patrons quieted. Anneli disappeared into the back room.

Ratigan shifted his feet. "So I asks her what the pervert looked like. She told me he was real ugly. Ugliest motherfucker she'd ever seen. Said she'd seen better looking catfish. So I says, 'did he smell?', and my girl says he was the foulest smelling son of a bitch you could ever imagine, smelled so bad it made you want to lop your nose off just to get rid of the stank. Finally, I ask my girl if this pervert was dumb. She tells me he was the dumbest, stupidest jaw-flapper she'd come across, dumber than a rock, dumber than a bowling ball, and that the pervert would be better off if his brains were made of whip cream."

Sanders fingered a pretzel, the salt nubs rough on his skin.

Ratigan bellowed in the mirror. "Now who could this *perv* be? I wonder, Bob. Maybe you could help me find him? It shouldn't be hard, what with the smell and all. And hey, I think I smell him now...."

Ratigan sniffed the air like a bear and slammed his colossal left hand on Sanders' shoulder. In the mirror, Sanders saw Ratigan's other hand coming at him in a fist.

Sanders swung around in an instant, connecting the glass beer mug to Ratigan's massive jaw. The glass shattered, gouging out a chunk of Ratigan's skin. Ratigan teetered backwards, eyes fluttering. He banged into a worn table, knocking the spindles out from the chairs and sending plastic ashtrays and cigarette butts flying.

Sanders grabbed a pretzel from the bar and chewed. The he strutted over to Ratigan and bent down. Ratigan's eyes were glassy, and blood trickled from the fresh wound. Ratigan tried to speak, but what came out made no sense. He lay there, sprawled out amongst the spindles like a fallen giant. He may have even caved in part of the decaying floor, too. Big fella.

Sanders waited until Ratigan made eye contact with him, then spoke. "These are my woods, Hoss. Always have been. When you come after me out there on the Silver grade, you chase the spirit of the woods. When you refuse me entrance to your land, you chase away the woods. One in the same, eh?"

Sanders stood and regarded the speechless patrons. Then he nodded and turned to the door. When he opened it, snow gusted into the building. Once outside in the low visibility, he slammed the door shut, flipping off the wind and snow like a switch behind him.

His modified snowmobile roared into the U.P. storm, his handlebar moustache turning to ice.

Day 3

Matt woke to rocks pinging the metal undercarriage of a vehicle. He bolted up, hit his head on the middle bunk, and ran outside in his boxers and t-shirt. The grey morning greeted him as he raced down the driveway, quads pumping. Screw the soreness.

"Hey!" he shouted. "Hey!"

When he reached Julip Road, he spotted an Ironville Police car coming from the north. The headlight was broken and the passenger front panel misshapen. Behind the windshield sat an officer with a crew cut and broad shoulders. The officer carried the aesthetic of the many Swedish immigrants in the area.

Matt's eyes shimmered and he waved his arms wildly. This was it, at last!

The officer scanned both sides of the road as the tires crunched gravel.

"Over here!" Matt shouted.

The officer signaled to Matt with two fingers to his brow. As the patrol car slowed, a yellow birch on the shack side of Julip Road snapped in half with a moist crack like a splintering turkey bone. The earth shook under Matt's feet as clouds of dust swirled above the road, suffusing with a vague distortion in the air.

The officer's casual here-we-go-again demeanor wiped right off his face.

We know what that is, don't we Matthew? the little voice said. *The trouble is that Officer Clueless has no idea.*

"Turn around!" Matt yelled. "Go!" He gestured violently to the north , then back like an over caffeinated runway marshall.

The officer scowled.

Shit.

***

Officer Bertil hadn't been up Julip way in quite some time. He tapped his fingers on the steering wheel and scanned the sedges and lady fern on either side of the road. The last time he was up here his wife Pam had accompanied him at Upper Black Falls. They'd had lunch on a slate slab framed by golden aspens. The upper Black had sluiced through slate grooves, and they'd watched brook trout darting across the dark stream bed. That tranquil spot was where they'd conceived Bobby, their first born. The memory made the woodland morning all the more beautiful.

Officer Bertil put the frisbee-sized cinnamon roll down on the passenger seat and held his distended belly. He'd gotten the roll from the Mountain Top restaurant back in Ironville. The place was a tourist attraction just for their damn rolls. Well, that and Mindy Jacobs, the young blonde waitress. She was the real attraction for many of the male residents. He imagined many of them only accompanied their wives to Sunday breakfast at the Mountain Top because of Mindy. Hell, Mindy might be responsible for bringing families back together across the U.P. with her taught ass and perky breasts. And a man could wrap both hands around her waist and touch fingers. At least that's how he imagined it.

The coursing sugar and images of Mindy were too much.

You selfish son of a bitch, he thought. *You're fantasizing about a girl half your age after thinking about the conception of your child and your sweet wife? Shame on you, pal. Shame on you.*

Swallowing a gob of guilt along with cinnamon and sugar, Officer Bertil turned right onto Julip Road. Soon the cruiser wound up the washboard incline, into the highlands and away from Lake Superior. The forest, shadow by shadow, swallowed the squad car in its dark maw.

The reason for the boonies patrol was a supposed call from a lost hiker. Headquarters had received the call last evening, but couldn't ascertain the precise location. The department sent out squad cars to parts of the county where the roads had a "J" in the name. Julip Road was on the list.

Bertil reached for his radio and burped.

"Charlie 102 to C-Com."

"Go ahead, Charlie 102."

"No sign of our 33 on lower Julip, over."

The radio hissed static as the car headed deeper into the U.P. jungle. Bertil hung the handset and scanned the dense vegetation and expanding shadows. He liked this area, liked the Hurons and the Black River. But damn if something wasn't keeping him on edge. He'd run an awful lot of 33's up here, but this one had a vagueness to it he couldn't crystalize. *Gah,* he thought. He pictured his wife smiling next to the Black River and his mind eased.

Bertil watched the woods on either side of the road in easy, timed intervals. But make no mistake, he had the eyes of an eagle, always looking for the tiniest movement.

As he drove on, slow and methodical, a trickle of irritation pooled in his gut. Tourist hikers didn't know their ass from a hole in the ground. He had nothing against the tourists, especially the pretty girls during the summers. But he held disdain for their numerous and ridiculous questions. A few of the pretty girls seemed to like his uniform too, their eyes sometimes lighting up as he walked over to them, his leather belt and holster creaking. He'd always rest his hand on his firearm, going for that extra dash of power and their eyes would flare even more. He wasn't a rock star, but in a way the gun trick was his guitar solo. Officer Bertil smiled and licked the sugar and cinnamon from the roof of his mouth.

Two deer on the western side of the road poked their heads above the browse, flicked their tails, and bounded away into maple and birch.

Fifty yards up the road a figure disappeared into the ferns. Bertil tapped the gas pedal and scooted the squad car ahead. As he peered into the brush the backside of a slender man revealed itself. The man carried a set of traps over his shoulder, the trap receptacles clanking together as if a deadly wind chime. An orange hunting cap covered his head, and he trotted away from the patrol car. Bertil lowered the passenger window and leaned over.

"Hello Skeet," he said.

The man with the orange hunting cap continued walking, the traps rattling louder.

"Don't make me get out of this fooking car," Bertil said, his voice rising. He knew Skeet from The Thirsty Boar, a local watering hole. Bertil had always considered the Thirsty Boar the Earth equivalent of the Star Wars Cantina.

Skeet whirled around with the submissiveness of the most obedient dog, greasy hair sticking out from his orange cap. His eyes narrowed.

"Come on over," Bertil said with a wave of his hand.

Skeet walked slowly to the squad car, but avoided putting his boots on the road.

"Whatcha up to?" Bertil asked, eyeing the trees behind Skeet as if his answer was preordained pointlessness.

Skeet looked at the ground and back into the woods. "Just collecting my traps," he said, running a finger along his hawkish nose.

"Possible call on a lost hiker. Seen anything?"

Skeet hawked a gob of black chew on a fern. "Saw a bear come up the ridge back here. A few grouse."

Bertil sighed. "No, not animals, Skeet. A person."

"Well, peoples are animals too."

The traps rattled in Skeet's trembling hands. Bertil couldn't tell if he was experiencing alcohol withdrawal or something else. Bertil looked down Julip Road and rubbed his temples with his thumb and forefinger. "Have you seen a *person* up here the last few days, Skeet?"

Skeet gazed into the understory and to the canopy. Then he removed his orange cap and wiped sweat from his brow. "Now that you say, I did see a man over at Blackie Falls a couple days back. He was fishin' the pool."

"Description?"

"Tall, jeans, checkered blue flannel. Brown hair. Strong as a buck. Oh, and I saw his truck too. Black Toyota with FIB plates."

"A FIB, eh?"

"Yup," Skeet said. "Probably had no tags for the fishin'. I says to him the warden would pinch him."

Bertil nodded and tapped his fingers on the door panel of his patrol car. "Anything else?"

"Notta. But if yer interested I have a bobcat hide back at shop. $75 a pelt. Could make a nice hat for the wifey."

"No thanks, Skeet. Maybe later."

Bertil raised the window and waved goodbye to Skeet with the sincerity of a beauty queen on a float.

Skeet watched the patrol car wind up the road, gravel popping like heated corn kernels underneath the chassis. Then he disappeared into a patch of bracken fern, two gray jays crying out above him.

Bertil crept his way south at five miles per hour, scanning the woods, each hundred yards deepening the sense of futility. And that was even *if* this was the distress call location. Most likely he was wasting his time. Almost all of these lost tourist cases ended up with the folks hiking out of one of the many logging roads. There were a few places where one could get lost for days. The Hurons was one of them.

Fookin eh, he thought, wiping sugar and frosting glaze from his lower lip. *There isn't anything up here.* It was settled. He'd go as far as that picnic spot with Pam, and that was it.

Bertil reached for the cup holder, drank his lukewarm coffee, and burped. He thought of Jennifer, his young daughter. *Ewww. Don't burp daddy, it's so gross!* He was often the target of etiquette corrections from the two ladies in his life. Sometimes they ganged up on him, but he liked the attention. Better to be a fat slob with people you love than a lonely fat slob.

As he rolled on, canopy shadows crept over the hood like sky witches.

Bertil gazed into a clump of ferns and saw a butterfly fluttering in a sunlight sword. *Jennifer would like that,* he thought. She was always asking him if he saw any animals on his patrols. He always had some lame answer, that he had seen such animals, but that he didn't have time for the shot. The truth was he'd been too lazy to get his ass out of the seat. Not anymore. He stopped the car, lowered his window, and reached into a small backpack on the front seat. Digital camera in hand, he braced his elbows on the window frame. Bertil peered through the viewfinder, trying to locate the butterfly. The shutter clicked. He removed his eye from the viewfinder and checked the LCD screen.

Darn, all blurry, he thought. *Sorry sweetheart. Maybe she'll like the photos anyway.*

As he continued down Julip Road, a breeze caressed his face. Offsetting the pleasantness of the breeze was the knowledge that the autumns were much warmer than he remembered ten years ago. Before he could roll the window back up, the sour stench of rotting flesh wafted into his car. After holding down a half-pound of cinnamon roll, Bertil stopped the car and hoisted his two hundred and sixty pound frame out of the vehicle. He brushed cinnamon roll crumbs off his uniform and stretched.

"Fooking slob," he said.

The sour stench came from the west side of the road, and he followed it with his nose like a trained bloodhound. The hard part was not following the smell, but rather keeping his meal down. He'd learned to trust his nose over the years—a useful tool for busting the occasional meth lab and marijuana field. And it was almost too easy to tell who was drinking and driving from his nose alone. The youngsters in the area who smoked pot were easy pickings, especially if they had any paraphernalia in the car. But he didn't always turn *that* evidence in. It relaxed him and helped with his back pain. To be fair, he never gave the kids more than a warning as long as their supply was under an ounce. Maybe they knew what he was up to. Oh well. It didn't matter as they couldn't do anything about it. Besides, they were focused on replenishing their stashes rather than vengeance. Perhaps he'd feel bad, or dishonest about it all, but the dang stuff was so dang helpful there was no point. Sometimes comfort and performance superseded morals. Yes indeedy. What he wouldn't give to have a little toke with Mindy Jacobs.

The stench worsened as he trudged through the lady ferns. A few feet ahead, red liquid dripped from a misshapen fern. Officer Bertil cupped his hand over his mouth to stop the gag reflux. When all was clear, he bent down and examined the blemished lady fern.

Strange. Real strange.

While blood dripped from the fern, it also dripped *onto* the fern. He slowly looked up, following the source. High in a tangled canopy of maple, aspen, and red oak, a moose carcass sprawled. Huge chunks were missing from its flank. The hooves were gone, chewed off into red and nubby spears, beaver-like. Half the face was eaten away, leaving a bony white jaw that seemed caught in a scream. Massive bite marks scarred the animal's hump. The belly had been sliced open, allowing intestines to hang and sway from the branches. Blood dripped down the intestinal rope like water trickling down a clogged garden hose.

See any animals, daddy?

He brushed away the thought and spit. Then he focused on the canopy, walking under the rope of intestine, careful not to get any blood on his uniform. As the wind shifted, a drop of blood splashed the back of his neck, trickling down the rolls of skin below his crew cut. He swept his hand along the rolls, smearing the blood like putrid sun tan lotion. The trunk of a maple was as good a place as any to wipe it off.

Right away, something else caught his attention. A shadow in the canopy. Another dead moose, but this carcass was an older kill. Crows fluttered into the canopy and picked at it. The crows completely avoided the fresh kill.

Officer Bertil remained quiet for several minutes, listening for a predator. A moment of *officer's intuition* socked him in the belly. Not a thing to ignore. No sir. He watched the crows peck and tear at the older carcass. One of the crows jabbed the eye and beaked up the slop with repeated head bobs, then cawed. The crows never approached the fresh kill, not even once. And it seemed they didn't even want to be near it, scooting back on an invisible line when they fluttered too close.

Bertil snapped a photo of the canopy and thumbed his radio. "Charlie 102 to C-Com."

"Go ahead, Charlie 102."

"I need Hendricks to do a 10-25 for biologist Michael Eggerts ASAP. We have a wildlife incident up on lower Julip Road."

"10-4. Do you need additional units?"

"10-54. Also, I'm running into a 10-1."

Static chewed apart the signal. He clipped the radio onto his chest and surveyed the woods. A rustling noise came from the bushes just over the ridge.

Go time. He palmed his firearm.

Wow mister, is that a real gun? the tourist girls would ask.

An enormous shape emerged on the crest of the ridge, loping towards him. It bellowed and huffed as branches and saplings snapped around it.

Bertil's overburdened-heart pounded as he licked away a bead of sweat from his upper lip. Then he raised his firearm. The creature emerged from shadows into daylight. A bull moose, breath steaming from its nostrils, eyes possessed by rage.

Bertil turned and dashed through the ferns.

The ground shook as the moose's hooves pummeled the forest floor. The immense antlers parted ferns and bushes, and it seemed the plants moved out of the way themselves before the bull could even touch them.

The moose bellowed again.

Officer Bertil searched for a tree, but they were too thin to offer protection. His only chance was the patrol car.

There was no need to look behind. He could hear and *feel* the moose gaining on him. He could picture it though, torturing himself with images of bulldozer antlers and manic eyes. At the last second he dove onto the patrol car, skimming the hood like a fat seal on a piece of ice. Unable to control his momentum, he slid off and thudded onto Julip Road. Bertil rolled and heard a sick crunch as the car lurched. The moose thrashed the vehicle with its huge antlers, punching holes in the metal siding. The leviathan huffed and kicked gravel, rocking the car as if it were merely a baby crib. Bertil lay flat on the road, tight against the driver's side wheel, his right leg under the squad car. He drew his firearm, creaking leather accompanying the crunch of gravel under keratin.

The space between the road and front bumper provided the only westward viewpoint. Soon a hoof appeared, and another. The moose's gigantic head swung around the front bumper in his direction. The antlers were poised to inflict maximum damage if need be. One of the weathered antler points was stained white from patrol car paint. Bertil aimed his firearm at the moose's right eye. If he could get a bullet in there, he had a shot at the brain.

The moose gazed at him, its breaths slowing. A moment later the moose emerged entirely from the front of the squad car, and Bertil's heart pounded in awe at the magnificent specimen. Rocks dug into his thighs and gut as the moose stood only a few feet away, staring at him with wary ungulate eyes.

What a fooking predicament, he thought. This is one he'd have to tell Jennifer. The animal story of a lifetime, the time daddy was charged by a moose.

Bertil took a deep breath, firearm locked onto the moose. A plump red ant scrambled across the chips of gravel in front of him like the Mars Rover.

The bull moose, now much calmer, turned his head and glanced up the road. Then it huffed and trotted east into the yellow birch. The last Bertil saw of the moose was its antlers rising over the understory as yellow, shedding leaves floated down. Hands shaking and stomach queasy, Officer Bertil picked himself up and swatted his uniform a few times. Satisfied the danger had passed, he holstered his firearm.

No one will believe this one, he thought.

Too bad he didn't have a video camera. In the budget-depleted U.P. they'd stripped the cars of any meager tech goodies. And what they had failed to even compare with what urban forces rolled with. Bertil sighed. He wished he had that on tape. He also wished he knew what the hell was going on around here. This was not even close to typical moose behavior. And the only animal capable of stringing up moose was a cougar or grizzly bear, two animals the U.P. didn't have. His ancestors had killed off cougars decades ago. If you caught a cougar back then, you were king of the woods. Every male who could hold a rifle or spring a trap wanted one, and soon there weren't any left to have. Many of the settlers didn't care for them, often blaming cougars for missing chickens and cattle. After a while, most people figured out the U.P. wasn't quality farmland or even ranchland. By that time it was too late. The cougars were gone.

He needed to speak with biologist Eggerts. This wasn't anything the police could solve, at least not yet.

Officer Bertil opened the trunk and took out a can of orange spray paint. Then he trudged to the other side of the squad car. The bull had maimed the panel above the passenger side tire and cracked the headlight.

Nothing a little taxpayer money couldn't fix, he thought.

Bertil aimed the can at a two foot section of the western embankment. The metal can hissed as it coated the grass orange. Next, he hoisted his big frame into the seat and pulled out his notebook, then looked into the woods where the moose were strung in the canopy. He made note of the deformed red maple and jagged boulder—something biologist Eggerts would find useful in trying to locate the carcasses.

The woods were quiet again but his heart was not. The trees beyond his windows mocked his uneasiness with outstretched limbs. Bertil shook his head, trying to lose the eerie feeling. *Ah,* he thought. *I know just the trick.* Bertil seized what remained of the cinnamon roll and tore off a chunk with his teeth. *This is what I do best when I'm nervous,* he thought. The eating calmed him, provided a center of gravity which had slipped away the last twenty minutes.

After washing down the roll with lukewarm coffee, he proceeded south into the wilderness at five miles per hour, sometimes creeping to ten. He scammed both side of the road, boring deep into the shadows where wood anemone peered back at him like the white eyes of an unknown creature.

Officer Bertil shook his head, lifted his arms off the wheel, and joined his fingers for a nice crack. *What does that to a moose?*

The road narrowed as he approached the spot where he and Pam had conceived Bobby. Although overgrown compared to all those years ago, the half-embedded road boulders were the giveaway, each offering their own identity, like a thumbprint. As he checked the steep western side of the road, movement caught his eye through the windshield. Sixty yards ahead, a disheveled young man waved his arms frantically. Bruises and cuts marred the man's arms and legs. Officer Bertil pressed two fingers to his brow and saluted, then nudged the gas pedal. The trees thirty yards up on the western embankment shook and parted.

Strange wind pattern, Bertil thought.

But when he examined the rest of the forest, nary a branch moved. Billowing clouds of dust materialized twenty yards in front of the squad car and he thought he felt the engine rumble as if out of balance.

Bertil jammed his foot on the brake. *Officer's intuition.* Big time.

The young man began waving him off. His dirty face was beat red and his arms swung wildly, trying to usher him away. And then the young man was blocked from his view, by some kind of distorted air, like the kind you see way up the road on hot days.

What the fook kind of drugs is this guy on? Officer Bertil reached for his radio, figuring he'd found a meth lab. Before his finger could press the button, the squad car lurched and shifted.

Earthquake? he thought. *A fooking earthquake?* He let go of the receiver and prepared to flee the vehicle. He'd watched enough TV to know you don't stay in your dang tootin' car.

The young man grew frantic and began to yell.

"Go! Go AWAY!" the man shouted.

I ain't going anywhere, buddy, he thought. *You might be going away though.*

A ten thousand pound weight fell from the sky, or at least that's what Bertil thought when the front end of his car pancaked into the ground, pulverizing the engine in an ear-shattering whine. Bertil's head smashed into the roof and the world sloshed around him, awash in distortions and reverb.

In the mental haze he reached for the gear shift and yanked into reverse, then hammered the gas pedal.

Oh fook! The engine, the engine is gone. For some reason he pictured Willy Wonka singing next to him in the passenger seat.

And isn't that a nice song? The engine, the engine is gone, oh yes, the engine, the engine is gone, let's all sing a song, the engine, the engine is gone.

The cruiser's smashed windshield dipped and bent within its frame. Bertil looked out in-between glass fragments, marveling at how the hood had flattened into the ground. Smoke snaked from the maimed hood into the U.P sky. But there was something off about what he thought was the sky. It was distorted, blurry. And this distortion moved, suffusing the smoke tendrils in its faint phosphorescence like blood in water.

Bertil reached for the door handle, but it wouldn't budge.

And isn't this such a nice song? The engine is gone, oh yes, the engine is gone. Darkness will sing its song, oh yes the engine has gone.

Don't panic, he thought. *Calm down.* He reached for the radio.

"Charlie 102 my car is—"

At once his words cut out and his chest tightened. He gagged as prickly sensations erupted all over his upper body. Without a choice, his thumb and forefinger released the receiver.

Oh, you've found darkness my friend, he thought. *Maybe if you grab your gun you can impress this thing like the tourist girls? You're having a heart attack. You're having a heart attack. You're having a heart attack.*

Bertil glimpsed his reflection in the rearview, his face purple and eyes bulging. The vehicle rocked back and forth and lifted into the air. He reached for anything, anything at all but couldn't move his arms. A soft cry escaped his lips, along with a dribble of cinnamon roll bile. Congested breathing grunted from his left, as if from elephantine lungs.

The patrol car rose thirty feet over Julip Road and rotated like a giant rotisserie chicken. The embankment, trees, and dusty road shifted and spun. With one final turn he was upside down looking south, Julip Road like some hideous sky which could never be flown and the earth as if an endless maw of which nothing stabilized.

The young man was no longer there.

Love you, Pam, Bertil thought. *Maybe we can revisit that picnic someday.*

As his strength escaped him, he realized his nearly-paralyzed fingers were near the siren switch. *He could do it. He could do it.* A deep breath (except he couldn't breathe at all), and exhale (nope) and a flick of the finger. He'd do it for Pam, do it for his cutie-pie daughter and Bobby. Yes he would. With spittle peppering from his lips and his vision blurring, Bertil managed to waggle his finger enough to flip the switch, and then he let whatever was squeezing him squeeze him further. The siren wail violated the quiet woods, shaking birds from the canopy like confetti.

The flipped squad car crossed into the maple and birch, holding thirty feet off the ground. Bertil couldn't tell for certain which direction, but had a feeling he was headed east.

That a real gun mister? they'd ask.

You bet, he'd respond, palm on holster. If there was something he could put his leg up on, he'd do that too.

He'd played the part so well. But maybe there was one last part he could play here, too. Officer Bertil reached for his firearm, this time for his life rather than for show.

He mustered as much strength as he could from his right arm and he felt something move across it—something solid but pliable. The sensation churned his stomach and he spit up bile. His fingers fumbled around the holster and unbuttoned the clasp. He pressed his palm tight against the holster so gravity would not steal this moment from him. Then Bertil wrapped his fingers around the 4006 Smith and Wesson and brought it to the roof with what seemed like more effort than anything he'd done in his life.

Whatever you are, I've got something for you, my friend, he thought. *I've got something special indeedy.* Officer Bertil fired a round through the roof. He straightened the barrel, face purple, eyes fixated to the roof corner. The roof of the car popped and dished as the vehicle was carried deeper into the woods. With the sirens blaring in his ears, Officer Bertil fired another shot into the roof, choking from the effort. Then he straightened the barrel with a trembling hand and fired another round that induced a berserk roar from the thing underneath him.

Gotcha.

Bertil fired another round, eliciting a freakish wail. The car plummeted and the ferns rushed up to him like a thousand green angels. His head smashed into the roof as the choking sensations increased, numbing all feeling. Slowly, his world dimmed.

See any cool animals, Daddy?

Officer Bertil fired one last shot out the window before his body went limp. His firearm thudded to the roof.

The upside down squad car elevated over the understory, sirens wailing and reflecting off the forest floor in vibrant patterns. The car ripped through leafy branches, collecting bits and pieces of trees as it went. Birds chittered and flew out of the canopy as the ghost car approached. The crows did not. Instead they watched from their perches with keen eyes. Four-legged animals rustled vegetation and snapped branches as they fled. Snowshoe hares tripped over roots in the scramble. Fishers tumbled from dead falls in haste. A goshawk collided with a branch, bruising a wing.

The flipped cruiser wailed deep into the northern forest, the emergency lights illuminating dark glades and exposing shadows that ought not be exposed. The car that carried the body of Officer Bertil as if a casket with no pallbearers paused at a small bog ringed by old growth hemlock—one of the few places the loggers missed.

Sirens shattered the stillness. A few creek chubs in the blackness swam frantically in all directions. The cruiser reached the rim of the bog, the water so dark the lights did not reflect. Then the car hurled through the air, the deafening sirens panning like an effect on a psychedelic record. Charlie 102 smashed into the murky water, splashing creek chubs and foul algae onto patches of dry ground. The inky water absorbed the cacophonous sirens, returning calm to the boreal forest. After a moment the sirens stopped altogether, replaced by one last electronic warble from the bottom of the forgotten bog. Ripples of dark water lapped at the slimy bank, and bubbles roiled up to the surface as if a big, metal crocodile lay waiting for prey.

Another secret for the Northwoods.

***

Matt screamed as he watched the squad car's front end smash into Julip Road, and then become vaguely blocked by a distortion. "Go!" he shouted. "Get the fuck out of here!"

Shut up you fool, the little voice said. *The Puller is busy. Make something of it.*

The poor officer clutched at his chest as his face reddened, no doubt wondering what was happening to him. Matt wanted to do whatever he could to help him. But instead he stood there, clenching his fists, helpless.

You can't save him, the anxiety voice said. *Look around. You can't even save yourself. But you have a chance...RIGHT NOW.*

He watched the suffering officer and grimaced, the taste of bile strong in the back of his throat. He was ashamed at what he was about to do, but the voice was right. He couldn't even save himself. What possible assistance could he afford anyone else?

The squad car lifted thirty feet off the road, then flipped over. For whatever stupid reason, an old lyric from a famous rock band crept into Matt's head.

There's a feeling I get when I look to the west, the little voice said.

At once the stasis left him, and he sprinted up the two track. His breath was calm, deliberate. He did not care about the cuts and scrapes and pain. Adrenaline took care of that.

Inside the shack, he yanked on his pants, flannel, and boots. He messed up a shoelace and panicked. He seized the kitchen knife, a box of matches, a jug of water. Then he put the blade in-between his teeth and went over to the bunk and retrieved the headlamp, stretching it over his head. He ran out of the shack not bothering to close the door.

As he ran up the path to the leaning post, police sirens went off. He sprinted past the leaning post and down towards the wall of alder and balsam fir that made up the western border of the orchard.

Sirens wailed across the countryside.

Danger Danger Danger

They clamored in his head and he ran like he'd just hopped a prison wall.

The sirens tracked east. This might be the only chance he had.

The dry orchard grass gave way to a cool mix of spruce, alder, and fir. Branches poked at his face, cutting his cheeks. His chest heaved as saliva trickled down the knife blade between his lips. Cobwebs caressed and then clung to his forehead. The pungent odor of rotting wood and moist soil permeated everything. He crashed through brush so thick that he threw himself against it in order to pass. Thorns tore at his clothes, their barbs sinking home and then ripping out.

Thorn bushes are the least of your worries, Matthew, the little voice said. *Keep moving west, old friend. The bog calls you.*

Matt huffed and flailed through the jungle, the water jug a four hundred pound weight in his hand, catching on every possible branch. There were no people trails leading into Twenty Mile Bog. But intermittent game trails crossed deadfalls and black pockets of stagnant water with unpredictable depths. Unlike the swamps down south, the water here was ice cold and something to avoid unless you enjoyed hypothermia.

The fir and spruce gave way to dead trees that punctured the bog like giant silver toothpicks. The bog carried less light overall, and the whole of it retained a blue cast, as if the black water sucked away brightness. Even the sky was not the same.

Off in the distance, the sirens, now a whimper rather than a roar.

Move Matthew, move! the little voice said.

He tripped over a fallen spruce, the water jug flying from his grasp. He spit out the knife before smacking into another dead tree. The petrified wood creaked like a rocking chair as his knee knocked into it. His other foot sunk into a hole filled with horizontal timber snags. He yanked his foot through the dead, grey branches, ripping them out of the hole. Something tickled his right ankle and he looked down at a northern widow spider. He swiped at it. The spider sensed his hand coming, reared up, and bit him on his index finger.

"Shit!" he shouted.

Hush, the little voice said.

Matt shook his hand, tossing the spider into the beaked sedge and alder.

A bright, red bump formed on his finger. Matt reached for the knife, now buried in the sedge. The blade was dirty from the soil and he wiped it along his pants before sliding it into his pocket, blade first. Then he examined his hand while pushing on the red bump. Northern widow spiders were considered dangerous, but only to those with pre-existing conditions. He didn't want to mess with the odds, so he reached into his back pocket for the knife. Then he held out his finger and dug the knife tip into the wound. Blood trickled from the inflamed lump. Pinching the lump, he massaged out any venom, and then cleansed it with water. Satisfied, he drank from the jug, filling his belly with the Black.

After the last, cold gulp, he held his breath and listened for the sirens. There…far off to the east, so faint. Without thinking he leapt over a snag and onto a spongy island of beaked sedge. Out before him stretched small, grassy islands spiked with at least one dead tree and surrounded by patches of stagnant water. The fresh scent of sweet grass permeated the air, with an undertone of muck. If he could travel from island to island, he should be all right.

Matt jumped, rattling the matches in his flannel pocket and sloshing the water in the jug. His foot sunk into a spongy island and he yanked it out.

Much better than a splash, he thought.

He had no idea how deep some of these water pockets were. He might end up soaking his boots or sucking water into his lungs as he sunk in over his head.

The still, black water reflected the dead snags and grasses in monochrome. Tiny ripples pinged out from the islands with every step.

The ground is very sensitive here, Matthew, the little voice said. *When the time comes, you best be very still.*

After two tough leaps, he caught his breath on an island, hands on his hips. Dead branches snapped to the west. He went to his knees, peering out between blades of sweet grass. Steps approached, and he felt them in the ground. Two white-tailed deer emerged, feeding on willow and bog birch. One of the deer sported a trophy set of antlers—the kind that misguided hunters spent thousands of dollars trying to find. Matt heard the deer chewing and grinding, their powerful jaws turning the vegetation into pulp.

He held his breath and listened for the sirens. They were no more. At last he stood and the deer bounded away from him, leaping from island to island, making a mockery of his progress. Their cotton white tails flagged high, warning others, but there was only him.

He could not hope to move as fine as they did across the bog. Nevertheless he aimed for the next island, clearing the water with as much grace as a human possessed.

Matthew, keep your ears open, the little voice said.

He had no doubt the Being would come looking for him after finishing with the patrol car. It had already gone to great lengths to pull him back into the orchard, following the strict radius of ACCEPTABLE MOVEMENT as he'd come to know it.

How could the Being even find me in the bog? he wondered. If it found him in this freaking tangle, with this head start, then he truly had no hope. He glanced up at the dead trees which now resembled crucifixes.

You know the Puller will come into the bog, Matthew, the little voice said. *It can find what it wants, when it wants. The question is how do you make it difficult?*

Matt stopped and cut a swath of fabric from the bottom of his flannel. Then he bent down and soaked the fabric in bog water. His fingers picked through the sedges and grass on his island, searching for a stone. After plying his fingers into the pungent soil, he grasped one. He tucked the gritty stone into the swath of flannel and wrapped it. Then he dipped it into the water again, adding more weight. Satisfied with the heft, he reared back and let the material fly as hard as he could to the north, triggering pain in his shoulder. The flannel and stone whipped across the sky, high above the dead trees and disappeared.

He jumped to another island, this one quaking below him. As he regained his balance the island began to tilt, dead tree and all towards a pocket of water. Before it could take him in, he climbed up the soil hump and leapt to another. The new island received him well. Behind him, the previous island tilted and crashed into the water, the dead tree groaning in displeasure at finally meeting the goop which it had avoided for so long. Two wood frogs skittered away from the sinking hump.

As the water settled, a bone-rattling roar came from the east.

MOVE! the little voice said.

He leapt wildly from island to island, missing several and soaking his jeans and boots in the freezing water.

Please no more, he thought. *No more jumping.* He looked up, hands on knees, water jug half-empty thanks to a leak. Then he thrust his numb legs forward. Always forward.

Fifty yards ahead lay a bigger island, this one ringed by a smattering of spruce and balsam fir—alive, not dead.

He struggled his way over, sometimes executing perfect jumps, other times...not so much.

The roar came again, closer this time. Low lying fog wafted between the dead trees, making visibility worse. He dragged himself to the edge of the last small island and prepared for one more jump. The black water lay still before him, almost smug. He went to jump, but his back foot slipped. Matt belly-flopped into the water, lashing small waves onto the bank. The shock of cold water and his fatigue pulled him under the black soup. Above him, the water jug floated on the wake like a fishing bobber. Silence enveloped the bog, as if no one had been slaving through it, as if it were a lie.

Underwater, he looked to the sky. Filtered sunlight shimmered above him in sepia waves. Dead trees circled him like surgeons who'd just taken off their masks, frowning.

I don't want to come up, he thought. *Why should I? This is peaceful. I should swallow the water...let myself become part of the bog. It's not such a bad way to go, and it's certainly superior to what the Being has in store for me.*

Underwater, he felt safe. The dread of the last few days slipped away under its protective blanket. Matt held out his arms and closed his eyes. *Love you mom*, he thought. *Love you too Andrea. Stacey and Dad, I'll be seeing you real soon, I hope. I'll be seeing you too Elmo. I'm sorry.*

But he didn't feel sorrow, instead he sensed hope in resolution to impossible conflict. *This is the way to go*, he thought. *This is humane.*

Matt took a big gulp and then another. Tiny bubbles escaped his mouth, rising to the silhouette of the floating jug and dim slats of light.

As he prepared to die, something bit his ankle, shooting bright pain through his leg.

The thing bit again.

He kicked to the surface, coughing and flailing his arms, desperate to get away from the biter. He aimed for the big island.

It's back, he thought. *It wouldn't even let me kill myself.*

Another bite on his ankle, and this time he was sure the creature hit bone. Matt groped and slapped at the muddy shore, pulling himself up the bank. There he wheezed and slumped to the spongy soil, wet hair splayed over his forehead, water dripping off his nose like a clogged gutter.

Blood seethed from several cuts on his ankle, but the wounds were not serious. They'd been inflicted by a much smaller animal than he'd imagined, but that realization took nothing away from the painful bites. He expelled the last bit of water from his lungs and slicked his hair back, clearing the bangs from his eyes. Then he checked the ground for a stick. Soon he found a fat one under an alive spruce tree. He gripped the stick like a spear fishermen and stood at water's edge, preparing to stab whatever it was if it came back to bite him. He clenched his jaw and waited.

Across the pool, movement caught his eye. A slick, elongated animal broke the surface. Two smaller versions followed the larger. The details were scarce in the weak light, and Matt wondered if there were other hostile creatures, things that had come here with the thing that was trapping him. Anything was possible in this shits n' giggles game of "Matt's Screwed."

The animals emerged from the water onto the grassy bank. The big one gazed at him, paws perched out in front. Matt squinted at it.

An otter, he thought. *A freaking otter.*

The female otter gazed at him, all slick head and dripping fur. Two baby otters appeared below her—one of them licking its paws. The mother sniffed and puckered her nose. Her whiskers emanated beyond the profile of her face, offering a cartoonish appearance. The two babies rolled and frolicked with each other at her feet, making snarky weasel noises. The mother otter made two, sharp clicking calls that drew the immediate attention of her family, and she wobbled out of sight. Her babies followed her, their whip-like tails swooshing back and forth, and then gone.

He checked his leg and noticed the bleeding had stopped. He wondered why the otter bit him, why she caused him pain.

To wake you up, Matthew, the voice said. *They wanted to wake you up.*

Matt shook his head, ashamed at his behavior under the water. He wasn't a quitter, but the peace was way too much to resist.

I know, the little voice said. *I wanted it too.*

Matt pushed through the wall of spruce that circled the island. There was maybe twenty by forty feet of dry land, but it had a sense of privacy. A big hemlock lay across the soft soil, missed by the loggers. Matt stepped on top of the log, looking for a place to sit and dry off. Halfway along the log he noticed a hole dug into the earth below it. He bent over, flipped on his headlamp (luckily he'd purchased the waterproof unit. His father had always told him, *buy cheap five times, buy quality once),* and peered into the hole. *Lesson learned, dad.* He thought. *Thank you.*

The hole led to a bigger chamber and he realized he was looking at a black bear den. No breathing sounds came from inside as far as he could tell. But then again, he wasn't a bear tracker or anything, so who knows what could be down there.

Might be a good place to hide, he thought, as the opening was wide enough for him to squeeze in. He had no doubt the Being would look for him in the bog. None.

As if on cue, a roar echoed across the landscape, closer than before.

Get in the hole, Matthew! the little voice said.

He returned to the bank and retrieved the floating milk jug with the stick. Then he used the stick to smear the muddy bank, wiping away handprints and footprints. He returned to the den jug in hand and crawled on his belly, grunting as his ribcage thumped into the dirt. His headlamp revealed gnarled, white roots in the ceiling, but a smooth floor. Once through the hole he shifted to his knees. Earthworms and aphids seethed from the walls, but they did not bother him. He wondered if this was Ernie's den—if this was how he'd avoided the hunters and trappers all these years.

The den surprised him with its comfort and security despite being in the middle of Twenty Mile Bog. And after all, he was experiencing some sort of freedom—a major relief compared to the last few days. He figured this was similar to the mindset of those persecuted during World War II. They too had taken to the woods, hiding from terror.

As he took in his surreal surroundings, he realized the bear could return any moment. His hands swept the floor for fresh bear sign, and he pulled up several clumps of coarse, black hair.

Looks like this bear hasn't foreclosed yet, the little voice said.

Tell me something I don't know, he said.

At least he had the knife. Matt reached into his back pocket, his splayed fingers finding nothing but denim.

"Shit," he said.

Shut your mouth, the voice said. *Do you want to give away your position?*

Matt turned towards the light, exasperated. He needed something to defend himself with, so he searched the island but came up empty. Then he retraced his steps to where he first emerged from the water. There on shore, half-covered in algae was the knife, the blade cool to the touch. A splash came from across the pool, followed by a ripple.

Weird, he thought.

What hasn't been weird? the voice said. *What makes this instance stand out? Context, Matthew.*

"Are you going to be a smart ass, or are you going to help?" he shot back.

Oh I think I've been more than helpful, the little voice said. *If you had liste—*

"Okay, Okay. You've been helpful. No need to bring up mistakes," Matt said.

Once back in the den, he nestled against the back wall, exhausted and cold. He wanted sleep so badly. Sleep was an escape, like the near-drowning which felt *oh so right*.

Matt gazed to the soft light beyond the den entrance. An occasional brown bat streaked across the sky, and a great-horned owl hooted somewhere in the gloom. Evening had settled upon Twenty Mile Bog. Frogs let loose an amphibian version of "It's a Small World After All," or so he imagined. *Interesting choice, fuckers*, he said.

Soon the narrow oval of light at the den entrance dissipated to blackness. He flicked the switch on his headlamp, making sure he turned to face the wall. The last thing he needed was the Being catching a flicker of light. Maybe it could sense the energy of the batteries, too. He hoped not.

The frogs wound down their symphony, but the owl had just started.

This is a good thing, he thought. *That owl will be my watchdog. When I hear it fly off or stop, you can bet that piece of shit is near.*

The Puller, Matthew, the little voice said.

"I hate what you named it," he whispered.

I hate it, period, the little voice said.

Matt nodded in agreement and tucked into a ball, his clothes still damp. Fortunately the bear den blocked the wind, allowing him to retain body heat.

Noises peeped up across the bog as the night grew richer. Here and there a frog croaked or a stick broke. His spine lit on fire with every noise, and it took five minutes for his body to stop trembling. It was like being on death row for a crime you didn't commit and hearing the pastor's footsteps every ten minutes. And the strength of the thing pacing outside his cell. He didn't even want to think about it. Impossible strength.

The bog noises faded and their absence was morphine. He thought of Andrea and his mother, of how they'd watched those damn movies from the 80's like *Dirty Dancing*. He remembered how they laughed and this laughter filled his heart as he drifted off. At one a.m. he woke to a nudge in his backside. He listened, puzzled at the sound of his breathing. It sounded labored. The spicy-sweet scent of body odor filled the den.

Maybe you're sick, he thought.

Matt listened to his breathing again. Strange. He held his breath, then flared his nostrils when he realized the noises weren't coming from him.

He fumbled for his headlamp switch.

The beam lit the den wall he faced, revealing a couple squirmy grubs. As he turned his head, the violet cone of light revealed a mass slumped against his body. The mass was thick with black fur. The furry heap rose and fell.

Alive. Breathing.

Heart racing, Matt craned his neck, careful not to disturb the massive animal. With a better perspective, he realized the animal was sleeping *against* him. A stench of bog algae and fruit farts wafted from the beast.

A freaking bear!

He forced himself to remain still, catching desperate utterances just before they passed his lips. He had to think, had to plan. A single bad move and this could be GAME OVER.

He bunched up, smashing his arms and legs against each other and the den wall.

Do you really think it's going to attack you, Matthew? the little voice asked. *It came into its den and laid down right next to you as if you were nature's pillow.*

Matt sighed.

No need to add more worries to your list. A bear is the least of your problems, Matthew.

The bear's midsection heaved as it snored, each snore ranging from frightening to comical.

The bear's face was turned away, its back snug against him. He followed its shape and saw a furry leg and an upturned paw, the pads worn and scarred.

The bear let loose a watery fart, filling the den with the scent of wild berries.

This made him hungry.

You sick bastard, the little voice said. *You sick, sick bastard.*

Matt chuckled, happy to one-up The Voice for once.

Resigned, he closed his eyes, took a deep breath, exhaled, and no longer feared the bear. Instead, awe and respect replaced fear. The damn thing was keeping him warm, too. He could even smell the wildness of it. This was an animal that roamed near his beloved shack—near the place that had always been home to him. Before The Being ruined everything.

It was never about the shack, Matthew, the little voice said. *Think about it.*

He listened to the bear snore, feeding off the power. Lying next to the creature, he sensed a positive force from the land he'd always loved. The bear represented everything—the woods, the rivers, the mountains. It was living proof of this vital ecosystem, an ecosystem that existed before The Being caught him and one that will exist long after The Being is gone.

Images of his Michigan experiences flashed before him: feasting on wild trout at the main pool of the Black River, fishing the tiny pools of the upper Black as a child, hiking the granite

Hurons with his father, eating wild berries by the bucket full, the lingering sunsets over Lake Superior, the sound of water sluicing through the slate canyons during spring runoff and movement in the woods, always movement in the woods. This place was a big, heaving, breathing ball of life, a peanut butter and jelly sandwich smashed down and squeezing out the sides.

Take a freaking bite, he thought.

The bear's flank rose and fell. Every exhale was medicine, filling the den with power.

Matt flicked off the light.

Maybe it never was about the shack, he thought. It was just a place to stay, an attempt to reconnect with the natural world. A portal, if you will. And maybe that's how the Being got here. Maybe from a portal.

His eyes flickered in the darkness, his breath silent compared to the boisterous bear.

Maybe you can find that portal, the little voice whispered. *Wouldn't that be a neat trick?*

It would be Houdini on steroids, he thought.

He clasped his hands together and accidentally elbowed the bear, triggering a grunt and a sloppy muzzle lick.

How did I get the knife back? he asked the little voice. *It must have fallen from my pocket when I was underwater and sunk to the bottom.*

There was no answer.

He tried again. *How did I get the knife back?*

Matt stared into the darkness, his upper lip quivering, waiting for an answer.

From a friend, the little voice said.

What friend? he asked.

You have friends, Matthew. Don't act so surprised. You've always had friends.

You mean Jim and the others back in the suburbs? he asked the voice.

No. I mean friends with a capital F, Matthew. You've always had them.

So a friend got my knife back?

Yes. And your friend woke you. You needed to be woken. Look around you. Look next to you! Is this normal to you? the little voice asked.

No, of course not, he thought. *It wasn't normal at all.*

Over time, the warmth of the bear dried his clothing. He turned on his side and smelled the rich black fur as the bear's lungs rumbled. This probably wasn't the famous Ernie, but perhaps a relative. This bear sported a darker coat, and was smaller, but not small. Wherever the bear came from, he was glad to have a protector for the night.

A twig snapped outside the den and his thoughts filled with the squad car rolling over and the choking officer. The remnants of the police sirens screeched into his brain. He blinked, trying to refresh the memories like a computer desktop. Yes, he was glad to have a guardian for the night.

Someone's looking out for me, he thought.

No Matthew, everyone is looking out for you, the little voice said. *Everyone.*

The warmth took him to dreamland, away from the domain of the Being.

Every Good Deed
15 Years Ago

John Kearns moved his prominent frame across the understory like a moose, fly rod in hand. His big forearms rippled, sleeves rolled up to his elbows. His size fourteen tan boots kicked through the colorful leaves. He was an animal, no different than a deer or a bear. At least that's how he felt.

It had been too long since he fished the Black and he'd worked too hard without a break. Susan had pleaded with him to go up north, promising to watch the kids in his absence. That was an offer he couldn't refuse.

John reached into a flannel pocket and found his Marlboro Reds. The sensation of the filter between his thumb and forefinger let his body know the fix was coming. He fingered into his jeans pocket and clasped a silver Zippo lighter. He snapped open the lid, relishing the mechanical ritual. His thumb pressed down on the spiked wheel, forcing up a flame. Then he leaned his face down into it, mouth puckering around the cigarette. After flicking the Zippo closed and sliding it back into his pocket, he gazed into the canopy, pulling deep on the cigarette.

A good day, he thought. A good fall day. No work, no people. The winding currents of the Black called his name.

The woods calmed him, and offered a pleasing display of maple, aspen, hemlock, and white pine. The silence honed his thoughts. *Things* were not pulling at him from all sides, and he was focused on the task at hand, slipping into a meditative state. His children meant the world to him, Susan too. They had their arguments, but so what. Everyone does. But while he loved his family like ferns love the rain, he needed time to himself. He figured this was something he inherited from his father, who was part-gypsy wanderer, part-interstate trucker. He hoped they'd never take this personally. This need, this natural craving was something deep inside him, something genetic he couldn't control. Besides, when he returned home he was a new man, a better person for them and for himself.

Colored leaves crunched under his boots as a ruffed grouse drummed its wings to the east. The slow beats crescendoed into a pounding rhythm. This commotion had a way of attracting many predators, and John often wondered how grouse survived. They were under attack on all fronts, the chicken of the Northwoods. If it wasn't goshawks or owls, it was coyote, fisher, bobcat, and pine marten. They were the woods drummer, perhaps playing a song for his arrival. Hard to beat that.

Whispering water caught his ears through the trees on his left. The good, fast-running, clean kind. *Ah the Black*, he thought. He headed towards the sound and after a hundred yards the forest gave way to a slate cliff that plunged into a deep pool. If he tried going down that way, he'd break a leg, or his neck. He watched the swirling water and wondered what it would be like to slip and fall into the frigid pool. John lit another smoke, relishing the sights and sounds of the Black. The rushing water and unique cuts and grooves of slate reminded him of things from a long time ago— things before he was born. One might call it an undefined spirituality. Whatever it was, it felt like home. Why, he could not say. No one had all the answers. Not even Big John.

He gazed upon the canyon like a shepherd to his flock. In the foam below the falls a coho salmon jumped, its top black and slick, its sides a silvery flash. He drew from his cigarette, admiring the waterway.

John moved upriver, attempting to find a way down. The canyon would not give way. He needed to work back into the forest and find the two track that followed this side of the Black.

He swept aside the branches of a gnarled spruce and heard a metallic clank to the north. A hundred yards ahead, chains rattled and tires spun. *Might be someone who needs help*, he thought. John hiked towards the noise, the Black flowing in the canyon to his left. Vibrant leaves crunched under his boots. Then the sound of chains and tires stopped and so did he.

A man cussed, and something growled.

Maybe these weren't people in need of help, but rather people he needed to avoid. Slowly, and engine roared to life and then dissipated.

Up ahead the stink of diesel permeated the air. Soon he came across a detached trailer, which looked like it had been used for boats and converted to a flatbed. Orange spray paint marked the side rail, spelling out PRIVATE PROPERTEE. A filthy khaki tarp covered the trailer, square shapes bulging underneath the fabric.

John moved closer. As he did, a growl emitted from under the tarp. *Could be hunting dogs,* he thought. The U.P. was famous for bear hunts, and this specific area was no exception. Over the years he'd seen plenty of hunters driving these woods, hounds caged in pickup beds waiting to be released. He stepped quietly to the trailer and a deep growl emitted once more.

John took a deep breath, set his fly rod against a maple, and unclasped a bungee cord from a corner of the trailer. A scratching sound came from below the tarp, followed by a whimper. John flipped the filthy tarp backwards on itself, revealing three steel cages. As the tarp flipped over, balls of fur wobbled away from him, some letting out growls, others whimpering and cowering.

John stood there, blinking. It took him a moment to realize what exactly he was seeing.

Unbelievable, the thought. Each steel cage contained a baby black bear. John clenched his fists. The bears looked emaciated and their hollow eyes dominated their faces. No food or water had been left inside the cages and two of the bears were panting. All of the bears were cubs.

Where the hell is their mother? he thought. Halfway through that thought, he had his answer. At the head of the trailer a large, dead bear lay, her chin resting on wood planks, her legs tucked to her sides. The cub in the closest cage pawed and whimpered at her.

While they were indeed cubs, they were also at an age where they *might* survive on their own. John imagined they'd be pushed away by their mother this season as she sought another mate—if she hadn't been gunned down by slobs.

John clenched his fists and spit.

The cubs seemed to relax just a bit, as their soft, leathery paws pattered on the cage floors. It was strange, but he felt they sensed he meant no harm.

You better, he said. *I'm here to rescue your asses.*

John examined the front of the cages. Each was secured with hanger wire woven in-between metal bars. He watched the cub as he untwisted the wire, making sure baby bear wasn't going to nip him. The bear sat at the far end of the cage, its rump against the bars, a curious expression in its eyes. As he fought the wire it sliced into his thumb, lubricating his fingers and making it difficult to grip the wire. John winced away the pain, and instead listened to the panting cubs and their little claws clacked against the floor. Urine and feces odor wafted from the cages, and a heady whiff of desperation.

Finally loose, he set the hangar wire so it could be pulled free in one swipe. He wanted to release the bears at the same time to avoid splitting them up. The bears came as a family, and he wanted them released as a family. As he untwisted the next wire, he listened for motors or footfalls, but heard nothing except the panting of the bears and the whispering Black far below. Their breath was a rotten gift spewed right into his face. John grinned, and for a moment relished the danger of being caught.

Caught. Interesting word. He realized he didn't care. He'd like to have a few words with the poachers, and maybe punch them in the face, too.

John took a break from untwisting and reached along his belt, near the right hip pocket. His fingers found a snap and he slid out a foldable buck knife. He unlocked the blade, all seven inches flashing in the morning sun. John set the knife onto the trailer, blade pointed away.

When he finished unraveling the wire on the second cage he walked over to the last. As he reached towards the wire, the bear thrust a paw through the metal bars at him. John jumped back, his heart pounding. The mangy little cub flashed its teeth and followed John with its eyes, anticipating the best moment to bite him.

Hey there fella, John said. *Calm down okay? If you go and sit back in the corner there I can get you out of here.*

John checked the woods for the poachers, sure they'd surprise him at any moment, but there was only the sound of the Black. He wiped his bloody fingers on his jeans, leaving a dark streak..

The aggressive cub withdrew its paw through the bars and retreated to the back of the cage. John untwisted the wire as drops of blood mixed with his sweat on the wooden trailer. The cub stared at him, head tilted to the side, tongue lolling. The bugger could jump at him any second and it contained an unpredictable fire in its eyes—true wildness if he ever saw it.

This is one I would not mess with, ever, he thought. *Bear has spunk.*

As if reading his thoughts, the bear growled, making him to back off the wire.

Whoa, calm down boy, he said. *You'll be out of here soon enough.*

The bear leapt at him, jamming both paws between the steel bars. The bear's tongue pushed between its fangs and dripped saliva. It growled deeply, face and paws trembling.

John stepped back.

The bear held this position for the next few minutes, so John lit a cigarette, the tan filter catching his bloody fingerprints like a cancerous police blotter. He took a drag and eyed the bear, waiting. With great amusement he pictured what the scene might look like later, the surprise and dismay on the slob poacher's faces upon returning to their trailer. He pulled on the cigarette again, exhaling into the canopy. Somewhere back in the hemlocks a raven   cawed.

The aggressive cub stood its ground, shaking and ramming into the cage door. John lit another cigarette and walked ten steps backwards. The bear calmed, then backed away from the cage door, vertical impressions in its fur where steel bars had been.

John backed up another five steps.

The quarrelsome bear followed suit, rump wobbling to and fro. And for the first time John saw the young bear's frame from the side. And the bear was a *he.* Although skinny, his frame was designed to hold plenty of weight. Even better, his legs, shoulders, and ribcage were oversized compared to his siblings. If he survived, he might be a real bruiser.

John squatted, arms balanced on his knees. He glared at the bear, willing it back to the far end of the cage.

Now look, he said, *I apologize for what these idiots did to you and your momma. But my friend, if you don't want to end up like your momma there, you need to let me finish the job.*

The bear growled and took two steps back.

That a boy, he said. *See? Nothing to worry about. I'm going to release you so you can grow big and fat like momma there, okay?*

John glanced over at the mother bear, lifeless and flat on the trailer with her arms tucked in. The quarrelsome cub loped to the side of the cage closest to its mother and pawed her through the bars.

She's gone, John said. *But you still have a chance, bruiser. I'm going to move closer now. I'm going to unravel this wire before the slobs come back, and you're going to let me, okay?*

The cub retreated to the far side of the cage, head titled to the side.

John worked the wire as ashes from the cigarette fell upon his fingers, mixing with the blood. When he finished he kept the last twist in place and stepped back. There, at least ready to go, stood all three cages and all three bears. But the doors pointed to him— to the east. *Towards the Black canyon*, he thought. *No good.* If the bears ran off in that direction, they'd have trouble accessing deeper woods away from the poachers. They might even be trapped between the two track and the river. The poachers could drive the road and re-capture them easily.

John walked around the trailer and glanced west. *Much better*, he thought. They'd have to cross Julip Road, but that was an easier barrier.

As he jumped onto the trailer, the bears scattered to the far sides of their cages. He grabbed each cage and spun them so the doors faced west. Two of the bears yipped and whimpered, and the trailer undulated like a see-saw as he walked upon it, yet the quarrelsome bear remained calm. John had been certain that one would try and nip his fingers. But the little bruiser did not, thankfully.

He bent over the cages from the rear, and lifted the wire from the first cage while swinging the door open. The first cub hesitated, eyes wide. After a good sniff of air, the cub jumped out of the cage and onto the leafy forest floor. Goosebumps peppered John's forearms. Initially, he thought the cub would run off into the woods. Instead, the bear sniffed the air, then leapt back onto the trailer and nuzzled up against its dead mother.

His heart sank, but there was no time for bad feelings. John pulled the wire from the next cage. The second bear slunk out, nervous as hell, then greeted its sibling on top of their mother. Soon, both cubs were mewling and pawing her rich, black fur.

John opened the door to the difficult bear's cage. The bear pushed so hard off the cage it jerked to the side as the bear leapt into the forest.

John sighed.

Good instinct, he thought. Maybe it was the only cub to learn from mother. The sound of crunching vegetation stopped and a little head poked out of the ferns.

Shit, he thought. The confrontational cub let loose several cries, eliciting return cries from his siblings. The second sibling stood on their mother, sniffing the air. It let out a mournful wail. The cub in the woods answered and ran towards its siblings, tongue lolling. The bear pulled itself onto the trailer and joined the others around their dead mother.

John walked to the other side of the trailer and retrieved his foldable Buck knife. Then he bent down and stuck the blade deep into the fleshy tire. He relished how it sunk into the rubber, how the air gushed out. He slashed the other tires and the bears looked around skittishly as the trailer lowered. Then John searched the trailer for the spare, finding it at the head. He jabbed the knife into it, twisting so the air gushed out faster. Then he sliced off the lighting wiring and wrapped the wires around the blade and sawed through.

The bears huddled on their mother, looking up at him with sorrow as he searched the head of the trailer. He opened a blood stained cooler, finding a bag of charcoal and lighter fluid.

They aren't going to leave momma, he thought, *so I'm going to have to make them.*

If he left momma, the bears would stick to her side. Then they'd be an easy recapture for the poachers.

Lighter fluid in hand, he approached the cubs. They stared at him, big eyes wild, snouts sniffing, paws shuffling.

I'm sorry for what I'm about to do, he said. *But I have to. We are your enemy. Always remember that.*

Then he screamed at the top of his lungs.

GET THE HELL OUT OF HERE NOW!

The bears cowered, pressing hard against their mother, covering her like the secret service would cover a president.

John feared his yelling would alert the poachers, but he needed to get the cubs out of here, now.

John kicked at the first cub and it bit his boot. Then he kicked at the other one, connecting with its ribs. The kicks were not hard, but they were enough to send a message. The quarrelsome bear swiped at his right leg, teeth bared. John kicked him in the rump with his left leg.

Go on, Get! Get the HELL out of here now!

John raised his hands in the air, making himself as big as possible. Then he jumped up and down on the trailer, rocking it back and forth. He kicked at the bears again, catching another in the rump. It yipped.

Go on GET!

John let out a fake growl, raised his arms high in the air, and stomped on the trailer. The cages and gear rattled.

The bears cautiously backed off the platform, not moving their eyes off him. They growled and clicked and snarled. John stood in front of their dead mother, blocking their path to her. He felt horrible, but not as bad as if he let the slobs get the cubs again.

The retreating cubs glared at him from the forest floor, not sure whether to attack or run. They wanted their momma, they missed her so. She was all they had known.

John jumped off the trailer and ran at them. They tumbled backwards in a cloud of fur and claws, squealing and huffing. Then they regrouped twenty yards away at the edge of the ferns. Two stood on their hind legs and watched him.

John climbed back on the trailer and doused their dead mother with charcoal fluid. The flammable liquid ran down her rich fur like vegetable oil over a stuffed toy animal. A smattering of fluid pooled around her eye and dripped onto the trailer floor. He poured the rest of the fluid over the platform and the tarp. Back on the ground, he grabbed a corner of the tarp and lit it with his Zippo lighter, holding it away from his body.

Flame licked the tarp corner and raced across the head of the trailer.

The bears looked on nervously from the ferns, two of them standing and swaying.

The flames grew, seizing their dead mother. A massive flame shot into the air upon catching her fur. The skin of the bear sizzled and John wanted to vomit as the smell of burnt hair and flesh filled his nostrils. One of the bears cried out.

John approached the cubs, his back to the flames that now engulfed the trailer. Black smoke mushroom-clouded to the canopy. He stared down the bears, screaming at the top of his lungs, eyes bulging.

GO! GO NOW! WE KILLED YOUR MOMMA! GO!

The inferno roared behind his bulging, red face like the devil in hell.

GO NOW! GO!

Two of the bears sprinted off. The difficult bear stood on hind legs and swayed, catching the scent of his mother, the intense flames reflected in his eyes, deep and red. The cub let out a God-awful wail that echoed across the forest and down into the Black canyon.

The bear dropped to all fours and stared at John Kearns. Then the bear ran off into the ferns, forever.

Day 4

First light crept into the den, illuminating the packed dirt and dangling roots. Matt awoke startled, looked for the bear, and realized he was alone. The taste of soil filled his mouth, and he felt part of the earth in the most literal sense.

He crawled out of the den, pausing every few feet to listen. Frogs croaked deep in the bog, getting in a last call before fall hardened into winter.

Keep moving, he thought. He needed to reach Gibbons Road, which would give him a chance to travel uninhibited by brush or water. Seven miles down Gibbons Road was a series of cabins, which made up Stiemkel's Resort.

Matt drank from the jug, watching the last of the fluid funnel down the clear plastic. For a second he thought about tossing the jug, but it might serve another purpose.

A bald eagle flapped its impressive wings across the southern horizon, looking more like a dinosaur than a bird. Upon seeing him, the eagle veered to the west.

Symbol of freedom my ass, he thought. He wanted to run after the bird and grab on for a ride. The eagle was smart to avoid humans; it didn't get to be a healthy adult by flying towards them, that's for sure.

He turned to the den, wondering if he should crawl back in and hide. Maybe that was his the way out of this, just waiting the Being out.

You could, you could, the little voice said. *You may be on to something.*

But with his matches lost to the bog, he had no means to keep warm should the temperatures dip even further. All he carried was his headlamp, a water jug, and a knife—not the best set of survival tools for freezing nights. Also, he wasn't sure how long the bear would tolerate him. One wrong move and the bear could be on him, possibly making enough noise to attract the Being.

Matt blinked up at the sun. The warm light was a relief from the gloomy skies that had dominated his trip. He basked in it, the rays lifting his spirits. Thirty yards to the east a ruffed grouse drummed, starting slow and building to a crescendo.

Matt paced the island perimeter, scoping a route through the bog. To the west, narrow islands spiked with dead trees led across the water. About a hundred yards out stood clumps of living trees, their dark green needles contrasting with the dead silver snags all around him. Gibbons Road was due west, so he proceeded in that direction. With the sun at his back, he left the sheltered island that had protected him through the night.

One good jump, then another. A huge log made up most of the new island, and ripples pinged out into the water with each step. He could hear his footfalls reverberate underwater, as if someone was down there with a stick banging away. Not good.

Matt jumped two more sections of water and worked his way across more grass humps, the healthy row of trees beckoning him. If he could reach them, he should have an easier time.

A stench of putrefied soil and vegetation wafted up to him as the sun's rays warmed much of the bog. Mist curled in dark pockets where sunlight failed to shine. The sun burned the back of his neck, and he swatted at a biting insect. Ahead of him, a group of Boreal Chickadees pecked a spruce for insects, their tiny brown heads twitching. As he watched them, his foot slipped into a hole laced with deadfall. He tried to brace the fall, but his hands only met water. With nothing to brace him, he smacked his face onto a log that jutted out of the murky bog. Matt screamed as pain ripped through his head. Even worse, the impact resounded into the water like a bass drum. The Boreal Chickadees fluttered above the treetops and scattered like a thinking cloud of dust.

Matt rubbed his aching jaw, trying to massage the pain away.

I'm done, he thought. *I just gave myself away.*

He paused, expecting a reply from the little voice. There was nothing.

Matt hugged the gnarled log, his foot still entangled in the snag hole. His heart thudded against the wood as sweat trickled off his nose into the stagnant water.

With each second, the bog grew quieter, almost achieving the utter stillness Matt had experience up to this point. But across the water, fifty yards towards where he'd started the day, two tremendous splashes ruptured the inky water. His first thought was that an elephant entered the bog. The water roiled as if pushed by two massive columns, and he realized the Being might be bipedal, similar to humans. The wake sloshed onto the grass islands, kicking up muck and other rotten debris.

Stay calm, stay down, he thought. *Stay down.*

The island shook with every splash, shuddering the dead trees. The log he clung to vibrated, shooting ripples into the water. As the elephantine splashes drew closer, Matt smelled the pungent muck that had been drudged up from the bottom. He thought he saw the air distort above the wake for just a second, like looking through a jug of creekwash.

The abnormal splashes stopped for a moment, then resumed in his direction. Forgotten branches skeletal in the depths cracked with muted notes.

Matt Kearns knew what was coming next. He was a little bitch who'd wandered too far from his master. He was the dog with the tail between its legs, submitting to the alpha.

Or was he?

The vibrations shuddered into him through the log. Bile crept up his esophagus and burned. The splashing ceased fifteen yards out as a flotilla of muck and grass floated towards him, interspersed with bubbles from the deep. Now there was no mistaking the distorted air above the water.

He heard the all-too-familiar heavy breathing, with bass notes that could only be produced by enormous lungs.

The Being moved towards him.

Concentric circles ringed out from where his log entered the water on a slant. Matt gripped the log so hard his hands ached. *He would no longer be the toy.* With whatever courage hadn't been beaten out of him, he reached for his knife. Then he waited, arm crooked behind his back. Slowly, he freed his foot from the snag.

The splashes came within ten feet and ceased. Matt blinked away the sweat in his eyes, waiting for the right moment to strike.

You can die on your terms, Matthew, the little voice said. *Or you can die on the Puller's terms.*

Matt dug his boot into the ground as his fingers tightened around the hilt.

Go Matthew, go, the little voice said.

Matt pushed off the grass hump with both feet and leapt into the air.

Get out of my woods! he shouted, his words echoing across the bog. Matt hung in the air, baring his teeth like a wild animal. For a moment he froze in time, a warrior fighting his last battle. Matt Kearns had returned. Whether he would die or not didn't matter. He'd taken control and brought the fight to the creature. As he hung in the air, he thought of Jeff Bridges' character at the end of "Thunderbolt and Lightfoot". He was proud.

I'm not your bitch, he thought. *These woods are not your bitch.*

In midair, Matt brought the knife down hard, and then he really did freeze.

The choking sensation was immediate and severe. A thousand needles poked and prodded his body.

There he hung over the bog like the world's saddest statue. The knife splashed into the water, sinking in the murk. Matt screamed and kicked the air.

Now I will die, he thought. *Kill me now, creature. No more play time. End the Matt Kearns Show. Do not renew the season. Can't you see ratings are down? Look around.*

Searing pain exploded inside his head as multi-hued flashing light obfuscated the bog. Then there was nothing.

***

"Want a blowjob?" the gorgeous brunette asked him, mouth parted, tongue nestled perfectly behind white teeth.

"Do I really need to answer that?" Matt said, a grin spreading across his face.

She ran a finger along his jaw line and up to the tip of his nose. Her mouth formed different shapes as she did this, as if she was in awe of her ability to turn him on and herself at the same time. Her lips moved closer.

"You *do* know that only good boys get head, right Matthew?" she said. "Have you been a good boy?"

Her hand slid down his stomach and worked under his shirt.

Matt felt himself harden and push against the inside of his jeans.

"You tell me," he said, grinning. In some ways, he thought this part was better than the actual sex. At least he always seemed to remember the teasing the most.

She moved one hand inside his jeans and slipped her other hand under her silk underwear. She worked her lips up to his neck and darted her tongue upon his skin like a snake searching for prey. Her breath was thick and musty, as if something had taken over her body—something not of this world.

Someone knocked on the door.

In the dim light, a Nordic-looking woman sauntered into the room. Feathered bangs covered half her face, her eyes as blue as Lake Superior.

The blonde' full lips were set in a dreamy smirk. She stalked onto the bed like a prowling feline and kneeled next to the brunette. Then she hugged the brunette from behind, her hair draping over the brunette's shoulders.

"I love you, Stacey," the blonde said.

"You're so sincere," Stacey muttered, her tongue warm and serpentine on Matt's neck.

The blonde kissed the nape of Stacey's neck and bundled her hair with a gentle, smooth motion.

Matt couldn't believe this was happening. These were classy women, not the kind you find clinging to rock stars in their trailers. They weren't going to fuck him because he was famous. They didn't want him because he was rich. He had neither. These women just wanted *him*, period. As he happily watched the women, he had the distinct sensation what they shared was not merely lust, but love. They were in love with each other and maybe they loved him too.

"Turn over," the blonde said to Stacey.

WAKE UP PERVERT! WAKE UP! the little voice said. *We have no time for that. Wake up.*

Matt's eyes opened to fuzzing black and white specks, the kind you see on your TV when the cable isn't plugged in. His head felt like a swollen watermelon. For a moment his thoughts drifted to *The Incident* in high school and the trapped coyote with its head pinned to the earth. The pain must have hammered the coyote's skull the way it now hammered his.

Open your eyes, Matthew, the little voice said. *Open your eyes before something opens them for you.*

He opened his eyelids halfway and peered into the darkness. A cool breeze stung his face, fresh from the Hurons. He found himself squinting at the night sky. No stars, though, just clouds. Crickets sang around him, the first time he'd heard them in days. The orchard grass swayed and caressed him that way it had since he was a little boy.

Matt rubbed his temples. When he pulled his hand back, blood caked his fingertips.

Must have gotten whacked pretty good, he thought. He closed his eyes, not wanting to be alive. *Nice dream, too. Wish I could've finished that one.*

At last he sat up and examined his surroundings. A shape loomed out of the orchard grass before him. The old leaning post.

Look behind you, idiot, the little voice said.

He turned.

Three big crows strutted behind him.

The first thing they go for is the eyes, Matthew, the voice said.

Matt whipped his hand in the air and the crows flew off into the night, cawing with disappointment. They'd have to peck out something else's eyes, perhaps something that wouldn't injure them in the process.

His muscles were rigid and hot-tight and he didn't feel attached to them, like they were chunks of ham stapled to his body. He wondered how much damage the Being was doing to him. There was a limit to the punishment a human could take. The thing had dragged him back through the bog, back to the orchard, and dumped him there like a cat toying with a mouse. *The bitch was back—the bitch of the ten acres.*

Matt stood and his knees wobbled. *Great.* That last hit did a number on his nerves, too. They were frosted, slow, frazzled. He wondered if it was permanent. He'd had his arm fall asleep before, and he'd woken in the night, frightened when he couldn't feel it. But that was because he'd fallen asleep on it.

Matt put one foot in front of the other, testing his strength. He moved okay, but limped. Despite achieving movement, his legs didn't feel right. At all.

Matt reached into his pocket and pulled out his trusty headlamp, then stretched the device onto his head, bloody temples or not. Slowly he scanned the orchard for his knife, then remembered it sunk in the bog when the Being had seized him. Didn't matter. There were other knives in the shack.

At least I don't have to carry that freaking water jug anymore, he thought. He could certainly thank the Being for that. On the way back to the shack, the headlamp beam illuminated his sideways truck. It seemed to wait there for him like an obedient dog.

I'll fix you, he thought.

You need to fix yourself first, the little voice said. *I don't think you can take too many more hits, Matthew.*

He knew this, and he also knew he needed to keep the Being entertained. If he remained still for too long, refusing to play the game, the Being might just finish him off and stalk the Northwoods for a new toy. Maybe that was a good thing. It would end the suffering.

A gnawing pain infiltrated his stomach. Hunger. But he wasn't the only one. Inside the shack, three furry rumps sat on the floor. A bag of Doritos lay shredded, the orange chips scattered across the musty floor. In-between the clicks chitters Matt could hear the little fur balls crunching his food. The raccoons were so enamored with their lucky-luck feast they didn't notice him. At first. When Matt reached the doorway, he stepped aside. His father had always told him *never corner an animal.*

Standing in the doorway and shouting would be mistake #1, his father would say if he were here. This was known as an *Operator Headspace Error* between him, his father, and Ron.

Matt knocked on the logs.

Furry thieves! He shouted.

The raccoons looked up and then slammed into each other. The fattest stumbled into the camp stove table, shaking the silverware drawer. They were all hefty raccoons with big, fat asses.

A second later the raccoons wobbled out in unison, snouts twitching. They veered around him and to the west, up towards the leaning post. One of the raccoons farted repeatedly as it scurried uphill.

Matt had always thought of this place as his one, true home—the place where he felt alive. The Northwoods gave him clarity and purpose, to live for nature and for nature to live for him. But now...Jesus Christ, what the hell was it now? He closed the massive door and secured the bolt.

The raccoons hadn't figured out how to open the cooler, although they were known to do such things. But they'd shredded the Kashi bars. *Damn.* He rooted around, looking for a Kashi bar that wasn't torn apart or coated in slobber. He found one and jammed the bar into his watering mouth.

You need to rebuild strength, the little voice said. *You will never survive this if you don't act like a normal person. Eat, sleep, drink. This isn't the movies where you stay up for five days straight and defeat your foe. You are a biological thing, Matthew, you must obey certain rules to function at acceptable levels...*

Matt finished the snack and fished in the bag for another. This time he found a peanut butter flavor, his favorite.

Next Matt checked for cuts or scrapes that weren't healing. Then he took the hand mirror off the shelf and checked hard to see places. He dabbed hydrogen peroxide on the worst scrapes, then cleaned the caked blood from his temple. And how could he forget the spider bite? The bump had receded and the redness was all but gone. He may have done more damage with the knife than the spider did with its fangs.

Stinging from head to finger, he picked up his backpack and withdrew fresh clothing. His current clothes were... *nasty.* He pulled a pair of blue jeans over his lean, stiff body and then a white t-shirt and red-checkered flannel. Although such a simple act, it went a long way to offering a glimpse of normalcy.

Untiled the voice chimed in, anyway.

They say that red can trigger aggression and passion, the little voice said. *Are you sure that's the best color choice? Is the Puller keeping you alive because something about you didn't offend? Be careful how you present yourself even in these remote woods, my friend.*

I don't give a shit what the Being thinks, he thought. *I need to find a weakness. If red antagonizes the Being, maybe I'm onto something.*

Matt didn't put his boots on. Instead, he set them before the fireplace and started a fire.

He held his hands to the flames, desperate for warmth. He hadn't realized how cold he was.

His fingers burned as they thawed. Nice. His thoughts flickered like the flames, from his family and to the Being.

He wondered why the Being left him alone at night.

A log spit a fire cherry and he dodged it. He picked up the ember with his naked hand and tossed it into the fire. That kind of pain was minuscule compared to what he'd been through. A joke, actually. *Haha, hehe.*

Why didn't the Being bother him at night? He blinked twice in the stillness, and the answer came to him from the tip of a flame: the Being sleeps at night.

Perhaps another test, Matthew? the little voice asked. *You could run out of here right now, full speed and maybe get out before the Puller knows you're gone.*

Matt felt the bump on his temple. He didn't want another knock, not today. And besides, he wasn't sure he'd survive any more of those. Also, how many escape attempts would the Being tolerate? Perhaps its quota changed based on mood. He'd forced the Being to search for him far and wide the last 24 hours. He didn't need the Being more angry than it already was. Oh no sir, he didn't need that at all.

Warmth toasted his bones as his skin pulled tight around the cuts and scrapes, the white blood cells fighting, weakening enemy forces. He stood slowly and went to the shelf. At the far end, near the wood-burning stove he found a stack of old newspapers with a yellow sticky note that said DO NOT THROW OUT. He pulled them down and returned to the fire.

They were newspaper clippings from across the U.P. Some of them contained local fishing stories which Ron and his father had enjoyed. Ron was even pictured in one of the clippings holding a trophy steelhead from the lower Black. Ron was wearing his aviator shades, cigarette tucked between his ear—a Ron trademark. The birch and pine of the lower Black framed him, and as Matt examined the photo, he smelled the air down there—the thickness of it amongst the seagulls and chokeberry bushes. Soon his eyes pooled with moisture, and the paper shook in his hand. He really missed his father and Ron. They'd taught him a great may things, but most of all he missed the humor.

One of the clippings covered the Michigan moose reintroduction. It featured a photo of a moose being dragged through the air by a helicopter: *Moose Are Back, read the caption.* The moose's legs dangled above the canopy and its head drooped—the effects of high dose tranquilizer.

He clenched the newspaper, wrinkling it. He thought of the moose which had tried to get inside the shack, how it desperately smashed against the logs only to be dragged off by something it could sense but not see.

Matt gazed into the fire, the softwood popping and crackling. His damp boots sizzled from the heat. The flames brightened the shack, making the slate rocks and stones look like a museum exhibit his mother used to take him to back in Chicago. *Old Town,* they'd called it. He remembered the quaint historic shops with no one in them except mannequins dressed for the time period. The streets were a buttery-looking cobblestone with frozen horse-drawn carriages here and there. Victorian street lamps lit the way with warm orbs. The memory always started with his mom walking by his side, handing him pieces of sesame candy.

Old Town was at the back of the museum—which one he couldn't be sure. All those big Chicago museums merged as one in his memories. Either way, Old Town was hidden away from the main attractions. Old Town was dark enough that such a thing would never be allowed today for fear of public safety. You couldn't buy anything at Old Town and you couldn't enter the stores, either. He could hear the clacking of shoes on cobblestone and the pre-recorded horse noises coming out of the carriage moldings as he and his mother walked past. Old Town only had one road and it didn't go very far. It dead-ended into a black papier-mâché wall. Tall curtains raised to the ceiling alongside it, obscuring the inner-workings of the museum. The papier-mâché wall had bulged as if consisting of boulders. A mannequin newspaper boy stood next to the wall holding a stack of papers, one held high in the air, front page facing the town.

Matt remembered his mom commenting on how dark it was. *Sometimes the darkness can be good,* she'd told him, walking past the gaslight glow windows of the Old Town post office. *The rest of the museum is so bright, honey. This is a nice place to take a break,* she'd said. He remembered the prerecorded sound the carriage rider announcing arrival into Old Town: *Whoa thar ponies! Whoa thar! By golly, we're at Old Town. Johnson, grab the luggage.*

The Old Town exhibit didn't last long. It was replaced by an interactive science section, lit with clinical mercilessness. Bright and shiny drew a crowd. Most visitors walked right passed Old Town as if it were a storage closet.

On their last visit, his mother had expressed disappointment when she realized Old Town was gone. To her, it was a place to escape, to get out from the sun, away from the magnifying glass of life. She had that look people get when hit with sudden disappointment, a pause that lingers a little too long, and finally a blink.

Old Town was only sixty yards or so of street. In some ways he *was* in Old Town, except here the fake rock wall was the Being. He longed for the papier-mâché wall and the mannequin paper boy. He longed for the voice of his mother, guiding him down the dim streets, pre-recorded piano music playing from the saloon as they walked past. He longed for understanding. Most of all, he wanted to *live*.

Sometimes the dark is a good thing, honey.

The Being rested at night.

You haven't tested the Puller at night, Matthew, the little voice said. *But I wouldn't bet on it. And what if...what if the Puller doesn't like it when you run at night? What if it decides to kill you right then and there? Maybe it's best not to test this theory.*

If he couldn't run at night, maybe he could work on other things. He stood and limped to the front window. His truck appeared, lying on its side like a defeated triceratops.

I need to get that thing upright, he thought. This struck a note like the melody of his mother's voice calling him home for dinner on a summer evening—*it's getting late.*

He *needed* his truck.

If anything else, he knew that now, and he was also certain he couldn't outrun the Being, ever. The truck, as fucked up as it was, was his only shot.

Matt's gaze shifted to the dead oak. Something the size of a small man perched on a broken limbs, head turning. A Great Grey owl. A blast of wind swayed the grass below the tree and the owl dropped off, sinking down into the bowl out of sight.

The thought of the carriage rider in Old Town came again, crackling audio through cheap speakers: *Whoa thar horses! Whoa!*

Matt reached deep inside his backpack, and pulled out his Canon S2 camera. The batteries were fresh, and he thanked himself for replacing them before the trip. He'd hoped this trip would be a chance to improve his camera skills. But he didn't take the camera from the bag because of pictures. Nope. Not at all. The feature he craved was the ability to record *audio*. He dove into the menu, thumbing the tiny buttons. Then he pressed the *record* switch and spoke into the S2:

Testing, testing one, two, three. Testing, testing one, two, three.

He pressed the stop button, then pressed the play button and set the volume to high. The audio played back loud enough to be heard across the orchard. A grin crossed his face.

Diversion, Matthew? the little voice asked.

Oh yes, he said. Matt didn't think the Being would let him get his truck upright. He'd almost gotten away the last time in it—at least he made it much farther than other attempts. He realized he was going to need something, anything to distract. The camera was one piece in the puzzle.

And how do you plan to get the truck upright? Rent a tractor? the voice asked.

This was an excellent question despite the sarcasm. The key to getting the truck upright was to give it just enough of a push so gravity would take care of the rest. But how? He didn't have the strength. Only the strongest man had a chance.

Matt stared out into the darkness. He no longer considered the night gloomy. As far as he was concerned, it was now a time of peace.

Somewhere in the orchard the Being rested. It was time for him to rest, too. In all this excitement he'd forgotten how bad his head pounded, each throb worse than the last. But *so what*.

He pressed record and spoke into the camera. When he was done, he sat cross-legged on the floor before the fire, camera in hand. He sighed and set the camera down, orange glow reflecting on the shiny back panel. Then he thumbed through the menus and found the play button.

His voice crackled out of the device and he smiled. His eyes caught the fire, flames dancing in their smooth, glossy surface. He didn't remember what he spoke into the camera, but as the audio played back, it became clear.

Whoa thar ponies. Whoa there! By Golly, we're at Old Town. Johnson, grab the luggage!

The Last One - 1928

Buzz Hawkins swung the axe into the stump two feet from his quiet photographer pal Aaron. Aaron covered his face with his hands.

Buzz laughed.

"You bastard," Aaron said.

"Come on, let's go. Mornin's always best," Buzz said, rolling up the sleeves on his khaki camp shirt. His face was rugged and tan, his hair thick black.

A 1925 Model T Ford truck rolled into camp, the engine coughing up smoke. Four hounds lurched in the bed, heads tilting and tongues lolling.

Aaron hoisted his Krauss Eka camera with the Tessar lens as the driver of the truck greeted them.

"Hey dar fellas, good morning to both of you!" the driver said. He was an older man with a plaid cap and a cob pipe wedged between his thick lips.

"Aye, good morning to you, Leaf," Buzz said. "Nice hounds you got here. I'll be honored to hunt by their side."

Buzz sauntered to the truck bed and patted the hounds one by one. After all, they'd be the ones doing the heavy lifting this morning. After greeting the dogs, Buzz entered his canvas tent and exited with the day's lunch packs and his Mauer Special Range rifle.

Aaron got inside Leaf's truck, his photo gear piled on top of him. The last thing he wanted was to get it wet, and damned if it always didn't rain this close to Lake Superior.

Leaf handed each man a steaming cup of coffee and they all shook hands. There was a distinct trace of electricity in the air. Aaron could taste it on his tongue like moonshine.

Buzz jumped onto the bed and smacked the flank of the tuck with an open hand. "Let her roll," he said.

Leaf leaned out the window with his tweed cap and cob pipe. Then he gave a thumbs up, clenching his teeth around the pipe stem. The hounds lurched back and forth, tongues flapping. Buzz stood on the bed, balancing himself on the black metal roof.

As they drove through the logging camp, canvas tents stretched for a hundred yards in all directions. The smells of fire, coffee, and cornbread wafted through the clutter. A brown haze clung to camp, present even when the wind howled. They'd gotten used to it. A track of railroad dead-ended into camp, but there were no trains today. The raging Erickson Fire had crossed the tracks four miles east. Stacks of old growth logs piled high into the sky, mostly red pine, white pine, and hemlock. Some of the trunks measured ten feet across.

Two miles east of camp, flames rose above the canopy as black smoke billowed into the sky. Sporadic gunshots came from far off as loggers shot animals fleeing the flames. Camp nights were raucous contests to see who had the biggest elk, caribou, lynx, bear, or mountain lion. The mountain lion always drew the most attention, and always guaranteed a winner. But no one had killed a mountain lion in at least a year. It was discussed that they might be gone.

The Model T drove for an hour along the big lake and turned up a fresh cut road, its tires jumping erratically on the washboard surface. The road was steep here, steeper than most new roads. All around them lay stumps as far as the horizon. When the truck crested the hill, Buzz tapped the roof with his open hand.

"Leaf, is this the new Julip grade?" he asked.

"That it is. Cut her eight months ago," Leaf said.

It didn't look like very good land, Aaron thought.

Buzz sighed from behind them.

Sensing the concern, Leaf responded. "We have a ways to go, Buzz. Where we're goin' the country is still untouched."

Buzz tapped the truck again. "Very good, very good. On with it then."

Leaf leaned back in his seat, put the truck in gear, and drove south up Julip Road.

Nothing but stumps.

Way back to the east a few hemlock and white pine loomed above the Black River Canyon, protected by direct orders from the state. They didn't want to scare away the tourists, wanted to keep the rivers looking nice.

After a half hour the road narrowed and hefty slate boulders protruding from the grade. The truck shook as it hit them, and Aaron worried about his gear. A few moments later the pleasant spice of sweet gale wafted towards him, and he knew a stream was close. To his right a considerable hill rose up to undulating sections of land, now stumps. It was a unique piece of high ground in these parts.

Buzz tapped on the truck and the vehicle groaned to a halt.

"I'd like to get a bearing," Buzz said.

"You're the boss, eh," Leaf said.

Leaf pulled the truck to the side of the road, got out, and walked to the bed.

"Come on boys, lets stretch them legs." The hounds jumped down, twirled, and panted by their master's side.

The men and the hounds walked up the hill towards the open piece of land.

Buzz halted at the top, his mouth agape. "You folks believe this view?"

"Beaut' isn't she?" Leaf said. The dogs panted at his feet and seemed to enjoy the view as well.

They looked out over a valley of stumps, and beyond that to the Huron Mountains. The exposed rock outcroppings held uncut hemlock and white pine.

"There she is," Buzz said, pointing at the ruggedness. "The home of the last mountain lion."

Leaf nodded in agreement and lit his pipe.

Buzz turned to Aaron, who was gawking at the view. "You going to take the photograph?"

Aaron shook his head. Although he respected Buzz, the tone of his voice could annoy. "Don't I always? What do you think I dragged this contraption up here for?"

Leaf snickered, and Buzz shot him a look.

"Let's get on with it," Buzz said, walking away. "I'm off to find that stream. I think it's on the other side of the grade."

"*That* stream is known as the Black," Leaf said before putting his lips to his pipe.

After a few minutes of absorbing the view, Aaron and Leaf headed downhill, the hounds on their heels.

At the truck, Buzz drank from a beading canteen, then handed the others theirs.

"Wonderful country, eh lads?" he said. "The river was just over there. No trout but the water was good n' clear."

Leaf nodded. "A man could not see finer."

Aaron lumbered into the passenger seat, his gear smashing into the window frame. He grumbled as sweat beaded on his face. Perhaps the fires and the heat were finally getting to him.

Buzz stood on the bed, balancing on the hood with both arms, rifle slung on his back. He reached into his shirt pocket and took his Camels, his Ronson chromium-plated cigarette lighter strapped to the pack with a fat rubber band. He quickly tilted his head down, trying to align cigarette to flame as the truck lurched. It took him five tries.

Progress was slow, the road no wider than the truck now.

I can walk faster than this, Aaron thought.

As if reading his mind, Buzz tapped the truck and Leaf slowed down.

"This is it," Buzz said. "We can make better time on foot."

Leaf spit onto the road. "There's a turnout ahead. Five more minutes, eh?"

After several minutes of verifiable truck-abuse, they reached the pullout, no more than a six foot wide gravel swath just off the main "road". Soon the men were slinging on their packs and canteens. Leaf draped a pair of black Zeiss binoculars around his neck.

Once comfortable with their gear, they hiked up the narrow road, boots trudging. The road carved around the base of a hulking granite mountain, then narrowed into a sliver.

"You always hear about *the end of the road*, fellas," Leaf said.

They chuckled and Buzz gave him a pat on the back.

The hounds sniffed the ground wildly, and Leaf threw an arm high, pointing up the granite mountain.

"Go get her boys. Go! Get on, get on!" He unlatched their collars and the hounds sprinted away, noses to the ground. Leaf watched them with the eyes of loving parent as they hustled up the outcroppings.

They followed the hounds throughout the late morning, making acceptable time for such rugged terrain. They climbed each granite shelf with labored breath, paused, and moved on to the next. When they reached the top, Buzz looked behind them.

"I've seen some views," Buzz said. "But this?"

"We must've climbed at least fifteen hundred feet," Aaron said.

"Wait till you see the view of the other valley, eh?" Leaf said with a gleam in his eye.

A group of stunted white pine clung to the mountain, growing out of a soil-catching depression in the granite. The men hiked across to the southern rim, glorious, cool wind rustling their hair.

"Tell me what you think of that, eh?" Leaf said.

Fifteen hundred feet below them a forest of virgin hemlock, red pine, and white pine choked the valley full. A series of granite mountains punched through the virgin forest, and trees clung to the domes, thinning as elevation increased.

"My God, Leaf. My God! We haven't gotten these yet."

"No we have not," Leaf said. "And by the looks of it, we may never. The company doesn't want to shoulder the cost of exploding all this granite to get a road in here."

"Jesus," Aaron said. "Is this how it used to look before us?"

"Yup," Leaf said.

Aaron's stomach churned and he felt a tinge of embarrassment.

Below them, down in the old growth forest, the hounds barked and howled, the cacophony rising up out of two hundred foot trees. The tree tips swayed in the breeze, and a goshawk watched them from a high, sun-dried branch. They might have been the first people it ever saw.

"They've picked up a scent, boys," Leaf said.

"Good. Lets not pass any more time up here then, lads," Buzz said.

Aaron looked down into the valley and frowned. "Maybe we shouldn't be doing this, fellas. Maybe we're supposed to leave this place alone."

Buzz looked at him, his widening eyes warning of a slap to the back of the head. Buzz would laugh, tell him it was a play slap, but there was just enough English to send a message.

Leaf raised the binoculars and they all went quiet, following his direction. The noon sun baked them through the layers of haze.

"There—the closest granite knob," Leaf said, pointing with his pipe. He handed the binoculars to Buzz, and Buzz swung them to his face with the precision of a combat officer.

"Yes, I see it. A fine trophy."

A mountain lion jumped from boulder to boulder, working up the granite dome between red pines. The hounds barked a hundred yards behind it, at the edge of the forest where it met granite slope.

The men worked their way down the first mountain. Each step brought them closer to the canopy, and finally they descended into the cool forest.

"Big woods," Buzz said, before drinking from his Army issue canteen.

"The biggest, eh?" Leaf said.

"Here's to Leaf and his well-trained hounds," Buzz said, tipping his canteen Leaf's way.

Leaf smiled and nodded with the cob pipe clenched between his teeth.

Aaron studied his fresh surroundings, mesmerized by the old growth forest. Slick moss draped the logs and rocks like the finest carpet. Squirrels chattered in the trees and the stillness pushed onto him.

They moved southwest, then stopped to fill their canteens in a creek. Spike Rush bunched up to the water's edge and chunky brook trout nipped the surface for bugs that dropped from the grass. The little rising circles trailed downstream, more apparent in the delicate crepuscular rays that pierced the canopy here and there.

"Last of the old country, eh?" Leaf said. "You won't find better."

Buzz moved well ahead of them now, his strength and speed superior as always. The hounds barked up ahead, each bark rising in intensity. Buzz gained speed and disappeared. Leaf shot Aaron a confused look.

"He always does that," Aaron said.

"I should have known, eh?" Leaf said. "Men like him—they do what they want when they want. I've seen my share of go-getters while guiding, and he's full of it all. This is why you two are friends?"

"They say opposites attract. Buzz helps me get photos I like, and I help him document."

"He bullies you, eh?"

"It's not always like that. He turns controlling on the hunts. It's part of him I accept. We all have our flaws."

"Yes we do, boy. Some more than others."

Aaron grunted as he shifted the wooden tripod across his shoulder. His canteen jangled in front of him and he swung an arm out, catching it, untwisting the cap and bringing it to his mouth. His light blonde locks lay clumped with sweat across his forehead. "How many mountain lions have your hounds treed?" Aaron asked.

"At least two dozen," Leaf said. Leaf lifted his cap, waving it at what few white hairs remained on his freckled scalp.

"How many have they lost?"

Leaf squinted into the canopy. "Plenty. The lion is a crafty animal, eh? Many go into the bogs and that's that."

"I've have hunted large swaths of the U.P. with Buzz," Aaron said. "We know this might be a last refuge, right. I guess my question is how many of the big cats are left?"

"You just saw it," Leaf said.

Aaron turned to Leaf, checking his face for a hint of sarcasm. There was none.

"How can that be? The country is wide, endless."

"Yes but the woods are gone in many places, and not all contain these granite mountains, eh? Roads cut through everything now except for the ground yer standing on."

Aaron's gentle mouth twisted into a frown. Chills crossed his back. *Everything they were doing, everything they had done was wrong,* he thought. These woods should not fall to the axe. This last lion should not fall to the rifle. He spit into the moss, trying to cleanse the bad taste from his mouth.

Buzz's voice floated back to them. "The hounds have her, up the mountain!"

Aaron and Leaf bolted through the forest and came upon the wall of granite. Then they picked their way up each boulder and ledge.

Above them, Buzz climbed the granite mountain like a bear, rifle in his right hand. Seventy yards ahead the hounds barked frantically. The trees thinned here, only growing in sandy pockets of soil collected in the crevasses. The hounds had their hinds to Buzz, muzzles jerking up and down. They retreated, attacked, and retreated again.

They had the lion trapped against a granite shelf.

A hound leapt forward and the mountain lion swatted at it, hissing and baring fangs. The lion's aquamarine eyes bored into the hounds with complete condescension, knowing full well it could take them all. As the lion caught a glimpse of Buzz, its eyes changed.

Buzz raised his rifle.

The mountain lion leapt forward, knocking a hound to the granite with a single, outstretched paw. The struck hound whimpered and the other hounds cleared like bowling pins. Buzz pulled the trigger and a puff of fine granite powder rose behind the lion. He shot again, hitting more rock, the bullet ricocheting off the mountain past his ear.

The lion, sensing an opening, leapt twenty feet and pounced on Buzz. The rifle clanked to the granite, useless. Buzz screamed and covered his face. The lion's claws shredded his shirt and gouging chunks from his torso. He screamed like a child, his face contorted with shock. Without hesitation the lion bit down, catching Buzz's left hand. Buzz pulled his arm back, screaming. But his hand did not come back with his arm. Buzz's missing hand flopped to the granite, the fingers twitching like spider legs. Blood sprayed from the stump, staining the muzzle of the big cat.

"It got my hand—it got my hand! It's gone! It's gone!"

Aaron vomited when he saw all the blood. Some of the blood pooled in a rocky depression, like a miniature Black River. Buzz sat there, rocking back and forth, holding the stump with his right hand.

Aaron turned and saw the lion bounding up mountain, its black-tipped tail disappearing between two boulders. Then he slid his belt off and bent down to Buzz.

"Take a deep breath. You need to calm down. I'm going to stop the bleeding, do you understand?"

Buzz rocked back and forth, gibberish and spittle flying from his lips.

"Calm," Aaron said. "You'll make the bleeding worse."

Buzz continued to rock, spouting nonsense.

Aaron cocked his arm back and hit Buzz in the chin as hard as he could. Buzz went limp and slouched to the mountain. Then Aaron wrapped his belt just above Buzz's elbow and cinched as tight as he could, keeping tension by pushing down on Buzz's shoulder.

"Hang in there buddy," Aaron said.

Leaf looked around, stunned.

"Leaf—are you with me? Leaf?"

"Need to round up my hounds," Leaf muttered. He walked away in a daze, then regained some vigor. "Come on, boys, get back now, you hear! Get on back!" Leaf clapped his hands and whistled, but the hounds did not return. Barking came from up mountain, as if cast down from the skies.

"We need to get him back to the truck *now*," Aaron said. "We can get your hounds later. They can handle themselves, right? I can get my camera gear later, too. You hear me, Leaf?"

Leaf looked up the mountain, his upper lip quivering, pipe clutched in his right hand.

"You take his legs, I'll take his torso," Aaron said.

They maneuvered back through the old growth forest, the hemlocks and white pine rising to formidable heights, shafts of light cutting through where it could. Buzz's face had taken a bad color, but they moved on, determined. They reached the base of the first mountain and worked up, zigzagging along the granite. When they crested the mountain a sea of stumps spread out below them, the horizon filled with flame and smoke. They struggled their way down and laid Buzz in the bed of the truck. Aaron took to his side, applying pressure to the wound.

"Hang in there," he said. "These woods aren't done with you yet."

***

A year later, a lone trapper told the patrons of a popular watering hole he heard four hounds barking on that first night, and one hound on the fourth.

Wrigley Field
Eight Months Ago

Big John Kearns coughed into his hand. Matt watched to make sure there was no blood. An obese woman sitting next to his father stared, and Matt stared back. His father adjusted his Cubs hat and returned his gaze to the game. A pair of seagulls glided over the field and landed in the empty upper deck, searching for scraps.

Eric Johnson, the Cubs shortstop was up to bat. No one was on base. The Cardinals pitcher, a lanky flamethrower, reared back. The baseball popped into the catcher's mitt and the ump signaled strike three.

The scent of warm pretzel dough and stale beer wafted down to them from the concourse. The wind blew out to center field, rippling the series of flags behind the bleachers.

His father coughed again and Matt cringed.

"The damn Cubs," his father said. "Not sure why I wanted to do this."

Matt turned to him. "It's the Cubs, dad. The important thing is that we got to do this."

Going to one last Cub's game was his father's wish. He'd chosen them among a myriad of activities in what was shaping up to be a losing fight against lung cancer.

"These guys can't even hit the baseball," his father said. "Don't they have the highest payroll in the league?"

Matt laughed and patted his father on the back.

"Come on now, you don't have to get all sentimental," his father said. "Just cause I'm dying is no reason to slather me with affection."

"You're not dying," Matt said, knowing full well this would be their last Cubs game.

"Well that's good to know," his father said sarcastically.

Matt smiled. His old man was still a smart ass, even now. Big John Kearns, hiker of the U.P. wilds, former smoker of Marlboro Reds. Big John Kerns, soon to be six feet under. The smile turned to a frown.

A popcorn vender stalked up the stairs past his seat and Matt paid for a super-sized bag. He grabbed a handful of the salty treat and held the bag out for his father.

"No thanks," his father said. "Not much of an appetite."

Matt nodded. The Cardinals were batting and had a runner at third with nobody out. The sky was a deep blue—as deep blue as Chicago got. Matt tasted the Lake Michigan water in the air. It permeated everything down here. The big lake always made its presence known. It was the giver of life in this area, and he often wondered why people didn't hold church on its shores every Sunday, thanking it. It was the life-giver, and it was real. You could touch it, feel it, jump into it. If you were good enough, you might swim up to the even bigger Lake Superior. Hell you could swim to the shack if you wanted to.

His father turned to him. "Thinking about up north again, aren't you?"

"How'd you know?"

"You always get that look in your eye. It's easy to spot. And maybe I *will* have some of that popcorn." His father dug out a handful and popped a few kernels into his mouth.

The Cardinals knocked in the runner on third with a sacrifice fly. The crowd quieted and the wind swirled across the upper deck.

"It's funny, isn't it?" his father said, gazing out at the horizon.

"What's funny?" Matt asked.

"How two places can be so different. Look around you, at all the buildings. Then think of up north, and how there are almost no people."

Matt nodded and chewed.

"The Huron Mountains are about a hundred thousand acres, and that's close to the size of this *county*," his father said in-between swallows of popcorn. "There are maybe a dozen people in the Hurons. There are a couple million here. Crazy if you think about it."

He agreed.

"You've got people shooting each other here for pennies. Up there, you've got none of that. Which makes me think it's all a people problem. All of it."

Matt watched a seagull arc the field.

The Cardinals knocked in two more runs, and the Cubs manager came out of the dugout to remove the pitcher.

Matt's father stared at the sky. A roar shook the stands, and an F-18 buzzed the field. The crowd applauded.

"I hate that jingoistic crap. Waste of gas, too. Are we North Korea now? Next thing you know, they'll start parading missiles and tanks around."

Matt chuckled and dug deeper into the popcorn. His father was on a roll.

Big John waited for the jet engine to fade. "Not everything is as it seems," he said, turning to Matt. "There are things out there bigger than all of us."

Matt's chewing slowed and he watched his father's big, blue eyes.

"Did I ever tell you about the time Ron and I caught that monster steelhead at lower Black Falls?"

Matt shook his head.

"You know how the falls are. Ron had put a size eight stimulator right behind the vertical logs. He was always a hell of a fisherman."

His father coughed again.

"The steelhead hit the fly and escaped the pool and headed downriver like a torpedo. We had to chase it through those jagged slate grooves and we almost slipped and killed ourselves. A hundred yards downstream it snagged on a submerged log. It wrapped so much line around the log it was caught like a dog to a lazy neighbor's tree. There was only a foot of line and the steelhead just swam there in the clear water, all forty inches. I tell you what, it was absolutely beautiful with the sun glinting off its flank. Ron and I watched it for a minute. It was like a jewel, Matt. A living, breathing jewel."

His father paused and gripped his cane.

"So what happened to it?" Matt asked.

"A minute later it broke off and swam downstream to Superior. It was the biggest fish we'd ever caught or seen in years of fishing the Black. But that's not what's important. While it was caught there, glinting in the light, I saw time curling off its fins in that pure water. Layers and layers of time. I saw beauty. I thought of your mother. I thought of you. I thought of Andrea and even Elmo."

"Dad—"

"—we are a moment, Matthew. And the best of that moment was my family."

Big John trembled and reached to hug his son. Matt gripped him, spilled his popcorn, and sobbed.

"You are *my* jewel. And soon here I'm going to watch you swim away, downstream. I'll be with you again, down at the big lake."

The crowd roared as Bobby Edstrom hit a double off the ivy.

Matt held his father and cried. And in him he felt the wild Northwoods and the beating heart of a lion.

Day 5

Matt Kearns bolted upright, police sirens faint in the distance. They came from down near Lake Superior, far to the north. At first he felt hope, but that turned into a sick feeling in his stomach. He didn't want them to come at all. Up here was death—or prison. They'd speed up here, deep into the woods, not realizing their blaring sirens were their funeral songs. Sure, if they did come, he might be able to use them as a distraction, but for how long?

Who cares? Let them come. Use any distraction you can, Matthew, the little voice said. *If they die, they die. You have no way of preventing that.*

I didn't do so well in the bog, Matt said.

You avoided the Puller for a day, the little voice said. *That's the best you have done so far.*

Best? he asked. *Yippee. I was just a dog on a longer leash.*

It was good practice and a lesson. You would be wise to remember it, the voice said.

He walked over to the window above the grungy couch and yanked the chair. The crusty nails groaned and bent and the chair gave way.

He didn't need it anymore. What he needed was to see.

Matt looked out at the big aspen and the outhouse. No sign of the Being, no sign of anything. He opened the shack door and urinated in the orchard grass. A cool breeze swept across the land, refreshing the still air and ushering images of lit pumpkins and laughter in the streets.

Matt limped up to the leaning post and gazed across the southern valley. The trees had begun to turn, their color morphing from green to saturated reds and yellows. The beauty almost made him forget his predicament for a moment, as wild and impossible and hopeless as it was. Denial was a heavy dose of comfort.

He grabbed the handles of the wheelbarrow and turned it down the path towards the shack. On the western wall of the shack he found a shovel behind the firewood, blade rusted but solid. He placed the shovel in the wheelbarrow and rolled it downhill to Julip Road. When he reached the road, he noticed several fallen aspen crossing the road seventy yards to the north, their cracked trunks white and fleshy. The downed trees were absent of chew marks from beavers, the only thing that caused a tree to fall like that other than wind.

Oh we know it's not a beaver, the little voice said. *Why would a beaver try and dam a road? Pull your head out of your ass, Matthew.*

"Go fuck yourself," he said. Matt forced the wheelbarrow into the thick ferns on the eastern side of the road, his teeth clenched.

The downed trees made him feel more isolated than he already was. If the Being did lay those trees, what was it protecting? What was the point? Was he that important? He doubted it. He was just a play thing, not food—*at least not yet.* One thing was certain—the downed trees were the action of a territorial creature. He shivered from his core and dropped the wheelbarrow handles.

What if there are other Beings?

Why else would it employ territorial behavior? His stomach gurgled and bile rose in his throat. He swallowed it down, pushing the thought away.

Please don't let that be true. Please.

The wheelbarrow snagged on the Goldie's ferns as they wrapped in the wheel spindle. Matt jammed it through like a fork through a salad. Bird sound echoed to the east, maybe a boreal chickadee. He maneuvered the wheelbarrow in-between the boot-snatching springs towards the Black. Then he removed his boots, took the shovel, and worked down into his half of the river, careful not to go any further. The cold rush groped him as he jammed the shovel blade beneath a rock. Air pockets welled up to the surface and floated downstream, disintegrating before his eyes. He reached into the icy water, pulled out a hunk of slate, and placed it on the steep bank. He thought of how the original landowners did the same many years ago when they built the fireplace. There was a sense of connection, of history repeating itself. He thought of his father and Ron doing the same thing for the fire pit and walkway.

Hey dad, I'm passing along the tradition, he said.

Fog ensconced the land as he pulled up boulder after boulder. Sometimes when he lifted a rock chubs darted away. He didn't see any brook trout. They were smart enough to stay away and probably a mile downriver by now.

Fog filtered through the aspens and maples like woodsmoke. The ferns were buried in it, which meant he was, too. At one point he had to reach through fog to sink his hand into the Black.

Soon the police sirens faded to nothing. A gray jay called from the east, back over the series of s-turns the Black made in this winding stretch. Leaves fluttered in the breeze above the layer of fog, the fresh greens of summer now encroached by red and yellow. Matt paused in the river, listening, sweating, eyes scanning. He knew the Being was watching him. Matt was sure if he stepped ten more feet across the river, he'd be pulled back. He didn't want any of that today (or ever). There was work to do.

Beat, he sat on the steep bank and admired his collection of boulders and rocks. Sunlight filtered through the fog in jagged shards, gleaming off the multihued rocks.

This should do it, he thought. He wiped his sweaty hair out of his eyes, lifted a boulder, and placed it in the wheelbarrow. The pudgy tire sunk down and the handles creaked as he rammed the loaded wheelbarrow through the vegetation. On the road, he stopped and studied the downed trees.

Maybe if those patrol cars had come a bit closer he might've...

You could use another distraction, the little voice said. *You may not have appreciated the bog, but you were free. I say let them come.*

He shook his head at no one and pushed across the road up the steep driveway. When he reached the truck he tried to dump the wheelbarrow sideways, but the right handle almost ripped off. So he stopped and unloaded the boulders one by one next to his old pickup. When he finished, he returned to the Black and retrieved the rest of the boulders, also dumping them near the pickup.

Sucking air and sweaty, he went into the shack and sat on a chair. He chugged water from a jug and ate saltine crackers and peanut butter. He didn't bother to use a knife, instead sticking the flimsy saltines into the jar, breaking most of them as he tried to scoop. Then he licked the peanut butter from his fingers, feeling a rush of energy. Satisfied, he pulled out the mangy box from under the bottom bunk and rummaged through it. He took duct tape, rope, and twine. Then he hoisted the dusty rope on his shoulder, took a knife from the hutch, and walked back to his old trusty truck, the one his father had so proudly handed him the day he got his driver's license. Five years ago now. So long ago, fading taillights on a dark highway.

He rolled out a long section of twine and cut it with the knife. Matt then wrapped the twine around the rusty truck frame closest to the passenger side door. This was repeated in four sections down the frame to the rear bumper, allowing multiple strands of twine to hang a few feet. He went back inside the shack and took one of the spotty blankets from Sucker's Bunk. Then he cut the blanket in half and did the same with the middle bunk blanket. When he finished the alterations (as his mother would say) he brought them out into the day, laying them flat upon the grass.

A demented picnic, he thought.

Matt cut holes one foot inside each blanket corner and wrapped duct tape through the inside of each hole, reinforcing them. He dragged a blanket corner towards one of the twine sections and tied the dangling threads to each corner. The blanket looked like an upside down parachute. He repeated this for the rest of the frame, using three corners of a blanket in two twine sections. When he finished he stepped back and examined his handy work. His truck looked like the world's worst parade float, decorated by the insane and feeble.

Then he bent down and picked up one of the boulders, placing it carefully inside the blanket pouch near the rear bumper. The twine creaked and groaned, but held. He reached out and plucked the twine like a harp string and it made a sour note. Next he filled the back blanket pouch with boulders and it sagged, the twine ripping into the tape.

He pushed the wheelbarrow back down to the Black. At midafternoon he placed the last boulder in the blanket pouch closest to the engine compartment. All pouches held, and looked like lead-filled balloons crashing to Earth.

He trudged into the shack and drank more water and ate more peanut butter, his upper back aching with each swallow. When he finished, he laid on the bottom bunk and stretched, his feet touching the logs.

Okay, you've got the weights in place. Now how do you plan to pull that thing down? he thought.

You can't do it, Matthew, the little voice said. *You're going to need help. Go on, go out there, tie the rope to the frame and see what happens. Give it a pull. Waste your time and energy on that. And speaking of energy, how much food do you have left? It can't be much.*

He wasn't worried about food. If he ran out, the orchard was full of tart apples. Sure, they might be dried and shrunken and horrible, but they were still sustenance. There were hundreds of the tart bastards littering the ground—enough to last for weeks.

Matt tied a section of thick rope to the rusty frame—right in the middle of the blanket pouches. The knot was almost impossible to tie. Then Matt walked the rope out to the big aspen and wound it around the trunk. Passing the trunk, he walked the rope halfway back to the truck. All he needed was a good pull and gravity would do the rest, right? The hanging weights should improve his chances, although he wasn't certain. His limbs tingled with anticipation. This could be it. *IT.* He had a feeling. He also had a feeling The Being was watching him.

He sighed, wrapped the end of the rope around his waist and gripped it with both hands. Then he pulled and watched the rope pick up slack. As he dug his heels in, his neck veins bulged. The truck didn't budge.

Matthew! Go inside now! the little voice said.

And then he heard it, booming footsteps and chopping air.

He dropped the rope and locked the huge door behind him. Out the window over the grungy couch, the rope lay slack against the aspen trunk. Then the end of the rope which he'd had around his waist lifted slowly into the air like a cobra out of a wicker basket. The rope hung there, limp end sagging, and then fell to the orchard grass. A groaning noise came from his truck. He turned to the front window and peered in-between the plywood. His poor truck shook and the front passenger tire spun in the air like a puppy doggy-paddling while held over water.

At once the truck stopped shaking. The twine and weights held.

You irritated it, Matthew, the little voice said.

"No shit?" he said.

Maybe you should try this at night, the voice said.

Matt thought of his mother in Old Town.

That's right, Matthew. Darkness isn't always a bad thing. For you Matthew, I think it may be a very good thing.

He glared out the window at his old pickup and clenched his fists. He'd worked his ass off to get those weights and now he was relegated to the shack.

Matt slumped onto the lower bunk and closed his eyes. He did not dream. An hour later he creaked open the massive door and peeked outside. Satisfied, he took a brown paper bag and limped outside, making a conscious effort not to go near the truck, instead heading up the path to the northwest corner of the orchard. Here the neglected apple trees grew thickest. Bushels of tart apples in various stages of decay punctuated the orchard grass. In one patch he found a big pile of bear shit complete with silky covering and buzzing fly groupies. He hoped whatever bear left this gift hadn't been killed by the Being. He had a hunch the Being didn't much care for intruders into its territory. Bears loved the orchard and the apples were an easy meal. They dwelled in the shadows of the neglected trees, their fat rumps high in the air, furry faces soaked with tart apple juice. Now *he* needed to feast on the apples. In the end, he wasn't all that different from the bears. He wondered if the bear that slept by his side in the bog feasted from the orchard.

One by one he snatched the tart apples from their grassy lairs and loaded them into the brown paper bag. He emptied the bag inside the shack and returned to fill it once again.

His work finished, he sat on the bunk and bit into one of the green monsters. His mouth puckered and his cheekbones sucked in. All moisture abandoned his mouth. Grimacing, he swallowed the torturous creation and washed it down with water, amplifying the sourness. And it didn't help that the apples stunk up the shack, too.

Matt looked out the door, frustrated. And then, for the first time since the bog, he contemplated suicide. It wasn't a long, drawn out moody thing. Just a quick flash, a clown's giggle.

Why don't I just take one of those kitchen knives to my wrists right now? He pictured himself panicking in the shack like a chicken on LSD, blood spurting from his wrists. He saw himself twitching on the floor like a mouse at the bottom of the anti-freeze bucket. This seemed far less ideal than the painless, watery death in the bog. Besides, if he did cut his wrists and die, his mother and Andrea would think he killed himself, that he was mentally unstable, that his trip up here was a suicide trip. The Being could have left and they'd never know why he did it. If he left a note describing the torment, that would only offer proof that he was truly insane. He *never, ever* wanted them to think anything along those lines. He loved them so much. If only he could see them again.

He bit into another tart monster, face puckering. The unpleasantness in his mouth pushed aside thoughts of suicide.

Rest and wait, Matthew, the little voice said. *The night time is the right time.*

Matt fetched wood from the side of the shack and split it near the door. Bright, raw shards laced the front walkway like shredded cheese.

He warmed his hands near the fireplace as the sun dipped towards the horizon. When it darkened he stretched his headlamp over his head, flicked the switch, and turned to the dead oak through the doorway. When at last the landscape settled into stillness he quietly approached the truck. Clumsily, he shined the beam across the orchard and up into the forest canopy.

Don't do that, the little voice said. *The last thing you want to do is shine the light around like a panicked hiker. You might have put that right into the Puller's eyes.*

"If it even has eyes," he said.

Matt climbed atop his truck and pried open the door. Then he held it open with one hand and used his other to find the seat lever. His fingers found the smooth metal grip and pulled. The seat loosened and he used his left hand to push the seat forward, keeping it in position with his elbow. He reached for a plastic bundle wrapped tight with a nylon strap and metal fastener. Once the object was secure in his grip, he drew his hand free as the seat slid back. Then he put an end of the bundle in his teeth, using his free had to push back up onto the side of the truck. He left his fingers in place so the door would close without noise. The door pinched his fingers, but anything was better than the alternative.

He jumped down from the truck, careful not to get caught in the twine and pouches. Hunching down on one knee, he unrolled the plastic bundle, revealing a heavy-duty tire change kit. Stumpy metal legs protruded from the bottom of the jack and a robust metal knob with an eye-hook emanated from the middle. A tire iron with a square hole in the middle lay next to the jack, two metal rods next to it. One of the rods featured a hook which attached to the jack opening. He attached the two rods together and put the square end into the tire iron receptacle, careful not to make noise. The last thing he needed was clanking metal. Night sounds seethed and receded around him, a bevy of crickets changing to frogs from Twenty Mile Bog, and then to the flapping wings of night birds over the southern valley.

Not too many days left for that, he thought.

An owl hooted from the north, reminding him he was not alone.

Oh you know you're not alone, Matthew, the little voice said. *The Puller is watching you. But who is watching the Puller?*

Maybe the owl, he thought.

The owl watches everything, doesn't it? the little voice asked.

Matt took the gear to the side of the truck that faced away from the shack. Then he examined the spot where the corner of the truck roof met the ground. He sighed when he realized it was right where the land dipped into the bowl. He'd have to stand on the slope in order for this to work, and he needed to find a suitable spot for the jack, someplace that would give him leverage. Placing the jack under the truck cap he and his father installed might cause the cap to rip off. There's no way it would hold the weight. The best bet was where the driver's side door met the roof. Matt placed the jack and rods on the grassy slope and retrieved the shovel from the wheelbarrow. Then he dug at the ground underneath the driver's side window, enough to allow space for the jack base to slide in. Once in place, Matt thumbed the jack receptacle, raising the telescoping arm so the playing card-sized piece of metal braced against the door and roof frame. He inserted the rod hook into the jack receptacle and twisted the tire iron. The jack rose and the truck groaned. Matt paused and listened for the Being, then gave it a few more twists. At last the jack base found solid footing, and the truck slowly moved up a quarter inch.

Holy cow it's working, he thought.

Darn right it's working, the little voice said. *It's a tire jack. What did you think it would do?*

A few more twists and the truck let out a beast of a moan. It now lay off the ground by a foot. The formerly-compressed grass unwrinkled towards the sky.

Matt paused, trying to hear anything. Had he alerted it? Nope. Just crickets and frogs.

More twists and the jack extended like the neck of a turtle. The roof of the truck was now two feet off the ground, tilted in the direction he wanted. He paused again, holding his breath, perking his ears. Nothing.

You better hurry, the little voice said. How *long do you think that's going to hold?*

The jack began sinking into the soil. Then the top of the jack began to wobble under the weight.

Shit!

Matt ran around the truck to the thick rope, flashlight beam erratic on the grass. The aspen with winding rope looked like one of those haunted spook trails his mother used to take him to on Halloween. He expected something to jump out at him— something bloody and nasty looking.

Oh no, we don't get that treatment here, the little voice said. *We get the super special no-see-um.*

Matt picked up the end of the rope and walked backwards towards his tilted truck. The rope tightened around the aspen as dust particles puffed out from the bark. He pulled, drawing the rope tighter. Then he reached up and flipped off the switch on his headlamp, just in case. He could feel the Being to the north, resting.

You two have spent some time together, the little voice said. *Maybe it's similar to when you get married. You can feel things after a while. Patterns, behavior.*

"Time for a divorce," he said.

Matt lurched back with everything he had, blood rushing to the scrapes and bruises on his body. His boots dug into the grassy soil and his face reddened. The truck moaned behind him like a submarine diving into deep fathoms. He waited for the sound of tires hitting ground but it never came.

Don't let that thing fall back, Matthew! the little voice said. *Let the rope down easy if you have to.*

After slipping on a pair of gloves to protect his blistered hands, Matt inspected the truck. The jack stood strong, sinking into the grass an inch or so but nothing problematic. With the jack stable, Matt limped up to the leaning post and then downhill to the wall of vegetation. A moment later he powered on his Canon S2. A sly grin crossed his face. It was oh-so nice to play offense for a change. He quickly turned the volume full blast and left the camera on an alder branch.

Back near his truck, he wrapped the rope around his waist and walked past the aspen tree to the north, causing the rope to go limp and slide down the trunk.

What are you doing, Matthew? the little voice asked. *You don't have time to waste!*

In a quick motion he pivoted to the truck and ran with all his might, arms pumping in the air. He passed the aspen, tightening the rope. As the rope cinched around his waist he ran harder. The rope tightened more. He grunted and threw himself forward in one last push. Without thinking, he swung around and yanked the rope with the ferociousness of a wolverine. Then he jammed his boot heels into the soil, eyes bulging, muscles ripping.

The truck groaned and creaked.

With no more to give, Matt collapsed onto his back, panting at the night sky. Venus. Breath. Constellation. Breath. There was nothing except the sensation of moving air, and then came a thud followed by chaotic, metallic rattling that shook the orchard. His heart pounded in his throat, but he refused to look behind him.

It flipped down the bowl, didn't it? he thought. Matt rolled onto his stomach and turned on his headlamp.

There she stood, upright, branches protruding from the cap. The truck his father had handed over to him when he first got his license. The truck they had bonded over.

The blanket pouches spilled boulders onto the ground and some of them were stacked under the passenger side tires. The tires were full of air. Lucky.

I said I would fix you, he cried. A tear trickled down his cheek and he wiped it away with an arm made of rubber. There he sat in awe of his old truck. For days it had laid there sideways, a ghastly reminder of his predicament, a tombstone for his suffering. Now she stood tall and proud. All two hundred thousand miles.

As he expected, the ground thundered in a rhythmic pattern, each new shake louder than the last. Matt stood, goose bumps peppering his forearms. As he got to his feet he held his arms out in a Jesus pose, then was slammed to the ground by what felt like a piano from the sky. His lungs expunged all their air, and he thought he heard a low octave note well out of tune before the blackness overtook him. The last thing he saw before entering darkness was the rusted wheel well of his old truck and the grey boulders from the Black.

Day 6

His eyes burned as if dipped in fiberglass. He tried to think of where he was, but nothing came except a loop of neurological dead ends. What was his name? He muttered something unintelligible and listened. A familiar, buzzing sound came from the blackness...a chainsaw. Then came screams. The chainsaw idled out in the fog of time.

Matt's eyes fluttered and he went to black.

He walked into a large, dimly-lit room with muted oil lamps spaced along log walls. A series of square windows on the far wall revealed a dark lake and the silhouettes of fir trees. A Wing and Son piano sat against the left wall, its keys worn and cracked. The wood flooring and wooden tables were all darkly-stained and the place felt like a deconstructed forest reimagined. Thick, Santa Fe-style rugs covered most of the floor. An extensive bar made with thick oak backed up to the square windows. People on the barstools looked out upon the dark water and trees. There must have been thirty of them, all women. "Dear Prudence" played from little black speakers tucked into each corner.

He approached the bar, the music louder, voices chattering in his ears. Matt sat at the far end and looked down the polished wood. The women's faces reflected the warmth of the room and the oil lamps—a pleasant, orange glow. They wore thick sweaters, some colorful. The women all had different hairstyles. Some of them smiled, others looked down at their drinks, wrapping both hands around the glasses and bottles. Some of them were in conversation. He recognized a few as ex-girlfriends.

The young bartender sat on a stool, sleeves rolled up, exposing hairy arms. A white towel hung limp in his left hand as he looked out to the dark lake and forest.

One of the women glanced Matt's way and walked over to him. Short blonde hair framed her china doll nose and full lips. A grey wool sweater hugged her hips, her fingers poking out the long sleeves.

Stacey.

He turned away.

"Matt—is that you?" she asked.

He rotated back towards her, embarrassed at his effort to hide. She held her fingers together monk-like, then pulled them apart and placed them on her hips.

"It is you! My God, it's been so long. What have you been up to?"

He gazed into her eyes, smiling nervously. She always had that effect on him. She'd been the most beautiful girl he'd ever known.

"Pouring foundations. You know, the usual."

She studied his face carefully, her eyes too sincere for this world. "Been taking any trips out west?"

"Nope. I should though." Matt wanted to hide. He wasn't expecting this...to ever see the love of his life again.

Stacey searched his eyes and smiled. "I still think about our trip to Grand Teton. Remember when that squirrel came up to our cabin and ran off with one of our powdered donuts?"

Matt laughed. "Didn't we name him 'Powder'?"

"Yes."

The thoughts of that alpine morning in the Tetons calmed him. He remembered wildflowers sprouting outside their rental cabin and butterflies flittering from one flower to the next, backlit by the sun. It might have been his favorite outdoor moment in his first trip to the Northern Rockies. They'd arrived in the park well after dark, unable to see the landscape until morning. Then they'd opened the door into a sunny alpine world. Matt thought he'd died and gone to heaven. He remembered standing in the doorway, mouth agape, Stacey's hand on his shoulder. *This is what we came for, isn't it*, she'd said, smiling.

"I still remember him running up the path, donut dragging behind him," Stacey said. "When he put it down, his little face was covered in white. And what about that moose, Matt? Do you remember the size of that thing? Geeze, and it came so close to us."

Matt looked into her eyes, measuring the excitement. She was happy to see him again. He was elated to see her—so much so that he was shaking, trying to cover it up with terse comments.

"It was a freak of nature," he said.

"And it had that collar around it. The one they use to track animals for research. Remember the velvety ropes hanging off its antlers? It looked like a Rastafarian moose!" she said, laughing.

"Ja mon, dat moose," Matt said.

Stacey burst out laughing, her pink tongue nestled behind her perfect teeth. She smiled at him. And then her smile faded to a frown.

"So why did we break up again? I was never really sure why."

The jukebox switched to "November Rain" by Guns n' Roses. Matt cleared his throat, searching for the right approach.

"It wasn't because of anyone else, I do know that." His eyes met hers, wanting her to see the truth in them.

"Same here. I've been thinking about it, though. Do you think...do you think it might have something to do with how amazing our trips were, and coming back to the suburbs was such a drag?"

Matt turned to the dark lake and woods. Silvery clouds passed above the tree tops, revealing pointed shapes in the sky. He thought it might be the Tetons.

"That might have something to do with it," he said. "To be honest, I withdrew when my father and Elmo died. I sat in my house for months. I didn't invite anyone over—I didn't want to see anyone. I'm sorry Stacey, I didn't mean to push you away. I care for you."

Stacey's eyes worked up and down the rising monoliths on the horizon. She bent down and looked into his eyes. "I don't believe you," she whispered.

"I'm telling the truth."

"No, not that. I don't believe you're telling me what you are truly up to. You aren't working foundations, are you?" her eyes radiated into his.

The sound of shuffling feet approached them.

"Can I get you two an animal?" the bartender asked. He reached down below the polished bar and pulled up an otter. The otter squirmed in his hands and bared its teeth.

Stacey jumped back from the bar.

"Whoa, where did you get that?" she asked, eyes wide.

"House special," the bartender said.

"What else do you have?" she asked.

"We've got raccoon, skunk, 'possum, fisher, and fox. Can I offer you any?"

"Hmm...no thanks. I'm good for now. Maybe later," she said.

The otter clicked and bobbed its head as the bartender placed it back below the bar.

"Okay, Just know that we *do* have a one animal minimum," he said, walking away.

The oil lamps hissed and sputtered as an edge of darkness crossed the room.

Stacey's eyes beamed into his once more.

"So what are you *really* up to, Matt? Tell the truth. I'm not trying to be a bitch, I just want to hear the truth, okay?"

Fog obscured the windows and Matt turned to her.

"I'm trapped," he said.

"Trapped? Where?"

"Up on Julip Road at the shack." His hands shook, knocking into a beer mug.

"Are you trapped in an old mine?"

"No."

"Is someone holding you hostage?"

Matt tried to control his hands by gripping his barstool. "Not someone. Something."

Stacey furrowed her brow. "What does it look like?"

"Don't know. I can't see it." He looked at her like a puppy that had just shit on the couch. He expected derision.

She turned, her lips pulling back to reveal her straight white teeth. She checked the other side of the bar to see if anyone was listening and turned back to him. Her eyes were wide, possessed, the whites almost abnormal. She leaned into his right ear and whispered.

"Then find a way to *see it*, Matthew."

"How?"

"You'll think of something," she said, draping her arms around his neck and sitting on his lap. She nestled her chin under his jaw and rested her head on his shoulder. "I miss you so much. Come back to me. I'm still out there in the suburbs, an island in the traffic seas."

He held her, gripping as tight as he could.

The fog blew away from the glass. When he looked back, the room was empty. The music stopped. His arms were wrapped in front of him, holding nothing but air. The oil lamps spat and flickered, casting shadows on the log walls. Shivering, Matt stood and walked towards the burgundy door. When he reached for the knob, it morphed to the shack door—humongous bolt and all. An animal scurried on the other side, yipping and barking. There was something odd about the bark. But what was it? He listened carefully and realized it contained human inflections. It sounded like *wake up, wake up*! Panting arose between the barks—maybe a small dog.

Matt opened the door.

Dull, grey light streamed into the room. A snowy forest of aspen stretched out before him, snowflakes falling with cold placidity. Paw prints trailed off into the painterly scene. Somewhere back in the trees the dog barked.

Wake up, wake up!

He trudged through the snow, following the tracks. When he reached the aspen, sunlight filtered in. The trees sprouted leaves before his eyes and the patches of snow melted. Yellow grass rose around him as he fell backwards onto the ground, staring at the sky. Light stung his eyes, and his head erupted in cascades of stabbing pain. His head felt detached from the rest of his body, and he couldn't move his legs. His opened his eyes as wide as he could make them, and *panicked*. No vision. No vision.

Am I blind? he thought. He tried to move his arms but they felt like cinderblocks. He blinked, his eyelashes scraping against a barrier. Something had been placed over his eyes. Tiny feet pattered in the grass around him.

Raise your arm, he thought. *Come on.*

Rather than trying to move his arm from the wrist or elbow, Matt used his shoulder, hoping to work his way down. Okay, good. His right shoulder moved and he exhaled. From there he was able to lift his elbow and the rest of his arm. Matt made a fist and released it. *Good.* His fingers were numb, but feeling trickled back soon enough. He reached for his eyes and grasped the barrier with tingling fingertips. It was the blue bandanna from inside his truck.

Weird. he thought. Almost as weird as the beady, black eyes of a crow staring at him from inches away. He turned to the left and another crow gazed at him, beak cocked.

"Get out!" he shouted, waving the bandana in the air. The birds ignored him, perhaps sensing he wasn't at full strength. In a show of force, Matt wiggle his toes and bent his knees. At last sensation returned to his legs. Wasting no time, he pushed himself up and got to one, wobbly knee. The world's worst hangover camped in his skull and vertigo overcame him as he vomited. Matt turned to the would-be-eye-stabbing crows, dizzy and pissed off.

"Get out, Go!" He waved the bandana. They stood ground.

Finally he stood, his legs buckling and almost giving way.

Christ, do I need a freaking walker? he thought. Matt whipped the bandana and the crows took notice, squawking and flying off across Julip Road. One of them glared back towards the orchard with its beady eyes.

Matt stumbled into the shack, dehydrated and head pounding. Sensation crept up his left arm, but his lungs were heavy and his breath ragged.

I'm sorry Matthew, the little voice said. *I'm so sorry.*

In all that pain he stopped and stared at the truck. It stood upright, a beautiful symbol of defiance. Matt grinned. It even hurt to smile, but it was so worth it.

With great care he strained onto the bottom bunk, cradling his head with his hands. Flashes of hot-white agony crackled through his skull and along his spine.

No more of those, Matthew, the little voice said. *No more. Get that aspirin from the shelf, stop some of the pain.*

Matt mumbled something back, not sure of what he said.

Despite wanting to vomit again, he pulled himself off the bunk and limped to the shelf. Five aspirin went down his throat with water from the Black.

Good, that's real good. That should take some of the edge off, the little voice said. *Go lie down now, Matthew. I'm sorry my friend...so sorry to see you like this.*

The mangy mattress and pillow provided comfort to his ravaged body. He drifted off into a stormy, black sea.

***

A gust of wind piped through a hole in the logs, waking him. Although his head still ached, Matt felt a semblance of normalcy. His limbs seemed to work okay, to, and he held up both arms and wiggled his fingers to prove it.

Good! I'm so happy for you, the little voice said. *I was worried.*

As he walked over to fish out a Kashi bar from his food stash, he heard a noise across the orchard, like birdsong. Matt held his breath and listened. The muffled cry amplified, mutating from bird call to a human voice pleading for help.

Matt limped out of the shack, snack bar dangling from his lips like a cigar.

"Someone, please help!" the voice cried out.

He hobbled north across the orchard, grass licking his jeans and slicking his boots. Up ahead in a depression came slight movement—a hand rising into the air, a green jacket sleeve. In a few seconds Matt was looking down upon a beat-up man in his fifties. The man had trimmed pepper hair, a matching moustache, and a wide face. A white patch on his vest read *Michigan DNR*. Blood trickled from a lump on his temple, and his nose looked broken.

"Thank God! Please help me," the man said. "I think I broke my leg. I can't feel my toes. Jesus."

"Welcome to the club," Matt said, bending down. He was glad to see someone else, to talk to another human. *I guess it's true when they say misery loves company,* he thought. He looked away, ashamed.

"You-you've been hurt too?" the man asked.

"You could say that," Matt said. "I've been trapped here for days."

The man looked around nervously. "Trapped? Where? We're outside, son."

Matt scanned the orchard edges and returned his gaze to the man. "In this orchard."

The man checked the tree line and then looked at him like he was crazy.

"Something grabbed me, put me here," the man said as he wiped his bloody nose with the back of his hand. "I was cutting fallen trees out on the road–then I felt numb and couldn't breathe. I was dragged through the trees and the next thing I know I'm lying here."

"The effects wear off after several hours, Mr. Can you feel your toes?"

"Yes, I think. But my limbs feel like dead weight."

"That will go away, trust me."

"Trust you? What are you talking about?"

Matt looked away, tears welling in his eyes. He fought them and turned to the anxious man. "I don't know. All I can tell you is that a force is holding me here, and that force put you here, too."

"Crazy talk, guy," the man said, his chest heaving and his eyes blinking rapidly.

No point in responding to that, Matt thought. Better to be the one asking questions at this moment. "What's your name?"

The man's panicking eyes met Matt's as he tossed aside a branch that had pierced his jacket. "Mike Eggerts."

***

The call concerning missing Officer Bertil haunted Mike Eggerts. The police had interviewed him as he was the last person Bertil tried to contact. Mike had met Bertil many times in the comings and goings around Ironville. They often passed each other on the road, exchanging friendly waves. Bertil was an upstanding and powerful young man.

He told the police he knew nothing, which of course was true. All he knew was that Bertil phoned in an animal situation. Eggerts had a good idea just what that was—slaughtered moose hanging high from the canopy. Eggerts shifted in his car seat and set the heater. The breeze from the big lake chilled the air down here, and the vegetation grew darker, with stout aspen and patches of blueberry and bracken fern. Eggerts adjusted his glasses, sliding them up from the tip of his nose.

The damn moose, he thought. They'd been a great source of anxiety for the department. Only he and a few other biologists had any idea what was going on. When they found these moose, they'd pull them down from the trees with grappling hooks and four of their strongest men, and even that was almost impossible. Once down, they'd bury the moose in places that most folks wouldn't come across. The public didn't need to know about this—at least until the department had some answers.

The DNR had a big problem on their hands.

They couldn't claim these strung-up moose were caused by mountain lions because there were no mountain lions left. And if by some miracle there were, Michigan wildlife laws failed to protect them. The timber bosses made sure the DNR had no teeth to protect rare animals. The last thing lumber companies wanted was valuable timber locked away by meaningless habitat designations. The greenies were always getting in the way of state wildlife affairs. Eggerts didn't think they should have a say. The state knew what was best for industry and for the wildlife that brought in tourist dollars. No one cared about mountain lions, lynx, or wolverine. The moose though? Different story. Moose can be hunted, and they're easy to observe if you know where to look. And many local shops were named after the animal. Hell, there was even Moose Tracks ice cream and Moose Drool beer.

Eggerts took a sip of his coffee, fresh from Finn's Market back in town. He liked going there in the mornings, the bright lighting and the calming music, the attractive ladies from town. He liked the way some of them wore no makeup, bedhead still intact, bags under their eyes. A few would ponytail up their hair. He thought they looked better that way, natural yet inferring a sense of purpose. After all, he was a natural guy. You don't get into wildlife biology because you like the fake stuff. You also don't get into wildlife biology because you dislike order. Everything was neatly explainable. Every reaction has a definable cause. The ladies in the market wore pony tails because their hair had not been washed; the eagle dies of lead poisoning because it consumed part of a deer which contained lead bullet fragments. These are neat, explainable packages with pretty ribbon bows. But there was one package which lay shredded, blood worms crawling in the wrappings, chewing off the bow. No matter how hard he tried, he couldn't close the box and finish the job.

Moose were still dying in puzzling ways.

Oh he knew some things. Had some guesses. But good science isn't about guessing. It's about *finding*. He knew most of the U.P. was second and third generation forest. Less than one percent of the original forest remained—most of it in the Huron Mountains. The loggers had taken the old trees, building the cities of Milwaukee, Chicago, and Detroit. He knew that severe habitat alteration drove out native animals and ushering in non-native species like raccoon and possum. Eggerts thought it possible their special moose hunter might be doing the same thing—moving into the new growth forests of the upper Midwest because it *preferred* the habitat.

His Chevy pickup rolled up the steep pitch at the beginning of Julip Road, pulling away from the Lake Superior lowlands and into the higher country. The woods had begun to turn, the yellows and reds bright through his windshield.

Need some rain, he thought. He also needed to ditch this bug. Eggerts put his hand to his mouth and coughed. Swine flu was a pain in the ass, although the last week was better than the previous two. He still didn't feel right and figured he might need antibiotics. On the passenger seat was a bottle of Vitamin C. He shook out two 500mg tabs, fine powder from the jar caking his palm. He popped them into his mouth in one smooth motion and wiped his hand on the seat bench. Within seconds energy seeped up his spine and the tickling in his lungs receded. Sucking away, he watched the colorful woods with a skeptical eye.

What does that to moose? Reveal yourself, hombre. Show me the goods, he thought. Their special hunter had shown him *some* goods, in the form of tracks. BIG tracks…the biggest he'd ever seen. But these tracks were of such enormous size that the human mind instantly triggered denial. At first Eggerts and his peers thought the flattened vegetation was a moose bedding area, but upon careful examination there were actual claw marks, or at least toenail marks. They had thought about sending in some of the keratin samples and puzzling fluids to the downstate lab, but that would arouse more questions from people they didn't want asking questions. Next thing you know every media outlet and conspiracy theorist blogger would be tramping the woods and scaring the thing off, if such a thing could be scared. And worse, the more people in the woods, the more this thing could take a swipe at. He and the five peers who knew wanted none of that. This was their responsibility, and they'd handle it as they saw fit.

Around Eggerts' neck hung a pocket camera which he kept on him at all times. The department was keen on documentation so long as it stayed within their circle. Top dog Anderson had issued cameras to all personnel in the Huron Mountain area, even those who had no idea what was going on. The orders were to document tracks and kills. However, they had plenty of those by now. What Eggerts *really* wanted was a picture of the damn thing. Jokes about Bigfoot, aliens, and flying saucers filled the halls of home office. Station Seven near the Huron Grade had even set a dead moose as bait, employing a series of oversized snares. No Luck. No surprise.

Whatever was doing this had brains.

Their special hunter wasn't going to stick its head or foot in some half-assed snare. He had far more respect for it to think such things.

Did it take Officer Bertil? So far, it hadn't killed people, at least as far as the department knew. But he wouldn't be surprised. Eggerts gripped the steering wheel hard enough to whiten his knuckles. He watched the woods. Always watching the woods.

It was out here, somewhere in the forest.

He thought about his home at the end of the pavement near the national forest. Five acres of aspen, maple, and balsam fir and a tidy log cabin with high ceilings and picture windows. He loved his life, but wondered if sticking his nose around this project would shorten it. The circumstances made him wish he'd raised a family, had kids running around and a pretty wife. There was no legacy, just his dogs, Emily and Raven. They were good pooches, fine golden labs who kept him company through the long Michigan winters. They were the loves of his life when you got down to it. Still, he wanted a family. His phone rang only with the voices of co-workers and drinking buddies.

And boy you can drink, can't you? he thought.

He and field biologist Glenn Summers participated in what the locals called "The Magnificent Mile." They'd hop from tavern to tavern, pounding down Bloody Mary's until they could barely walk. There were no worries of police—not on those roads. Law enforcement was so underfunded the locals got away with many things. There were certain freedoms one had here in the great north.

But what was freedom without people to make choices? Ironville was a dying town—all the young people moving to Minneapolis or Chicago. The young wanted a taste of the big city and suburbs. He didn't like the crowding. He also didn't want his town to die. The Scandinavian and Nordic-influenced population produced more women than men—most of them attractive with blonde hair. For a while there it seemed as if Ironville had been created just for Mike Eggerts.

The truck bounced along the rough road as plastic rattled behind the dashboard. Between ferns, a streak of orange paint marked the possible spot Bertil had seen before trying to contact him. Eggerts stopped the truck and got out.

Yup, he said to no one, examining the dead moose in the trees. He took the camera from around his neck, thumbed the power button, and snapped a few shots. Eggerts rubbed his mustache with his right hand and checked the LCD screen. He scrutinized the forest floor, found two tracks, and crouched down. When he finished taking pictures, he walked the scene perimeter. He found nothing—not a hair, not a patch of skin. Vegetation rustled to the west and he reached down to his hip, feeling for his can of bear spray. His peers had laughed at him, preferring to carry guns. But what good was a gun on a ghost? No one had seen the creature. At least with the bear spray he had a wall of deterrent. The spray delivered a massive cone of blinding capsaicin. This was how grizzly biologists and hunters stopped thousand pound grizzly bears out west. If it worked on those brutes, it had a good chance to work on this thing, too. Many of the guys in the department were poor shots. When you combined poor marksmanship with an animal capable of yanking moose into the canopy, your chances of deterring the animal were low. Numerous bear spray studies in Alaska also concluded that spray was more effective than firearms by a forty percent margin. When presented with this data, his peers still chuckled. In some sick way he hoped to be proven right. *You'll see*, he'd told them. When Rick Martin—their field coordinator—disappeared two weeks ago near the Hurons, Eggerts had an idea why. They all did. Rick had laughed at him, told him bear spray wouldn't stop a red fox.

He unsnapped the button on the bear spray holster, slid out the can, and aimed to the west. The mountain maple rustled and a white-tailed buck sauntered out.

Eggerts holstered the bear spray and turned back to the truck. It took four turns of the key to get the engine going. Quality.

Eggerts thought about turning around, back north where the elevation was lower and the light was better, but there was something up the road he wanted to see. The DNR had completed a trout restoration project way up on the headwaters of the Black a couple years ago. He'd like to document any progress. Mostly, he wanted to scout a possible fishing trip, seeking first dibs on the benefits of their hard work.

You won't tell anyone, will you, old dog? he thought.

As Eggerts drove deeper into the maw of the Hurons, his mind wandered to Finn's Market and how Abby Stenson had smiled at him. For years he'd visited Finn's in the a.m., hoping to strike a conversation with one of the local beauties. And God damn if he didn't make first contact today. He still couldn't believe Abby invited him over for dinner. She'd smiled at him, her manner nervous, words faltering. Of course he'd accepted. He'd been keen on her for a long, long time. Had his recent weight loss played a part? Probably. Like anything, you have to practice to get good. And playing the social game means you have to work at looking your best. If you're in college, you better damn well study. And if you're lonely and want to meet women, you better get your fat ass in shape.

Eggerts grinned and nudged the truck over the bumps. Better a short, sharp knock than lunging all over the road.

Julip Road narrowed, hunks of rock prominent in the grade like exposed fossils. Up ahead downed trees crossed the road—maybe four or five. Eggerts parked the truck ten feet from the blockade, got out, and examined the trunks. There were no teeth marks at the base, eliminating beaver activity. The raw, fresh wood was splintered and stringy—a sign that the wind had knocked the trees down. Eggerts sighed. The problem with this conclusion? No other signs of disturbance existed in the surrounding vegetation. Someone or something had slammed these trees to the ground like an elephant. The wind doesn't pick out four or five trees and annihilate them—it doesn't work that way.

Eggerts returned to the pickup and lifted the plastic chainsaw case from the bed. The case looked like a coffin for leprechauns. After unlatching the case, he hoisted out a beat up chainsaw. A pair of plastic goggles lay in the case, and he stretched them over his face. Eggerts grasped the starter handle and gave a good yank. The nylon on his jacket sleeve sung as it rubbed his chest, and then the chainsaw sung with it.

A flock of chickadees flew off to the east.

Eggerts needed to work this in manageable sections... focused, organized, methodical. The chainsaw ripped into the chunky wood, sending bright splinters into the air all around him. The whining of the saw receded and peaked, muffled when buried deep, screaming when free. His arms vibrated and the sensation of slicing through the trunk reminded him of sex. And then another sensation overcame him: Chest tightness. Eggerts scanned the woods around him, trying to shake off the weird feeling. And now his limbs didn't feel right....

I'm having a heart attack, he thought. *I did well-I lost weight—please not this!*

The sensations grew stronger, his face turning red from the pressure. Eggerts went to pound his chest with his right fist and dropped the sputtering chainsaw. But his fist never reached his chest.

The chainsaw lay on the trunks and branches, cradled there like a mother giving comfort to the enemy.

Eggerts collapsed and clutched his throat. His arms numbed and dropped to his sides. He looked at his feet but couldn't see them. Instead, his lower body was a blur.

I took the medicine, he thought. *My cholesterol is good. Dr. Enders said the lab work was fine. I haven't had dinner with Abby yet. This can't happen, God!*

Something lifted him into the air. Then he was dragged through the woods on the western embankment. Each beat of his heart pounded in his head and throbbed in his limbs. A deep, black sadness overcame him and he knew he wasn't dealing with God. No, it wasn't anything close.

We meet at last, Eggerts thought.

The image of Rick Martin laughing at him filled his mind. *Bear spray wouldn't stop a red fox,* he'd laughed. HAHA BEAR SPRAY WON'T STOP A RED FOX! WATCHA CARRYING THAT FOR HEEEHAW! RED FOX RED FOX RED FOX.

The world of light drew away from him. Branches slapped against his body, and he saw a meadow or clearing. A strong wind hit him—or was he being hurled through the sky? The world spun violently and he crashed into the ground.

***

Mike Eggerts spat onto the orchard, hands on his knees. "You're telling me that you can't see this thing?"

Matt became aware of his appearance in Eggerts' nervous eyes—the cuts and scrapes, the dirty clothes. He looked like he worked at a remote meth lab. And when Eggerts reached down for his bear spray Matt knew that's precisely what he was thinking.

"I know it's hard to believe," Matt said. "But you're going to have to accept it." He made firm eye contact with Eggerts, driving the point home. "This is why I'm here. This is why you're here. If you try to leave, you'll be brought back...or worse."

"Brought back?"

"The same way you came here. Picked up and dropped really freaking hard."

Eggerts finally stood, and almost stumbled over. "My truck," he said. "The road."

"I wouldn't do that," Matt said.

"I'll do what I God damn well please, guy," Eggerts said. "Which is the quickest way back to my truck?"

Sweat beaded down Eggerts' face, mixing with blood from the gash on his forehead.

"You don't get it. There is no safest way back to the truck. Trust me." Matt clenched his fists, poking a fingernail into his skin.

Eggerts looked beyond him into the orchard, eyes widening as he caught a glimpse of the shack roof. He began limping in that direction and brushed past Matt.

"Wait," Matt shouted, trotting after him. He grabbed Eggerts left arm, twisting him back. Eggerts recoiled with surprising quickness and palmed his bear spray canister.

"You see this, guy?" Eggerts said, his upper lip quivering. "This is biologist-approved bear spray. Touch me again and I'll use it."

The stink of fear emitted from Eggerts in waves. Matt's only choice was to react to Eggerts rather than forcing him elsewhere. "When you come to the shack you'll see a two track," Matt said. "Follow it downhill to Julip Road. But please, please do not go back to the spot you came from. Please Mr. Eggerts."

Eggerts removed his hand from the bear spray holster and limped to the sad excuse of a driveway. Between steps, Eggerts eyed Matt. "You got a meth operation here?" Eggerts asked.

"Does it look like it?" Matt asked.

Eggerts glanced at the tie downs and the sections of blanket underneath. Some of the blankets bulged with rocks. Eggerts eyed the rope dangling from the truck, and Matt realized the contraption looked like a system for manipulating heavy equipment such as barrels.

"Yes, it kind of does," Eggerts said.

Matt raised his palms in the air. "Busted. You found me. I store tons of it in the shack. Need a pick-me-up?"

Eggerts pointed a finger at him, his eyes wide. "Keep away from me. I'm serious."

Matt followed Eggerts to the road, careful to keep his distance.

"Where's the God damned truck?" Eggerts asked. He spun around, hand on bear spray. "Answer me, guy. Where is it?"

Matt looked him in the eyes and laid his palm on his heart, trying to show this idiot he was sincere. He enunciated his words like a well-trained politician. "Your truck was moved by the Being. The same force that moved you, moved the truck."

He could almost see Eggerts thoughts swirling in a murky sea of mistrust and fear, never quite finding daylight or reason.

***

Eggerts turned towards the fallen trees. Maybe it was possible the thing that grabbed him was the same creature hunting the moose. But invisible? Bullshit. In all his formal education, he'd never encountered invisible mega-fauna. Maybe what seized him wasn't the creature at all, but a device used by the meth lab to keep out intruders. The U.S. Navy had frequency generators-round dishes aimed by soldiers. These generators emitted frequencies that paralyzed and confused humans. When someone or something screws with your nervous system, your entire reality shifts. You can hallucinate, and even imagine things that never happened.

Eggerts grimaced and palmed his bear spray holster. Then he licked his lips, tasting a bit of blood in his indecision. They'd pinged him with the frequency generator, making him convulse and hallucinate. Then they'd dragged him into the orchard and stolen his truck, maybe for scrap parts. And here he stood next to this filthy guy, someone who pleaded with him not to walk towards the road.

Nothing had grabbed him.

There was no invisible creature. He hallucinated the entire thing and now his life was in real danger.

"I want you to back up there, guy," Eggerts said, unsheathing the bear spray and aiming. "This will put you down forty minutes. It will not be pleasant." Eggerts backed away from Matt and shuffled onto the rugged road.

"Mr. Eggerts, you need to calm down. Please listen to me—"

"—you and your group need to let me leave—WITH my truck."

"I don't have your truck—"

"—ah bullshit, guy. You have it, and you're going to show me where it is." Eggerts aimed the can of bear spray at Matt's eyes.

***

Matt looked beyond Eggerts' shoulder at the downed trees. They were close to where the dead deer had laid a few days ago—a lifetime ago.

Then Eggerts' eyes flashed, and Matt wondered if he was about to make a run for it.

Of course he was.

Eggerts backpedalled, occasionally glancing behind him for direction. The rest of the time he kept his eyes on Matt. "If you try to approach, I'll use the spray," Eggerts said. "It goes thirty—"

"—I know how bear spray works," Matt said. "But do you know how the Being works? Because I do. It only lets you get so far before it either pulls you back or kills you. And if you keep going, that's exactly what's going to happen to you. And trust me when I say this, you do *not* want that to happen."

Eggerts inched closer to the downed trees and Matt started towards him.

"Stay away."

"Please listen to me."

***

Eggerts was certain the meth junkie was going to kill him. Those wild eyes, stained clothes, weird cuts, and ridiculous tales of supernatural bullshit. Eggerts couldn't see a weapon, but that didn't matter. They had the frequency generator and that was all they needed. Maybe they even got off on it.

"I can't let you do this," Matt said, moving towards him, palms out. "I can't let you get hurt."

"You can't let *me* get hurt? *You're* the one who's *going* to hurt me!" Eggerts screamed. "Stay back!" He shuffled backwards and tripped over the first downed tree.

Matt inched closer, well within bear spray range.

"I'm not going to hurt you. I've been coming up here for years with my dad. I'm from a suburb of Chicago. Mapleton, as a matter of fact. Did you see my truck plates? Illinois. Why would I drive all the way up here to make meth? Stupid, huh? You have to believe me. You're in great danger."

***

Another threat from the mangy addict and more false promises. Eggerts popped the safety cap off the bear spray and slid his thumb over the trigger. The orange cap tumbled to the dry road and when it hit earth, the earth shook. The cap flipped and hit the earth again, and once more the earth shook. Two more flips, each one incurring thunder. At least that's what Eggerts thought. Now the cap lay motionless on the road, but the ground still trembled—each shake louder than the previous. Before Eggerts could press the trigger, he began to choke. His limbs numbed. Every ounce of his flesh pricked with little pins, or maybe little teeth. His face began to look like a swollen plum. Something unseen whipped the air above him, a hundred mad slave-drivers. Eggerts felt the breeze from it on his face.

They're hitting me with the frequency generator again, he thought. *But this time they're going to kill me.*

"Tell them to turn it off" he garbled to Matt. "Make them stop!"

***

"I'm not doing anything," Matt said. He dropped to his knees, ran his hands through his hair and sobbed. He'd tried to warn Eggerts, but the last thing he needed was to be debilitated from bear spray. How he wished Eggerts never brought the stuff. He'd have tackled the stubborn asshole to the ground and beaten him into submission.

Eggert's face swelled like a puffer fish. Distorted vocalizations belched out his mouth like rotten egg farts.

"I'm sorry. I'm so freaking sorry," Matt said, sobbing. Eggerts began to lift off the ground, his feet and hands wriggling.

Matt turned his back.

It wants me to watch, doesn't it? Then he ran up the driveway, collapsing in front of the shack.

***

Just a hallucination, Eggerts thought, even though he could no longer feel his limbs. *Don't worry, these small frequency generators aren't powerful enough to kill you, old buddy. They need to be much larger and carried by heavy-duty trucks.*

Light danced in Eggerts' brain, white spots flickering and pulsating. He felt himself lifting off the ground, hovering above the road like an Anglo Saxon totem pole. *You're going to be all right buddy. A hallucination. Close your eyes and it will be over soon.*

Through grotesque visual disturbances Eggerts realized he was hovering over the road, except there was no up or down, but a constant, smooth motion and the paralyzing sensation. Eggerts floated up the steep driveway as if on an escalator. *Just a hallucination,* he repeated to himself. Through patches of boiling red and flickering white spots, he saw the meth dealer. He was sitting on the ground, hands cradling his head.

Who was holding the frequency dish?

The visual distortions receded for a moment, allowing him to view the shack. Empty cabin, empty truck. So where was the dish? Eggerts looked down at the sobbing meth guy who now only came through in waves. Eggerts floated to within feet of him, the pressure on his chest excruciating. The meth guy looked up, screamed, and looked away. And then the meth guy went stiff. Eggerts watched him choke and spit, then rise into the air at his own level. Meth guy's limbs were still, too.

If he's incapacitated, who's holding the frequency dish? And why would they do it to one of their own? Eggerts left the world for a nod and returned, his vision ruptured by explosions of white. It was becoming harder to grasp a thought, to process information. The meth guy's face turned a deep red. Behind him, two tracks cut through the soil, heading down into the grassy bowl. The size of the tracks screamed moose and a horrible thought crossed his mind:

There was no frequency generator, no meth lab.

Instead, this was the beast that had eluded the department.

An intense pressure besieged him, and he saw an image of his beloved golden retrievers, tongues out, gentle eyes happy to see him. *Goodbye, buddies*, he thought. *Goodbye.* Then Mike Eggerts' world went dark, forever.

***

Matt looked on, frozen. The Being was forcing him to watch Eggerts' face, all red and bloated like a baboon's ass. Eggerts mouth had stopped moving, as if the muscle had been severed, his eyes red with a million bursting blood vessels. A grotesque sound like someone wringing out a thick, damp towel came from his face and neck. Tiny red spots burst through Eggerts' skin like a terrible rash. And then Matt saw something else. He saw a classic U.P. summer sunset, deep red from the humidity. He saw his father walking across the orchard, ever-present cigarette in his mouth. His father smiled at him, anxious to get down to the Black for a bit of fishing. He saw Stacey on that evening after their first Cubs game, her sunburned body recoiling from his touch. He'd sprayed the anti-sunburn mist across her legs and arms, and she'd sighed, the portable fan tousling her hair in the dark bedroom. The feeling of relief, her warm hand on his thigh, her lips on his neck. He focused on what his mind presented to him, not his eyes. What his eyes focused on couldn't be real. Only nightmares.

Elmo ran up to him in a meadow of yellow flowers, his tongue lolling and his eyes filled with love. His friend Trent, running across the orchard from a weasel, laughter from his friends as they watched. The turbulent waters of the Black, fresh with oxygen bubbles and the deep grooves of rock in the riverbed, mysterious nooks where bigger trout finned. Sunrises, sunsets, trees bowing in the wind, the scent of pine sap and bog flowers rich in the air. A chorus of frogs at dusk lulling the day-things to sleep, Upper Black Falls a whisper across the southern valley, often confused with the wind, but there, always there.

He wanted to flee but could not move.

Spittle flew from his mouth and mixed with Eggerts' gunk on the grass. The stench of fecal matter and blood filled the air around him, forcing him to gag.

It's going to kill me this time, Matt thought. *I've finally pissed it off enough. Good. Freaking good!*

Images of his mother, of Andrea, of his father, of Elmo, and Stacey shuffled through his mind like a deck of cards and then the Being dropped him. He lay there, arching his back and sucking air. Blood rushed back into his head, clearing the random white blotches from his vision.

Still in the grip of the Puller, Eggerts' body spasmed as gunk flew from his nose, mouth, and eye sockets. Eggerts' tongue had turned rotten green and flopped out the side of his mouth. His loose eyeballs jangled above his cheekbones, making viscous slapping sounds. Matt turned away and crawled to the shack, listening to what sounded like clam chowder slopping onto the grass. "Please, please end this," he said, waiting for a final verdict.

It never came.

Matt crawled into the shack and closed the door. He'd never seen anything like that in his life. The vision of Eggerts had torn out a piece of his soul, lit it on fire, stomped it, grilled it, shit on it, and then dumped it into a volcano. He'd never get it back no matter what happened.

He was a nice man, a DNR employee, Matt said, sobbing into his hands on the bottom bunk. *Why did this happen?* he asked the empty shack. He listened, expecting the voice to answer back. *Where are you?* he asked. *Where are you with your pithy comments now?* Matt waited. The voice did not respond.

Matt peered through the window above the couch. What was left of Eggerts lay slumped in the grass. Matt waited there, hoping the shaking and panic would settle. Slowly, his confusion and rage shifted focus into survival. He kneeled on the couch and stared out the window, tears drying, breath slowing.

Survival.

There was something Eggerts had that he needed.

After a half hour Matt opened the door and peeked around both sides of the shack. Then he limped over to Eggerts, following the stench and guts, determined to avoid what had once been his face. Matt undid the latch on the bloody belt buckle and removed the belt. The bear spray holster slid free onto the ground, empty. After wiping the holster in the grass, he searched Eggerts' pockets. No luck.

A camera on a shoelace necklace hung from Eggerts' neck. Matt untied the bloody knot and placed the camera onto the grass, figuring the batteries might come in handy.

Then Matt turned his back to Eggerts, bent down, and lifted his soiled ankles. He dragged Eggerts across the driveway and down into the bowl where the old farm house once stood. After finding an appropriate spot, he limped back to the truck and cut a blanket pouch from the frame. Down in the bowl he laid the blankets upon Eggerts, setting a slate boulder at each corner.

Not much of a burial, Mike, but this is all I got right now, he said. *May you rest in peace. I tried to help you, friend. Please forgive me.*

Matt limped away, the pit of his stomach acidic and sour. He vomited onto the grass and continued on as if it were a sneeze. Tremors began to seize his hands and shivered hard enough to rattle his teeth. *Shit,* he thought. Behind him, along the trees of Julip Road a murder of crows called out, sensing blood on the grass.

Enough, Matt thought.

Where the hell are you? he asked the voice. *You abandon me now after all this?* He waited for a response, but only the crows answered with their mocking caws.

That's what I thought, Matt said.

The voice was gone.

He was alone—in a place he'd always considered his home. Now it was nothing more than torture and isolation, dragging him

hour by hour on a prolonged death-arc. The fantasy he lived for—
the sunny days, the humming grasshoppers, the wildflowers—
faded into lifeless purgatory. Even the memories here with his
father no longer held power or reverence. There was nowhere to
retreat, mentally or physically. His only choice was to fight. Fight
or die. A pathetic pep talk, at that. He had no fight left.

Matt Kearns limped into the shack and grasped a knife from the
hutch. He sighed and turned his left wrist up, exposing the delicate
underside. He flexed, making the veins pop. The rusty steak knife
contrasted with the pink tendons and thick, worm-like arteries.

"Do it, you freaking coward," he said. "Just slice right in like a
Thanksgiving turkey and get it over with." His hands trembled as
alarms rattled off in his mind like a thousand broken bank
windows. Slowly, he dug the knife point into skin. He wasn't
going to be all pretty with his cutting. Oh no, this wasn't going to
be a Martha Stewart suicide. The plan was to hack away, gouging
across the arteries. No reason to take longer than needed.

Surprising himself, he raised the blade, arm cocked like a spring
trap. Before he could make the final cut, images of the rescued
fisher popped into his mind. He saw it squirming in the air and
slamming down like a furry puppet on crack. He saw it leap again
and again, only to be yanked back down by the trap chain. Yet
despite the torture, the fisher never gave up. It didn't matter that
the chain was there. The fisher *tried*.

Would the fisher kill itself?

Why would it? Freedom lay just beyond the trap. The fisher had
sniffed freedom and that was that. *His* problem was he could see
and smell his own painful death approaching. Like the moment a
driver realizes they've allowed too little time to brake, and
surrender to the inevitable crunch of metal.

Matt held the trembling blade. In his mind he saw Andrea,
laughing and smiling at a joke he'd made.

At once he dropped the knife to the floor. Then he crumbled to
his knees and cradled his head. Random slideshows of happier
times flashed in his skull: his mother getting sprayed after he'd
wrapped the sink nozzle with a rubber band, and Andrea smiling
as Elmo went down the slide at the park. He thought of Stacey, her
face resting on his chest in their Grand Teton cabin, the

wildflowers blooming in meadows. He still had reasons to live, still had reasons to fight.

Matt lay on the bunk, salvaging stable, sane thoughts like a computer scanning a hard drive for errors. He drank from the water jug, which helped. Then he rose, took the knife off the floor, and limped outside. At his old truck he sliced off a blanket pouch and left the twine attached. He paused several times on the way down the driveway to listen.

Do not piss it off again, he thought. *It might be the last time.* As he approached the downed trees on Julip Road, he saw a red metal canister lying on the ground. The bear spray. But he did not approach the canister, instead he tossed the blanket pouch forward like a shore fishermen trying to net fish.

The pouch landed behind the canister.

Matt reeled the twine, hoping for a catch. The blanket dragged across the road, wiping the dust smooth and then catching the bear spray in a fold of cloth. Yes! Finally something was going his way.

When he picked up the can, he sighed and kicked gravel.

The can was empty.

Something had stepped on it, puncturing the side. A picture of a grizzly bear was painted on the side, along with a big paw print. The paw print had a circle around it and a slash through the circle. Matt tossed the can aside. Then he glanced towards the downed trees and tried to hold back a genuine smile. There, resting atop the trees was a chain saw. Matt flung the blanket, but it pulled up just short. He took two steps forward, expecting the all too familiar choking numbness.

Nothing.

Another toss of the pouch. This time he caught the back end of the saw. *Yes!* Slowly, he reeled in the pouch and the cloth tore as it caught blade.

Do you really want to do this? he thought. The chainsaw might make *IT* mad. Then again, what choice did he have?

He hadn't developed a specific plan for the saw, but what kind of dumbass would pass on it now? Matt pulled with enthusiasm, the twine digging into his skin. The saw moved six inches and he paused. Two branches full of hook-like twigs blocked the path forward. Off to the east, a ruffed grouse beat its wings to a crescendo. Matt thought of the weekend his father and he fished for pike at Mattheson State Park. They liked to fish *the soup*, as his father called it. And as an ambush species, the pike liked *the soup*, too. He and his father would cast spinner baits(wacky lures with rubber skirts, a metal arm bent at a 90 degree angle, and a flashy spinning blade attached to a swivel). The vibrations and flashes were too much for the pike. They hit the lures hard and fought even harder. To get to the pike, they had to cast the spinner baits into submerged trees, exposed reeds, and lily pads. If they made a poor cast, they'd lose the $6 lure forever. No one much cared for that, especially his father. He'd rather of drowned trying to save a snagged lure than lose it. On one particular cast, years and years ago, Matt had wrapped his line around a half-submerged tree. As he'd reeled, he'd seen the line dragging over the exposed branch. If he'd kept reeling, he'd have hooked the lure right onto the bark.

Good job, his father had said. *What you want to do here Matty is get the lure about two feet behind the snag. Keep the line tight so it doesn't fall back. But don't pull up. Now what you want to do is yank that sucker while holding the rod high. Make your bait fling over the branches, see. And make sure you're wearing your polarized glasses.*

He'd followed his father's instructions, and the spinner bait had flipped over the branches and plopped into the water ten feet from the boat. He'd reeled in, smiling.

Matt raised the twine high in his hands, turned, and yanked. As the saw ripped through the branches, the twine tightened, and he pulled harder. The sound of snapping branches gave way to metal scraping along gravel. Before he could get too excited, he paused and scanned the forest. A breeze tousled his hair, then rustled the maples and aspen on the orchard side of the road. He felt *IT* watching him.

Matt waited for a retort from the voice, perhaps something along the lines of, *no shit, it's always watching you!* but there was nothing. He actually missed the sarcasm. It was like his best friend had deserted him in his greatest time of need. The voice had always been there when his anxiety peaked. Always.

Maybe I finally outgrew it, he thought. Many psychologists said young adults often grow into, then out of certain mental conditions. For some it might be obsessive compulsive disorder. For others it might be voices. Maybe it was his time.

Matt lifted the chainsaw, relishing the heft and potential violence. Then he balled up the pouch in his left arm and limped up the driveway.

He set the chainsaw under the front awning in case it rained, even though it hadn't rained a drop the last week. So odd. The U.P. was famous for shitty weather. Now, the stage was set for wildfire, a condition Matt had never experienced in the U.P..

He kicked a section of orchard grass, listening to the wispy crunchiness.

Fire, he thought.

Matt kicked another patch of grass then caressed the dry blades with his fingers. A devious chill trickled along his spine. Sure, he might kill himself by lighting the place up, but at least the Being wouldn't win. And if he didn't die, maybe it would serve as a distraction. With a renewed sense of purpose, he unscrewed the gas cap on the chainsaw, then poured gas into the plastic cup. He held the noxious brew to his eyes and studied the orchard.

There was something about the northern section he didn't like.

He had a hunch the Being always came from this spot, right where the orchard met hardwoods. If he was planning to set a fire, *that* was the place.

Payback can be fun, he thought.

A gust blew down from the Hurons, bending the orchard grass to the north. The rustling vegetation seemed to whisper *do it...do it.*

He went into the shack and snatched another lighter, a relic from the Huron Bay Tavern which had burned down five years ago. *How poetic*, he thought, staring at the lighter as if it held his life in its worn, black plastic. He hobbled to his truck and lifted the handle on the passenger side door, making sure the thing would open as he bolted from the fire. The keys dangled from the ignition switch, winking back at him like a pot of gold. As he limped across the orchard, he whistled a tune, the melody clear but the writer escaping his mind—what was left of it anyway.

Oh, it was slipping away, he was sure of it.

A person couldn't endure this and not lose something. For every traumatic incident, he gave away a piece of himself. Whatever youthful sheen he'd had scrubbed away days ago.

Matt was careful not to step on half-buried apples. The last thing he needed was a sprained ankle as he tried to outrun a fire. And oh, this fire *would* be a dandy, with the wind lending a helping hand. He thought of the glove character on Hamburger Helper boxes, its beady eyes and stupid, red nose. The wind was his little gloved hamburger helper, hehe. He continued whistling, crunching through the dry grass with dare he admit it, a spring in his step?

The older hardwoods swayed up ahead. The forest groaned, almost asking for it. Or was it protesting? There were no signs of wildlife—not even a bird. Whistling, he tipped the plastic cup and limped around, spreading a thin line of gasoline. The grass bent towards the northern forest. The wind whispered in his ears.

Do it...do it.

When the cup emptied, he thumbed the lighter wheel. He stared into the tiny flame, entranced by the organic glow.

This one's for dad, he said.

Before flame could meet grass, something rustled in the ferns. Matt released his thumb from the wheel. A shape formed behind the trees, then faded.

A moose.

And here he was about to torch the moose's home. Shameful. Selfish. But then again, so what? It was either burn baby burn, or die.

The moose clomped deeper into the forest.

Leave, Matt said. *Now!*

He wasn't going to let the Being have any more fun. Matt set the cup down and limped into the ferns.

Go! he shouted at the moose. The moose's high shoulders swished between two sapling maples just ahead. He trudged on, pain streaking up his legs. A new infection?

The forest darkened. Fireflies glinted in far off glades, lighting the ferns in intermittent bursts. He limped up a ridge of red pines as they swayed above him. For a moment he thought he saw the moose disappear into the understory. He followed it, wondering why the Being was letting him travel so far. Was this freedom, at last? His heart beat faster. Maybe the moose was leading him through a loophole. Matt lumbered on, into the dogberry towards a clearing.

As the view cleared, several holes appeared in the spongy forest floor. The three foot wide holes were bordered by chunks of green moss and pungent forest litter. Strangely, a silk-like material stretched across each gap.

He stood there, dumbfounded.

Off to the east a woodpecker tapped a tree for insects. Deep breathing cut the air behind him and on the second breath something shoved him into the mossy ground. Matt pushed himself up, his eyes inches above the holes and their translucent, silky coverings. He checked behind him for the assaulter, seeing nothing but forest. Still, he knew it was there, watching him, waiting. So much for his Freedom Fries.

Matt crawled to the edge of the closest hole and examined the silky covering. The smell reminded him of Elmer's glue—the stuff that never held anything together except art paper. Matt reached out to the white strands and caressed them. He plucked one of the strands and it released a note. Other notes followed from other holes and aligned into a melody, perhaps something from his childhood. The chiming was wonderful, rising through the canopy and into the sky. Slowly, each strand of silk began to vibrate.

Matt reached out and gave a good pluck. The melody rose in tempo and changed key randomly, ushering an atonal jingle across the woods.

The woodpecker stopped.

Frogs paused their ribbitting. The trees looked on with indifference. The tempo and key changed. Faster now, faster. Matt held his hands to his ears and stood.

A clicking sound rose up from his feet, and he spun. *Danger danger,* his mind warned him. *No, stay,* an unidentified voice whispered. *Stay and see the new ones.* The calming thoughts brought on by the first musical notes sucked away like water into a sink drain, only to reveal cold stainless steel.

He blinked twice and took a slow, deep breath. How the he'll he'd gotten into the woods he had no idea. The last thing he remembered was holding the plastic cup over the orchard grass.

The wind shifted in this forest glade and it occurred to him he'd been misled out to this patch of woods for a reason. He searched for moose tracks, finding nothing but vegetation and his own pathetic boot prints.

The clicking came again, this time followed by tearing as if someone was shucking corn. Most of the silky hole coverings were torn and ragged tufts of white fibers poked up.

More clicking.

Pain wracked Matt's right leg and he cried out.

He looked down and saw a tear in his jeans above the ankle.

You need to run, and you need to run now.

Matt hobbled south through the forest. Vegetation smashed behind him, followed by the intense clicking. He thought about looking back, to catch even the slightest glimpse of what was behind him, but thought better. Soon the orchard appeared beyond the hardwoods, his guiding light out of this dark place. At last he crossed into the orchard, smelling the gas he'd poured earlier. As he ran, he watched the ground for half-buried apples. A botanical slip would be the end of him, and never had he been more sure of any outcome in his life. He chose to keep his eyes on the ground as he ran. He navigated the orchard by observing the contours of the land, the sand pits under a few of the aspen that used to hold pens for pigs and cattle, to the gentle dips and rises. This was his orchard, his home, and every inch of it was etched into his mind.

Run to the shack and slam the door, he thought. *Do not look back or you will die. Do not stop or you will die. Do not fall or you will die. When you are in the shack, board up the other window.*

Matt dodged numerous tart apples, his boots landing solid in the empty spaces, then launching despite the pain. The last time he ran through the orchard like this was when he played a joke on his friend Bill Engles. Bears scared the shit out of Bill. One summer they were walking the orchard, trying to flush grouse for the hell of it. Bill was also interested in finding a woodcock, the cantankerous Northwoods bird known for its unusual mating displays. As they'd walked back to the shack, unsuccessful, Matt had paused, looked back behind him and shouted "bear!" Bill had froze in horror, and when he'd tried to run away he'd fallen on his face. He'd lumbered up, face contorted with fear, and tripped over his own feet again. Matt had turned to him, laughing and telling him it was all a joke. Bill had asked why a friend would do such a thing. It was a damn good question.

Now who's afraid? Matt thought. If only Bill could see him now.

Matt passed a sandy patch behind a big apple tree. The shade was a good place to set a water trough for pigs and horses. Ron had told him they used to flock there on warm summer days, sucking at the water and whipping their tails. He and his father used to find old horseshoes buried in the sand. Weathered logs connected below the tree, half-buried in the hillside.

Matt hobbled up the hill to the west side of the shack, cutting in-between thorn bushes as they ripped into his clothing. A second later whatever was behind him rustled into the same bushes and wailed. Matt couldn't help but laugh as the things chittered and thrashed in the thorns. Finally he reached the shack door and slammed the iron bolt down. Then he ran over to the window above the grungy couch and lifted the chair, hammering the back rest into the logs. Sweaty and exhausted, he slumped onto the remaining chair and listened for the death that followed him back to his childhood sanctuary.

Click clack snap!

A few seconds later his follower arrived and slammed against the logs. The obnoxious clicking and scraping circled the shack, and it occurred to Matt there were several of them. Awesome sauce.

After scrabbling around the logs, the things sensed he was inside and slashed at the wood, as if someone was stabbing a pair of scissors along the exterior walls. Matt held his breath and listened. The scraping never quite climbed the walls, instead staying below four feet.

Quickly, Matt scanned the shack for weapons. When he moved the creatures grew excited, clacking and slashing on the west wall. Matt's first instinct was to sprint out there with the chainsaw and swing it wildly around him, and he stood to do just that.

I don't think so, the little voice said.

Matt's eyes moistened and he wiped at them with a trembling hand. *You're back?* He said. *You're back!* He gazed to the roof, raised his arms, and clenched his fists.

You aren't going to go out there and do that, Matthew, the little voice said. *You'll be killed.*

Maybe so. Matt turned to the southern window and peered out. The dead oak loomed in the frame, his truck to the left of it. All around him the clacking ceased, but he knew the creatures were still out there. That's how these things operated. He wasn't buying their act.

He caught a glimpse of himself in the window and rubbed the stubble on his face. He looked like he'd aged twenty years. His stomach rumbled, so he knifed peanut butter onto a few slices of bread. There was no time for manners, peanut butter sticking to his stubble. He had to eat, had to drink. Taking care of himself was the only way he'd win. Weakness was not an option.

Matt had a good idea there were at least four of these new creatures out there, waiting for him to make a mistake. He also had a good idea that if he hurt *any* of them, the Being would strike in a way he would not wake from. The moose shadow in the woods had to be a decoy, perhaps pheromones given off by the Being to make him go to the nest.

Strange that the shadow arrived just as I was about to light the place up, he thought.

It wanted you to go to the nest, the little voice said.

Why? he asked, triggering the creatures into a fit with his voice.

To teach the younglings how to hunt, the little voice said. *That's how big cats in Africa train their cubs. They capture young gazelles, place them near the cubs and let them bat it around until one of them figures out how to kill. Then they eat.*

The southern window shattered and the creatures squealed. Chunks of glass clattered against the plywood barrier and crunched to the floor.

Clack snap scrape!

Dry fall air filtered into the shack, cleansing the mustiness. All at once the obnoxious clicking stopped, replaced with an odd, curious low squealing.

They could smell him.

Matt held his breath and listened. The things gurgled and whined, and he swore he also heard a hint of jubilation. The good news was they had not damaged the plywood or the door. If they had, he'd have no choice but to smash their heads in, if they even had heads.

The things congregated below the broken window, panting. Every so often an impatient squeal piped into the shack.

Perhaps they are hungry, the little voice said. *Give them a tasty treat.*

Tasty treat? Matt checked the shack, his mind racing but never finding a suitable object.

West wall between bunk and hutch, Matthew, the little voice said.

The anti-freeze mouse trap.

The bloated mice were still in the bucket, soaked in the poisonous fluid. He'd never had a chance to clean it out. Matt took the log grabber from the fireplace and clamped down on a dead mouse. As he raised it, the stench of rotten flesh punched him in the face. He gagged and maneuvered the mouse across the shack like a scientist relocating a dangerous test object. At the broken window, he poked the grabber in-between the plywood slats and panes. With the flick of his wrist the mouse plopped onto the grass. Pattering feet and frenzied squeals erupted below the window as flesh tore and bones popped. Matt repeated this with the other dead mice and waited for the poison to work.

Soon the sound of the little devils faded. He sat on his bunk for twenty minutes, beads of sweat forming on his temples, his hands twitching. He thought of the chainsaw. If they did break in, he wanted a tool capable of inflicting real damage—not a flimsy kitchen knife. Sure, he had the fire poker, but compared to a chainsaw?

Matt placed his ear against the huge door and listened. Nothing. He loosened the bolt and pulled it back from the edge. He paused again. Nothing.

Okay, at the count of three, run out there and grab it. You outran these freaks before, and you can do it again.

Matt swung the heavy door open and juked to the left, grabbing the chainsaw and pulling it back in. The metal chassis slammed in-between the door and frame, sending painful shocks up his arm.

Then he felt something tear into his ankle.

Matt screamed and kicked, and his boot met something hard, maybe the creature's skull. It let out a surprised squeal, and he slammed the door shut. The creatures clicked and scraped at the lower third of the door, furious at his escape.

"Haha," Matt said.

He set the chainsaw on the floor and examined his left ankle. A four inch gash seeped blood, staining the torn fabric. After limping to the shelf, he dabbled the cut with peroxide and grimaced. The white gauze was cool on his skin as he wrapped the wound.

A crazy urge tugged at him, and he laughed as the things thumped and squealed against the door. Over the last few days he'd gotten used to providing entertainment for the Being. But he was damned if he was going to let these things do the same. A moment later he slid out the cardboard box from under the bunk and grabbed the bear trap. Much of the trap was rusted, but seemed functional. The heft was most assuring. Here was a weapon, here was something he could use. Sure, it was worthless against the Being, but these smaller bastards? Ha.

His father once told him the trap had belonged to the farmers who originally owned this place. He set the receptacle on the floor and pried open the jaws with a kitchen knife. Slowly, he poked the silver dollar-sized trigger plate with the knife and the jaws snapped shut around the blade. Then he pulled the knife out and dabbed peanut butter on the trigger plate. It might be a strong enough scent to lure in one of the little freaks.

Matt chuckled, relishing the potential violence aimed at his tormentors. Most days, people dreamt of sunshine, the beach, or getting laid.

Next he leaned against the door and listened. Nothing. He opened the door and using the log grabber, snuck the trap receptacle through the crack, the rusty metal chain sliding out the door like a snake. Once the trap was set in the grass he released the grabber. Then he took the last two feet of chain, laid it flat on the ground and closed the door over it.

The scraping and clacking started up again, along with pattering feet in the grass. Matt kneeled, two hands on the chain. The trap snapped shut and a shriek echoed across the property. A moment later, the shriek was followed by the monstrous train sound he'd heard during the northern lights. Deep, black dread sludged over him and his mouth dried to the texture of cardboard.

Um...you've pissed it off, Matthew, the little voice said. *I'm afraid the tango you two are dancing is coming to an end.*

The metal chain yanked outside the door. Fish on! Matt reached for peanut butter-covered kitchen knife. He laughed like a lunatic, holding the chain in his left hand and swinging open the door. He yanked the chain and felt the weight of a medium-sized dog. With a quickness that surprised him, the knife whistled down deep into a thick piece of meat. Crimson slime splurged onto his arm and at once the tension and squealing ceased. The business end of the trap fell towards the ground and then stopped just above the grass, supported by whatever he'd stabbed. Matt yanked the entire thing inside and shut the door. Outside, the Being roared, its approaching steps shaking the property with the authority of a Panzer.

Without thinking, Matt plunged the knife into the thing he'd caught again and again, sometimes hitting shack floor, other times sinking into flesh. He counted every stab, laughing like a madman, each stab weaker and less accurate than the last. Blood covered the entry way like melted chocolate, and trails of slime dripped down the door. He stuck his hand into the slop like a finger painting, then raised it and laughed. He wore it well.

Huuuooohar

The steps rumbled the shack walls and shook loose wood particles from the ceiling. The Being had no reason to conceal its steps this time. Matt laughed again, half his face covered in slime, contrasting with the whites of his eyes. He slapped his stained hand to his face and snickered.

Huuuooohar

The sound blasted through the east window, blowing the glass apart and tossing the nailed chair across the room. The chair socked Matt in the ribs as he turned, and his lungs expunged air in a grotesque cough. He dropped to the floor, holding his ribs. Glass particles crumbled from his hair and sparkled on the ground.

Huuuuooohar

Another roar blasted through the open window with a foamy spray of phlegm and hot breath. *First time I've seen that,* he thought, pressed tight to the musty floor. Rough, elephantine breathing filled the shack, followed by frenetic sniffing.

Keep down and be still, the little voice said.

Matt lay flat behind the center table, obscured from its view. He tried to breathe when the Being did, and held his breath when it did.

After several moments, the sniffing and huffing dissipated.

Whew, the voice said.

As Matt prepared to push himself up, his groin vibrated. Metallic rattling shuddered the shelf above the grungy couch—the coins and metal knick-knacks doing the jitterbug. Then the silverware and dishes joined in the dance. The triple bunk joined in, too. The lid covers on the iron stove rattled, almost lifting off the stovetop like blown manhole covers. Soot belched from the hearth. Dust and wood particles crumbled from the rafters and log walls, blooming inside the shack like a murky cloud. The trap chain rattled at his feet and he saw the knife sticking out of the unseen creature, hanging in the air, half the blade missing. The bloody handle vibrated, making a sick humming sound. Pieces of the white paste used to cobble the slate boulders on the fireplace crumbled to the floor. The lighters, matches, lantern mantles, and lantern buzzed and shook. Sure this was *it,* Matt held his hands over his head and curled into the fetal position.

Be still, Matthew. Do not move, the little voice said.

He followed the advice, making no sound as the world collapsed around him. Four mice scurried from the northeast corner and scrambled down the logs onto the red couch. They huddled for a moment, looked around nervously, then fled through the open window. The Being pounded the roof, sending down shards of wood, insects, and spider webs. The detached webs floated in space and time, avoiding the violent shaking like a starship ghosting past an imploding planet. Matt's teeth chattered and the tips of his boots slammed into the wooden floor, shooting pain from his toes to his knees. The log beams in the pitched ceiling groaned and decades old sawdust crumbled down like fine sand. Some of it settled on the back of his hands and got into his hair. He sucked in dust and a clump of spider web, then gagged and spit the crap out of his mouth.

And then the shaking stopped as if it never happened.

The ground rumbled, but each rumble was farther and farther from the shack, and then nothing.

Matt sighed and let his forehead touch the shack floor. He thought of Stacey, of Elmo, and his father. He loved them, but he wasn't ready to see them just yet.

Yes, Matthew, the little voice said. *That's the spirit.*

His left ear twitched as a spider web strand glided past the intricate folds leading to the ear canal. Then the ear twitched again, catching something far off. His cochlea vibrated into action, processing the vibrations to the brain: A voice. A voice near the leaning post.

"Hey dar! Anyone home?"

***

Bob Sanders was pissed off. Someone stole his lucky trap, and he was going to find out who. The bastards even took the God damned nail. He'd used that exact nail on that exact tree twenty years now. Who had the right to break tradition, eh? He gazed at the tire tracks along the road near the stolen trap. They headed east towards Julip Road. Sanders sat on his Yamaha four wheeler, an 870 Wingmaster pump action strapped to his back. If he flushed up any grouse or woodcock along the way, so be it.

"Fook the DNR, eh?"he said to the forest. Sanders and his friends liked to call them *Do Nothing Right*. This always got a laugh at Spencer's over in Ironville. No one liked the DNR, at least not people who didn't work for 'em. They meddled in the affairs of locals and pinched too many of 'em. Sanders flipped on his copper-tinted, heavy-duty marksman glasses and twisted the acceleration handle. The four wheeler scooted down the road, happy to absorb the puddles and bumps.

The stolen trap wasn't the only thing bothering Sanders. He'd never seen so few animals. Where were all the deer and moose? The grouse were few and far between and the woodcock nowhere to be found.

The sides of the road closed in on him, the chokeberry and alder almost suffocating. He reached behind and touched the smooth barrel of the shotgun. The vibrations from the four wheeler buzzed into his groin, pleasing him. He'd always loved the combination of motors and nature. There was something triumphant about it. Being boss was great, and make no mistake about it, he was the boss of these woods. He'd been blessed to be a human, and he damn well planned to take advantage of it. Sanders pitied the suckers and tourists who visited the woods thinking it was fooking Disney Land. The truth is these animals killed and ate each other, sometimes in ways you'd never want to see or even imagine. He'd often ask the bright-eyed tourists at the Hilltop restaurant if they ever saw a black bear eat a deer fawn alive. He'd seen it. Tried to unsee it. *Fook the bears eh?,* he thought. They'd eat him too if they could. If he laid down in the middle of the God damned woods and sat there, you bet your ass they'd try and feed. This ain't Disney Land, eh? This is nature. Eat or be eaten, kill or be killed.

The fishers were part of the problem too, along with the coyotes. Just like insurance companies, Bob Sanders had his own policy: shoot on sight.

He chuckled, bobbing down the two track, master of these woods. As the four wheeler vibrated his groin, he thought of Melinda, twenty years younger than he. It was his confidence that attracted her. He wasn't some waffling hippie pontificating every facet of life. She also liked the Shangri-La he'd created up here— the cottage far away from the intrusion of town life. She liked his decisiveness and his tone. You bet they had disagreements, eh? But she always fell in line on *The Bob Sanders' Train.* In some ways he was like an animal, lots of doing, not much thinking.

Sanders spit into the wind, and the gob sucked away from his face and shot behind the four wheeler. He figured the place needed the rain.

The engine whine dipped and peaked as the four wheeler navigated the ruts. Sanders rocked side to side, flowing with the movement like a rodeo rider.

Soon he arrived at one of his secret trails. The horizontal, carved wooden branch hanging across a young birch was his little tell. He moved the pile of brush he'd placed there, passed the four wheeler through, and replaced the brush. No big deal. Sanders had them all over the countryside. It was far easier to check his traps and bait stations from the four wheeler than to walk everywhere. He had trails across county land, private property, and paper company land. Most of them didn't allow four wheelers so he had to keep things secret. This particular trail he was riding led to the old orchard to the north—one of his top secret honey holes. Most people kept lists of favorite music or movies. Not him. He kept lists of the best hunting places— kept them rolled up on yellow notepad paper in his coffee cupboard. From time to time he'd pull the list out, relishing the opening of each dry fold. He liked to read it on the toilet. It made him feel good as he worked out a fresh shit, dreaming of the sunshine and all the critters waiting for him. Sometimes he'd re-order the favorite spots in his mind, but never mess with the order on the paper. That'd be like dicking with the Ten Commandments.

Most of the four legged animals that frequented the orchard liked the apples. But the apple lovers had a problem, eh? They were followed by animals that wanted to eat them. And in the case of bears, they liked to eat the apples *and* the animals that liked to eat apples. And wouldn't you know it? He liked to eat the bears. So guess who wins, eh?

Sanders gripped the four wheeler's handle and the knobby tires rolled to a stop. He marveled at the silence of the valley and the thick growth of alder, chokecherry, and birch. The place was a damn jungle. Most of the trees were no taller than fifteen feet. Animals loved the thickness—especially birds, hare, weasels, and bears. Sanders felt closed in, though. Visibility was nil compared to mature forests. If a bear wanted to, it could charge him through the brush and he'd never know it until the fooker was on top of him. *Another good reason to have the shotgun today eh?* he thought.

But there were other reasons for the shotgun. For the first time ever, he felt strange in these woods. An unexplainable sadness crept over him, so he unzipped his fanny pack and slipped out a can of Pabst Blue Ribbon. Sanders cracked open the tab and foam soaked the handlebars. *Shit*, he thought, raising the foaming can to his lips. He sucked off the foam, some of it sticking to his moustache. The beer was a touch warm but that was okay, eh?

The four wheeler lurched down the narrow path, the jungle brushing against his shirt. Thirty feet down trail, something darted out.

A ruffed grouse.

Sanders braked, swung his shotgun from his back, and pointed it with eerie precision. Before he could pull the trigger, the grouse disappeared into the stubby brush towards Twenty Mile Bog.

Well shoot, eh?

He didn't care for the bog much. For starters, he couldn't get his four wheeler back there. The country was too dense. The biggest game used it as a refuge, too. A certain bear had eluded him for years there—a trophy specimen if there ever was one. He'd caught a glimpse of the hoss four years ago in the orchard. The son of a bitch was gorging on apples, standing on hind legs and batting them down from the trees. He'd forgotten his rifle at the time and only had his shotgun. No good. The bear had caught wind of him and had stormed downhill to the west, out into the bog. Ever since, he brought slugs along.

His four wheeler puttered along, the exhaust like the panting of a happy puppy. Once in a while Sanders splashed through puddles. The air grew thick with the scent of sweet gale. Here and there birds flitted across the trail, a few plucking worms from the soft soil. These were of no use to him. Not enough meat on them bones. A familiar track caught Sanders' eye, and he pulled over. Bear prints.

I see you, fooker, he thought, his heart pumping faster like it always did when the hunt began.

The tracks pointed towards the bog, and Sanders' cocky grin twisted into a grimace. He never followed them into the bog, and the animals damn well knew it. The bear probably heard him puttering down the road and headed right for it.

Sanders drove on and then braked at a tiny clearing. His leather hunting boots creaked as the heels thudded into the earth. His boots meant business, and he walked in a way that inferred complete authority. Many an animal's last breath was spent under those boots. He'd crush furbearers like pine marten and fisher under the thick vibram soles. This was an approved kill method by the state. Approach the trapped animal, jab your boot in its face, and the animal will roll onto its back while biting the boot. This is a fatal mistake for the critter. All he needed to do then was let gravity take over, squeezing the life out of the animal, crushing ribs, lungs, and heart with his weight. Sanders enjoyed that moment the most—when the eyes, full of life, faded to a dull grey. *No-one-home-time.* Sanders *controlled* their fate, and then he controlled their body afterwards, either taxidermy or food for the crows. As if giving thanks, a crow passed overhead and cawed at his presence. He never shot the crows. Ever.

Bad luck, he thought. *Just plain bad luck.*

The crow flew north towards the orchard, the same direction he was headed. Sanders watched it cross the sky like Boba Fett watching the Millennium Falcon as it left the Cantina.

Sanders bent down in a small grassy clearing next to a twisted chokecherry. His camo shirt hung over his waist, flapping in the breeze. Sanders flipped up his field glasses and examined his trap. Empty. All empty trap were taken back to the cottage and rubbed out, removing all potential scent. Sanders did this by soaking them in the Silver River, staked down on the river bed. He never could've done that with the old traps, but with these 400 grade stainless steel wonders he sure could.

Sanders took a hammer from the plastic ATV toolbox. Below the toolbox was a yellow bumper sticker spelling out: *COYOTES....SMOKE A PACK A DAY!*

Sanders stepped into the brush and pried the u-nail out of the tree, grinning at all the claw marks along the steel shank. He put the nail in his pocket, making sure to button it. He'd lost too many knick knacks over the years bouncing around on the trails, and there was no doubt he'd be the one to run over the God damned nail since he was *the* trail user in this little corner of the world. After a while he'd learned to lock stuff down. Everything out here was in order and he was master of this order. But one issue stuck in his gut: the absence of animals this season. Every time he checked his traps, the cold reality slapped his face like his wife did when she'd found out about Melinda. That wasn't such an abnormal thing as the furry punks learned to avoid traps— especially if they smelled like Pabst Blue Ribbon. *Cut down on your drinking*! Janie would always tell him in her condescending voice. *Your liver gonna give out on you, eh? An' God ain't making no more livers for Bob Sanders, trust me on that one!*

Gah, he thought. His balls shriveled just thinking about her.

Sanders wrapped up the steel trap and tucked it inside the toolbox. Then he drove the four wheeler down his secret, convoluted path through chokecherry, alder, and birch. Sanders thought of Melinda's curves and playful demeanor. He remembered what she'd told him when they first screwed, how she picked up copies of Bob Seger's *Beautiful Loser* and Neil Young's *Everybody Knows This is Nowhere,* and said with a smirk, *Neil and Bob...get it, Bob? Kneel and Bob....* She'd tossed the albums aside and knelt before him, almost tipping over from drunkenness. The memory should've freed his balls out of their frightened state, but his balls remained tucked away, almost painful. And something else was bothering him. Sanders braked, killed the engine, and listened. He'd been in these woods a long, long time. He'd never had this kind of feeling before, not even after Jim Alberston's freaky UFO stories out at the cottage, or listening to the Art Bell radio program alone at night (something he eventually learned not to do). Out here in the bush, away from society he'd grown accustomed to heightened, unpolluted senses. He knew how to find animals—could even smell 'em sometimes. Sanders knew to watch his back for bears or a charging bull moose. Hell, he sensed the damn things before they made their move.

In the great U.P. wilds he craved sex more than normal—even more so than in Ironville thanks to the pulp plants that fouled the air. All that fresh air helped blood flow. These were feelings he'd come to know with regularity. His appetite was also ravenous out here, and he consumed vast quantities of bear steaks, venison, and fried grouse. These desirable proteins further enhanced his feeling of the wild. Hell, they made him part of it. Every fiber of his being was in one way or another connected to the U.P. landscape. When he ate trout from the Silver, he became part of it, part of the cold water and frothy bubbles from underwater crevices and graveled bottoms, shuddering from the deep, shaded recesses, as deep down as a fish could go. When he shot a bald eagle last season and grilled it, he felt as if he might even be able to fly. Out here it was hunt, fish, eat, fook, and *drink*—a blissful existence. What the hell else could a guy want? None of this was hippy dippy bullshit. That was for the liars, the fakes. These were facts. And while he was always fearful of bears in a common sense way, what he felt now was something far different. A real and protracted sense of danger enveloped his senses and that's what made his balls shrink on this warm fall day. Like wading into the deeper pools of the Silver during spring runoff, up to his waist and feeling out the river bed in front of him with the tip of his boots. Shadows glommed in the depths, and you weren't sure if your next step would submerge you, waders filling with frigid water, triggering a shock heart attack. When your front boot swung in the murk, you retreated a few steps. There, a few feet from the precipice you enjoyed fishing, happy and safe.

The fools walked forward with both boots.

Those were the ones he'd read about in the paper every spring. And right now, he was walking forward with both boots, shit-eating grin, fishing pole in hand like a dumb tourist.

That isn't Bob Sanders, he thought. *Fookin' a no.*

Sanders examined his winding, illegal trail, a taste of copper in his dry mouth. He sloshed his beer can around to make sure no insects had flown inside and took a drink. His wife's voice assaulted him once again. *You ain't so different from the coyotes,* she'd once told him. *You stick your snout in all kinds of bullshit! One day you ain't gonna be able to pull your snout out of what you stick it into, eh Bob?*

"Shut your fooking pie hole," he mumbled to no one.

Without hesitating, Sanders turned the four wheeler around in a skillful five point maneuver. He wanted out.

Just before he sped off, something swished through the stunted woods ahead of him. The grass parted below a birch and he glimpsed chocolate-colored fur. Then Sanders heard a squeaking noise.

"Fookin' fisher!" he said. Sanders revved the four wheeler and gave chase. The trophy fisher bounded up the trail, using the open ground to gain speed. Sanders followed, only able to go so fast without flying off the seat. He gripped the bars with sweaty, eager hands. His eyes were electric behind his field glasses.

"Yeeeehoooo!" he shouted into the woods. "Yeeeehoooo!"

The fisher bobbed like an overgrown squirrel, its thick and luxurious tail not all that different from a fox's except in color.

How'd you avoid my trap, fooker? Sanders thought. *Doesn't matter, eh? Soon you'll be on my wall, a lone trophy in this season of not-so-plenty.*

The four wheeler gained on the fisher and Sanders unslung his shotgun. At the last moment, the fisher darted into thick brush and disappeared. Sanders killed the engine and entered the woods, where he crouched in the shadows. His breath was heavy, and sweat beaded on his nose and forehead. Sanders thought he heard the little fooker panting behind a grove of alder. After five minutes, he walked back to the four wheeler. As he sat down, he couldn't believe it. The fisher was back on the trail, thirty yards up! He cranked the engine and gave chase, closing in on the little bastard as he had before.

Hey, you ain't a very smart guy, eh? he thought. The fisher gained speed, leaping over the water holes that Sanders had to lurch through. He went too fast through one of them and splashed his shirt sleeves with mud. The fisher continued to lead him down trail, almost to the orchard and Ron's place. He and Ron had shared a few drinks over the years, but Ron had no idea of the four wheeler trail he'd illegally hacked through his property. The key was making sure the trail ended well before the orchard. He always outsmarted tourists from Chicago, even if they did own property up here. That didn't mean nothing.

The fisher reached trail's end and disappeared into the vegetation near the orchard. Sanders parked the four wheeler, grabbed his beer, and pursued. As he pushed through the brush, his face caught branches of colorful, dying leaves. *That's what the field glasses are for, eh?* The barrel of his shotgun snagged and he snaked sideways to loosen it, performing a strange dance.

I can catch the bastard out in the open in the orchard, he thought. Sanders licked his lips in anticipation.

The lower forest spit him out.

He stumbled into the knee-high orchard grass, tossed his beer, and spread his legs for balance. The sun parted the clouds, watering his eyes behind his field glasses. Sanders glanced uphill towards the leaning post. The furry fooker loped away not more than a few yards from him, squeaking and chittering. He unslung the shotgun and aimed it up slope, knees bent. Then the fisher did something no animal had ever done to him in all his years in these woods: it turned and ran *at* him.

What the fookin' a Christ? he thought.

The surprise maneuver froze Sanders in his tracks. The fisher raced to his right and paused near his boot, then behind it.

What the fook? he thought. But he knew better. Only the direst of circumstances would make an animal behave in such a way. The god damned thing was using him as a shield. Before Sanders could turn and pull the trigger, the fisher leapt into the wall of lower forest, squeaking and bounding into obscurity.

Sanders sat there, gun in hands, numb. A sense of appreciation for the fisher overcame him— something he hadn't felt before.

He outsmarted me, he thought. Huis wife Janie's irritating voice shrieked in his mind. *Oh, stop acting like that's a first, eh Bob?*

Then Bob heard a sound he'd never heard before in the U.P.—a sharp, obnoxious clicking. This was turning out to be a day of firsts in the shadow of the Hurons.

Sanders looked up towards the leaning post while thumbing his right flannel pocket for the slugs. He needed to feel them, to know they were there. The clicking moved closer. Then the knee-high grass parted near the leaning post.

"What the foo—"

Click! Clack! Click!

"Anyone here?" he shouted. "Hey dar, you here Matty?"

The orchard grass parted in a continual line, right at him. Behind this line, just to the left more grass parted, and it too emitted a clicking noise. Then *both* rows of parting grass drew closer. Behind these, another row of grass parted.

Three, he thought.

Sanders strained his eyes, expecting to see the small animal responsible for the bending grass. There was nothing. But things *were* indeed coming at him—the orchard grass betrayed them. In all his life, his eyes had never lied to him. And he wasn't about to let his brain lie to him, neither. Sanders thought back to his pa, fresh from the Korean War and their visits to the firing range. He and his pa never saw eye to eye except on guns. When his aim was shaky, his pa would slap him on the back a bit too hard, as if to snap him out of a slumber and offer cold advice: *You gotta learn to shoot, boy. Someday it may save your life. The most important thing you can remember boy is to hold your breath and make yourself a statue like so.* His pa had gripped his gun, forearms bulging, eyes calm. He'd inhaled and then pulled the trigger. The bullet thwacked the paper bulls eye and ripped through the haystack behind it into the dirt bank.

Click! Clack! Click!

Sanders aimed just ahead of the first row of parting grass, inhaled, and fired. All movement and sound slowed. His ma had told him great athletes experience everything at slower speeds, and this was how they made remarkable plays. They were given physical intelligence. *Everyone has a gift,* his ma had said, God Bless her. And Bob Sanders did have that gift. In situations that seemed impossibly fast for most people, he was calm.

The shotgun shell ejected from the chamber, to his left. As it reached its peak in the air, Sanders heard a sickening crunch and the first row of parting grass stopped. Thick, snot-like blood oozed onto the ground. Then Sanders heard another noise and just about pissed himself.

Huuuooohar

It came from near the shack. The ground trembled under his feet, not all that different from the Silver River in spring as it pummeled floating trees into the canyon walls. *Two left,* he thought. Sanders aimed at the second row of parting grass, now way too close. The muzzle flashed with brilliant orange as shotgun pellets peppered the creature, spraying droplets of blood. Sanders licked his lips, tasting the foul slime. Bile surged up his throat and he forced it back down with a burning gulp.

The second row of parting grass stopped.

Three left in the chamber, he thought. The ground rumbled.

Huuuooohar

The third row of parting grass reached his feet and a terrible pain seized his left leg. The thing had sliced him above the boot, tearing his jeans open. Sanders kicked firmly—not in a way meant to deliver damage, but in a way to flip the thing in front of him, like someone trying to lift a soccer ball. Then he'd have a good shot once it parted the grass again. Another pain from his shin, and then a breath-sucking pinch followed by razor teeth. Sanders jammed the shotgun barrel at his boot, using it to jab the thing away. Another bite ripped his flesh and he screamed.

It's eating me alive, he thought. Sweat beaded on his face as he planted his left boot and kicked at the thing with his right. His toe found the mark and the thing grunted. Sanders retreated five steps, aimed the shotgun down, and fired at the moving grass. The red and copper shell spun from the chamber, high into the fall day. At once the grass ceased moving. A chunky horse fly landed on the blood and dipped its probing feelers into the mess.

One left, he thought.

The thing that made the big noise. Big mamma. Big *motherfooking* mamma.

Sanders lowered the shotgun and loaded the three slugs into the chamber. He checked the orchard grass. Nothing. He surveyed the leaning post, knees bent in a shooting position. His ears throbbed with anticipation, his eyes darting to the tiniest sound.

Something chopped the air above him like a whip.

The wind picked up from the south, rustling tree tops in the southern valley. Oh how he wanted to climb onto his four wheeler and haul ass back to the cottage, to lie in Melinda's arms.

Then his chest tightened, and he choked.

Next, his arms numbed and flopped at his side, and a punishing constricting sensation overcame his entire body. Somehow, he held onto the gun as spittle burst from his lips.

Then he saw Matty Kearns near the leaning post, running towards him with a chain saw.

***

If you go out there, you will die, the little voice said.

"Don't care," he said.

Another shotgun blast ripped across the orchard. Matt stood and paced like a caged animal.

You'll die…do you understand that? the little voice said.

"I'm not going to stand by and do nothing this time. Someone needs my help and I'm going to offer it." Matt opened the door, dragged the dead thing by the trap chain, and swung it into the grass. It thumped to the ground like a waterlogged volleyball. Matt took the chainsaw, pressed the safety button, and yanked the plastic handle. The saw rumbled to life as he gunned the accelerator. He raised the blade into the air and revved, making the saw buzz like a colony of pissed off wasps.

Another shotgun blast.

Matt staggered up the path to the leaning post, holding the chainsaw out in front of him, his eyes wild. When he crested the ridge he saw Bob Sanders downhill to the south, at the wall of vegetation. Sanders was rigid and surrounded by bloody grass. Portions of his body were distorted.

He must've taken out the little things, Matt thought. *Good job, Sanders. Good fucking job.* Matt hobbled downhill and shouted his lungs out. "Bob, aim high! Shoot the head!"

Matt hunched over to avoid crossfire and tailed off to the left of Sanders, swinging the chainsaw low and wide. He grimaced like a wolverine as his forearm muscles rippled. The chainsaw met flesh, throwing an arc of blood across the grass.

Huuuooohar

Something smashed into Matt's chest and he was thrown uphill ten feet, the chainsaw daggering into the ground and going silent.

Matt looked downhill in time to see Sanders get into a shooter's stance. A thunderous crack ruptured the orchard and a spectacular orange flame erupted from the barrel.

The Being roared.

"Yes!" Matt shouted. "Freaking yes!"

Another flash from the barrel, and another roar.

Sanders aimed the barrel towards the ground. "This might cripple the fooker, eh Matty Boy? I done good here, didn't I?"

A tremendous orange flame shot from the barrel, and the Being wailed in pain. Sanders pulled the gun back to reload, and as he did, he was hit by a train. Then he flew into the air, high as an eagle.

***

I'll miss you, Melinda, Sanders thought. The southern valley stretched out below him, colorful and endless. As he flew so high, he glimpsed his four wheeler trail winding through the forest. He saw puddles of bog water, and the impenetrable tangle of Twenty Mile Bog to the west.

Such a beautiful view, he thought. He'd never seen it like this before.

The trees beckoned him, pulling him closer to their sharp branches and the hard, sandy soil. A moment later he disappeared into the canopy, the branches ripping into him and obscuring the cloudless autumn sky like dirt from a cemetery worker's shovel. There'd be no sauna or Pabst Blue Ribbon tonight.

***

Matt played dead.

This time, the Being did not try to muffle its footsteps. It shook the orchard in a tantrum, vibrating his rib cage as he lay flat against the ground. Elephantine huffing came from down near the creatures Sanders had killed. Matt wanted to run, the panic triggering a fight-or-flight response. His nerves were fried. Fried in those nasty fast food fat fryers where they dropped fifty pound cubes of lard.

Yes, the little voice said. *Run back to the shack!*

There was no reason to dissent. Matt picked himself up and hobbled off. Halfway down the path the orchard rumbled and he was swatted to the ground, all breath expunged from his lungs.

Something kicked him in the head with enough force to roll him on his back. The world faded and dimmed and the last thing he saw was the arm-like branches of the dead oak. It leaned over him, laughing and pointing. Then he realized it might be his headstone. Maybe it had always been there, waiting for him to roll under it.

***

The chirping of crickets and frogs rained in his mind. Points of light flashed behind his eyes. The incessant hooting of an owl tickled his ears.

That owl is close, he thought.

Matt shivered and smelled moist grass and soil, so moist it almost smells like a fish. The Milky Way stretched out before him, cold and striking. He tried to lift his left eyelid but it wouldn't budge. Matt felt a sticky substance there, probably blood. Or maybe a crow pecked his eye out and there was nothing there but slop pooled in the socket. He reached again and sighed when he touched the lid.

It let me live, he thought.

Yes it did, the little voice said. *Maybe it wants to keep you around for its next batch of offspring.*

Not cool. He'd already been a soft target for the offspring, and had no intention of playing that role again. He took a breath and winced as sharp pain radiated across his chest.

"I think I broke a rib," he mumbled to no one. He realized, with creeping gloom, that his breathing was erratic. He could feel his heart beating abnormally between stabs of pain. He brought two fingers to his crusty eye lid and pried it open. Above the eye he discovered a bump that seemed to cover half his forehead.

High in the dead oak loomed the silhouette of a great horned owl, the stars speckling behind it. The owl hooted and he realized just how loud their calls were.

He thought of Sanders emptying his shotgun and smiled. Then he sat up in the orchard grass, shivering. His face felt warm and sweat—strange considering the chill in the air. As he stood, his knees wobbled and his calves spasmed, teetering him back to the ground. His face tingled and a warm sensation crept under his cheeks and forehead. Sweat dripped from his upper lip and nose. He placed a hand on his forehead. Yep, warm as a radiator.

You have a fever, Matthew, the little voice said.

"Tell me something I don't know," he mumbled, trying to stand. His jaw felt like it was a big, rusty hinge and he touched the bottom of his face to make sure it was still all there. With great effort, Matt slumped towards the shack, dragging his right leg behind him. The owl watched from its roost, maybe to see if he stirred any mice from the grass.

At last he reached the bunk and stretched the headlamp over his swollen head. He flipped the switch, illuminating the shack with sterile light that removed all color. His right arm itched and he removed his red-checkered flannel. Dirty yellow puss oozed out of the branch wound from a week ago. He poured peroxide on it, grimacing at the sting. The brown fluid pooled, then dripped down his arm onto the floor. Peroxide bubbled and foamed in the wound and he wanted to vomit, but let loose a dry gag instead. A long drink of water helped, although it was almost empty. Next Matt wrapped gauze around the wound and put his flannel back on. He shivered violently, then huddled in his own arms.

A breeze poured through the broken window above the couch. He thought about ripping down the shelf and boarding it up, then realized it might be a good idea to have two exits tonight. As far as he knew, the clicking freaks were all dead. If they weren't they'd have feasted on him as he lay knocked out under the dead oak. Still, he didn't like the idea of an open window. He slid out the cardboard box from under the bunk and taped it to the logs. Halfway through the process, he lost his balance and vomited onto the couch.

When he recovered, he bent down near the mouse bucket and took the lantern. The glass was cracked but it still looked useable, and white gas sloshed around inside. He found a lighter and a fresh mantle that looked like a baby's sock. The lantern lit for maybe the last time and he turned the intensity dial, bathing the shack in organic light.

Matt flicked off his headlamp and glanced around. Memories embedded everything. The old man loved this place as much as he did. He wondered what his father would do, how he'd approach this situation. He sat, waiting for an answer but there was only the stillness of the country and his shivering.

Your father would leave immediately, the little voice said. *He'd know that he had twenty four hours or he'd be dead.*

"Easier said than done," Matt said. His mind raced with absurd plans. The only plan based on reality was running to the truck and driving away. Fine. Maybe this time it might work. But he needed a distraction, something to get him going fast enough so the Being could never catch up.

Matt coughed yellow phlegm into his palm and wiped it onto the blanket, then shivered again. But this time it wasn't from the fever. For the first time in his life, he was certain of death. It hit him like a n NFL defensive end, popping his dazed mindset into cold reality. If he didn't leave tomorrow, he'd die. He'd die from infection, or from one, final attack.

The wind carried the scent of sweet gale up from the Black. He thought of the trout finning in the dark water and gentle riffles under the Milky Way. Cold. So cold. He took his black North Face jacket out of his backpack and laid it over himself.

Ah...the waters of the upper Black, he thought. His eyelids fluttered and he dozed off into paradise, away from the darkness.

He woke at two a.m., teeth chattering. He crawled under the blankets, his legs rigid and unresponsive. For a moment he wondered if it was ten degrees in the shack. Thoughts of Stacey popped into his mind, her warm smile and laughter comforting him.

"I'm s-s-sorry if I f-f-failed you guys" he said. The fever wracked him and he shuddered. When he closed his eyes, he felt the frenzied bacteria colonizing the highways of his arteries and the fertile soil of muscle tissue. The bacteria weren't all that different from the Being. He couldn't see them, yet they still disabled him, trapping him.

"Why d-d-don't you go f-f-find the Being and invade its b-body," he mumbled. "That's the b-bad guy."

Mother nature doesn't choose sides, the little voice said. *She just is, Matthew.*

"I g-g-guess I c-caught the the bad e-end of i-it, huh?" he asked.

Yes, you did, the voice said.

"I'm g-g-going to die, aren't I?" he asked.

There was no response.

Matt slipped into vivid dreams of color and action. Objects and people swirled around him—his mother, his father, Stacey, and Andrea. Stacey walked towards him in a park, then away like a yoyo. In his dream he jostled from the bumps of Julip Road as he laid on a cot in his father's old pickup. His father looked through the rear sliding window of the cab, grinning, letting him know they'd arrived. It was all so pretty. Everyone he loved made an appearance, and they loped from scene to scene. He relished it all, happy to see them, excited to feel their energy. The peace and finality warmed his heart. He shook his father's hand, then embraced him, telling him how happy he was to see him.

Matt woke at three a.m., convulsing under the covers, teeth knocking so hard they cut his tongue. He spit blood on the covers and laughed. "This is f-fun!" he said to no one. "Best f-fun I've had in a l-long time. So glad I c-c—came."

Het thought of Chad Figgins farting on the top bunk, and laughed. The fart had smelled of rotten eggs and had cleared the shack. He laughed again and coughed. Then, insidiously, he thought of the knife rack in the hutch. Without further thought he lifted his head and tried to move.

Time to end this.

But severe vertigo overtook him and he faded to black. He dreamed of a snowy aspen forest with a stream winding through. All around he heard the slick sound of parting snow. The Being was coming towards him, but this time there were more, and they didn't want him as a play thing. He stumbled through snowdrifts in his fevered clumsiness. On the last fall, a white robin landed on the ground before him, its delicate feet sinking into the glistening powder. He lifted his face, his chin covered with snow. The bird closed and opened its beak like an animatronic robot.

You didn't do it right, the bird said. *Now it's got you.*

He woke at 3:40 a.m., beads of sweat dotting his skin like tent condensation. Matt wiped his hand across his forehead and marveled at the blood and sweat. Something hissed to his right and his heart skipped. Just the lantern using the last bit of gas. The dying light flickered across the walls, perhaps the last time he'd see them. Light finally gave way to darkness and the shack he'd known was no more.

He turned on his headlamp and studied the plywood plank above him, following the grooves with fatigued eyes. The light was erratic as he shivered. Various shapes and patterns were ingrained in the wood. In the upper left, a bald eagle and a cloud. Below that, a man standing, maybe his father. The man looked at something far away. On the ground, behind the man lay a crumpled body. To the right of the body he saw tall grass and a line of trees. Next to this were no shapes or patterns at all. Something big blocked out the scene, and he had a good idea what it was.

"I'm going to die today," he said. "I'm going to die today and no one is going to know how or why."

His eyes filled with pointless, dehydrating fluid. He blinked it away.

For the first time in his life, Matt Kearns asked something of God, if there was such a thing.

"Please God, don't let me die. I've lasted this long. Please."

Matt rolled onto his side and curled into the fetal position. Outside, wind caressed the old logs and the orchard grass sighed. He rolled onto his back, the weakening lamplight shining on the plywood. The big, consuming shapeless thing disappeared. The crumpled body now stood next to the man, and below them, running at their feet was Elmo.

"Oh how I miss you, old buddy," he said.

The infection bore deep, and he closed his eyes.

Day 7

Matt woke sore and with a stomach that wouldn't stop rumbling. The room spun on him, making the nausea worse.

His sister had told him about vertigo while she was in medical school. She had said it only lasted a short while. Still, this knowledge didn't help much. As the room spun, the couch and shelf jerked like he was on the Tilt-a-Whirl. He coughed, spraying phlegm onto the covers. His head throbbed and the shivers persisted, although his teeth no longer knocked. It took all his energy to initiate movement. He angled his legs off the bunk and the spinning grew milder and sort of manageable. He stood, reached out to the table, and fell forward. The sturdy table caught his fall. Then he pushed himself up, using the slate fireplace for balance. The rocks were smooth and cold on his hand and he swore he felt the hum of the Black River in their depths.

Matt shook his head, trying to chase away the vertigo, but instead an intense throb rocked his skull and shot sparks across his vision.

Wonderful.

He stumbled past the fireplace, reaching for the shelf. The shelf bowed under his weight, but held. He grasped the aspirin bottle and swallowed four orange pills. They clung to his dry throat but he forced them down anyway. Sweat dripped from his chin, only to be absorbed by the grungy red couch. Fresh air streamed in from behind the taped cardboard and froze the sweat to his skin. He forced himself over to the stove table, his knees knocking.

Dull morning light crept into the shack, tinting everything monochrome. He felt like a man waking in his own coffin. He took several deep breaths, dismayed at how labored and rough his lungs sounded.

Not much longer now.

The time for escape had passed and now he'd rot away in the shack, sick and helpless.

Everything was so quiet—more so than at any other time he'd come to the U.P. Matt slumped against the stove table and looked out towards the dead oak.

Something looked back.

He looked away, his heart jumping into his throat, his nerves lighting afire. He came alive, raging through the pain and fever and looked out again.

Still there.

Sitting next to the dead oak. Matt blinked, just to double-check.

"Dear God," he said. "Now this?"

He tried to make sense of the shape, of the tail, of the round aquamarine eyes and the flat, orange nose. Whiskers protruded from each side of the thing's muzzle.

The animal licked its nose and watched him, sitting patiently like a house cat. The head was enormous, topped off with symmetric ears rounded at the tips. The ears flicked to the side and then pointed at him, catching the sound of his ragged breathing. He marveled at its brown coat and thick, long tail that batted the air. Matt didn't want to say or think the word, but yet here it was. His sore jaw opened and he mumbled the words:

Mountain lion.

Impossible, he thought. *They were killed off decades ago. All the biologists said so. This was fact.*

As if bored by his line of thought, the mountain lion let out a gaping yawn in the dull morning light, revealing knife-sized teeth. Next, the mountain lion gazed at the shack with what Matt perceived as hungry eyes.

He couldn't believe how powerful the lion's back legs were. He remembered reading that mountain lions had an eighteen foot vertical leap and a forty foot horizontal leap—from a crouched position. By design, North American mountain lions featured disproportionate hind legs, more so than any other wildcat. If he opened the door, the mountain lion could easily reach him in a single jump. If he decided to run, the lion would catch him. No person can outrun 45 miles per hour.

Trapped in freaking stereo, Matt thought. *Lion on the left of me, Being on the right. Stuck in the shack with you.*

He coughed up a yellow hunk of phlegm and it splattered onto the camp stove. The lion's ears twitched, then settled.

As he watched the mountain lion, the morning grew brighter, frost on the orchard grass reflecting clouds and light. Out behind the dead oak and the lion, far onto the horizon the exposed rock of the Huron's glowed a subtle red. Matt perceived a wildness he'd never known in this country. The U.P. was always wilder than Chicago, sure, but having a mountain lion sitting here after a hundred years of supposed extinction redefined the landscape's character. The shadows in the vegetation seemed richer, and the air crackled with possibility.

The mountain lion's eyes penetrated him, as if it could wait him out forever. Then the lion sniffed the dead thing Matt had flung out there. After getting a good whiff, the lion backed up like a kitten surprised by a bug. The lion arched its head and sneezed. Then it slunk down into the bowl, its thick, black-tipped tail disappearing amidst the grass like a bull snake.

Matt tried to remain still, holding back shivers and a cough. He had no idea what he should do.

What you need to do is get the hell out of here, today, the little voice said. *I don't care how sick you are, Matthew. You have to do it.*

Matt nodded and took a sip of water. Then he stumbled over to the pile of tart apples and forced himself to suck one. Surprisingly, the bitter juice made him feel better. He took a few tart apples and sat on the bunk, thinking about the mountain lion, about how they hunted the sick and weak.

He was a perfect candidate.

As he sipped more water and sucked the tart monsters, the shivering lessened along with the cramping. He flexed and stretched his limbs, feeling a tightness around the wound in his right arm. His skin tickled with oozing puss as it leaked down his forearm.

Needing more boost, Matt reached down into the blue cooler and dug around, coming up with a packet of powder. The packet had been put there by his mother. *Take your Emergen-C every day*, she'd said. *They'll give you a boost, Matthew. Would your own mother lie to you?*

The Emergen-C pouches contained vitamins in a sugary powder. Simply mix with water and drink. So he did.

And wouldn't you know it? His mother had been right. Some of the fog cleared from his mind, and his limbs tingled. Better than nothing.

Matt Kearns stood and examined the shelf full of knick-knacks. These items had fascinated him throughout his life. He stared at the fireplace, admiring the smooth stones and ancient poster for the last time. He glanced around the shack, taking in every part of it, memories of his father cooking, card games, animal stories, and laughter. He fed on all of this, his little escape from the world up on Julip Road. He raised his hand to his forehead and saluted the place. He'd never been in the military but was compelled to do so anyway.

Slowly he twisted into his jacket, wincing. Then he tied his boot laces and took two big knives from the hutch. Satisfied with his choice of cutlery, he reached for the fireplace poker. The density of the weapon pleased him—a good device for keeping a mountain lion at bay.

Matt opened the huge shack door for perhaps the last time, and scanned the property for the lion. Then he turned to face the inside of the shack. For a moment he thought he saw his father cooking on the camp stove, smiling.

"Goodbye," he said, closing the heavy door. He turned away and limped to his truck. Although his legs were stronger than the previous night, they were far from ideal. At the truck, Matt bent over and cut the last blanket pouch from the frame. He emptied it of boulders and dragged the parachute-looking device behind him as the orchard grass slicked it with dew.

Almost at the leaning post now, dragging the pouch behind him, head down. Maybe the mountain lion would jump him and slash his jugular. Even in that horrible scenario he'd get the last laugh over the Being.

At the leaning post he gazed out upon the southern valley and the Hurons. The forest of chokecherry, birch, and alder stretched out below him, the occasional balsam fir and red pine puncturing the canopy. Birds flittered from the far off trees as wind rustled the branches. *Somewhere down there, a mountain lion still lives,* he thought. *And maybe it will kill me today.*

Matt glanced towards the southern edge of the orchard, at the wall of stunted forest. He thought about going after the shotgun Sanders had dropped. Then he remembered the boundaries. He couldn't risk it. The last time he went down to the edge, he'd paid. Matt slumped into the grass on his knees.

"This was our spot," he cried. "This was our place."

Never in a million years did he think he'd ever die in the orchard. Even when he was a child he knew the place held a special magic for him.

A twig snapped in the wall of trees and a ghost emerged.

The mountain lion.

It gazed upon him as if sizing him up for a morning snack. In all his many outdoor trips, Matt had never experienced an animal look at him like he was dinner.

"Come on," he mumbled to the lion. "Do it. I want you to."

The mountain lion sniffed the air and turned back into the vegetation. A last flick of black-tipped tail was swallowed by alder.

Matt limped down to the place where Sanders had massacred the offspring. Wind rattled the leaves at the wall of forest and he wanted to run, but then thought better. His breath was heavy and erratic. He thought he felt his heart skip out of rhythm, and remembered the doctors had a name for it: atrial fibrillation. Dizziness seized him and the world darkened, then returned. Sweat beaded on his forehead and he wiped it away with an arm made of grinding glass.

Matt reached into the stained grass, feeling for the dead creatures. His hands came across something like pig skin, smooth but with occasional hairs. His hand worked over the object, feeling something that may have been deep set wrinkles like the back of a fat man's head. His fingers groped dozens of tiny, swollen holes, the work of Sanders' copper shot. Finally he felt a limb of sorts and ran his hand along it. The piggish skin segued into a smooth shell-type surface, like what a crab would have. Matt held the limb where it met the piggish body, then sawed through the meat. Pulling with his left hand, the limb separated in a soggy squish.

Matt put the knife back in his pocket and ran both hands to the end of the limb. *So, this was what made the clicking sounds,* he thought. He returned to the leaning post with his prize, checking behind him every few steps for the mountain lion.

Nothing.

He placed the limb in the blanket pouch and grabbed the fireplace poker. A heap of phlegm expunged from his lungs as he wheezed on his knees.

The lion could run out at any moment and snap my neck, he thought. He'd feel the weight of it on his back, and then nothing. At least it would be a clean kill, far more merciful than the Being's offspring.

Matt took one last look across the southern valley to the Hurons, then limped north down the leaning post hill. Soon he arrived at the second biggest tree in the orchard, an old aspen that shaded a remnant sandpit.

A long time ago the sand pit was populated by pigs and horses. They drank cool water in the trough, brought up from the Black via aqueducts spread across the property. The aspen tree was much smaller then, providing minimal shade. The animals found it did the job just fine. Over the years, the pit collected horse shoes. A log wall three feet high cornered into the hill, making sure the sandy soil did not erode into the aqueduct and trough. The forest was younger, recovering from massive clear cuts. A man could see a deer when looking out into the southern valley. The only surviving old growth trees hid back in Twenty Mile Bog and the Huron Mountains. Wind had blown soil from the clear cuts, slowing new growth. After most of the woods were cut, fires raged, scorching the soil. The forest was never the same.

Before the pigs and horses, before the farmers scratched out a living, the orchard wasn't an orchard. Instead, it was a grove of old growth white pine and hemlock, many trees rising two hundred feet. Lichen grew along the shaded forest floor and caribou fed on the lichen. Mountain lions hunted the caribou. The wolverine, long gone from these parts, weaved in and out of the thick trunks always searching for food, sometimes stealing mountain lion kills.

The view from the leaning post always existed, except a person had to look beyond thick trunks amidst a massive, mediaeval forest to see. The woods were cooler and the streams swarmed with six pound brook trout known as Coasters. The coasters were poached off and the practice of using the rivers to run logs scarred the riverbeds, destroying precious spawning grounds forever.

The wilderness was endless.

And in the end, the wilderness was turned inside out to build Chicago, Detroit, and Milwaukee. Now it stood, scarred, beaten, and missing most of the great pines. The loggers, miners, and farmers left after realizing this wasn't fertile ground. The loggers cut too fast, too hard and ran themselves out of business. Paper companies bought the land for mass production, which they still own. The paper companies did not seek the old growth pine, but rather the pulpy, fast-growing hardwoods which they harvested at increased rates.

In 1900, Julip Road was graded for the loggers and the forest leveled. Loggers dragged the giant white pine and hemlock from where the orchard now sits and ran them down the Black or took them by road. Sometimes, they used railroad. The old track laid two miles south of the shack in the valley, long since faded into the stunted forest. The railroad company pulled most of the track for the iron after decommission.

The rivers were dead for years.

Haze filled the sky for decades as fires up to a million acres in size scorched the land.

What was dark, foreboding, and ancient had become bright, open, and light. An invasive species has found this land, not all that different from the white-tailed deer taking over for the caribou. Matt had no idea where it came from. The Being saw *something* about this place it liked.

But is it really an invasive species? he asked the land. *Could this be something from Earth?* Maybe man had poked the forest too many times, too deep. Maybe the Being was a defense mechanism, something that sprang forth when certain boundaries were breached, a last protector of the ecosystem. Maybe *they* were the intruders and this thing was sent to beat back the human horde.

Oh how the woods had burned. How the insides of the giant trees lay splayed open, revealing the raw, yellow flesh to the sun. The wounds were deep, the pain ceaseless. Millions of animals died in the fires. The white eyes and mental smiles of the sooty-skinned men, the black skies and stumps. The sound of gunfire everywhere, the cadence of running animals, deep red flames roaring behind them, nostrils dilating, surviving the blaze only to run into the camps of men with rifles pointed. The last breath of the caribou, the last breath of the mountain lion and wolverine rising into the ashen, burning skies. Men danced around the campfires with hats of fur, animal heads displayed in the growing sprawl of cabins and cottages.

When the fires died down and the men went back to the cities, stillness engulfed the land—a stillness only mother nature could understand. This stillness triggered alarms and reactions—mechanisms man could not grasp at this juncture in the species evolution. Every landscape makes a unique sound. Humans cannot hear this sound. They were never designed to, and Matt understood this now. It is the sound of forever, of ancient woodlands, granite outcroppings, and the echoes of river canyons. Somehow, something heard these alarms and responded, a common understanding shared. The white-tailed deer smells something in the air, telling it to move north to unoccupied habitat that had recently become suitable for its needs. Perhaps the thing that now occupied the orchard responded the same way.

Why didn't it come earlier? he asked the land. But he knew Mother Nature works in a very slow and methodical fashion. Like all things, change takes time. And the creature now occupying the orchard was part of that change.

The orchard grass crunched under his feet, like it always had. He walked with the weight of generations of fools upon his shoulders. He spit, cursing them all.

"Yeah, well, that wasn't me," he said.

He had no intention of paying for damage he didn't cause. He reached the sandpit in the shade of the giant aspen and kicked the sand with his boots. His head pounded and his body was as responsive as a piece of lumber, but not enough to deter him from such a simple task.

Matt laid the blanket pouch upon the grass and jabbed the sand with the fireplace poker and his boots, loosening it, digging down into it. His toe struck something hard and he pried the object out with the poker. An old horseshoe. He dusted the horseshoe off and read the engraving: *Mary the White Horse, Julip Road Farm, 1962.* Ron had told him about a magnificent white horse up here, when the orchard was enclosed by a fence. Ron had first seen the horse prancing and neighing amidst the apple blossoms as they fluttered in the wind. The horse had died the year before Ron purchased the land, and he believed a well-hidden grave was placed near the leaning post, as that was the horse's favorite location.

Matt placed the horseshoe onto the sand to mark the location of the invisible creature's claw. As he looked down, he noticed a slight appearance of the limb. His heart pounded. At last! Slowly, his grin twisted into a frown as he examined the limb. It looked like the arm of a hairless sloth connected to a multihued lobster claw. The inside of the claw contained a perforated, saw-like blade that led to pinchers. Octopus-like tentacles sagged from the severed end of the limb, each tentacle filled with tiny suction cups on the underside. The skin—if you could call it that—was embroidered with shimmering pigmentation that bent and fragmented in the grey light. Looking at it mesmerized him and he turned away.

It had to be the pigment, he thought. *That's what makes them invisible. And when they die, these effects die too.*

Matt opened the blanket pouch and began dumping cold sand onto it. When it was full, he took the twine ends and wrapped them around his wrist. Exhausted, he sat in the sand and shivered. His eyes darted around the orchard, seeing images of him and his father playing catch on the hill, the collegiate-approved football spinning through the air. He thought of the clay pigeon contests they'd have, the sound of the crickets and the taste of a warm beer at sunset. One dusk he and his father saw anxious bats out before nightfall, their bodies exposed in the light. *See, even bats screw up,* his father had said to him. That had been their first trip after The Incident.

Now he saw nothing at all, not even a bird. The animals had learned to stay clear of this place the last week. He guessed most of them moved on the night of the northern lights.

A branch snapped and Matt looked downhill to the western edge of the orchard.

Two eyes stared back.

The mountain lion gazed at Matt as it stood on all fours, tail swapping the brush. Then it sat on its haunches and licked its chops, then its nose.

"Come and get me," Matt said, his teeth chattering. "Come on!" A crazed look crossed his face, and what had been the whites of his eyes were now deep red. Knots on his head leaked yellow puss and he laughed as he touched one of the lumps. He crossed his arms for warmth, gazed to the monochromatic sky, and spoke:

"Stacey, mom, dad, Andrea, I'm so sorry. I could've been a better son, a better person. At times I was detached and self-involved. *Really* self-involved. I don't know if it's my generation or just me, but either way it's not an excuse. I want you all to know I love you very much. And to Stacey, dad, and Elmo, I'll be seeing you real soon. I want that breakfast you always used to cook up here dad—you know, the canned hash browns, scrambled eggs, and pancakes without lumps. Elmo old buddy, we'll walk together again my friend. Trust me on this. And to Stacey, I was and am an asshole. I want to apologize to you for that. I loved you and still do. I didn't know how to deal with what happened to my father. Please forgive me."

Matt let his words carry away in the Huron breeze, and shivered. He checked the mountain lion. Still there, still watching. The scent of sweet gale wafted across the orchard, and three colorful leaves tumbled in the air.

"And to mother nature," he said, "I'm sorry for what they did to you here. I'm sorry for the extinctions and the poachers and the freaking fires. Please understand that none of this was my fault. I played no part. Thank you for hearing me out."

Satisfied with his last words, he shivered and spat, fighting back unshed tears.

The mountain lion continued to watch him.

"Come on," Matt said.

Slowly, he went to one knee and picked up the offspring limb. He took it in both hands, one hand gripping the upper claw, the other the lower. Matt exhaled a raspy breath and coughed.

Then he forced the claw open and slammed it shut. At first it didn't make a sound, but as he repeated the action, the clicking started.

Click! Clack! Click!

"Come on you bastard."

Click clack click clack!

"I've got your *baaaaaby*! HAHAHA!"

Click! Clack!

His eyes grew wild as he slammed the claw harder, the cracks echoing across the orchard. Matt looked behind him. The mountain lion had slunk back into the brush, but he could see its eyes peering through the vegetation.

Matt turned away from the animal.

Click clack!

He emitted a gritty, hollow laugh, salty tears rolling down his filthy cheeks.

All at once monstrous footsteps shook the orchard. This time the Being made no effort to fool him. Each tremor grew in raucousness until individual steps blurred into one long rumble.

An elephantine huffing sound came from above, and the stink of the thing's breath wafted towards him. The last behemoth step rattled the half-buried fence. The air distorted in front of Matt, and he tossed the claw to the ground.

Do or die, he mumbled. And in that moment, he thought he heard the soft neighing of a horse.

Matt swung the blanket pouch with his left arm as hard as he could, flinging it into the air and stumbling to the ground. The pouch traveled forty feet up and dumped the sand into the sky as gravity took over. The sand poured down as if from a broken hourglass. Instead of hitting ground, the sand sprinkled over the Being, sifting down the featureless shape. As more sand layered upon it, he realized the Being was at least thirty feet tall. Sand traced down the thing's enormous head and he thought he saw a blinking eye as sand rolled off an oversized lid. Each feature appeared like a statue and then disappeared as the sand shifted. All he wanted was for sand to stick so he could see where the godforsaken thing was. A moment later, sand found its mark in the moist eyes and along the edges of the mouth. It founds its mark along the glistening tentacles. It stuck in the pores of the sucker cups, arrayed under the numerous tentacles by the thousands. Thin white hairs coated much of the Being, enough to catch sand. The features were never static. It moved and the sand moved, creating a new feature set. The shifting biological puzzle was impossible to piece together. He could tell the mouth was enormous, and that the Being featured two gigantic eyes. There was no nose to speak of, at least that he could see. The powerful legs remained hidden, the sand sifting from the vast frame of the Being and falling clear. The tentacles—some up to forty feet long—flowed out behind the Being's backside. Sand gummed-up the undersides of the suckers, revealing the snaking half-visible tentacles. One of the sandy tentacles whipped towards him. Matt spun to the ground and dodged the tentacle as it sliced the air above him. A tremor wracked his spine and he glanced behind him, down towards the forest edge. The aquamarine eyes of the mountain lion beamed back, a violent sea rocking inside them.

He looked up in time to see a tentacle reaching for him, the suction cups spreading wide to grip their prey.

So these are what paralyzed me, he thought. *I bet they contain poison, too.* Matt seized the fireplace poker and thrust it into a suction cup. The suction cup instinctively wrapped around the iron and he shoved it forward, bursting the cup.

The Being slammed its unseen feet into the ground. Matt lost his balance and tumbled into the sand pit.

Patches of sand shifted on the Being's frame, revealing new features. The mouth opened wide, far bigger than a great white shark. Rows of teeth lined the mouth, dwarfing any butcher's knife. The Being bent down to him, its tentacles bunching high in the air behind it as if someone had tied them together and was holding them from a platform in the sky.

"I'm sorry," Matt said.

And then the mouth closed in on him.

Cold wind blew from the south, down from the Hurons. It fluttered the aspen leaves. The rustling was enough to cover the steps of something wild, something from another time. The mountain lion leapt from its hiding place, eyes blazing. The big paws of the ghost cat thumped the orchard soil, beating down into the granite below, sending messages from a long time ago. It took only one second to cross fifty feet of orchard, and then the mountain lion leapt into the air, letting out a scream that pierced the ears of a young Matthew Kearns. The lion rose twenty feet, limbs fully extended. As it flew past the aspen branches, the lion curled its paws in a grip-lock. A moment later the lion was on the Being's neck, scratching and biting with the violence of a thousand mass murderers.

Huuuooohar

The lion evaded a tentacle and climbed the Being's head.

The Being turned from Matt and shot its suspended tentacles towards its head. The lion countered each tentacle with a dodge, and when the Being brought all tentacles down, the mountain lion jumped off and retreated, its coat and face stained with blood.

Run Matthew, Run! The truck! The truck! the little voice said.

He picked himself up and stumbled forward, shivers wracking his body. He wheezed and stumbled towards his truck through the orchard, the place he'd run as a child, chasing hoppers or catching a ball from his father. His legs flopped out before him like he was wearing clown shoes. His left foot wobbled and he fell forward, his sturdy right leg saving a fall. The ground shook with the steps of the Being as it dealt with the mountain lion behind him. Up ahead, the dead oak seemed to wave him on with its gnarled, worn branches. Matt hobbled to the truck like a newborn colt, always on the verge of falling. He flung the door open and turned the key.

Nothing.

He turned the key again, giving it gas. Nothing. The battery light blinked back at him.

"Come on, come on, old girl," he said. "Have I ever let you down?"

He looked out the windshield, up the path to the leaning post. The top of the Being's head emerged, the tentacles splaying out behind it, and then gathering steam towards their prey.

The mountain lion roared.

He turned the key and the engine flopped. Matt slammed the gas and turned the key again.

The engine tried to catch.

It spun twice and he gave it more gas. The engine responded with more chatter. Matt gave it more gas, and the clanked and sputtered.

His eyes filled with tears and goose bumps flared across his limbs. He put the truck in reverse and sped down the two track.

Huuuooohar

The land shook as the trees parted along the path to the leaning post. Small patches of sand clung to the Being's frame, betraying it. He stomped the accelerator, feeling the tires rip the soil. He knew if he was on the driveway or not just by how it felt—no need to look behind. Matt jerked the steering wheel back and forth, watching out the front windshield, dismayed as the vague Being thrashed closer. He blinked, and when he opened his eyes the mountain lion was on the Being's skull again, biting and clawing. The Being shook the lion off, flinging it into the bowl of the old farmhouse.

"Oh freaking Christ!" Matt shouted.

The Being stormed to within twenty feet of his truck, the ground violent with its movement.

Matt closed his eyes, expecting to feel the choking and numbness, his final suction cup ride. When he opened them he saw something rip through the orchard grass near the outhouse. The thing was tan-colored with a black snout. Another creature followed right behind, growling and baring its teeth. Both animals featured long tails and sharp, pointed ears.

Coyotes.

They leapt through the air, landing where the Being's feet would be, slashing and tearing. The Being whipped one of its many tentacles at its feet, swatting a coyote away. The coyote yipped as it flew through the air and disappeared into the bowl. A second later the mountain lion leapt from the bowl and clawed the Being's head, gouging out flesh chunks. The thing bellowed and swung at the mountain lion with one tentacle while swinging at the coyote with another. The lion dodged the tentacle and tore deeper into the Being's head. While all this was going on, the remaining coyote tore and slashed at the Being's feet—or at least what he thought were its feet.

The truck whined and bottomed out on Julip Road, snapping Matt's head into the seat. He recovered and swung the wheel to the right and jammed the truck into first gear. The tires ripped through gravel as he sped towards the downed trees. Matt shifted gears and stomped the gas pedal and the truck smashed over the downed trees, sending flurries of leaves into the air behind him. He fisted into third gear and mashed the pedal, but the truck was sluggish. He checked the side mirror and his heart skipped when he saw sandy patches in the air behind him, the tentacles whipping and reaching. Matt dropped the truck into second gear and the engine screamed. Redlining hard, Matt shifted into third, trying to catch momentum. He felt the back of the truck slide and in the mirror he saw a sandy tentacle holding onto it, with another tentacle reaching around to his window.

His mouth dried and his heart sank into his nauseous stomach.

And then the truck came to a screeching halt no more than half a mile from the shack. Matt jammed the pedal, spinning and screeching the tires. He checked the mirror and saw the tentacles encasing the truck, their tips almost at the passenger and driver windows.

"Let me go!" he shouted, jamming the gas and gripping the wheel with both hands.

Rumbling emanated from the woods on the eastern side of the road, and then the sound of flattening vegetation. A dark object the size of a small car thundered out of the alder and crashed into the Being.

The Being roared in pain.

The animal bared its teeth as its massive paws pinned one of the Being's tentacles. It bit down, cut the tentacle in half, and spit the dead part out. The Being swung another, and this one also caught in the bear's mouth, and again was bitten in half and tossed aside.

Matt looked back at the freakish bear and saw something in its eyes. The radiating colors of fire.

Hit the gas! the little voice said. *Wake up!*

Matt shifted the truck into first gear and mashed the pedal. The truck sped away from the Being while the bear swatted and bit tentacles. As the battle grew smaller in his mirror, the mountain lion once again clawed and bit into the thing's head. The leaves and branches that arced over Julip Road were parted in the clash as the Being tried to catch the truck. Matt heard yipping from behind and saw the coyotes at the Beings' feet, slashing and biting. Its tentacles swung wildly through the air as it ran, each one thinking for itself and choosing a specific target. Its mouth opened and closed, hoping to catch an animal that got too close. The coyotes leapt back from the tentacles, the bear instead choosing to bite them in half. The sheared tentacle chunks writhed on the road, suction cups squealing and ejecting an oily substance. Dodging branches and tentacles, the mountain lion dug deeper into the thing's skull, drawing more blood. The bellows and cries of the Being rattled the metal tailgate. Soon, the sound of tearing flesh and scratching echoed through the dense second growth forest along Julip Road. Electricity trickled up Matt's spine and his eyes filled with fluid. This time it didn't feel so useless.

He was crying for his friends—ones he never expected to have.

The last thing Matt Kearns ever saw on upper Julip Road was the tiny shape of a fisher crawling up the front of the Being and attacking its eyes.

Matt shifted into third and gave more gas. His old truck obliged. She always felt at home on the gravel roads. The hardwoods blurred by him, the pines long gone. Julip Road finally spit him onto the pavement of Highway 5, and he looked back, but there was nothing except the dark tunnel of roadway as it wound into the highlands. Matt sped to U.S. 2, out where the Forest Service kept the highway trees tall but clear cut the rest. He was not going to stop until he had to.

He wept as the cold Northwoods air streamed into the cab. The truck rattled and whined as he watched the alder and knee-high grass on the embankment.

You always had friends, the little voice said. *Always. You and your father made friends and never even knew it.*

Matt looked to the tree line of pine and aspen for answers. For anything. "I know," he said, wiping tears away. He patted the dashboard like a dog and leaned back. "And damned if the friends you don't know are the ones that really matter."

The old truck rolled into the day, one headlight working like a flashlight trying to find its way in the woods.

He never heard the voice again.

**

The coyotes came upon one of those wheeled machines they didn't care for. It let the men come closer and they'd shoot the metal wasps from it. This one was obnoxious red. It glared at them with its one eye. They sniffed around it, smelling the stink of man everywhere. They smelled the pungent yeast odor, too. These scents always came together. One time she drank from one of the odor cans and got dizzy.

The coyote lifted her nose and caught scent of man, not too far from this spot. Together she and her mate worked through the short woods. These woods were very thick. Colorful leaves fell on their coats and her mate looked into the sky and yipped, parting his mouth and showing his teeth and tongue. She liked the way he looked and liked his muzzle. He glanced at her, perking his ears, amber eyes widening.

They followed the scent and stopped in the bushes sixty feet from *The Man*.

**

Bob Sanders lay on the ground, moaning and slowly emerging from the black. He raised a bloody hand in the air, propping it up with his elbow. His right leg was bent behind his back and a branch pierced his left leg. Pain ravaged his nerves like fire as he tried to move.

"Love these woods and I don't mind dyin' in 'em," he mumbled. Sanders reached for his shotgun with his right hand, but it wasn't there. His shooter's glove gripped only leaves and soil. Sanders heard panting and lifted his head off the ground, chin pressed to his chest.

Coyotes. Watching him.

"Eat and be eaten, eh?" he said. "So you come to finally top Sanders, eh? Good on you! You have that right. It's survival of the fittest out here and I ain't so fit right now, eh?" Sanders laughed and grimaced at the pain. Maybe he broke ribs, too.

"Well come on, fur balls! Get me while I'm fresh, eh?"

The coyotes approached and his self-deprecating sarcasm vanished into a blizzard of fear.

"No—I don't wanna go this way," he told them, trying to kick away.

The coyotes trotted to him, side by side. They were within five feet now, staring into his soul.

"Go on, get gone! Back to the bog, fur balls! You like the bog, don't you? Everything loves the fooking bog up here, eh?"

His eyes grew wide and his frowning lips quivered. He tried to squirm away but a hot flash of pain put that plan to rest. Bummer, eh? These were two healthy coyotes and he couldn't do a god damned thing.

One of the coyotes bit him on the boot.

"Get off me...get offff meeee!" He reached into his front pocket for his Buck Master knife, but it must have fallen out during his flight.

Each coyote chomped into a boot, their teeth scraping his toes. Then the coyotes backed up, their paws digging into the soft soil and leaves.

"Bastards! Get off a me and go back to the bog!"

The pulling straightened his legs, eliciting a sick crack from a bone in the left. Sanders screamed. He hoped Melinda heard it.

The coyotes pulled him through the brush, up and over branches and forest litter that cut into his back. Sanders faded in and out of consciousness. His eyes rolled in his head, pupils disappearing under the sockets. The canopy and sky flickered and ghosted.

Sanders woke in sunlight, mosquitos buzzing his ears. The smell of oil and rubber filled his nostrils. He tilted his head and found himself staring right at his four wheeler. The coyotes were gone, the only souvenir a sharp pain in his toes.

"My fookin' four wheeler," he said. He grabbed the handlebar with his good hand and dragged himself alongside it. Then Sanders draped his good arm over the seat and pulled himself up, his legs splayed out behind him. He managed to balance his chest on the seat to support his weight. Sanders screamed as his ankle twisted, the anguish echoing across the southern valley. He almost fainted, but recovered and groped the plastic toolbox on the rear equipment tray. Then he reached inside, took his yellow waterproof radio, and turned it on.

"Melinda, y-you there?" He waited, listening to the crackle. There was a low beep and then a click.

"Bob! Where are ya? My God, I thought you went camping and drinkin' again. I didn't catch your location, eh?"

Sanders cracked a smile.

"I'm on the trail I cut near Ron's place. You remember, eh?"

"Yep. Be there in a few. Ya hurt?"

He looked down at his bloody clothes and mangled legs.

"No," he said. "See you soon, eh?" Sanders slumped over the rear of the four wheeler and onto the trail. Then he screamed in agony. Slowly, he propped himself against the back of the four wheeler, clenching his teeth. He turned his head and saw the yellow bumper sticker. Sanders read it several times and spit. He reached his good hand and used one of his unkempt fingernails to catch a corner. Sanders picked at it, piece by piece. Then he crumpled the sticker into a ball and tossed it into a puddle.

***

They ran through the orchard, playing. She was faster so he had to chase her. Their tails bounced high above the grass, like furry sails on the ocean. They ran to the old wooden post, up where the sky got big. She raised her snout into the air, sniffing the breeze. The colorful forest stretched out below her. They ran downhill to the place where things got cool and dark, where the apple trees were fewer and the grass taller. She liked the way it was cooler there. She smelled something in the grass, something she might be able to eat. She bent her head down and grabbed one of the apples and chewed. She spit it out, then shook her head, backing away from the thing.

They ran up and down the undulations of the orchard, nipping and yipping at each other, smelling the clean air. She paused and he stopped behind her. The grass quivered and swayed in the breeze.

These are good woods.

The End

Acknowledgments

The Puller would not exist if not for Sarah Welsh. Her support and encouragement kept me writing through a difficult time. I'd also like to thank my editor, Gary Lucas and my literary agent, Laura Wood.

Michael Hodges resides in the Northern Rockies, where the pine forests still keep secrets. Over twenty of his short stories have appeared in various magazines and anthologies.

You can find out more at his official site:
michaelhodgesfiction.com

Made in the USA
San Bernardino, CA
26 June 2016